Song of Mornius

Song of Mornius

Book One of The Talenkai Chronicles

Diane E. Steinbach

Dedication

With love to my mother, Jeanette E. Steinbach, for her unfailing belief in me, to my Aunt Eve and Uncle Warren Luy for their encouragement, to Lynne Haase Shanholtzer for her devoted friendship and support, and to the wordsmiths Judy, Doranna, Damon, Kit, Jo, Elenora, Susan, Hannah, and Esther for their advice along the way.
And to you, Stephen R. Donaldson, for inspiring me to write in the first place.

Acknowledgments

I would like to thank my content editor, Dr. Debra Doyle, Ph.D, also my line and copy editor, Judith Tarr, as well as editors Bethany Pennypacker, Starshadow, and Elizabeth Wright for helping me to make my first novel shine. Thanks also to the talented artist, Jason Moser (cover art and interior illustrations — maverickdesignworks.com), and to Paul D. Hoffmaster III (back cover photo) and Jeremy S. Bancroft (artistic input) for their advice and support.

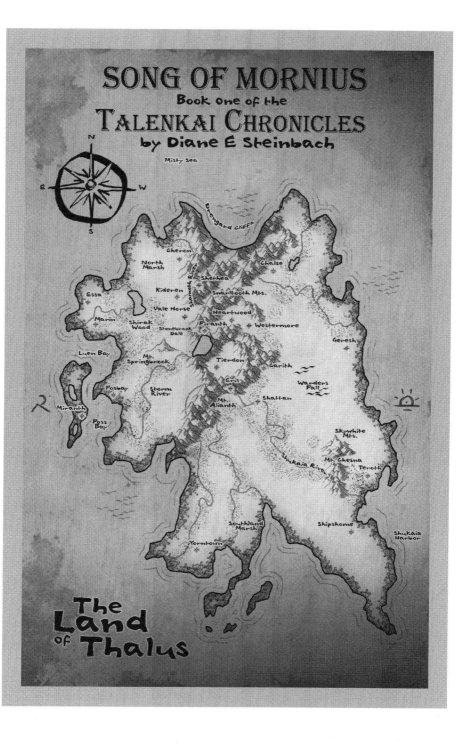

Chapter 1

*D*azed, Gaelin examined his hands. His knees were folded to the side where he sat, the red pool widening across the floor. He slanted his gaze to the ax on his lap, the rivulets of blood sliding along the edge of the weapon he cradled.

The silence dragged out while he gaped at the wreckage his fury had made in the little room. A shaft of dusty light from the cabin's tiny window flooded in above him, brightening as the morning sun climbed to breach the mountain.

"*Gaelin, run!*" the ringing voice repeated inside his head.

With painful stiffness, he braced the ax's head on the floorboards and pushed, drawing his body into a crouch over its wooden handle. He stood, swaying as he lurched to the blood-spattered door.

"Run," he told himself, his fingers fumbling to release the latch. "Move. Do it! *Run.*"

The wind struck his face as he hurried out, the chill air clearing his thoughts. He blinked, dazzled by the dawn's white brilliance on the frosty ground. Dragging the ax, he stumbled from the dwelling his stepfather had taken by force, to thrust himself toward the remains of the barn.

Reaching the heap of rotted boards, he squatted beneath the sagging entrance, rounding his shoulder to avoid two of the five nails he had not been able to bend.

He saw his bed, a long cattle-feed trough he had filled with leaves and straw, sitting against a wall below the cracked rafters. "I need you, Father," he called. The ax thumped the soggy floor as he knelt next to his nest to frantically dig through the debris within. "I can't do this alone!"

"*Run!*" said the voice again in his mind, and Gaelin nodded, grasping at last the highly polished wood of his staff. He yanked it from the moldering straw, raising its heavy crown to keep its bluish gem from the floor.

"No one can take you from me, now," he addressed it, recalling how his mother had told him the heirloom's name the day she had died. "Mornius," he repeated, stroking the iron talons encasing the stone. His head bowed, he hunched over his knees, his matted hair swinging to cover his face. "I can't believe I *murdered* him! I'm—"

"*Trust me in this, Gaelin,*" the voice in his head interjected, "*you must run.*"

For a moment longer, he hugged the staff, mesmerized as he peered into the depths of its multicolored crystal. How many times had he slept on his makeshift bed, transfixed by a sliver of moonlight through the splinters above him? He had heard the staff then, too, which had been his only friend, speaking to him in the dead of night to instruct him about the world.

"Father," he said to the staff Mornius's mysterious occupant, and not for the first time. "I need you with me."

"*I am,*" the voice avowed through the turmoil of his thoughts, and Gaelin lifted his head. He raised his staff, braced it in front of his knees, and stood.

"Where shall I go?" he asked the jutting timbers, the flattened half of the ancient barn where the structure had struck the trees, ending its long-ago plummet from the sky. He frowned as he glanced at his blood-soaked gray tunic and worn leggings, the only clothing he possessed to protect him from the cold.

There was the beaver cloak above the trapdoor leading to the cellar, he recalled, and his stepfather's woolen hat. To get at them, he would have to reenter the little house and walk across its floor. *I can't go back in there*, he thought wildly. *I won't be able to—* He gulped as he envisioned himself tripping to land on something soft and still horribly warm.

Gaelin ducked low to exit the barn and trudged the way he had come, clenching the ax's gory haft in his right hand as he gripped Mornius in his other. He faltered as he neared the eerie silence of the ramshackle cabin, his knees threatening to buckle.

Arriving at the front window, he stopped short. With a grimace, he rubbed his itchy chin along the collar of his tunic—to scrape the drying blood from his beard. He caught a salty tang, and tilting his neck, he heard it—a faint buzzing of insects from beneath the door.

He staggered back, the cabin and barn spinning around him as he flung aside the ax. Then he bolted, sprinting past the woodpile and into the forest, pelting as hard as he could. Down the steep slopes he ran, sliding and leaping below the stunted bluebark trees and into the moaning wind, desperate to escape the scene of his crime, the site of Seth Lavahl's murder.

His lungs burned in his chest, and still he pushed on, thrashing through clove-leaf, the plants staining his sleeves purple. A tree root tripped him, snagging the toe of his boot. With a yell, he pitched forward, rolling to land on the crinkly leaves with his legs spread. Through a haze of fatigue, he studied the trail in front of him sinking out of sight into the undergrowth below, a narrow track stamped out by deer.

Gingerly he massaged the base of his thumb, feeling again the ax's splintered handle against his palm. He raised his knees to his chest, light pulsing from his staff beside his feet, flashing out from Mornius's gem.

As his breathing steadied, he peered through the boughs overhead, squinting at the sun's blur above the trees.

I'll never have to see it again. He glowered at the thought of the cabin that had been his prison, the only building he had known, other than the barn, for nineteen years. As if from a distance, he heard the pulse of Mornius's power rustle the leaves and then felt the heat of the staff's fire reach his spine, the magic's bluish tendrils clearing his sight. The sensation was familiar. *Not too much*, he reminded the spirit in his staff. *Or you'll make me ill.*

Reaching out, he caught Mornius's wooden shaft and shook it once to quell its fire, grunting with satisfaction at the strength in his arm. He had worked hard to prepare for this, to build up his body to escape from Seth Lavahl and have the chance for a normal life.

"To get away," he said, "not kill! Why didn't I flee after he fell? I could have just run!"

He scowled at the path before him. "Now I deserve to die," he said, eyeing the winding track that no longer promised freedom for him, but death. "I killed someone!"

3

He shifted to his knees. His staff's iron-shod heel rang hollow on the trail, reminding him how close winter was. With a shuddering sigh, he lurched to his feet and once more ventured downward, and as the byway sloped sharply to the right, gravity hurried him faster, thrusting him blundering and out of control through the fern-stalks.

He groaned in relief when at last the grade leveled out, and then spied a drop-off to his right with a jagged line of treetops jutting up from below. "There should be a trail down there leading to Kideren." He shivered. "With its people and . . ."

Rubbing at his forehead, he hastened across a narrow meadow, slowing as he sloshed his way through a frigid stream. He breathed deeply, struggling to remember a conversation from a summer ago with Delbert, his eldest stepbrother. After Delbert and his younger sibling, Jax, had rebelled against their overbearing father, Gaelin had approached the older boy.

"What's it like to live in a town?" Gaelin had asked, and to his surprise, Delbert had responded.

"Kideren's people," Gaelin whispered to the brooding trees, his brow furrowed as he recalled Delbert's description. "Governed by"— he paused, fighting to recollect—"Enforcers . . ."

He toppled back, his shoulders colliding with a low-hanging branch. In his mind, he saw figures in black flowing garments cluster around him, their features resembling his stepfather's, all of them pointing at his face, their furious cries demanding justice.

"I deserve it," he said to the gemstone in his staff. "However they decide to punish me, you will allow them!"

He broke once more into a jog as the sun reached its zenith above, turning his thoughts to more pleasant things as he descended the narrow path—the year he had spent plotting to break out and his efforts to improve his endurance. The constant chores were not enough. He had forced himself to race up the steep mountain, to run and jump carrying armloads of wood.

It's my fault she died, he thought as he remembered his mother. *If I hadn't been born, she'd still be alive!*

Gaelin halted to position the staff, bracing its heel on the ground below him while he climbed down a rocky protrusion. He grimaced, recalling himself at eight years old, meeting Sareh, his mother, for the final time in the barn's concealing shadow. Never would he forget her tears as she gave him the heavy staff.

"*This was Garrick's,*" Sareh had said, stroking his hair and holding him close, "*the father you never knew. He never fought with this, Gaelin, but your great-grandfather's father did. Mornius—that's its name. I kept it hidden for you in the ravine.*

"*Gaelin, Seth knows!*" she had warned him. "*I don't know how, but you must hide this again before he sees it. No matter what happens, never let that bastard or his sons near it. Promise me!*"

Gaelin started as the drumming rain brought him back to himself, and the growing awareness of how far he had traveled. He jerked to a stop, glimpsing above the treetops the swollen black clouds, their edges tinted orange by the setting sun. Peering through the misty boughs in front of him, he spotted blocky shapes in the twilight. *Kideren!* he thought. *It has to be!*

As he squatted behind his staff, he gasped when three rain-blurred figures briefly appeared, sloshing through the mud as they crossed between the two closest buildings.

Fear locked him in place. Then the deluge's chill reached his bones, forcing him at last into motion. His muscles quaking, he ventured through slimy puddles and over a narrow path of stone to press his palm against the rear of the nearest building.

Again he froze, gaping at the traces of red on his fingers, at his scarred wrists, and the clove-leaf's magenta stains on his tunic's gray sleeves. *At least the blood's washing away*, he thought, glancing at his soaked-through clothes. *But not fast enough. I look like a killer.*

He cringed as the water pelted his shoulders and head and trickled down his back. Cautiously he crept around the side of the building, collapsing at the base of its checkered green-and-white front.

The citizens of Kideren veered from the stony path, preferring to splash through the muck as they passed him by. Their gazes were averted, shielded from the sight of him helpless in the storm. With a soft groan, he sank onto his rump on the drenched stones, hunching forward to hug his knees.

He cowered when a man in leather armor loomed before him and knelt down, his wide belt creaking. Gaelin, turning his face from the stranger's concern, focused on his elbows where they rested on his knees, and on the pinkish rain sluicing over his wrists. Without delay the stranger gave him a tap.

5

"Hard times in Kideren, aren't they?" the man called, his voice projected over the storm.

Gaelin slanted his gaze at the man's gentle expression and then ducked his head. He studied the bruise on his thumb, the pale white gleam of his knuckles beneath his freckled skin.

"You'll freeze out here!" The man bent close, water trickling in rivulets along the boiled hide of his armor. "It's getting dark. Why aren't you home?"

"I don't have . . ." Gaelin thumped his soggy shoulders against the building. "I'm not *from—*"

"What's this you're covered with?" the man interrupted, catching the tainted rainwater dripping from Gaelin's sleeve in his palm.

"Blood," the man said, sniffing what he held. He tipped his hand, flicking the red-tinged liquid onto the stones. "What happened to you? I see bruises, but where are you bleeding?"

Gaelin glanced up, forcing himself to meet the stranger's regard. "Seth Lavahl," he said over the hissing rain. "I was trying to escape! He wanted to kill me!"

The stranger frowned and leaned closer. "Kill you? Lavahl's just a drunk. Mean, yes, but I can't imagine he would—"

"He kept me on Mount Desheya! He killed my father and stole his cabin . . . forced my mother to be his slave! He *killed* her!"

Bending down, the stranger probed Gaelin's shattered cheekbone. "You're talking about the smith, am I right?" he asked. "I had no idea he had a stepson."

Eyes closed, Gaelin nodded.

"Why would Lavahl kill your mother? Or *you*, for that matter?"

Shifting uneasily, Gaelin wrung his hands. "I tried to escape; that's why. When he cornered me, I grabbed what I could—the ax he had left on the table."

Gaelin grunted as, quick as a blink, the man snatched up his wrist, then pushed back the dripping sleeve of his tunic. At the stranger's touch, he shuddered, watching how the man traced the jagged scars marring his skin. "Years," said the stranger, his quiet voice barely audible, and Gaelin, feeling his face go hot, jerked free.

"Please. I must see the Enforcers. I left him dead on the floor! I can't return to that . . . place."

"We'll sort it out later," the man replied. "Get up, now. You'll

6

catch your death, sitting here!"

Arms, firm and gentle, raised him to his feet. Gaelin tottered, but the larger man supported and turned him, after which they shambled like comrades through the rain.

Chapter 2

The persistent rapping of knuckles on the wooden surface before him jerked up Gaelin's head. Bewildered, he peered through a haze of exhaustion at the man seated opposite him across the little table, a man in his early thirties, he guessed, who had been kind enough to rescue him from the rain.

"I said," repeated the stranger, with an air of dwindling patience, "I'm Terrek Florne, son of Lucian. My father owns Vale Horse, the Stonebrook Dale ranch. We're south of Kideren. You can see the border of our land through the trees beyond the city. And you are?"

Gaelin gripped his staff, tipping it to vertical as he strove to meet his companion's forthright gaze. Again his weary mind reeled, pulling him out of the present to show him what he had done—how his stepfather had tried to run after flinging the chair at him and how he had leapt to pursue and kill the older man.

In his mind, he saw Seth Lavahl toppling onto his stomach and dragging his body through a swath of his own blood. Gaelin remembered standing over the dying man, his arms rising and falling, the warm red fluid splashing his neck, the sound of splintering bone in his ears.

"*You* are?" the stranger repeated.

Gaelin focused again on the other's bearded face. "Lavahl. Gae . . . lin," he said. After years of being called "runt" or "it," he had left his real name far away, in another time.

He risked a furtive glance at the steaming bowl before him, his stomach twisting into knots as he leaned back, staring at his lap. He studied the bruise on the hand he held out of sight under the table. He could almost feel the ax's haft in his grasp, the weight of the weapon lending momentum to his strokes.

With a shudder, he raised his head, blinking to clear his vision. In the tavern's amber light, his benefactor's eyes were hazel, he realized, and not brown, filled with motes of fire, a fierce determination belying his kindness.

Around their table, large men were pressing close. Gaelin tensed at the acrid smells they brought with them, of roy—a beverage of barley, yeast and chimara flowers—or worse, the fermented potato brew preferred by his stepfather. Despite himself, Gaelin cringed. Then he tilted his staff to lean against it.

"I had a friend who lived in Kideren," his rescuer said, eyeing him, "who owned a grakan he'd raised from a cub. Matar gave it love, kept it gentle, but after his death, his younger brother, Alandari, took over. You've heard this story, Gaelin? You know it?"

Gaelin chewed at his lip. He did not want to know. More men were crowding into the tavern. Tucking his feet under his chair, he locked his gaze on the soft-spoken stranger facing him. *No, he has a name,* Gaelin chided himself, *Terrek Florne,* and now he read anger in his companion's gold-flecked stare.

"The great bear lost weight," said Terrek. "I saw it once and I could count every rib. Matar's brother had a cruel streak and liked to hear it howl. Until one day, the beast turned on Alandari and ripped out his throat. I know because my brother, Camron, found him torn to pieces in their barn. The sight of it . . ." Terrek scowled at his hands. "My only brother is dear to me. His exposure to that death unraveled him. Camron lost his senses, and for a time, I had to care for him."

Gaelin regarded the cloth next to his bowl, the fabric tinged with blood from between his fingers, reminders of Seth Lavahl. In the stoneware vessel steamed the stew he could not bring himself to eat. "Was the beast destroyed?" he asked pointedly, raising his voice over the tavern's din.

Terrek grimaced and shook his head. Watching him, Gaelin picked up his wooden utensil at last and dunked it into his stew.

"Eat up," said Terrek. "We need to talk."

Gaelin toyed with his food while Terrek ate, again letting his mind wander. With a practiced shake, he dropped his auburn hair over his eyes and glanced out the window at the pub's glowing lantern.

Terrek, he thought, squinting at the man across the table.

9

Distracted by the tavern's noise, Gaelin cast about at the men and women standing near. *Did Seth Lavahl come here? How many of these people know him?*

As Terrek set aside his spoon, Gaelin peered at him from beneath his matted hair. "I have to *confess*!" Gaelin blurted. "I can't live with what I've done. The Enforcers would listen to you."

Terrek frowned at his hands and wiped them calmly with his napkin. "Am I to understand you're asking to die?"

Gaelin looked at the bowl in front of him and nodded.

"Well, forget it," Terrek said. "We don't kill people for defending themselves." Leaning his weight against the back of his chair, Terrek appraised him. "If you were stronger, I'd recruit you. I need warriors, criminals or not. You have no home or place to go. I'd take you on, but for your safety, I can't let myself—"

"That's fine. I don't want to be a burden."

"Let me finish." Terrek reached across the table, and Gaelin felt the larger man's fingers touch his forehead, flicking the hair from his eyes. "You're no warrior, and I'm off to battle things you wouldn't believe: magic-warped humans we call dachs. They're all muscle and toughened skin. They're strong and hard to kill. Some have wings, but the ones who don't are still plenty lethal with their poisonous spines. The cult that makes them . . . Erebos's slavers . . . I'd be putting you at risk. My father wants me to *protect* Kideren and Vale Horse. I'm not going to cause the deaths of unskilled men!"

"I'm strong enough," Gaelin countered. "I could learn to fight. I could care for your animals until I do."

"You're what, sixteen?" Terrek lifted his tankard of mulled wine to sip at its contents, then licked his lips. "You'd look even younger if we cleaned you up. You've hardly any beard."

"*Nineteen*," said Gaelin. "I'm nineteen." Angrily he pointed to the right side of his jaw. "I was burned here so now it won't grow. That's all."

"Still, you've been up on that mountain. Now you're scared to death just sitting there. Have you never seen people?"

Gaelin met his steady regard. "No. I've never seen anyone."

"It's no wonder you seem younger," Terrek said, "which leads me to my problem. I've aided you with food, or I will if you ever eat it. So now what? Do I just leave you here, out in the cold and homeless?

You don't have much meat on you . . . which, come to think of it, how did you make it down the mountain without freezing? You managed it in one day?"

"If Seth Lavahl can get here to drink . . ." Gaelin stopped, taken aback at his own sarcasm. Again he glanced at his staff, and at the glowing blue stone with its streaks of violet, green, and amber at Mornius's crown. "I ran; that's how," he muttered, while across the table, Terrek inhaled sharply as he focused on the gem.

"This is old," Terrek said with a gesture toward the staff's crystal. "Familiar, too." Reaching out, he waited for Gaelin's permission and then touched Mornius's bottomwood shaft. "I *know* this." Carefully he tilted the staff to examine the caged gem. "I studied artifacts from Earth at university. "There are many. If you travel any distance, Gaelin, you will find that there are even whole buildings from Earth—relics, we like to call them—strewn across this world."

"I know," said Gaelin. "That's what the barn was, where I slept. It's the word my mother used."

"Really?" Terrek cocked his head. "I didn't realize we had any that large near Kideren. Lesser things like rocks are less familiar, though the elves might know of this. They like to use what quartz they can find from Earth to channel their power. This one's beautiful, Gaelin. Is it yours?"

Gaelin nodded. "My father gave it to my mother after he had a premonition of his death. Seth Lavahl wanted their home. He was in town shoeing my father's horse. Or at least that's what my mother told me. He had heard that my father had a barn high up on the mountain and wanted it. So he came in the night and slit my father's throat. The barn wasn't useable, but he didn't get to see that until dawn."

"Killed for a barn?" Terrek scowled at his bowl. "I never liked him. I saw him trying to shoe a fractious colt once. He got mad at the little beast and threw a hammer at its head. He missed his target, of course, intoxicated as I'm sure he was, but still . . . I guess it shouldn't surprise me."

Gaelin sighed. "Before her death, my mother told me my great-grandfather's father fought with this staff. She didn't tell me how, just that he was the first who did. Sometimes the staff helps me, too, and I can't explain . . . But today was different. I got here by myself."

"Your staff has a name. Did you know that? If I'm not mistaken, this is Mornius you carry, and the gem is called the Skystone. The stone is a relic from Earth. It contains—"

"I didn't realize the stone had a na—" Gaelin broke off at the sudden intensity of Terrek's gaze, the flare of warning in his eyes as he stared up.

Gaelin heard the slow creaking of the floorboards beneath him. He sensed the presence of someone large and very masculine looming behind his back.

"You're Florne?" a gravelly voice asked. "The one with the army?"

As the man spoke, his tone rough and slurred from too much ale, Gaelin cringed. For one wild moment, he feared Seth Lavahl had reassembled himself and trailed him down the mountain.

"I would hardly call it that," Terrek said, leaning back in his chair. "I lead a brave rabble of men, many of them hired to defend my father's interests, as well as Kideren itself, and *you*."

"So Florne Recluse gave you a job, did he?" the big drunk snarled. "How nice. Did he give you those fancy titles, too, *Commander*?"

Terrek nodded. "As a matter of fact, he did. He thought the younger men would respond better—"

"You talked my brother into joining you and now he's dead, isn't he?" the man pressed. "Why else wouldn't he return with you?"

With a slight shake of his head, Terrek motioned Gaelin to stay still. Then, standing, he thrust back his chair. "Your brother had a mind of his own, Lars. *Feyin* Broudel wanted to fight! Death is coming for Kideren, and he wanted to stop it."

"For Kideren, you say?" Hands clenched, the big man leaned into Gaelin's peripheral vision, and Gaelin gasped at the fury he saw on the ruddy face. "Death for Kideren? Is that the lie you're telling these days? Is that what you're telling this . . . Hades's blazes, what a *stink*! What's this filth you've dragged in?"

"Someone," said Terrek, "I'd prefer to sit with more than you, and yes, death, for all of us, or worse. People don't just die, you know. They're changed into dachs, or bodachs, as we once called them. Ever see one, Lars? I have. During my stay at university, I saw paintings of monsters from Earth called demons. Monsters, and that's what the dachs are!"

"Is that how Feyin was killed?" the man returned. "Fighting your 'demons' for you? You think your puny band can stop them, but all you do is slay more good men, as you destroyed my brother! What's your count up to now, *Lordling*? Fifty, sixty men? Against what . . . *thousands*?"

"One hundred and twenty-two, last time I checked." Terrek softened his voice. "Look, I'm sorry about your brother, but he died defending his home. We fight the cult, Lars, my volunteers and the men my father hired. Which is more than you do sitting here waiting for them to take you. If people like you weren't so bli—"

"*Fight?*" Broudel sputtered. "With ignorant children?"

A second man charged at Terrek's back. Larger than the first, he had circled around while Lars spoke. When Terrek fell under the jabs of his attacker's fists, the tavern's patrons threw aside their chairs and stood.

From a shadowed niche flanking the bar, four men in travel-stained garments leapt to Terrek's aid, charging into the battle with their swords drawn.

Heart pounding, Gaelin bolted from his seat as sounds of combat filled the little room, driving him to cower in a corner near the door.

Terrek, clambering to his feet, managed to throw a punch at the largest man before Lars Broudel hooked him around his neck. As Terrek went rigid, Gaelin saw Broudel braced behind him and holding him fast. Frozen with dread, Gaelin watched the drunk draw his sword, and with deliberate slowness, stab his blade through Terrek's torso.

An older man sprang to Terrek's defense, smashing a half-empty bottle over the enraged Broudel's head. Ignoring him, the drunk adjusted his stance to support Terrek's weight as he twisted the hilt. With blood on his lips, Terrek sank to the floor.

Gaelin gawked at the red pool spreading out from beneath his benefactor's ribs. It reminded him of his capacity for violence—the life he had taken earlier that day. In his grasp, his staff trembled, its blue-violet stone flaring above him. His consciousness separated from his body as an unfamiliar other arrived to manipulate him. As an observer, he witnessed his limbs moving, scrabbling him across the creaky floor to kneel below the battling men.

Gaelin clamped his staff against his side with his arm as he clung to the wounded man, the room spinning fast around him, the shouts from the combatants muted above him, their movements slowed.

Far in the distance, he heard a fathomless voice as pressure mounted in his chest, threatening to tear him apart. Desperate for air, Gaelin mastered himself once more and seized Terrek's wrist, hauling at the armored man's dead weight with all the strength he could muster.

"Hang on!" he yelled. Muscles burned over his bruised ribs as he heaved backward. Through the doorway he struggled, dragging the dying Terrek out into the rainy night. Then he knelt.

"*You're filth, you know that?*" came Seth Lavahl's voice from the storm of his past. "*You miserable runt! Why did I ever let you live? I have no—*"

Gaelin hammered his left fist on the flagstones next to his knee. He shuddered as the pain cleared his head. "You *listened*," he said, bending over the stricken man. "You wanted to *help* me."

As Gaelin gripped Mornius, the agony in his chest shifted to his fingers. A force like fire thrust his hand down, bringing the weight of the Skystone to bear against his companion's wound.

Energy blasted from the stone, forming a cool, silvery current under the driving rain. Eyes closed, Gaelin threw back his head, his writhing body taken by a power he could not control.

At last a comforting darkness settled upon him, and he sensed himself falling, his body collapsing on the stony path. He managed a breath, and then another.

An arm slid beneath his back, lifting him into a seated position. Dazed, Gaelin squinted at the figure kneeling beside him, a man's blurry face he could not make out. "I should die," he murmured. "I've killed someone."

"After you saved my life?" a familiar voice asked. "I think not!"

Gaelin started when he recognized Terrek supporting his back. "You're alive? What happened? What did I do?"

"For now, I am," said Terrek. "Thanks to your staff. It has made you a healer, I see. Well, now I know."

"Know what?" Reaching out, his fingertips tingling, Gaelin searched the wet stones and the mud for his staff.

Terrek chuckled. "What you might do for my men."

Chapter 3

*A*valar Mistavere turned her back from the storm's renewed assault. The cruel wind blasted her little boat, thrusting her stumbling from the windrunner's prow. In dismay, she caught the taste of land in the salty air, the tang of driftweed rotting on stone.

She clung to the sturdy port rail, holding on tight as the slash of a distant shoreline appeared between the pitching swells. "Impossible!" she groaned. She inspected her boat's slackened sail above her and nodded. The scraps she had pieced together snapped and rippled, flinging water at her sodden hair.

"Shortened canvas, as Captain Kurgenrock would want, and yes, Uncle, I am running at an angle. So how in Hothra's bloody coral could I have come so far? This squall—has it been with me all night?" She glared up at the roiling black clouds. *I am a giant,* she fumed in silence. *You shall not break me!*

Lightning forked behind the waves, and she tensed at the jolt through her bones, the magic within her flesh echoing the storm's rage. She toppled to her knees, ducking her head as she hastened beneath the boom and hauled herself up onto the helm's raised seat.

Breakers splashed the protruding rocks to the port side of her boat, the five looming smudges she craned her neck to see. Bracing her feet at the back of the mast, she seized the tiller, tacking once more to cut through the wind. With a flick of her head, she shook the hair from her eyes, and frantically dug one-handed for her map, groping with red swollen fingers into the breast pocket of her shearling vest to retrieve the soggy parchment. She stared when the drawing flew open, the wind shredding it in her grasp, flinging its tatters to the deck.

As if it were the backdrop of a dream, she knew the seaboard ahead, recognizing the curve of its bay. She had beheld sketches of the lofty cliffs beyond the gray beach in her lessons at Freedom Hall. The long, jagged gouges in the vertical rock were unmistakable.

Ever since her childhood, she recalled, she had longed for this—to voyage to Thalus, the land her people feared. Yet, now that it was within her sight, she was gasping for breath, tightness balling in her chest.

Avalar groaned where she sat at the helm, watching the mist coalesce below the faraway cliffs. Now she discerned phantoms in the fog, remnants of ghosts from the memories she had inherited from her father. Limned in silver on the sand, the specters of the doomed giants swayed in the wind, their wails barely audible as they opened their arms to the sea.

She gaped, leaning forward over her knees. *You did see them, Father,* she thought, *the ones who arrived too late. Is this why you forbade me to come here? To protect me from the truth? I am no child!*

She bowed her head, her tears burning her cheeks as she sensed the helplessness her father, Grevelin, had felt. She hated her magic, the power that uncovered his past and the wounds he had striven to hide.

Torrents pelted her exposed face and neck, the downpour obscuring her view of the haunted shore. Limp with grief for her long-lost people, she sagged above the tiller.

"This cannot be Thalus," she reasoned aloud. "The slavers' land is farther than this; it lies to the south from our home on Hothra Isle."

Again she froze, whimpering under her breath as the cliffs reappeared. Visions knifed through her head. Within a wave's breaking crest, she glimpsed her father's boyhood in the tunnels beneath the ground, felt the magic in his flesh, the agony he had suffered when his captors had turned it against him.

Avalar, frowning, peered through the deluge at the slavers' former homeland. *Why would humans crave our power?* she wondered. *How could they hold us in thrall as they did?*

She leaned back on her seat, her fingers aching as she gripped the windrunner's helm. *No haunted shore will stop me,* she thought, steering hard to port and between the threatening rocks. *Once my people learn what I have done, they, too, shall come here. Our grain crops shall flourish once more in this land!*

Her magic revived within her muscles, strengthened by the gale buffeting her body and the splashing of seawater across her back. Through the haze in her eyes, she saw the clouds gather angrily above her head, rotating like a ponderous wheel.

She howled, clinging to the tiller as her boat shot sideways, buoyed by the corkwood trimming the base of its hull. Clambering to her feet, she caught the stiff fabric flapping over her head with her free hand and leaned back, anchoring the drenched sail with her weight.

A massive rock filled her vision, jutting black and ominous from its watery cradle. With her left hand still clutching the canvas, she pressed hard against the tiller, struggling to slew her little boat to starboard, to *turn . . .*

The prow crumpled upon the stone. Water gushed around her ankles.

"Sephrym, help me!" Avalar threw herself forward, clinging to the mast as she felt the frigid ocean swelling around her legs, her little boat spinning into a trough. Another wave crashed down with brutal strength, breaking her windrunner's keel, then tearing her from the mast and into the sea.

Over swirls of debris and gray sand, she tumbled with her mouth clamped shut, shocked by the water's bitter cold. Battling the vicious drag of the undertow, she strained to swim toward the brownish foam tossing on the surface. She thrashed free from her shearling vest and kicked hard, her efforts hampered by the weight of her deer-hide leggings. A wave helped her, lifted her. She screamed when she was flung against the rock.

"Father!" Scraping along the sharp stone, Avalar squinted at the remains of her boat. Beyond its scattered wreckage rose Thalus's frosty shore, already seeking her life.

"Hold on!" cried a voice. She gasped when small hard fingers snagged her wrist. Glancing up, she glimpsed white-feathered wings flailing behind her back and a slim, elven body descending.

"No!" Avalar lashed out with her fists, battling for the hope her people needed, the call to her heart she had yearned to answer since her childhood. She knew the creature tugging at her limb. She

17

recognized his voice, his stern eyes above his tight-lipped mouth. He meant to take her home.

"You shall *not*!" she raged. "You will not stop me! You—"

A calming heat filled her chest. Dazed, she gaped at the sky, feeling her limbs go numb. Hands grasped her tunic, gripping her at the nape of her neck and again at her waist. She heard the static crackling through his wings, his magic strengthening them to lift her up, soaking wet, and carry her ashore. Numbly she collapsed on the rocky beach.

"You are young, Avalar," her rescuer said, "and you have much to learn. Indeed, why in all that is magic would you battle a tempest and let it destroy your beautiful racer? Did you forget what you are?"

She looked up. Before her stood Ponu, the mightiest of the elven wizards sworn to protect her people. He was her father's friend; she knew he would want to take her home. She sat and locked her elbows around her knees, narrowing her eyes at the winged elf.

"You did," Ponu continued. "Avalar, you are a *giant*. All you had to do was shout a command—*Avaunt storm!*—and the waves would have stilled for you."

"Ponu," she said. Avalar examined him. He was a thin, crooked-mouthed creature whose head, whenever she stood near him, barely reached her hips.

His attire she knew well: the cream-colored vest that had fascinated her as a child with its many pockets of secret treasure, and the mysterious pouches dangling from his wide shan-hide belt.

His bare arms were dripping, his tunic and vest cinched above his hips. The quilted leather that made up the back of his vest hung loose, out of the way of his muscular wings. He kept his doeskin leggings fastened in the old style, she noted, laced tight down the sides and tucked into his fur-lined boots.

Ponu bowed with a flourish and gestured to the cliffs towering behind them. "Behold!" he said, his smooth skin and youthful timbre of his voice belying his great age. Leaning forward, Avalar strained to hear him over the rhythmic thunder of the surf, the warbling shrieks of the wind. "These are the Drengards, the ancient protectors of Thalus!"

Her nerves tingled along her neck as a gentle touch of his magic enhanced her hearing.

"Avalar," said Ponu, "it was from this cove that your people escaped. Why would you want to return here? Do you not recall what your father went through?"

"Of course I do." Hunched against the cold, she scanned the curved shoreline, hunting in vain for a way to evade him. *He is Ponu,* she reminded herself, *the eyes and ears of Sephrym, our great protector. Does he have his staff? If it is here . . .* She glowered, envisioning the power of the crystal—the elf transferring her home.

"The memories of my people are woven forever through my magic," she said. "If I relax my sight, I glimpse the slaves waiting here, just as my father did when he was forced to abandon them. They are his ghosts, not mine, and they shall *not* hinder me."

"They're not ghosts. You do realize that, I hope."

Avalar clenched her jaw. "It matters not! I experience what they went through as though I have *become* them!"

"This is not what you expected, is it?" Ponu said. He hurried on as she tightened her lips. "Avalar, I thought we had discussed this plan of yours. I tried to warn you. I explained how foolish this was."

She straightened under the freezing rain as much as she could. "But later you approved," she said. "You were supporting me. You assisted me with my boat. You even collected scraps for my sail!"

"Yes." Droplets flew as he shook out his wings. "I contributed your bits and pieces—the things you needed for your race boat. It was a patchwork canvas, marking you as a novice. I never suspected you'd attempt to bring it here!"

"Your staff of magic shows you everything, does it not? I thought you had checked it, Ponu. I thought you knew!" She curled her fingers, her digits digging into the pebbly sand. "I told you at Freedom Hall the day I first heard its voice," she said, "long ago, when I was yet a child, but you laughed at me! You refused to even *consider*—"

"What, that Redeemer sang to you? You still believe Govorian's Bloodsword compels you here?"

"I do!" Avalar gritted her teeth. A pocket of warm air touched her face when he stepped closer. "The world created the blade, and now in one night I have gained Thalus, flown here on the wings of this storm. How can this be when I am but a novice? I will tell you. The Circle's magic wants me here."

"Avalar—"

"No!" she interjected. "You could be wrong! You have erred before!"

"And I will again, I assure you," Ponu agreed, wiping the sleet from his eyes. "This is what I know. The humans who enslaved your people are dead, yet the power they worshipped endures. Erebos the Destroyer has new followers now, whole armies of magic-warped humans. How would you fight them, Giant? Even if you tamed an Azkhar well enough to ride it, yours is the old magic, Talenkai magic. Erebos's power comes from the stars. One touch of it would kill you."

Avalar stiffened when he caught her wrist, and the fire of his thoughts probed her mind. Gasping, she snatched back her hand.

"You seek the dance," he said. "The Talhaidor. You intend to reach the mountain city of Tierdon and learn the Swordslore from the Eris Masters there. What, were Grevelin's lessons not enough for you?"

She returned his glare. "My father teaches how to butcher the Sundor Khan. They are naught but simple beasts; they deserve to thrive as much as we do."

"They are not so 'simple,' as you call it," Ponu said, "when they destroy entire villages. Or when they devour the elves who strive to protect your people! How can you claim that they deserve—"

"So we murder them," Avalar broke in, "to defend those elves. Very well, am I so wrong to desire a different road? On Thalus, I shall learn to fight with skill, sword to sword."

Ponu, scowling, contemplated the sea. "I hope you realize how this will break your father once he discovers you are gone. You are all he has left of Alaysha, your mother. Avalar, he—"

"Yes, my mother," she said, "who died giving birth to me. She never recovered from the slavers' abuse. Ponu, what has this to do with my purpose on Thalus, and why should it concern you? Redeemer sang to *me*. I am here at its bidding."

"How can you ask that?" Ponu rubbed at his forehead. "Your father is friend-bonded to me, so of course it concerns me. I will be forced to endure his pain, and this is a critical time for this world. I cannot be distracted by your father's heart." He paused. "I could *transfer* you home with my staff, or fly you there over the sea."

Avalar hissed. "Do that and I shall free myself and fall. And afterward you can tell my father how you slew me."

Ponu stood. Seated as she was, his head came to her chest. She could feel the heat from his body, the soothing pocket of comfortable air he created around them both.

"The Talhaidor of Tierdon is a beautiful dance, but it is not the way of giants, and it cannot stop Erebos." As Ponu thought aloud, Avalar saw bursts of lightning reflect in his eyes from across the sea. "Only power can defeat a warder. The Destroyer understands this very well and so he hides, gaining strength in his mountain. The others trapped here with him . . ." The elf-mage sighed. "He's already slain Tythos. Before Holram could even hope to withstand Erebos, he would need to get stronger."

She surveyed him intently while he rubbed his chin. In the bunch and release of the muscles across his forehead, she could see his quick mind work. "Tierdon is by my home, Giant," he said. "Look."

Startled by this change, Avalar moved out of his way when Ponu knelt, giving him room to poke his finger into the rocky sand. Carefully, his slender arm dripping, he drew a curved line and a circle.

"If you head west," Ponu instructed, "you'll find the Shamath River. It spills into the sea. Beside the falls, there is a stairway carved into the cliff. Climb it. When you reach the top, follow the river. It will take you through the mountains to this point." Ponu tapped the circle he had dug, its thin line filling with water. "A lake called Crinath. This is where you veer east along the shore. There is a trail to Tierdon that begins"—he buried his thumb in a clump of tiny pebbles—"here."

His feathers rustled when he stood. "If you must make this journey, you shall go the way I tell you. This route is the safest path I know over the Snarltooths."

He hesitated, watching her face as if to gauge her reaction. "Now answer me this," he said severely. "It is the truth your leader, Trentor, asks all warriors to acknowledge before they leave for the North: What three things on this world will slay you?"

Avalar brushed the moisture from her lip as the rain flattened his map. "A Sherkon Raider," she said, "for he values his blood sport above all else."

"Correct." Ponu nodded. "What next?"

"A human, for he craves power."

"Indeed," said Ponu. "While there are no Raiders here on Thalus, there are many humans. Beware of them, Avalar. They will kill whatever they fear."

She met his troubled regard. "The third thing is what I am," she said, "a giant—for she will surrender her life to protect the weak."

"Your people are threatened by extinction," said Ponu. "You can no longer afford to protect the vulnerable. You shall keep to this path of doing what the weapon wants, and nothing more." Stretching back his shoulders, he glanced at the sea. "This feels wrong. There are other ways to prove your worth, Giant. The Sundor Khan are raiding again near Kadoth. You're old enough now, and trained. I will convince your father to allow you to fight."

"No." Avalar wrung the seawater from her thick blond braid. "I am not here to prove my worth. Govorian's blade quickened the blood of my people to make them lust for battle. It gave them the courage to rebel. Yet still we are not free. Because of this, the sword is uneasy. It will not rest until I do as it bids."

Lowering her head, she scrutinized her drenched garments, the ripples trickling from her elbows to her wrists. "I have come to find freedom for giants. To remind my people of what they are. Until I do, they will remain as slaves controlled by fear."

Ponu, his brow furrowed, licked his lips. "Talenkai will fail without its magic, and without your people to anchor it. What if you should die, Avalar? There are not enough giants as it is."

Avalar grinned at his concern. "Now it is you who have forgotten what I am," she teased. "As a giant, I have the world defending me. You asked why I failed to stop the storm. Mayhap I craved the challenge, Ponu."

He snorted and read the sky, the purple diagonal slash along the horizon. "That would be like you," he admitted, "but no amount of courage is enough. Nor is the weather's protection or your skill with a blade. In case you have not noticed, your supplies are missing, Avalar. Here."

Ponu faced the thundering surf and opened his wings. Briskly he clapped twice, and Avalar gasped when her stores appeared in front of her, tangled in glistening seaweed. The packs were heavy with brine, bloated with pockets of air. Yet still she could spot her sword in its scabbard underneath a bundle, with her rolled shelter lying close by.

"Your provisions were submerged under the wreckage," the winged elf told her. With his toe, he prodded the soggy tangle. "If the foodstuffs are spoiled, I shall fetch you more. I will not have you starve, Giant."

Avalar shifted to her knees, her every muscle bruised and sore. The rain hammered her wet tunic as she bent over the pile. Bracing the first sack between her thighs, she fumbled with its knots.

"I use reef-bulbs," she said. "They do not hold as much, but what they do stays dry. It was a trick my uncle Kurg taught me." She withdrew a hollow blue sphere from the sack and gave it a shake. "The bulbs are resistant to water," she explained, and with her thumbs she pried it open. "Do you see?"

Ponu's white elven brows lifted toward his hairline. As she replaced the bulb among the others, the frown returned to his ageless face. "Your uncle's knowledge serves you well. Though I doubt Kurgenrock would approve of your presence here."

Avalar stumbled to her feet. "I thank you for my life."

He grunted. "I didn't save it so you could stand out here and freeze," he said. "Come now, Giant. There is a small cave half a league down this beach. If you follow me this way"—he jerked his head—"I will be pleased to show you."

"No." She slung the first pack over her shoulder. Most of her stores she would leave behind; she had packed them only for the sea. "I shall find it myself!"

She wheeled in the direction he pointed, the sodden bundle thudding against her when she stopped to meet his stare. "I have been protected all my life," she said. "This I shall do on my own."

Ponu looked toward the jumble of boulders by the cliff. With two running steps, he launched himself, flying to land on the rocks. Flaring his feathered wings for balance, he bent at the waist and reached between two large slabs.

Avalar squinted through the storm, struggling to see the crystal staff he plucked from the stones.

A flash of gray exploded from the gap. The lean-bodied creature, whooping furiously, leapt at Ponu's boot. Avalar watched it climb. She recognized Saemson, the agile little beast the elf kept as his companion. Ponu tilted his head, and the ferret darted under his hair. Then calmly he assessed her, his violet eyes gleaming.

"We'll speak again!" he shouted. "When you are ready!"

Avalar blinked. With a movement too swift to follow, Ponu *transferred*, removing himself from her sight. Already the pocket of warmth he had created dissipated, and the sleet pounded harder still.

"Sails," she whispered.

She was alone.

Chapter 4

Ponu, hesitating at the mouth of his cave, leaned on his staff and squinted behind him into the tunnel from which he had come. Within the darkness, he glimpsed the row of descending torches, brands that when kindled by his magic illuminated the steep narrow path to his workroom.

Random images danced along his gnarled staff's crystalline shaft, a kaleidoscope of possible futures distracting him from his thoughts. Scowling, he wedged the staff, one of the very few objects he still retained from his homeworld, into a crack in the stone that formed the entrance to his home.

"You're supposed to be making my life easier," he chided as he eyed the Staff of Time. *When* will that happen aga—"

He caught himself with a wince. "Talking to inanimate objects now, are we?" Sighing, he withdrew an egg-shaped quartz from one of his belt's dangling pouches. Gripping the Star Crystal from Earth, he pivoted in a circle, clearing away the snow with his booted feet to expose the grayish ice of his mirror. *Sephrym's Eye*, he reflected, thinking its name as he peered intently down.

Power surged as Ponu focused on the warder Sephrym, a celestial being whose thought-energy, an alien force perilous to Talenkai's magic, drew nearer to the six outer worlds orbiting its sun. The warder, responding to his call, directed its fire through the stone Ponu held to channel and shield its power, the energy spilling in translucent streamers to the ice at his feet.

Easy does it, Ponu thought to the entity, his eyes closed in concentration. *Just a smidge, that's it, and a bit more. You're too close, Sephrym! Here, let me compensate.*

Licking his dry lips, Ponu crouched to touch the same fire

Sephrym gathered to make stars. Through the conduit that was the stone from Earth, he guided the great being's power, swirling it in glowing patterns over the ice. It melted and merged, a magic he shaped with his thoughts, resembling liquid metal as it heated the frozen water, expanding it into a silvery pool.

Carefully he submerged his curled fingers, pressing the stone under the glassy surface as he bent to block out the sun. Above his knuckles, his likeness winked out, and from the shadows the tiny ripples made, Avalar's image formed.

He inspected her salvaged supplies as she did, his view shifting to peer over her shoulder while she sorted them out, her braided hair flicking with her movements. She squatted in a dry patch at the rear of the cave to which he had sent her, in a corner behind its slanted ceiling.

Leaning back, Ponu raised the Star Crystal above the water to broaden his field of vision. Avalar's image wavered across the pool, stiffening at the edges where the fluid hardened. The giant donned her bracers, mail shirt and armor, oblivious to his scrutiny or the lurking threat of Sephrym's fire.

He saw her shrug on her furry cloak and soon after organize her gear. Nodding his approval, he followed her trek westward to the falls. Frozen at the top by the late-autumn ice storms, the Shamath River plunged in plumes of rising mist to the sea below. Beside the pounding, roaring water, she ascended the slippery stone in stages, the bundles on her back pulling her off balance in the angry wind.

Her daring made his blood thunder in his ears. Unable to withstand the sight any longer, he visualized Mornius instead, Holram's staff. He pictured the relic from Earth mounted at Mornius's crown, the beautiful Skystone, a blue gem laced with violet and flecks of green.

The Star Crystal he grasped, the Skystone's paler twin, flared in response against his palm. Then more tendrils of Sephrym's energy lanced between his fingers, tumbling to the water at his feet. He waited, squinting, until a fire glimmered faintly within his pool, a shimmer of interest from Mornius's distant stone.

A soft sapphire light answered his will, drawing into focus another image, that of a gaunt-faced human male, his brown eyes glaring beneath his auburn hair. Ponu recognized the youth. For

many cycles, he had observed Gaelin Lavahl through his icy mirror. Free of his stepfather's abuse, the staff-wielder strode confidently as he journeyed among the warriors. In his hand he held the staff, Mornius, its radiant stone pulsing with its trapped warder's potency.

As Ponu looked up, he gestured to the vision in his pool. "See the fire within the Earth gem?" he called to Sephrym. "Gaelin's adventures are rousing your son Holram, forced to dwell inside the stone! Holram's time for rest is ending. Let him try, great Warder. He has Gaelin now to help him. Give us this final chance!"

He spotted Sephrym's light, like a star above the wispy clouds, reluctantly fading from his view.

"Yes." Ponu climbed to his feet. "There *is* still hope. Gaelin Lavahl travels to Tierdon, as does Avalar the giant."

He sighed. *A young human and a young giant,* he thought, *both searching, and both led. Perhaps they can save the world. We must let them try.*

"While I stay here doing nothing," Ponu added wryly, rubbing his burning eyes. "No, wait. There is one thing I can do."

He retrieved a gildstone lion from the inner pocket of his vest. Bending stiffly, he set the little statue at his feet. It warmed when he stroked it, stretching beneath his palm. "Yelsa Min." Breathing its name, he welcomed it as it grew. "I wish for the forest kings to hearken to me, for Sephrym himself commands them. You will follow the giant unseen while the hunters track her through your eyes. If she falters, the prowlers must guard her well."

The beast roared, tossing its shaggy mane. Ponu stumbled back as, with a powerful kick, the lion sprang forward.

It slipped on the packed snow near the mouth of his cave, its massive paws scrambling. In silence, he observed the magical cat plowing tirelessly through the drifts, its tail flicking as it vanished into the sun's white glare.

Ponu scowled at his Staff of Time in its crevice next to the cave. The tool from his homeworld flashed in the sunshine, showing him hints of possible futures within its depths, but nothing to ease his heart.

THE DARK WATER lapped at the rocky shelf by Felrina Vlyn's feet. She knelt, leaning over the edge of the underground pool to scrub at the crimson traces on her skin.

Still the screaming resounded in her memory from the previous night. The cropper's death had been a painful one, which was often the case with growers who failed in their duties.

"He made his choice," she whispered to the sunken chamber. "Arawn's life force cannot quicken without blood. The blood is life. That farmer . . ." She wiped her fingers on the front of her black robe to dry them, rubbing as if it might erase what the ritual had done.

Slowly she stood, clutching her Blazenstone staff while she searched the troubled water.

It's hard, yes, she consoled herself, *but Erebos can't create New Earth until he's stronger. He needs blood and pain, the elements of birth, to bring him to full strength. You're helping him, Felrina! You're helping your people.*

"Yes, I am," she said with a nod. "That's all I want. I just wish Terrek were here. He used to *believe* in me. I just wish he understood!"

One day he will, she thought. *He'll know the truth and you'll be the one to show him!*

"Indeed," she breathed to the tarn's oily surface. "I will save him *and* make him love me again. I just wish I—"

She tensed when Arawn's spirit stirred in the murky depths to answer Erebos's will. Now the pool reflected more than the stalactite above her. She beheld the one thing her god, the Destroyer, feared the most: the staff known as Mornius.

"Talking to yourself, Felrina?" Allastor Mens padded toward her along the damp stone shelf that enclosed the water, his black garments rustling softly.

Felrina glowered at the pasty-faced leader of her order, despising him for what he was, the wild-eyed fanatic he was becoming. Though his power was no stronger than hers, she sensed a quality about it, a warped heat devouring him. "Sometimes I have to," she said. "After that horrible death last night . . ."

"'Horrible'?" Mens asked. "I honored that cropper. I gave him some of my finest work. You felt it yourself, Felrina, how his death empowered Erebos. We all did—everyone in that room."

She shifted her gaze to the pond's fetid water. "You didn't have to enjoy it so much, did you? I found the gray-robes' vomit on the floor behind the chairs."

"They'll get used to it," Mens said with a laugh. "And yes, I *enjoy* thinking about New Earth. We'll have it soon. Erebos will see to that, with no more *elves* and their confounded rules. I do enjoy my work, and so should you, Felrina. Erebos knows it when you don't."

Mens leaned over the tarn and sneered. "Oh look, Gaelin Lavahl," he said, jerking his head at the image the water revealed. His mocking tone echoed in the sunken chamber.

"Get out of here, Mens!" Felrina said. Then she knelt to stare at the pool's flat calm, scrutinizing the vision before her.

His smile malicious, Mens flipped his staff over. On the edge of her sight, she saw him plunge the bloodstone straight down into the tarn's black heart where dead Arawn's magic endured.

Mens motioned to the water. "Arawn's strength belongs to me, and here you are, wasting it."

"I am not." She caressed her staff's polished wood, studying the ruddy gem mounted in its crown. The Earth rock flickered in its twisted cage of steel. It was alien, she knew, a fragment from the planet her people had lost. Though the carnelian itself was devoid of magic, with it she could tighten Erebos's focus, allowing the trapped warder's power to affect the world. "Gaelin Lavahl could be a threat. There's a *maker* in his staff, remember? A creator of suns."

"Holram?" Mens snorted. "Erebos destroyed his priest, Jaegar Othelion, in the first war. What danger is he now?"

Lifting his staff, Mens bent to sniff with relish at the blood-tinged water rippling along its length. "Come *on*, Felrina! Lavahl is just a boy!"

She ignored him. His power of reason was gone, consumed by the old magic in the pool that had long ago been corrupted by Arawn's touch. Chanting, she drove her awareness deep into the tarn to find the soul of the great wizard. "Gaelin Lavahl," she whispered, "carrying Mornius, his staff . . . Why show me this, Arawn? Where does he go?"

The picture drew back. Felrina glimpsed a ring of white mountains with rolling fields tucked between them, and a town, its architecture both human and elvish, nestled behind the early morning mist. She reeled at the sight. Without the black-robe gripping her elbow, she would have toppled into the water.

"Heartwood?" She turned, clutching at Mens's bony shoulder. "We must stop him before he gets there! The Seeker elves . . . What if

Song of Mornius

they show him the truth?"

"The elves won't interfere," Mens gritted. She shuddered when he leaned against her, his fingers smoothing her brown hair. "And so what if they do? My forces obliterated Kideren, didn't they? You think I should worry about an illiterate *brat*?"

Felrina winced at his reference to her former home, the beloved community she had helped bring to ruin. She covered her ears with her hands, muting his nasal voice as best she could.

Once more she bent to the pool, resting her weight on her forearms while she studied the water's reflection, the moving images Arawn's dark skill had conjured.

Chapter 5

Gaelin Lavahl hiked on the rutted path leading to the town of Heartwood, a trail that rose and fell, curving between the white highland hills. A silvery mist hung over the forest flanking the valley to his left. He watched as the fog dispersed, the branches of the distant trees becoming more distinct as he crested the ridge to peer downward at the little town.

A round cluster of buildings and homes jutted below him, their angled rooftops glimmering in the light of the new dawn. Squinting hard, he surveyed the village. Though it was smaller than Kideren, he saw that Heartwood endured, its five unpaved streets joined together as spokes to the hub that was the bustling central market.

The Snarltooth's jagged peaks loomed to his left and right, towering high above the hills and forest at his back. To the south, the valley descended to where the village nestled. Beyond Heartwood, he spotted more icy fields, acres of land left barren after the harvest.

He pressed his cloak to his throat, glancing at the folds of fuzzy blue yarn covering his chest with interwoven charcoal-colored nubs. Gaelin scowled when he recalled his nights in the freezing barn on Mount Desheya and how desperately he had wished then for such a garment. Clutching his staff, he started at a sliding trot down the frozen slope.

Laughter rang from the town, drowning out for a moment the grinding sound of his footsteps. He stopped halfway to scan the many houses, their snowy shingles now level with his sight, their green-gold pennants fluttering above their shuttered windows. Somehow, the town remained undamaged by Erebos's cult, while the larger city of Kideren had fallen prey to the dark warder's army.

He frowned. He still could taste the blood in his mouth where he had bitten his tongue during the slaughter he had witnessed in Kideren. Even now, days later, he continued to find bits of ash clinging to his scalp. The gray flecks had floated leagues upon the air to the cliff where Terrek and his men had stood powerless to defend the city from the invading dachs.

The path leveled out as it neared Heartwood, the mud mixing with the dung of horses and cattle. Gaelin jerked to a halt, staring at a row of thorny sticks no higher than his waist that barred his way. He hesitated, fingering the rough twine holding the dead branches together before untying the fence's rickety gate.

The town reeked of humanity, the stale raw sewage of a nearby drop-shed and the exposed refuse ditch dug out by dogs. Sneezing, he rubbed his burning eyelids to clear away his tears, the brewery's yeasty odor making him gag.

As the roadway widened to enter Heartwood, people began swarming past him, an excited mob in homespun and furs hurrying him along. *These townsfolk don't know yet*, he thought as he approached the market. *Kideren was their capital city. Surely some of these people had family there!*

He broke away, pushing himself from the crowd. Heartwood's stench he could not avoid, but its ignorance, he would.

His destination stood tall and majestic beyond the town's perimeter. The elven temple brooded above Heartwood's lesser buildings, its long, alabaster face a disapproving pattern of light and shadow.

As he walked, Gaelin admired the curve of the temple's domed summit, the passing reflection of clouds on the adjacent hall's crystalline roof.

Reaching the town's outer buildings, he ducked between them and skulked toward the temple, skirting rusted plows and broken kegs and pottery. He vaulted over the remains of a collapsed wagon, falling backward when his cloak snagged on a nail. Pausing to catch his breath, he worked the cloth free and flipped it behind his shoulder.

At the base of the temple, he stopped, clenching his fists. Finally, lifting his staff, he forced himself up the steps. Crossing the threshold, he ventured in quietly.

The arched corridor was empty beyond its colored-glass doors and from a distance, he heard a tinkling of wooden chimes in the wind. Inhaling, he smiled at the perfumed air. The incense reminded him of chimara flowers or, from a very old memory, his mother's baked cinnamon apples.

His muscles relaxing, he took a step, and then with a sigh, settled on the floor to remove his boots. All around him, voices chanted in reverent tones as gradually the scented air changed. *Rain on leaves*, he thought, identifying the smell.

He lurched to his feet and proceeded down the hallway, padding stealthily as he savored the air caressing his skin, feeling how it beckoned him on. With each slow breath he steadied more, the tightness easing in his chest.

A hand clasped his wrist, pivoting him toward an open doorway. He recoiled, throwing his weight sideways in an effort to escape the Seeker Elf he had failed to hear, but who now stood close by.

The elf, frowning, reached past his flailing limbs. Gaelin froze when light fingertips brushed his cheek. He searched the elf's moss-colored eyes and found their depths filled with gentle concern. Sighing, he bowed his head.

"Good," said the stranger. "Come."

ASSISTED BY HIS guide, Gaelin stepped through the narrow doorway into a circular room. The candle-lit chamber was small, the mosaic on its floor depicting three wide tree trunks under a blue canopy of leaves. Sixteen silver-haired elves, clad in robes of ivory or blue, sat in a circle, each behind a glowing white candle. Alone and gripping his staff, he entered their midst.

"What is your language?" a sharp voice demanded. It came from a wizened individual seated on a golden pillow at the center of the ring. "You speak Thalusian, yes, but what of the elven common tongue? For nine hundred cycles, your race has existed on this world, yet in all that time, have any of you mastered even the simple phrases our infants know?"

With a rustling of ivory robes, the ancient elf stood. Raising his arms, he held out his hands, his palms toward Gaelin. "No? Well, tell me this, young human. We recognize the staff you hold. Mornius is dear to us. How did it come to you?"

Gaelin met the mage's piercing regard. "My father gave it to my mother before my birth."

"You stand here among us with an ancient Earth relic," said the elder. "Are you not afraid we will reclaim it? We understand the threat of its power, whereas you do not. Such might, in your ignorant hands, is a peril to us."

A pressure alighted on Gaelin's shattered cheekbone, invisible fingers probing his hurt. "A friend told me to come here," he said. "He assured me I could trust you and thought maybe you'd help us."

His skin prickled under his tunic when the feathery touches on his face, still unseen, lowered to his tightly bandaged ribs. Peering into the seer's glistening green eyes, Gaelin felt a pulse of warmth soothe his skin and gradually remove his pain.

"How brazen of your friend," said the elf, "to presume to know what we might do. Now, in your heart, I perceive your name, Gaelin Othelion, though at this moment you shun your rightful title. Indeed, Holram marks you as his, yet you deny him to follow a human?"

Gaelin glared in response. "Terrek saved my life. I'd follow him anywhere."

The mage's silvery brows furrowed. His gaze dropped to the tree design at his feet. "Anywhere?"

Gaelin nodded

"We hear you, Staff-Wielder," said the darker-haired novice Gaelin recognized as his guide. Clad in blue robes, the younger elf sat straight next to the elder, his legs folded alongside him on the marble floor. "The pain of your body is naught compared to the wreckage of your soul. We may ease your bruises and broken bones, but we cannot succor your spirit, not without preparation."

"Stay with us," the senior elf advised. "Allow us to defend you as we do our magic, the Circle of fire, water, air, soil, stone, and the flesh of giants. We shall remedy your hurts as we strive to mend all things. Let us comfort you, Gaelin, known as Lavahl."

Gaelin stared at the elves before him, their lithe bodies behind their candles. Despite his efforts to hide his inner turmoil, still he could see how they sensed it.

"That's not what we need, though," he said, his voice thick in his throat. "Erebos's hordes destroyed Kideren. They waited until we were leagues away; then all we could do was stand helpless while the winged dachs came like a shadow across the sky.

"They took Chalse first," said Gaelin, "Kideren's sister city. Terrek's father sent a rider from Vale Horse with the news. We are here to turn the cult's army from Heartwood if we can."

"They have visited us already," the elf said. "I assure you, our shield held."

Gaelin hesitated. "If you mean your little fence, how can that stand up to . . . ?" He stopped at the seer's knowing look.

"Appearances," the eldest mage said, "often defy reality. If not for your vocabulary, I would take you for a foundling raised by animals, as many human children were after your people first arrived. Yet you are not what you pretend to be, and neither is our fence."

Gaelin cleared his throat, feeling his cheeks go hot. "We have to save Tierdon, where Terrek's brother lives. If you could help us guard that city or give us a weapon we could use . . ." Slowly he lifted his staff. "Or am I holding one here? Can Mornius kill?"

A hush filled the chamber while the ancient elder reseated himself. Through the lengthening silence, Gaelin shifted from foot to foot and watched while sixteen pairs of glittering eyes tracked his every move.

"Holram does not take life," the old leader said, finally. "From this warder comes heat, health, and light, only."

Gaelin scanned the seer's upturned face. "Could I make it kill?"

"Terrek Florne is important to you," observed the novice.

"Yes," said the elder. "These are your leader's desires we hear from your mouth. His words, not yours. What is it *you* wish, Staff-Wielder?"

Gaelin peered at the mysterial elves. He glimpsed flashes of fire in their troubled gazes, a blue-needled forest burning alive. "You want to know what *I* . . ." He pounded his fist against his hip. "I want to fight at Terrek's side. Mornius heals, but that's not enough."

36

Ivory robes flared when the eldest stood once more. "I am Cojahra, Master Seeker," he said, raising his hand. "I salute Holram, the child of Sephrym, our warder."

The elven ring came to their feet and bowed. Then, as they each took a knee, Gaelin groaned. "No, I don't deserve that."

"Though he is not of our magic," said Cojahra, "we revere Holram's spirit as well. He helped Sephrym breathe new life into our sun." With a nod, Cojahra lowered his arm. "As his priest, we will honor you also."

"But I don't . . ." Gaelin faltered when he met the mage's quiet stare. "Please, I care nothing about warders. I just need to know"— again he lifted his staff—"can I use this to kill?"

Cojahra shook his head. "Mornius carries power within its stone, yes, the essence of Holram, who was banished long ago. His purpose is to gather light and the potential for life. He is a creator of *suns*, Gaelin Lavahl."

"Suns?" Gaelin scowled at the elf.

"Indeed," Cojahra continued, "yet he has fallen. He sleeps now in the staff, and while he does, your thoughts manipulate his power. You influence what it does.

"But know this, young human. Holram's need for rest is ending. Once he wakes, *he* will direct his power, not you. When he does, your roles will be reversed and you will need to accept his authority. He will control *you*."

Gaelin considered the candlelight flickering on the opposite wall, the wavering shadows of the kneeling elves. "So Mornius can kill. Terrek was right."

Again, the young elf stood, followed once more by the others. "Until Holram reunites with his power, Mornius is yours to wield. You direct its song. But hear my father, for he asks that you remain with us. Holram rouses, and Erebos knows this. To stop Holram, the dark warder will seek to slay you. If he finds you before Holram can prepare, we will lose all hope."

Gaelin straightened. "My mother *died* because of me. I need that to count for something; I can't do it hiding here."

He watched while the senior magus lifted up his hands. "Our way is one of peace, Gaelin Lavahl. We commit ourselves to healing, to preserving the Circle, which holds our magic. We cannot join you in this endeavor or aid you with our power.

"Hear me," Cojahra went on, "these victims of Erebos whom you name bodachs after mythical creatures from your Earth are still as human as you are, wounded against their will. We desire health for them, not more harm. If you intend to commit murder, even in self-defense, you will not have our support. It is not the fault of humans the Destroyer came to our world. Yet he is trapped here, a threat to everything we cherish. Only Holram can stop him. That is his purpose: to *prevent* death."

"I understand." Gaelin bowed to the mage. "But he wouldn't be killing the dachs. I would. And I know nothing about . . ."

"Then *stay*," Cojahra said, "and let us instruct you."

Gaelin straightened. "There *is* something in my staff. It knows what I'm feeling; sometimes it even talks to me. All my life it's been there, but it's never done anything to protect me. It never *could* . . ." He searched for the right words. "You called it a warder. If that's true, it should have been able to save me, but it didn't. No." He glanced at Mornius. "I believe it is my *father's* spirit I sense in the staff, the one I never knew. My mother called him a wizard. I think he watches me somehow, and he would help me if he could."

"I see how the man you become grasps the truth," Cojahra said, "while this child you remain denies it. Do as you will. In your way, you speak truly. Holram is a father to you, just as Sephrym is the father to us all. Your warder does empower you, though you realize it not, and as he rouses, his aid will grow stronger."

The younger elf approached him. "Come," he said. "Let me lead you."

Despite the draft on his skin as he left the tiny room, Gaelin could hear nothing from outside the temple. The friendly chimes were silent now, undisturbed by the wintry wind.

Gaelin sniffed at the air. "I guess I failed," he said.

"Failed? Was there a test?" The novice's wispy brows lifted toward his silver-black hair, his eyes narrowing. "There is no failure in you."

Gaelin gaped at him. "Why do you care how I feel? I don't even know your name!"

"Would knowing my name make a difference?" The mage-in-training smiled. "We are brothers in spirit, you and I, Seekers in our way."

Gaelin pondered this in silence while his escort brought him to the outer doors. "Can't I know?"

"I will give you my name if you answer a question for me." The elf stepped to block his way. In the background Gaelin heard the chimes renewing their song, quietly at first, a sweet, random music.

A smile tugged at his lips, his heart calming while he bent to pull on his boots. The thought of enduring Heartwood's crowded streets terrified him, but the music stilled his fear, the air soothing him with smells of sweet berries and clover.

Frowning, the young elf studied him. "Why Terrek Florne?" he asked. "Are you not tired of violence? I see scars in you now, and also in the child you used to be. Your mind has walls. This fortress keeps you safe, but it does not permit you to grow. Who is this human you swear your fealty to? How is it you can trust him?"

"You don't understand," Gaelin said. "I wanted to die for what I did. I went to Kideren hoping to be punished, but no one would see me. Not until Terrek. He stopped in the rain and *listened*. I've known bad people, Elf. Terrek is not one of them."

"Peace, Gaelin Lavahl. Your eyes convey what your words cannot." The novice chuckled. "As to my name, I am Everove, the youngest of my order. Cojahra is my father."

Gaelin sighed. "I was afraid to come here. I'm not good around people."

Smiling, Everove opened the doors. He squinted up at the pale sun. "Light—it nourishes life and fills our hearts with hope. Be at peace, Gaelin Lavahl, for your true name awaits you. It is my wish you may find it along the way."

Gaelin ventured past him, then turned for a final glimpse of his face. But the young elf was gone, lost behind a bright ray of sunshine and the temple's glass doors.

Chapter 6

With cautious steps, Avalar walked above the steep riverbank, slowing warily when the trees thinned in front of her. She could see how the stream slanted east, winding out across the valley toward the outline of mountains through the mist. For a moment she paused at the smell of smoke, feeling magic in the air tingle against her skin. "A fire," she whispered, glancing at the sky. "Someone is close."

She arched her back, shifting her pack higher on her shoulders. Veering to the left, she abandoned the openness of the river for the trees. A crunching noise drew her attention to her feet, to the brown petals of clove-leaf she crushed as she skirted the meadow.

She heard a cry of distress, a sound like a wounded racka in a snare. "Sails! Is something hurt?" Gripping her sword, she froze when the voice wailed again. It came from the bend in the river behind her, as if the turbulent water grieved at being left alone.

Instinct called her, awakening racial memories. Despite her fear, they compelled her to action, turning her from the trees and the west-risen sun. *I am sorry, Ponu*, she thought, *but I must defend the weak. This is what giants do!*

Once more, she approached the river, tentatively descending the slope. Within her, a memory lived. She heard through her father's ears the long-ago shriek of human-warped magic—felt the pain tearing at his heart. Sweat gathered on her brow. The skin of her back flinched, anticipating punishment, a cruel whip's painful lash.

She bared her teeth, focusing with effort on her immediate surroundings. As she reached the high bank, she cast her pack onto a clump of grass, freeing her limbs for battle.

A moan rose up from below. Kneeling, Avalar peered over the

edge.

Panic flattened her to the ground before she could think.

Lying there, her cheek pressed against the frozen dirt, she winced while the past and the present collided in her mind. Her basic instincts clashed inside, her urge to flee or fight, and her desire to protect. The voices of murdered slaves yowled within the vault of her skull, warning her with one united cry: "*Human!*"

Avalar groaned, scrabbling at the hard soil under her. The high-pitched wail rose for the third time, a terrified keening. Still quaking, she sat, hugging her ankles as she confronted the river.

"Please," a soft voice groaned. "Help me!"

Pressing her chin to her knees, Avalar rocked.

Fear sharpened the voice. "Who's *there?*"

Her breath caught in her chest. She was a giant, a guardian of her world. No memory of slavery could deprive her of that. It was the identity and purpose of her people, and it dwelled, burning deep, in her heart. *Come, Giant. It is just one human.* She crawled again to the bank and looked down.

He was small, with spindly limbs. Because of his tears, he had not seen her yet, at least not clearly. She could still abandon him and leave him to starve, or worse. The memories he conjured were strong, urging her to *flee* with all of her strength, yet his helplessness stopped her.

His face was contorted as he lay sprawled on his back, his chest heaving. His left arm had flopped over the stones and his other clutched at a jumble of wood, a gnarled stump thrown out by the wild current. The skid marks on the bank behind him revealed how he had slipped from above to become ensnared. Now he lay trapped beneath the twisted roots, his left leg pinned.

Raising her gaze, she scanned the narrow clearing. He was far from any habitation and utterly alone. No one would find him here.

"Mother!" The human sobbed. Avalar, watching him, caught the timbre of his voice, the childish quaver. *Why, he is just a baby*, she thought.

She drew erect and unbuckled her sword. "I hear you," she called in his language. She saw his face slant toward her. Any lingering doubt vanished at his stark expression of fear.

Avalar dropped her weapon and knelt. "Rest easy," she said. "I am

41

here to succor you if I can. There is no one else."

He whimpered when she rolled onto her stomach atop the ledge and lowered her hips. Blindly she explored with her boot. The boulders beside his left hip were stable beneath her, held in place by layers of mud. She centered her weight and turned.

His lips quivered, his brown eyes bulging at the sight of her. Groaning, he strained to break free.

Avalar crouched to touch his elbow. "Peace, little one. I will help you. Where are you injured?"

For a moment more he struggled before he sagged against the rocks, his eyes closed while he gasped for air. "My *leg*!"

"Nothing more?" Suddenly curious, she stroked his velvety cheek. He cringed as she patted back his grimy hair. "I shall see you to your home," she told him. "But first you must tell me where you hurt."

The boy shivered as he stared at her. "My leg," he said again. "My . . . my ankle!"

Avalar twitched off her Sundor Khan cloak. It was heavy even for her. *Yet it will warm him*, she thought. She tucked it around the child and then settled on her haunches next to him, bracing her heels against the tangled wood.

"How come you're so big?" he asked.

She smiled, flicking him a glance. "How are you so small?" she countered as, still grinning, she drew back her feet.

The stump recoiled as she kicked it, exploding from the mud to splash down into the rushing water.

She removed what remained of the roots, disposing of them as well. At last, turning to the child, she lifted his leg and cradled it. He cried out while she did so, clutching at her fingers as she settled back, setting his wounded ankle on the pillow of her thigh. Her attention on his face, she unlaced his boot and opened the worn leather flaps.

"It *hurts*!" the child moaned.

"Shh, I know," she said, uncovering the foot. The flesh was a yellowish purple, the skin abraded along one side. Softly she probed the child's bones from the calf on down.

"You have bruised your ankle and toes," she said. "Fear not, tiny human. You will mend. How long were you trapped here?"

His eyes glistened. "Mother sent me out for wood after I finished my supper, and a prowler chased me. They've been hunting around

Firanth. They take our chickens."

"A prowler?" Avalar blinked at the boy. She knew of the ancient catlike people but had no idea the race still existed on Thalus. "And you escaped?"

The boy nodded. "I played dead," he answered, a note of pride in his piping voice. "Prowlers only eat what they kill, you know."

"Yes," she said. "It was fortunate you recognized the danger. For no human can see a magical creature unless it wishes it. Indeed, he *was* hunting you."

The child raised his head, watching as she stood. She lifted him up to the level of her chin, stretched him out atop the bank, and scrambled up to join him. She set to work, splinting his leg and foot using fragments of bark from the stump, then binding it with leather scavenged from her stores.

"We must get you home," she said, climbing to her feet. Once more, she strapped on her sword and wriggled her pack onto her armored shoulders. He looked up expectantly, and she bent to scoop him into her arms. "How far is this Firanth?"

He gestured to the west. "Half . . . half a league! I thought I was going to die! The prowler said he wanted to . . . play, but I—"

"Ah!" she interrupted as she hurried toward the meadow. "I know what he meant by 'play.' His kind are cousins to creatures I am familiar with—the Sherkon Raiders. Prowlers are not as fearsome or as big."

The child's eyes went wide. "They are pirates," she replied to his silent question. "The Sherkon Raiders inhabit Tholuna, the southern continent where my people lived. Their appearance is much like the creature you saw, with size and strength enough to tackle a giant, which is one reason we live on Hothra now."

She sighed as she envisioned the heavily maned, leonine warriors who patrolled the Misty Sea. "It is well they avoid this colder climate," she said. "They would slay humans. They would slay a *giant* if they could. 'Play' is everything to them. My people would block their ships. We would drive their vessels into temperate waters, far away from vulnerable targets. Now, with so few of us left, that duty falls to the elves."

Avalar bared her teeth in a voiceless snarl, yearning for the day the Raiders would cease to exist, driven into extinction as they had slaughtered so many.

The boy groaned in her arms, and she regarded him with concern. "Not long now," she reassured him. Reaching the trees, she turned sideways to squeeze her pack between their frozen branches. "What are you called?"

"Kray." His gaze found hers. "You're a giant?"

"Yes, indeed," she answered, moving farther into the forest. "I am Avalar Mistavere. Do I frighten you?"

"No," he said. "Giants are always bad in my mother's stories, though. They stomp on people and . . ."

"Real giants do not stomp," she said, laughing. "We are taller than you humans, but most of the time we are not *that* large. We would rather lend our strength and stamina to the world. As important as our magic is, little Kray, it is not wholly what we are."

"How come you're here?" he asked.

"It has to do with a sword called Redeemer," she told him. "A magical blade our leader discovered long ago. It was a tool of salvation created for giants, wrought by no living hand. Legend has it that our magic formed the sword from caches of bloodstones within the ground. No one knows the sword's origin, or how our savior, Thresher Govorian, managed to find it and have the skill to wield it. He was a farmer's son. He had never held such a weapon in his life."

"Redeemer." Kray smiled, staring up as though he imagined the bloodstone sword nestled among the boughs.

The sunlight faded in the deepening forest. "The Bloodsword," she said. "For as long as I have lived, it has been on display in the treasure hall on Hothra. When I was a child, it sang to me. It made me see I needed to come here, to learn to fight, but also . . ."

She swatted away an icicle falling from the tree limb above her.

"Also?" Kray prompted.

Smiling, Avalar clomped over the frozen bones of a thorny bush and the silver-leafed fern beyond. "Giants should live as they were meant to," she said. "I will show my people that they can."

The boy sighed. She wondered at his stamina, and yet his brow and cheeks seemed deathly pale, his lips tinged blue. She quickened her pace. *What if he dies?* she thought.

Voices shattered the stillness before her, and Avalar jerked to a halt. She squatted down, listening hard while the approaching strangers called back and forth. She heard a rhythmic thwacking, multiple blades hewing through the frozen brush.

Avalar loosened her pack and let it drop. Then she stood, gripping her sword's hilt.

Kray's lids fluttered open. "Mother?"

Avalar gasped. Once again, she was plagued by visions and memories not her own. Almost she could feel the brutal weight pressing the back of her neck, the low, rocky ceiling of the mines. Grakan roared and whined through the darkness. Giants screamed as their magic was harvested, ripped by force from their bodies by the slavers.

A figure, reeking of smoke, crashed through the trees in front of her and froze. Even on the hillock where he stood, the top of his parka's green hood barely cleared her hip. The boy strained forward in her grasp, yet Avalar ignored him. She snatched out her sword, standing poised on the balls of her feet.

"Uncle Sherin!" the boy cried.

Avalar waited. Kray's voice was distant to her ears, lost behind the memory of her father's pain and fear. She stood ready as the adult human approached, her weapon whistling as she slashed at the air.

She widened her stance when more humans ventured into view. She counted four, one woman accompanied by three older men, all hollow-eyed and starving. Circling her, the newcomers brandished their sticks and machetes—puny threats she deflected with her sword.

Only the boy clutching at her arm steadied her pounding heart. "Don't fight them," he pleaded, glancing up. "Please! She's my mother!"

"Back away!" Avalar warned the strangers. "Do it and I shall give you this child; do it *not* ..." Her control shattered, and she howled. "Get *away!*"

Kray's mother stumbled as she complied, her face haggard. "Kray?" she called. "Are you injured?"

"The giant saved me!" Kray yelled over the indignant cries of the watching men. "I fell in the river. A prowler chased me!"

The woman hesitated, and Avalar scanned her closely, glimpsing beneath the grime and careworn features the protective mother she was to Kray, not so unlike the parents of giant children. "She is very beautiful, Kray," Avalar said. "What is her name?"

"Lianna Middleton!" the boy answered as he stretched out his arms. "Mother!"

Lianna waved the others back behind the trees. Reluctantly, the men obeyed, arguing in their rough Thalusian tongue.

Avalar bent to lay the child on the ground, freeing him from her heavy cloak. She met Lianna's stare. "Please," Avalar said. Again she spoke in the same guttural language she had used with Kray, feeling grateful for the first time in her life for her tedious lessons at Freedom Hall. "You are famished, and I have food."

The little people went very still, and Avalar opened her pack, sensing how their hungry gazes tracked her every move, their interest intensifying. "Your son was injured, and I succored him. Now, if I may, I wish to give you aid. Have the prowlers taken so much? How many of you have perished?"

Lianna motioned to the trees. "Sherin, my brother, take Kray. Do it now."

A tall, balding man skulked forward to claim the boy. Avalar allowed it, winking at Kray while his uncle swept him up, hastening the child away from her sight.

She lifted a greenish sphere from her opened pack, the color of reef-bulb she had designated for dried fish. Carefully she placed it on the frozen ground and stepped back. "Hold it with your knees," Avalar instructed the woman, "and press along the seam to pry it open. It's smelly, but it will lend you strength for your journey home."

Hesitantly Lianna lowered her weapon and Avalar smiled, hoping belatedly it would not be taken as a threat. "Prowlers prefer their own territory," Avalar said. "It seems to me they have claimed this area. I am not wise, but I say you would do well to settle elsewhere."

Nodding a mute farewell, Avalar retreated. She ducked under the branch of a massive pine, keeping her sword at the ready while checking repeatedly behind her. Focused as she was on putting as many trees as possible between her and the humans, Avalar failed to notice how the winter birds had hushed.

A swift, soft panting alerted her. She spotted the dark smudge of a figure crouched low beneath a fern, the glimmer of its steady amber eyes peering up.

Avalar stopped short. "Are you pursuing these humans?" she asked. "Should I be hunting you?"

"Fish," the creature hissed. "Grubby paws, I smell. Give me!"

Avalar considered the hidden figure. Despite its petite stature, she felt a tingle of fear. "You are rude," she told it. "Why should I give you anything?"

"I notter trail humans," came the sibilant voice. "Fish better." It paused, and Avalar heard a quick series of grunting breaths. "Fish, give me!"

"Show yourself," said Avalar. "Let me see you first."

The branches swayed. Slowly the creature stalked toward her, bounding into her sight. It was lithe and lean, its color that of pale sunlight filtered through leaves both golden and brown.

Avalar caught her breath, stunned by the prowler's unexpected beauty.

The predator was naked, its flat, lean muscles sliding beneath a short, tawny-red coat dappling into gray along its flanks and shoulders. Stripes of ebony reached from its calves and elbows to its furry black paws. It was small, half the size of a human, its limbs designed for running on all fours. Its sharp ears flicked in her direction, pricking atop its domed skull.

As Avalar watched, the hooded, wide-spaced eyes glinted up at her, the blunt muzzle lifting, jaws parting into a needle-toothed smile. "She-prowler," the creature purred. "Beautiful, yes? You like?"

Avalar inclined her head, entranced by the creature's golden stare. "You *are* beautiful," she said. "Were you following me? What is your name?"

A raspy thrumming came from the carnivore's throat. "I, Shetra. I notter harm giant. Notter hurt life of world. Prowler protect!"

"Good," Avalar told her. "For I am battle-trained by Grevelin Mistavere. No giant knows combat so well as he."

The catlike creature lashed her rust-colored tail. "I notter match for giant. Fish?"

Avalar snorted. Again, she shrugged off her pack, keeping her blade at the ready for the predator to see.

Her last reef-bulb landed with a soft crunch at the prowler's feet, but on impulse Avalar leaned in, the threat of her blade holding the creature back. "Promise," she said, "none of your people will stalk these humans. If they do, I shall know it. We giants have a way of knowing these things. We thwarted your Raider cousins in the south, and if we must, we will stop *you*."

Shetra's breath puffed her cheeks with an agitated rhythm. "No prowler hunt. Cruel human take human meat, notter prowler!"

"You lie," Avalar said. "Last night a child was injured by one of *your* kind."

"Shem." Shetra opened her jaws in a toothy yawn of disgust. "Bad

48

male is outsider. Heem hurt here." With a splay-toed paw, she tapped at her temple. "Notter good."

Avalar drew back her weapon, surrendering her last bulb. "To protect the humans, I will kill this Shem if I find him. If you have love for him at all, warn him to leave this land at once."

Shetra sprang forward and fastened her jaws on the glistening green sphere. A second great leap took her sailing over the low-hanging branches of the trees.

Avalar stared at the spot where the prowler had been. Something sinister preyed on the town of Firanth, feasting on its people.

She forced her thoughts to more immediate things like hunting for her dinner and replenishing her stores. "I am your companion once more," she told the river. "Until I reach this Lake Crinath, where we shall again part ways, for I am marching to Tierdon!"

Ponu had mentioned a path between the mountains. Yet right now, from where she stood, it seemed unlikely they would ever end.

Chapter 7

$\mathcal{G}$aelin sighed as he braced himself on his staff. He stood on a hill with his shoulders to the wind more than a league away from the town of Heartwood. A few hours ago, he had visited the Seeker elves' temple, strolling barefoot next to Everove through its pristine hall, oblivious to the doom tightening a noose around Heartwood's inhabitants. Now, viewed from a distance, the cluster of peaked rooftops glittered like hammered blacksteel under the rays of the setting sun, the alabaster temple gleaming pink and gold behind them.

The appearance of Terrek on his plunging white gelding at the base of the sanctuary's steps, and afterward the wild ride into the hills, had shocked out of him any lingering benefit he had gained from the temple's tranquility.

"We ride to battle!" Terrek had shouted, and Gaelin's wrist still ached where Terrek had seized him to help him mount. They had ridden hunched over the racing horse, reining Duncan from side to side to avoid the dachs' diving attacks from above, the winged creatures striking at them with primitive sabers.

At least twenty humans from Heartwood had joined Terrek's forces, or so it seemed to Gaelin as Terrek threaded his lathered horse around the heaps of dead branches and other debris the men had piled between the two hills.

"The dachs fear sunlight," Gaelin mused with a glance at the clouds. He recalled Terrek's hasty explanation to his new men: "*They attack any burning thing. We'll lure them to the fires and come down at them from both sides!*"

A bell ringing from the town interrupted Gaelin's reflections, and he saw Heartwood's streets emptying below, the fearful people hurrying into their darkened shops and homes.

He started when Mornius's pulsing gem crackled close to his ear, and a quiet, stern voice entered his awareness, entwining itself with his thoughts: "*I am here.*"

Gaelin winced at the pressure mounting in his temples. A sickness roiled in his belly, the familiar nausea he experienced whenever he heard the staff's voice inside his head. He pulled his blue cloak higher up his neck, hugging its folds to his chest while he watched the sun settle behind the mountains.

The forest, separating the valley from the surrounding peaks, spread out along the fringes of the harvested fields. He could see a commotion in the dimming treetops and in the woodland's outgrowth of pines between the town and himself. The branches moved where the enemy crouched, the dachs waiting for the cover of dusk as obligingly the twilight gathered, creeping out across the rolling hills.

It'll be different this time, Gaelin reminded himself, his fingertips tingling. *Terrek expects me to kill.*

AS THE LAST streaks of daylight faded in the east, a flock of winged dachs, with their long gray bodies and lashing tails, exploded from the trees on all sides. Screaming, they arrowed toward the blazing fires the warriors had built, hurling fistfuls of snow or dirt in their haste to extinguish the flames.

"*Now!*" Terrek's breath plumed as he shouted, and when his horse reared up, his fighters charged. Down the twin hills they rushed in their mismatched armor, their weapons flailing at the descending winged horde.

More black figures burst from the forest with their sabers drawn, Erebos's flightless dach army pouring from a shadow behind the benighted pines. Gaelin rubbed his eyes. The mind-touch from his staff, its earlier intrusion of words in his skull, had made him feel oddly detached. He squatted, cognizant of the men launching arrows and spears at their winged foes above him.

He saw movement in the distance beyond the trees. The flimsy fence that surrounded Heartwood was growing. Touched by the golden light from the bonfires, the circle of dead sticks came alive under their knotted twine, their new branches sprouting, weaving together as they rose swiftly to the height of the town's gabled roofs, the sharp thorns forming a defensive dome.

A hand slapped his cheek, jerking him back to his place on the hill and the clash of men and dachs in front of him. He flinched when hard fingers seized his shoulder.

"Gaelin!" Terrek yelled into his face. "Do it *now!*"

Gaelin lifted his gaze, groaning at the pain knifing through his head. Terrek's eyes were intense, his expression fierce as the pressure of his grip triggered memories—Seth Lavahl and his years of torment. Crying out, Gaelin recoiled. "Stop! Let me—"

"*Release him!*"

Gaelin tottered. The booming voice came from his throat, but it was not his own. In shock, he stumbled and fell, and a flash of white light from Mornius smote Terrek's chest, sending him careening into his horse.

Gaelin stared at his staff's dissolving power, the lavender-blue tongues of it rippling down his arms. He fought to breathe, to see Terrek's stunned dismay through the glare of Mornius's multicolored gem. "I'm sorry!" he called. "I don't know what happened. I didn't *mean—*"

Terrek wheeled to parry a dach's blow aimed for his neck, grunting as he threw his attacker back. The creature paused, the fanned spikes along its spine exuding poison, and Gaelin caught a glimpse of the enemy's face, its human skin melted and stiffened to form scales. The open mouth twisted into a pointy-toothed grimace, its crimson eyes blazing over the ridge of its nose.

Gaelin staggered when a fighter crashed into him as he tried to climb to his feet. Everywhere he looked, the mindless creatures struggled. He had observed them from afar, but never so close. *They're people*, he thought, *tortured like me.*

Mornius's Skystone flared above his hand while from some

distant, echoing place, he heard weeping.

"Grakan's teeth!" Terrek's voice seemed muted as he yelled, "Vyergin, *stop!*"

"*They suffer.*" Gaelin cringed when the voice within his skull drowned out his benefactor's words. He transferred Mornius to his left hand, the staff's power swirling between his fingers. Frantic now, he skidded after Terrek across the shadowed half of the hill, his staff vibrating against his palm.

A scream, cut short from somewhere below him, sent him ducking behind the trunk of a tree as a clamor rose, the clash of metal and the thumps of weapons striking flesh. Under his staff's pale light, Gaelin spotted several bloodied men struggling past the bluebark pine concealing him, their legs trembling as they continued to fight the pursuing dachs.

A battle-ax's wooden shaft protruded from a body nearby. Without thinking, Gaelin lunged for it, grabbed at its haft, and yanked it free. He sprinted, catching up to the last dach, swinging the ax wildly at the creature's shoulder.

Instinctively Gaelin heaved backward, dislodging the steel blade. He spun around, cleaving his adversary's temple as it collapsed.

Fluid jetted, the hot blood splattering him, and he lurched, gagging, to his knees, the ax falling from his grasp. In a flash of brutal memory, Gaelin visualized Seth Lavahl's dismemberment. Once more, he breathed the stench of his crime; transfixed, he gaped at his hands.

He winced, two swords clanging close to his head. Wren Neche joined him, his slim blade deflecting the dach's attack. Beyond Wren, metal flickered under the moonlight—the enemy's sabers felling warriors he knew, men like Terrek, who needed him to kill.

"*They suffer!*" said the voice, and Gaelin howled.

To kill!

Gaelin clambered upright, anger swelling in his chest, slashing crimson across his sight. Against his will the staff erupted, blasts of blue power bursting from its gem in all directions. He blinked, dazzled by Mornius's brilliance, its alien magic exploding through the trees and setting the ground afire.

The dachs screamed. Blistered bodies tumbled and fell, twisting in agony under each consecutive pulse from the stone.

"Lavahl!" Wren shouted. "*Behind* you!"

He wheeled, and another blast shocked him. More creatures fell, their writhing shapes curling, melting like wax into smoldering ruin.

Gaelin shambled among the ashy husks that had been his foe. He sensed the presence rousing in his staff, the entity in the Skystone longing to heal the misery it saw, and yet the warder's efforts only intensified the staff's power, the magic whipping into a frenzy.

Gaelin crested the hill and saw the bowman he knew as Grenner sprawled on his back. At once his mind cleared, the fire from his staff sputtering out. The wounded man stared at the stars, his hand gripping his mail. Gaelin stumbled toward him. "Did you drop your bow?" he asked, kneeling at Grenner's hip. "I don't see any blood."

"My side!" the marksman wheezed. "A polearm hit me. I can't . . . breathe!"

Closing his eyes, Gaelin tilted his staff above Grenner's hand. *Grenner, the one who likes to whistle*, he thought. He pictured the fighter strong and whole as he positioned Mornius higher. Because of his inner turmoil, he had lost control of the staff's power. Yet now he focused, reaching with his mind into the Skystone.

Grenner lashed out, and Gaelin hissed as the bowman gripped his forearm. Lowering his staff, Gaelin pressed its stone against the warrior's chest. Power crackled, spilling in ripples over his fingers. Grenner's legs thrashed and then stilled.

Gaelin sat back when Grenner released him, his hand tingling as he set Mornius in the grass. He bent, probing his patient through the rings of protective mail, finding the broken ribs knitted and whole.

Grenner staggered to his feet and grinned.

"Stay." Through a haze of fatigue, Gaelin reached to detain the determined battler. "You need rest."

Grenner pulled free. "We'll stop them, Staff-Wielder!" he cried. "This won't be like Kideren!"

Gaelin opened his mouth to protest, but the warrior was already striding across the hill with his sword drawn. Dazedly, Gaelin bent to collect his staff before limping to follow.

The forest burned below him, its flames glowing orange over the lumps of the blackened trees. Gaelin stumbled as he neared the base of the hill, overwhelmed by the destruction his staff had caused, his hand shielding his eyes from the noxious smoke.

The flightless dachs huddled, trapped between the bonfires and the reduced ranks of Terrek's men. Their bloodshot eyes staring, the hapless creatures cringed at their airborne counterparts' attempts to save them. In a cluster, they gibbered and sobbed.

Gaelin screwed his eyes shut. From far away, he heard the dachs' screaming and the ugly thud of metal on flesh as Terrek's fighters finished their work.

Terrek rose in his stirrups, his bloody blade held high, his white horse pawing the smoldering ground. The weary men—many of them carrying or dragging the wounded—converged toward their commander.

Gaelin leaned on Mornius. The cries of the injured caught hold of him, driving him through the worst of the carnage. The hills and trees wavered in his dwindling sight as he fought to stay erect. His shoulders aching, he raised his staff.

Terrek waved back over his triumphant men. When he shouted, his words were unintelligible, yet Gaelin caught the note of command in his voice.

Gaelin sank to his knees and pressed his cheek against Mornius's crystal. His consciousness penetrated the gem, the Skystone's intricate matrix guiding him deep into a restless fog.

As the mist brightened around him, he heard the sound of weeping, spied a figure transforming itself while he watched—first into a dragon, next a wolf, and then a man. After a final convulsion, the entity became a lion stretching out its massive forepaws, and Gaelin felt its power filling his chest, a frigid pressure ensnaring his heart.

He struggled for breath, feeling the ice spread through his arms. His fingers clenched. Healing fire erupted from Mornius's stone, arcing across the hills.

Gaelin slumped, his head bowed as he embraced the staff and pressed it to his chest. Heedless of the bloody grass, he rolled over onto his face as the light pulsing beside him went dark.

Chapter 8

Gaelin stirred, drawn from the mist by a rock and sway of motion, the grinding crunch of hooves breaking through the frozen crust. He sensed a pressure holding him still, the feel of hands clamped over his ribs.

Voices spoke above him. He saw glimmers of firelight and the golden rise of another dawn. Someone shifted him, and for a time he rode, his chin tapping against his chest.

He shivered at the kiss of wind on his cheek, finding himself stretched atop a blanket. Beneath his back and his cushion of layered wool, a squeaky wooden floor jerked as it moved. He heard the neighing of several horses, smelled grain and the sweet scent of hay—until the sky tipped him over, spinning him into the fog.

Then he was facedown, his cheek against the frosted ground. He caught a confused glimpse of a misty stream below him as someone raised him up, an impression in the stiffened grass where his body had been. "Thirsty," he mumbled, batting at the arms holding him still.

"Let's try some soup," Vyergin said. "The lad needs fluids."

Gaelin nodded, staring at the smudge of sunlight through the branches. He licked his lips at the thought of Vyergin's broth, smiling at the crackle of a nearby fire as his mind began to drift.

∞ ∞ ∞

Song of Mornius

GAELIN AWOKE TANGLED in blankets, the taste of salt on his tongue and sweat trickling down his neck. Dreamily he gaped at the tent's slanted ceiling, his ears catching the sound of whispering snowflakes.

As his head cleared, he rolled onto his stomach, wriggling forward under his covers. He peered through the crack of the tent's door-flap at the pale sky and the looming white peaks. The trees in his view dwarfed the figure he spied by the central fire. They were the massive kingskies, a silvery blue conifer he had not seen around Heartwood.

He kicked at the blankets and lifted up onto his elbows for a better glimpse of the man seated beside the flames. He recognized Terrek, watching as the commander inclined his body toward the blaze.

Climbing upright, Gaelin picked his way from the shelter.

A line of spear points glittered to his right, their shafts propped against the trees. All around him, the warriors struck their tents or knelt to pack their gear. Behind the shelters that were still erect, the horses rattled their pails, eagerly lipping the last of their grain.

Terrek glanced up, the muscles tightening around his mouth beneath his regrowth of sandy beard. "Nice to see you awake."

Gaelin squatted near the fire and yawned. The kettle spat water at the flames, sending puffs of steam to mingle with the smoke. "How far have we come?"

The lines deepened between Terrek's brows. His leather cuirass squeaked when he shifted on the knotty log. "The attack was the day before yesterday," he said. "Heartwood is safe. I'm not sure if you saw it, but the elves raised a dome over the town no dachs could breach."

Gaelin stared. "Two *days*?"

"We've journeyed twenty leagues since the battle on the hills," said Terrek. "The mountains slowed us a bit, but our new ponies got us through."

"Ponies?" Gaelin looked again at the trees where the tethered animals munched their grain.

"Adapted to higher elevations, yes," Terrek said. "They have tougher feet too, though they still need pads under their shoes to protect them from the snow. We stopped at Westermore to have the horses we kept reshod, and while we were waiting, we swapped out the wagons, got three sleds for our provisions, and I've hired wranglers to help with the animals. It cost a heavy shukna, but my father's credit was good.

"Oh, and"—bending forward, Terrek snatched up a stick from beside his legs and poked it at the fire—"remind me later; I have some new gear for you in my pack. We bought more blankets, too." He gestured to the nubby fabric covering his lap. "It gets colder where we're going."

Gaelin lowered his head when the clearing around him canted sideways. He braced against the stump behind him and pushed himself up to claim it as his seat.

"Dizzy?" Terrek asked, concerned.

Gaelin nodded. "Did someone . . . *carry* me?"

Terrek dropped the stick and stood. "That was Jahn Oburne. The trail got steep for a while and I had my horse to deal with. We feared you might fall."

Oburne. Gaelin cast about the camp through the random spits of snow, but the swarthy lieutenant was missing along with several warriors. *Scouting party*, he thought with a frown. Turning back, he met Terrek's gaze. "I'm tired of riding. Today I'm going to walk."

"You will not." Terrek reseated himself while Silva, clad in his black guard's armor and mail, brought his breakfast.

At the sight of the steamy porridge, Gaelin heard his stomach gurgle loudly. Laughing, Terrek offered him the wooden bowl and motioned to Silva to fetch another. With a grin, the guard sauntered off.

Gaelin sampled the fehley, its honey savor and nutty smell making him ravenous. Three sticky spoonfuls of the porridge were already hot in his belly before he remembered and jerked up his head. "Thank you."

Still chuckling, Terrek bent, lifting the kettle with Vyergin's fire stick. While Gaelin watched, he poured them both chimara tea. "You're welcome." Terrek passed him a mug. "It's no wonder you're hungry. Vyergin got some broth into you yesterday though, which was more than I could do."

"Vyergin?" Feeling his muscles tense, Gaelin scowled across the fire at the grizzled captain helping the wranglers load the sleds. His body trembling, Gaelin hunched over his bowl and mug.

"He's not a bad man," said Terrek. "He did what he had to. Those things on your scalp would have infested us as well, so we had to do something. And how did you thank us for our help? You scratched up Vyergin's neck. I didn't see him giving *you* any scars."

"It was humiliating. He hurt me." Gaelin, setting aside his bowl with its crooked metal spoon, slanted a resentful glare at his benefactor. "You both did, and then you *buried* my hair!"

"We had to get rid of it somehow," Terrek said. "The elves have their rules we have to follow. We couldn't *burn* it; imagine the smell!" He paused. "Look, there's bad hurting, like what your stepfather did, and then there's the kind that helps, the way healers do. Think about it. You feel better, do you not? Your sores are healed?"

"I guess." For a time, Gaelin sipped the soothing tea, trying to forget the echo of his screams—his helpless thrashing while the two grown men had held him down.

He stared at an object behind the fire, a battle-ax propped against a mottled rock. The sight made him yearn for his staff, for the reassurance of a nobler kind of power. After a moment, he glanced up, seeing Terrek accept a second bowl from his bald-pated guard and begin to eat.

"It's yours if you want it," Terrek said around a mouthful of porridge.

Gaelin blinked. "What is?"

"The weapon you're admiring. I hear you fought well during the battle. You won the right to wield it when you killed your first dach."

"No." With a shudder, Gaelin grimaced.

"That's a shame," Terrek replied. "It's a beautiful ax."

Gaelin eyed the weapon and nodded. "The elves in the temple," he said, hoping to change the subject, "used a word I didn't know. They said humans have been here for nine hundred cycles. What are cycles—years? And what did they mean? Were we someplace else before?"

"Indeed, we were," Terrek said. "We had our own world, a planet we called Earth. I studied this at university, and I've heard legends, too. My father told me them, and his father . . . you know."

Gaelin glowered at his tea. "No, I don't. I never had a father."

"Well, you're welcome to have mine." Terrek stretched out his leg and laughed at Silva's startled reaction. Grinning, he passed his bowl to the armored man.

"Sorry, Gaelin," he said. "It's just that Lucian, my father, is a difficult man. People make him uneasy, so as a rule, he avoids them. He has a head for business, though, and an uncanny rapport with horses, but if your heart is hurting, forget it, he's impossible. I'm here for the same reason my mother left: to escape his abuse. I requested he give me a task, which he did—to watch over both his land and Kideren, where we get our supplies."

Gaelin traced the rim of his mug with his finger. "I don't think your father would like me very much. I—"

"Do you want me to answer you or not?" Terrek cut in, and meeting his gaze, Gaelin nodded.

"Very well," Terrek said. "It's easiest if you close your eyes and imagine a starry sky. Do you have it?" Gaelin nodded. "Good," Terrek's voice continued. "Now arrange your stars into two clusters, keeping one nearby and the other far away." He hesitated again. "On Earth, we called those groupings 'galaxies.' Each had millions of stars, all like the sun you see in the sky, with worlds that move around them.

"Earth existed in the galaxy you placed at a distance, while the planet we stand on orbits a star in the one that's closer. Now forget the stars. See the blackness you put between them?" Again Gaelin nodded. "We were taken across that by an energy being named Sephrym who was trying to save this world. Perhaps the elves mentioned him?"

"They did," said Gaelin. "They talked about Holram, too, and something called Erebos. He's Holram's enemy and he wants me dead."

"Erebos is the one who attacked Earth. He's a creator of darkness who enjoys torture and feeding off suffering. Earth's warder, Holram, tried to stop him but failed. He wasn't strong enough. Another defender of suns, Tythos, came to help, but the Destroyer defeated them both."

"Are these things gods?" Gaelin picked a blue petal of chimara from his tea, his lids heavy under the brew's calming influence.

Terrek jabbed his stick at the fire, sending a skittering of sparks across the snow. "They're like custodians," he said, "though I'm sure they've inspired some strange beliefs on many worlds. But nothing exists outside of nature, Gaelin. These beings die like everything else. Holram wasn't killed in this battle with Erebos, but he was gravely wounded, as was Tythos—both of them reduced to shadows of what they were.

"Holram knew we were doomed. By attacking the Earth's sun, infusing it with his power until it exploded, he was trying to use our destruction to protect other worlds from Erebos."

As Gaelin frowned, Terrek chuckled. "It's a *myth*, Gaelin. Don't take it to heart. Yes, there might be truth in it . . . somewhere. These creatures *do* exist, as you know." Terrek sighed. "You have proof of that in your staff. They have no bodies, yet they live.

"When I was younger," he continued, his amber eyes glinting, "I had to cross Warder's Fall to get from Geresh City to Shattan. Except for the trees the elves planted along the roadway—which I hear they still have to tend constantly—the rest of the land was dead where the warders were cast down. I saw no plants or trees, nothing as far as I could see. The ground was poisoned. It is dead now."

"This Sephrym . . ." Gaelin shifted closer to the fire's heat, his gaze on Terrek. "He's another of these things?"

"Yes, and the only one who is Erebos's equal." Terrek gestured to the sun's pale disk beyond the clouds. "Nine hundred years ago, *that* was dying. Sephrym was working to revive it, as he's always done before. He looked for . . . power from other failing stars. Sensing our sun's imminent destruction, he reached from this, the Denevaar galaxy, into our own.

"Magic binds the universe. The more planets like this one are allowed to perish, the more the stars themselves will drift apart. Sephrym would do anything, even cross the divide between galaxies, to preserve this world. He ensnared the heat from our dying sun and caught by mistake the battling warders, bringing *them* here as well. Holram and Tythos made a final grab at Earth before they were taken, and that's how we were transported."

Gaelin glared at his friend. "I don't know these words," he muttered. "Universe and galaxies?"

"Because they're not from here," Terrek said. "They come from old Earth books we study. We've lost our wisdom, Gaelin. The theory goes that Sephrym didn't want or need *physical* matter, so he cast us down. And now here we are, refugees on a world that spins in the wrong direction around a sun that never dies." He cleared his throat. "That's something I learned at university. It's why we see the sun rising in the west here. On Earth it was reversed."

"And how charming we're stuck with Erebos, too, who wants to torture us," said Oburne's sarcastic voice.

Gaelin jumped when snow crunched behind him. He glimpsed rippling brown fur and scooted over, giving way when Oburne passed by to settle his bulk on the log next to Terrek.

"Oh, Sephrym, the *wise and magnificent*," Oburne intoned, "casting aside *warders*, of all things—who happen to be lethal to his precious world." Oburne snorted. "Stop making him out to be the hero, Terrek. If he had just *killed* Erebos then and there, we'd have no cult butchering us now."

"True enough," Terrek admitted, "but he was trying to save his star. I don't think he cared what else he ensnared."

"Anyway, it's just a myth." Oburne shrugged back his weighty cloak. "Superstition and nonsense, lad. Pay it no heed."

"Tell that to his *staff*," Terrek said. "Gaelin, fetch Mornius for us, will you? I'd like to introduce Holram to Mister Skeptic here."

Gaelin braced himself to rise, but Oburne gripped him and held him still. "No, boy," the warrior said in a gruff voice. "That's not necessary."

"So he's in my staff." Gaelin looked across Oburne's barrel chest at his friend. "This Holram." Embarrassed, he swallowed. "I'm sorry, I don't—"

"The crystal on your staff comes from Earth," Terrek explained. "It's dead; it has no magic. The power of these beings is lethal to this world, so they must hide in dead stone. First, Holram fled to a temple—a petrified tree near Tierdon—but he found it too restrictive; he couldn't move as he wished. So the elves made your staff for the Skystone and found a human to carry it. That would be your ancestor, Gaelin. Jaegar Othelion.

"As for Erebos, he slew Tythos upon arriving on this planet and wounded this land during his flight to the mountains. There he found an extinct volcano to hide in after he destroyed what life Mount Chesna still had. Now Talenkai serves as his shield from his enemy,

Sephrym, until Erebos becomes strong enough to break free."

"Holram . . . didn't mean to kill the way he did," Gaelin said. He set his mug on the log beside Oburne and stood. From the nearby tent, he sensed his staff's hold on him. "Holram wanted to heal the dachs, but I interfered."

"They were trying to slaughter us, Gaelin," Terrek replied. "It was hardly the right time to be helping them."

Gaelin heard a soft clink as Terrek placed his cup on the frozen ground. "You were disoriented, Wren told me, and I saw it a few times myself during the battle. Perhaps your state of mind confused the warder."

"Wren tells you everything I do?" Gaelin jerked up his head. "He needs to mind his own business. I can take care of myself!"

Terrek leaned back from the fire to survey him from behind Oburne's shoulders. "Wren saved your hide at Heartwood, so I made him your guard. Don't be stubborn, Gaelin. You refused the ax you won. You won't even carry a knife."

"It's fine," muttered Gaelin. Once again he peered at the tent, feeling the yearning for his staff in his bones. "I'll accept the guard, but I—"

"You saved *my* life, too," Terrek interjected. "I won't pressure you to use Mornius. But as long as you're with us, you'll have Wren Neche guarding your back."

Gaelin winced, his mouth dry as he recalled the ugly wound Lars Broudel had inflicted on Terrek in the pub at Kideren. At that time, he had wanted to die. He had committed murder, proving to be all the terrible things his stepfather had thought him.

Voices rose in the distance, the yells of the warriors carrying across the snow as they practiced their drills.

Gaelin glanced at the trees that concealed the men from his view. *I'll never be like them,* he realized, flexing his arm. He had enough strength to wield a weapon if he had to, but he lacked the heart for it, a fact he was keenly aware of. *I wouldn't have enough endurance, either.*

"Gaelin?" Terrek leaned toward him.

"I'd like to fight." Gaelin stopped, unsure if he had spoken aloud. "I'd like to learn to ride horses and use a sword, but when I think about hurting the dachs . . ." He rubbed at his mouth. "They're people, Terrek. They can't help what they are and . . . in a way I was like them. I know how it feels to be seen as less than a *person*."

Terrek cleared his throat. "Ask Caven Roth what he went through and how he uses his pain to fight. It gives him courage."

"And my hurts help me to know where other people are injured," Gaelin countered. "Enough to guide the staff to make them well. I fight, too, against their suffering.

"I believe Mornius can kill, but I'm not a warrior, and I'm its wielder. There must be a reason for that."

"A valid point," said Terrek. "Holram chose *you*, didn't he? If he had wanted a fighter, he could have picked someone else. One of your stepbrothers, perhaps, and as a result none of my men would be healed and I'd be dead right now."

After a pause, Gaelin nodded.

"Today you'll ride with me," Terrek told him. "You're one of us; you belong here as much as any of these men. Understood?"

"Even if I decide not to fight or . . . do as you ask?"

Terrek's grin was fierce. "Even so."

Chapter 9

*G*aelin held tightly to Terrek's saddle, his body swaying with Duncan's lurching steps. His thighs gripping the cantle, he fought to stay centered on the horse's broad hips as the animal's muscles worked beneath him.

Slabs of ice and weathered shale crunched in the heavy silence, collapsing under the weight of the sleds. It was the third day, and they were crossing below the summit of the endless white peaks. Panting for breath, Gaelin winced at the ache in his lower back and hips.

Abruptly Terrek reined in his horse. He turned in his saddle and squinted, his tired eyes surveying the line of dispirited men. "We rest here!" he called.

With a grateful sigh, Gaelin dropped from Duncan's rump. Pain stabbed through his ankles as his feet hit the ice, and the muscles above his knees spasmed. He limped with Mornius to the rocky debris below the ledge and plopped onto the rubble, reclining against the layers of stone.

Wren Neche, clad in black armor signifying his status as a guard, strode toward him. A thin scar running from his temple to his chin twisted his lip forever into a fierce expression. Not once had Gaelin seen the young man smile, yet his manner was welcoming as he knelt, unstopping his flask and handing it over.

Gaelin took his time sipping the hill-folk ale as he savored Wren's company—a man he sensed was close to his own age. He recognized the taste of the beverage in his mouth, a sweet brew known as "roy" that had been popular in Kideren. He swallowed and then sighed, enjoying the bite of the alcohol in his throat. From the corner of his vision, he saw the new guard slide off his pack, the scar stretching the left corner of his mouth down. Gaelin recalled what Terrek had said about Caven Roth, how he had implied that other people in the company had suffered, too. "I'm sorry," he said.

Wren glanced at him and shrugged. "You're not the only one having trouble. Terrek's wise to let us rest, even if it delays us a bit."

"No." Gaelin gestured to Wren's disfigurement. "If we'd known each other sooner, my staff could have healed that."

As Wren's fingertips explored his scar, water gurgled overhead, trickling red across the shale from the glacier above them. Unable to meet Wren's stare, Gaelin averted his gaze, the guard staying his hand when he tried to return the dented container. "You keep it," Wren said. "I have another and I don't need two."

Wincing at the pain in his temple, Gaelin hooked the metal flask to his belt. He staggered to his feet and then hesitated, shaking the snow from his cloak. Braced on his staff, he scanned the people around him. A few of the warriors were sprawled in the drifts beyond the ledge, while most clustered together, huddled beneath the stony shelf.

Terrek waited out in the open, standing apart from his men, his back bent while he tended to his mount. Approaching him, Gaelin noticed Duncan's drooping head. "He looks tired," said Gaelin when Terrek glanced over.

"He's hungry," Terrek said, rubbing a salve deep into the animal's hoof he held lifted and propped against his knee. "And *cold*. I need to get him to where I can dry him off and throw on his blanket. We'll make for those trees and break camp for the night." He pointed and Gaelin peered through the mist, glimpsing the outline of branches below.

"See the fog?" Terrek said. "No wind."

"How long do you think until we get there? How many—" Gaelin broke off when Duncan lipped at his friend's hair.

Chuckling, Terrek caressed the horse under his grayish mane, then quickly sobered. "A few hours, if the weather holds. Threats like that"—he jerked his head at the murky horizon— "could spell our deaths, and Tierdon's."

Gaelin lurched forward a few paces with his staff and halted, mesmerized by the advancing clouds. "What you said about . . ." He paused.

"About what?" asked Terrek.

Gaelin, watching the distant mountains darken one by one, spoke over his shoulder. "Something you told me earlier about your father. You said he was hard to bear when you're hurting, and that's why you're here. Why were you hurting?"

He risked a glance at Terrek. The commander's expression was thoughtful as he ran his hands down the animal's sturdy legs.

"I lost a good friend." Terrek patted the horse and then straightened. "She was a neighbor of ours. My brother, Camron, adored her. He thought of her as his big sister. But to me she was more.

"Felrina Vlyn was the brave one who always had to go first in front of us boys. Things change, I guess. A cleric from Erebos's cult came to Kideren seeking converts. She was bored with her life, and so she was taken in. I tried, but I could not dissuade her. I think she expected us to follow her again, but we didn't."

Gaelin turned, observing as Terrek worked his way around Duncan's wide rump to the animal's opposite side.

"The priests strive to convince people that the Destroyer will free them from the elves' control," Terrek went on, "and that their god is going to make them a new Earth. Felrina's a bright woman, but Erebos got into her head. So she left with them, bragging to us about how she was going to save humanity—and she took her mouse of a father, Nithra, with her."

"So now she's your enemy," said Gaelin.

Terrek nodded. "I guess so. I have to believe one day she'll be forced to see the truth, and when that happens"—his jaw hardened—"I fear for her."

Hoping to change the subject, Gaelin motioned to Terrek's horse. "My legs can't take his back anymore. I need to walk."

Calmly Terrek appraised him before stooping to tighten the frozen girth. "You're still not well. You've been frail since Heartwood."

"What about the sleds?" Gaelin asked, pointing. "You let me ride in one after the battle, remember?"

"That was a *wagon*. Those sleds aren't meant to carry people. Sitting there alone, you'd freeze to death."

Gaelin jumped back when Terrek mounted, avoiding Duncan's restless hooves. Behind him he heard the grunts of the warriors climbing to their feet and hurrying to re-form their line.

"What I need is for you to recover." Terrek reined the horse in close and leaned over to thrust out his gloved hand. "Now climb up. It's time to go." Catching Gaelin's upper arm, he lowered his voice. "You'll do as I say now. Or do you *want* to stay sick?" His grip tightened, and Gaelin was dragged off the ice—to dangle in Terrek's strong grasp.

Gaelin's face burned as the men around him laughed. He pulled himself onto the horse, settling his weight on the green-gold pad that extended beyond the saddle.

For a moment he sat still, breathing hard and clenching his staff, feeling the horse's wide haunches tilt beneath him. All at once something snapped, a blistering anger blurring his sight. Desperately, he pulled against Terrek's sudden grasp on his belt, struggling in vain to lift Mornius enough to dismount.

Terrek backed his horse under the lone bluebark pine jutting from the cliff. Gaelin yelped when, with a heavy thump, the branches gave way, dropping their snowy burden upon him. He yelled and sputtered, the coldness chilling his neck as Duncan leapt forward.

"That's the same thing I did to Terrek," said a gravelly voice at his back, "when he was a boy. You won't have the luxury to ride much longer. Appreciate it while you can."

Gaelin tensed, recognizing the man leading his dappled gray horse. "I did detect a slight limp," Captain Vyergin said, stopping beside them. "It's the right foreleg."

Terrek nodded. "Duncan's cracked his hoof. I don't think it's bad, but he—"

"I see it," said Vyergin. "You used my salve. Good man. Once it dries, it will form a nice patch. Just keep him off the ice." Stroking his gelding's thick neck, Vyergin met Gaelin's regard. "You don't get to be a savage anymore, my lad. If you want to remain here among us, show some respect.

"Let's hope he makes it to Tierdon!" Vyergin called to Terrek as he hurried with his horse to join the men.

Gaelin shot a glance over his shoulder at the captain, then gripped the cantle with his thighs, the muddle of his thoughts interrupted by Duncan's lumbering start. He heard the crunching of hooves and booted feet as the warriors followed—the hissing runners of the sleds when, with protesting squeals, the ponies hastened by to again pack the trail.

Gaelin let his mind wander. He watched the sun bury itself behind the ridge to the east, and the red-tinged darkening clouds. After what felt like hours, the horse stumbled to a halt beneath his aching thighs and turned.

"No fires," Terrek announced with a glance at his men, his words drawing a groan from several raw throats. "We're too exposed out here. Gather blankets. We'll pitch half the tents and pack ourselves in. We may not sleep, but at least we'll stay warm."

∞ ∞ ∞

FELRINA, PERCHED ON the lowest ledge in the watery chamber, spun away from the pool's black depths. "Tierdon?"

Her voice echoed down the adjoining tunnels. Confronting her leader, she lifted her staff, tilting its Blazenstone. "You haven't the balls for it, Mens. And anyway, the Masterswords would stop you. They have a powerful friend—the winged creator of Tierdon."

Snorting, Mens picked at a sore on his jaw. "The Eris elves focus on one thing now," he said. "They care for the *trees*. They don't even teach the Talhaidor anymore. They have humans doing that."

"No." Felrina grimaced. "The history preserved at Tierdon is precious to them." She closed her eyes, attuning her ears to the lapping sound of the water. She could sense Arawn's spirit drifting toward her below the surface of the tarn. The former enslaver of the giants was listening, considering in silence their every word.

She scowled at the swirls of oil on the water, the remnants of fat from the many humans she had formed into dachs. *Mens is changing, too*, she observed. The old magic he wielded feasted on his flesh like a coiled and hungry worm. His attempts to master the bloodstone mounted atop his staff was slowly taking his life.

While I remain as I am. She examined her arms, what little of

69

herself she could see under her flowing robes. *After he dies*—she risked a glance at her superior—*I would be leader.*

"If I conquered Tierdon," Mens went on, "if I had my winged horde pierce its heart, think of the message that would send to the elves!"

Felrina nodded. His voice sounded wet to her ears, his inhalations wheezing in his bony chest.

"The elves would fear me, and your precious Terrek would cower at my feet! I'd make him grovel to *you*, Felrina, and beg for his life!"

Mens's wide black eyes caught the light from across the room, the smoking torch held high by her faithful apprentice. Something about his expression tugged at her, conjuring thoughts of the future Erebos planned. "If you succeeded, we would . . ."

"*Yes!*" Mens tossed his head. "We'd finally get our world, created by Erebos for humans alone with no elves to answer to!"

Felrina studied him. She doubted very much he would live to see that day. Even now, he was nothing but bones, his skin stretched taut over his skull. Yet he was animated by the thought of more killing.

"All you think about is war." She glanced at the lanky figure next to the torch. Respectful as always, her apprentice, Gulgrin, peered back. "We can't do anything without food, and our suppliers have refused us. Without their tithe, how will we survive the winter?"

Mens humphed. "That's your problem. If the croppers aren't so willing, *confiscate* their animals and hoarded goods. Seize them, too, while you're at it. You can make them into warriors for me."

If only I could! she thought. *I hate begging, and the farmers know it, but if I lose them to Mens, we'd have nothing to sustain us.*

"What about later?" she said. "When the grain stores are empty and there are no sleds bringing us more? How will you fight if your warriors are starving?"

As her leader bit his lip, she frowned, recalling the deep-thinking man he had been when she had first met him. For a moment, she ached for the younger Mens, for the sane human being who had persuaded her to leave her home in Kideren.

"They won't go hungry," said Mens. "Not if you give me what I need. I'll feed them the croppers if I have to."

"Feed them the . . . ?" She caught her breath.

"Why does that shock you?" he asked. "What do you suppose

happens to the captives I consider unfit for the altar? Do you think I send them on their way? We can't keep prisoners if we're short on provisions ourselves, and my forces must be fed. If the farmers won't cooperate, give them to me, Felrina. I'll put them to use."

"I just assumed you found some way to . . . get rid of them."

"Indeed I have," Mens said. "First I ram hooks through here." He jabbed his thumb into the skin beneath his chin. "And out the mouth. Then we dangle two or three at a time above my fighters. The blood gets the creatures excited, until the prisoners drop, their jaws ripped from their skulls."

"No!" Felrina covered her mouth, but the cry had already escaped her lips. As her Blazenstone staff flared beside her, she paused and clutched at her stomach beneath her robes.

He nodded at her reaction. "It's a waste, to be sure, but since most are still alive when my warriors begin to feed, Erebos is also strengthened by these deaths. He's always there. If you want the truth, I think he does something so the prisoners don't bleed out."

"So the process takes time," Felrina said in a tone of feigned approval. She winced at the dryness in her throat. "Good. But doesn't that deprive us of fodder for our communions? There are fewer for you, too, for . . . the work it is you do, and for the poisonings in our dungeons. These are the deaths that benefit Erebos the most. We can't afford to—"

She stopped, cringing when a shadow fell over them both. Darkness took shape above her, a dragon unfurling its massive wings. "Erebos is here!" she hissed.

"He senses your distress, my dear. As do I. You know, Felrina, sometimes I think your heart's not in it," Mens told her. "Every day we achieve so much. Where is your enthusiasm for your work?"

She tipped back her head, spreading her arms as she searched the granite ceiling for her god. "Great Lord, believe in me, for I *do* believe in you and our objective here. I just feel we ought to rethink—"

"So be creative!" Mens gestured to the pool's flat calm. "You have a warder's power at your command, and Arawn's skill. Make better dachs. Design them so they don't need food, and then we wouldn't have to worry, would we?"

Felrina glared at him. "Don't be absurd. I can reshape the bones and skin into wings, but I *cannot* change what the internal organs do. Even Arawn has limits."

Mens averted his eyes from her staff's bright flame, the conduit to Erebos's power that he so openly craved. Again she glanced up, watching as the dragon's oppressive silhouette faded into the rocks.

"The point is I need better warriors." Mens thumped the granite floor with his bloodstone staff. "If you don't produce them soon, Felrina, I will indeed feed the croppers to my dachs. And once I'm finished, I'll test how long *you* can hang by your jaw. Do you hear?"

She nodded, her sweaty hands tingling.

Chapter 10

*A*valar felt her pulse quicken in her throat as she ventured into the shadow of the elven city below its crystal domes. She craned her neck, staring at the top of Tierdon's winged entrance. Joined at the tips and wrought of agate-veined marble, the feathered symbol of freedom created a stylized archway.

She smiled despite herself. Awed as she was by this glimpse of elven architecture, she could almost ignore the tumult she caused when she strode between the gate's open doors, the humans crowding to see her.

As Tierdon's denizens pressed in close, she reached for her sword, her fingers clenching its pommel. Inhaling deeply, she glanced over the many gawking faces, the townsfolk around her gaping upward. Exhaling, she laughed, her amusement bubbling from her lips before she could stop it. Teasingly she mimicked her audience's rudeness, goggling back openmouthed at the curious horde.

Her response prompted a snicker from the mob, and Avalar found its source, a youngish man with doe-soft brown eyes, smiling at her. She stumbled as his gaze called to her heart, unraveling her fear and mistrust.

Taking a knee, she marveled at what she spied behind his eyes, the power of his soul transfixing her. "What *are* you?" she asked.

He swept her a bow and grinned, his ruddy tail of tied-back hair flopping forward alongside his neck. "The museum's curator, at your service, my dear. I'm Camron Florne. Did the elves summon you?"

Avalar considered his flawless skin with its downy hint of a beard. Small freckles dotted the bridge of his nose, fanning out across his cheeks.

"I called myself," she told him. "I seek the Masterswords'

academy. Do you know of it?"

"Of course I do," he said, and as he smiled, Avalar noted how easy it was for his handsome features to do so. She cleared her throat, seeing the people around them begin to disperse. She had come expecting trouble, a confrontation at the very least. Never had she imagined she would find an ally so soon.

The young man reached to grip her thumb. "Would you care for an escort?"

Avalar curled her fingers around his knuckles. "Surely, I am not the first giant you have seen. How else could you be so fearless?"

"Fearless?" He laughed. "Are you kidding? I've always wanted to meet a giant. You're like the heroes from the old Earth comics I've read. We have a collection of them I can show you."

"And *you*!" Avalar snatched a shaky breath. "I begin to see why the elves have given humans their aid."

"Oh really?" Camron's laughter was strained. "Well, I don't. We had our world, and our greed destroyed it. We were doomed long before the warders' battle brought us here."

Avalar released him and stood. "Mayhap," she said, "in time, your kind will learn from its mistakes, as we giants have. No species is perfect, Camron Florne. Not even the elves." She grimaced at his puzzlement. "Hear me now. I have questions as well to ponder and answers I must learn. Perhaps you may teach me ere I go. You are unlike the others here. The vibrations I feel . . . If I block my sight, it is almost as though you were a giant."

"It's probably my eyes," said Camron. "My brother, Terrek, always blamed them for the way I won over the girls. Or maybe he's right that I have magic. When I was a child, I saw an Azkhar fly over our ranch. We're not supposed to be able to see them, but I did. It was big and very blue. When I described it to Terrek, he called it my lucky dragon. He said if I ever see it again, I should make a wish."

Avalar smiled. "Perhaps the Stormfury, which is what I like to call them, was as enchanted by your spirit as I am now. It has naught to do with the windows through which you see, Camron Florne. I am a giant. I am familiar with such things. Your spirit lies *behind* the walls of your flesh, and there I discern your fire."

"Please!" Camron humphed. "I'm just a human, while you, my dear, are the magic's living heart. We're as opposite as we can be."

Avalar touched his brow with her thumb, brushing wisps of red hair from his face. "Everything has energy of some kind. Yours is foreign; that is all." She shifted her pack, wincing when the straps abraded her raw skin under her tunic. Camron hurried to her side.

"I can carry something, Lady . . ."

"Avalar." Releasing one of her three pouches of frozen meat, she lowered it into his grasp. "Avalar Mistavere, daughter of Grevelin Mistavere, protector of the . . ."

"North," Camron finished. He swayed on his feet, struggling to balance his load.

She caught his arm; with a flex of her hand, she compelled him to look up. "You know of him?"

He grinned. "I'll tell you on the way. Come."

Turning, Camron pushed with his shoulders, clearing a path for her through the remains of the crowd. Avalar, following hard on his heels, hunched forward as she struggled to readjust her pack.

"I know the names of *many* giants," said Camron, raising his voice above the banter from the gaggle of children trailing them. "Working in the museum has taught me a lot about this world. Grevelin Mistavere was a slave, was he not?"

Avalar sighed, her attention lifting from the little girl skipping by her knee to the sparkling domes above her. Constructed from strands of interlaced crystal into an almost invisible shield, they stretched over the buildings and streets, protecting the city from snow. "Indeed. Most of the surviving slaves yet live, even after a hundred and twenty cycles, though many cannot have children. This is why our magic stops us from aging once we reach maturity. Trentor, our leader, tells us this will continue until enough of our dead have been replaced."

When Avalar ducked around a bright red awning, again she caused a stir. With a piercing cry, a wire-haired dog shot off down the street. She watched with mild amusement as the tiny black creature scurried away, then focused beyond it.

"What is that?" She motioned to a lofty structure that dominated the square. Her gaze lingered on the central statue in the plaza in front of the tall building—a large white raptor with wings spread wide, its silver talons curled around a gildstone disk representing the sun.

Camron followed her stare. "That," he said proudly, "is the museum, my place of employment. Impressive, isn't it?"

Together they circled the monument. The children raced to climb the stones cemented and wired in place next to the sculpted bird.

"Come back down; you know the rules," Camron called in a firm voice. "Not without your parents!" He stopped with his hands on his hips, waiting until the last child—the inquisitive girl—trundled off.

"Those are the viewing rocks," Camron explained to Avalar. "And that beautiful statue, my dear giant, honors Tierdon's builder. He was a winged elf, they say, unique to this world, and not from it."

"Yes, my people know of him." Avalar risked a glance at the sky. *Can you see me in your ice mirror, Ponu?* she thought. *Behold! I am among humans!*

Camron stopped and motioned to the museum. The wedge-shaped structure crouched atop a fleet of stairs, its alabaster pillars holding high its conical roof. "Do you want to see the interior? We have fabulous treasures within from all of the cultures on Thalus."

"I would like that very much, Camron Florne," Avalar said. Wriggling her shoulders, she shifted her burden. "Mayhap after I am settled. *If* I am settled, for I know not if the elves will approve of my presence here."

He clasped her wrist. "Of course they'll welcome you. You're a giant. How could they not?"

Avalar paused, admiring the museum's walls, the intricate weave of granite and harvested gildstone that marked it as Ponu's work. "The elves strive to protect giants," she said. "The Eris might try to force me home."

Camron released her and scrambled up the overlapping boulders parallel to the sculpture. He stopped when he reached the level of her nose, to set her bundle near him. Grinning, he flopped onto his stomach across an overhang of rock and propped up his chin.

"I'll never understand why the elves consider humans a threat to giants," he said. "Your males are twice our size! Is it because we warp the old magic? Well, none of us touch it anymore because now we know better. In fact, we avoid contact with your native creatures as much as we can. Look around you, Giant. Do you see *anything* magical? No! Racka-hares in the fields have more power than we do."

Avalar's mood darkened. Deliberately she shrugged off her pack, arranging her thoughts as she strove to rest her shoulders.

"You are young," she said, "as am I. Bethink you. Some of you did touch our magic once, and with it, you enslaved and tortured us! By calling yourselves powerless, you demean my people."

Camron scooted toward her, his fierce stare meeting hers. "But how is it fair to us that we have to live apart? There are no slavers of the giants anymore! Think of what we could gain from each other, my dear, if you sailed your ships to Thalus. You have a history more ancient than the elves, and we humans have insights to contribute, too, the knowledge we've preserved from our forebears!"

Avalar cleared her throat. Forgotten was Tierdon's grandeur. Even the winged statue honoring Ponu blurred from her sight, replaced by the blazing spirit she glimpsed before her. "My people have no interest in the wisdom you bring from Earth," she said and then drew a sharp breath at the harshness of her words.

She remembered Kray—how her initial reactions to the child's family in Firanth had been violent as well. *It is the memories again,* she realized sadly. *Oh, Grevelin, my father, how much your sufferings plague me now! It has been over a hundred and twenty cycles since you escaped your chains, yet still, I feel your anguish!*

Camron winced, though his smile remained steady. "Not all of our advancements are harmful to this—" He stopped, seeing her discomfort. "I'm sorry, my dear. I've made you uneasy. If you could, though, please explain one thing. Why must the giants live isolated now? What is it the elves fear?"

"If I were older and had more sense, I would *never* . . . !" Avalar studied the stone beneath her tired feet. The flat white granite was dry around the sculpture, shielded by the dome's arch above.

Camron, tucking his knees under his stomach and chest, rolled himself back to sit on the protruding rock, his legs folded by his hip. "What?" he asked.

"*Tell* anyone," she said. "It is not something giants discuss. It is a weakness of ours, a defect, some might say. It captures two spirits and makes them one, altogether dependent upon each other. "The elves are fearful because my people are rare now on this world and because Talenkai's survival—its power—depends on giants. So now we have restraints upon our hearts, placed there by our magic at the urging of the elves.

"And yet, this does not stop a giant from bonding with an outsider. This fate befell my father when he bonded to an elf, and I am forced to witness his pain whenever they part. I have often tried to console him."

"Avalar, I know what friend-bonding is. There's no need to explain it further. Not if it hurts you."

She slanted her gaze to meet his. "Then you do understand!"

He blinked. "I do?"

"A heart cannot be fettered. Nor can it be controlled. If a young giant's heart should bond in this way to a human, that giant would perish ere he reaches his prime—from his friend dying of old age. Do you not see? No giant can die while we are yet so few. The magic needs us!"

Camron grimaced. "Death of the magic—of the world—if one of you dies? *That's* what the elves fear?"

"Yes! This world would not endure it. Talenkai is ancient, Camron Florne. Without its magic, it would be dust, and so would we."

He seized her bundle and sprang from the rock, landing with a thud on the frozen stone. "It's wrong that *giants* should be restricted! Talenkai is your world. If anyone should have to be isolated, *humans* should!"

Avalar grinned. "But you breed like squeakers! Every farm I have passed had hordes of your little ones. No," she said with a chuckle. "Your people would not fare well on Hothra."

Camron glowered. "I've heard tell of these children. They were abandoned when their parents were taken, left alone and at the mercy of winter. Humans enslave *humans* now, Giant."

She followed his lead and hefted her pack, grunting when it thumped her spine. Already he was striding across the common, his back rigid beneath his heavy load.

How alike we are, Avalar thought. *Mayhap this is indeed what the elves fear.*

"Wait," she called. All around her, people were stopping to watch, but she saw only Camron, his red hair fluttering in the wind. "Camron, I am sorry! Camron, wait!"

Breathing heavily, he halted. "We do *not* 'breed like squeakers,'" he said. "Each family is limited to three children, and that's it. I've seen those youngsters you speak of—starved to death along the road. I've had to bury them, the kids who lost their parents, and little babies, who never had a *chance.*"

"Who would do such a thing?" Avalar spoke carefully. "Why would humans wish to enslave other . . . humans?"

"Enslave," Camron gritted, "is an understatement. The cult *mutilates* their captives, transforming them into creatures forced to destroy what they love! My brother, Terrek, says my black moods do nothing at all to change the way it is, but I can't control how this sickens me, seeing those children!"

Avalar tilted his head up, forcing his grieving gaze to meet her own. "It is well that I am here, Camron Florne. When it comes to battle, I know naught of the finer art—the dance of blade against blade. Your Eris elves shall teach me. And once I learn, I will free those lost parents, if any at all still endure. Those children shall be avenged. Like my ancestors, I shall defend the vulnerable who are in need."

He urged her over to where people huddled in groups on the stony steps, their conversations halting when she neared. As Avalar swept them a bow, Camron smiled. "I'm glad to see you relax, Giant. You seemed so . . . uneasy when you first arrived."

"Indeed, I was," she admitted. *Word of my arrival is spreading,* she thought as more men and women emerged from the various buildings.

"They've never seen your kind," Camron said under his breath. "Like me, I think many have wanted to. See that?" Camron indicated an L-shaped building tucked behind the museum, its walls merging boulders with hardened red clay. He laughed when, unimpressed, she wrinkled her nose. "That's the arena, where the Masterswords fight."

Avalar surveyed the barnlike structure clearly not of Ponu's making. *Even the Maerfolk's ice homes are less crude,* she thought, turning to her companion. "Show me where they *are,* Camron Florne! Allow me to prove my worth!"

He nodded. "Wait, and they will come to you."

She raised her brows as he patted her knuckles, and for the first time, she took notice of his jacket. Bright blue worm-cloth adorned its front, set between panels of darker blue suede. Seashell buttons fastened the silky fabric at his throat and ran diagonally across his lean torso.

Camron stepped back. Grinning, he spread his arms and rotated on his heel, displaying both his coat and black leggings. "Like it?" he asked. "My uniform."

She chuckled. "You have . . . done this before."

"For the elves I have, yes," said Camron. "I am their employee. My brother brought me here to escape our father, who was being too tough on me, or at least that's what Terrek thought. I couldn't please him, you see. I had no desire to carry on his work."

Avalar dropped her gaze as Camron drifted close again, allowing her to touch the garment he wore. "How long must I wait?" Glancing over her shoulder at the square, she spotted a man with an easel not far from the large statue, his keen eyes studying her face. *No doubt, he seeks to record this great moment*, she mused with a snort.

"There." Camron's voice was soft. She followed his gesture and stared.

A pair of men approached, their jet capes rippling as they advanced without fear. Stopping to confront her, the older of the two men flipped back his cloak to reveal the distinctive ebony hilt and red tassels of his Talhaidor sword. Avalar fell to her knees at the sight. In one smooth motion, she drew her own blade and placed it at his feet.

"Roshar Navaren," Camron said in a tone of awe.

Avalar met the newcomer's stare as he scrutinized her, his steely blue eyes intense beneath his knitted gray brows.

"You are human," she said, focusing on his short silver beard, the hint of dark hair on his wrists beneath his sleeves. "Yet you dress as a Master."

Roshar's lips twitched as he regarded her coolly above the sharp ridge of his nose. "You offer your blade," he noted. "Giant, have you come to learn?"

She straightened where she stood. "I have. But where are the elves to teach me?"

"They live among the trees, in the shadow of Alianth's peak," the swordsman replied. "We are the last of their students in Tierdon. They've chosen us to act in their stead while they tend to their hearts' work: the trees of their forest." He paused. "Tell me why you have journeyed so far. It cannot be just for this. What else calls you from the safety of Hothra's shores?"

"Giants broke their chains," she told him. "Yet still we are not free. I wish to remind my people of what they are."

His eyebrows lifted. "There is more to this than what you're telling me. I—"

"It is a private thing," she cut him off, shifting her feet on the frozen stone. She transferred her attention to Roshar's companion— a sandy-haired young man who mimicked his mentor's stance and stern demeanor. "Are any of you familiar with giants?" she asked, hoping to change the subject. "Have you seen us fight?"

The three men shook their heads. Roshar cleared his throat, fingering his sword's polished hilt. "We know the legend of Redeemer, the sword that liberated your people. We've heard the old tales as well, of your battles against the Sherkon Raiders. Still, none of us has seen a giant. In fact, until now, we've doubted you exist."

Avalar lifted her sword. Shrugging off her bundles, she climbed again to her feet. "Well, we do," she said. "And we fight like this."

She demonstrated, exaggerating her movements as she cut at the air with a firm, level sweep. "Our weight follows our strokes, reinforcing with our backs and shoulders. This is fighting with power, not precision. It works well against the Sundor Khan, but what I seek is skill—the finesse of the Talhaidor, the joining of mind to weapon so that I—"

Avalar, startled by the younger Master's grimace of pain, hastened to sheathe her weapon. Roshar, his gaze locked on hers, placed a calming hand on his companion.

Once more she dropped to her knees. "I intend no harm!" she exclaimed. "I am here to learn to bond with my weapon. Will you not teach me?"

Ruthlessly Roshar evaluated her. He rubbed his chin and then glanced toward the L-shaped arena. "You cannot train there," he said. "The ceiling's too low for you. But we do have other places. Tye Warren here can give you a tour."

Still trembling, Tye raised his head to meet Avalar's concern. "Her heart lies open like a book, Master Navaren," he said, "though her magic makes reading it difficult. She speaks the truth; she seeks the Swordslore and nothing more."

Brows raised, Avalar turned to Camron. "A soothsayer?" she

asked. "You said humans had no magic." Camron ducked his head, yet not enough to hide his smile. Avalar glared. "I am not amused, Camron Florne. I have heard of new magic, the power of the warders from beyond our world. You humans brought it with you and it is a grave threat. If this is—"

"Relax, Giant." Camron grabbed her wrist. "Tye's magic comes from his mind and heart, as we discussed. You are safe, believe me."

Tye stepped close and looked up, and Avalar blinked, entranced by the youth's golden eyes. "Come," he said. "There are rooms in this city intended for giants. Please, allow me to guide you. Along the way I will explain the first stages of the Talhaidor."

Avalar bent to retrieve her pack.

"Go," Camron said with a laugh. "Your dance awaits you, my dear."

Chapter 11

Gaelin, struggling to lift his heavy legs, trudged behind Terrek as they walked alongside his horse. He squinted at the glare above them, the overhanging glacial ice atop the frozen shale. When Terrek bent to examine his mount, Gaelin glanced back over his shoulder, scanning the warriors' wind-burned faces as they appeared around the base of the cliff.

At the sight of their torn and chapped lips, he reached to explore his own mouth, staring at the smear of crimson on his glove as Vyergin passed by him. Through a haze of fatigue, Gaelin watched as the captain, leading his gray horse down the line, halted at intervals to encourage the men.

With a low curse, Terrek stopped. As he raised Duncan's sagging head, Gaelin watched him cup the gelding's pinkish nostrils with his palms, then lean in to blow between his thumbs. Rubbing the horse's muzzle, Terrek looked up and gestured to the three wranglers waiting nearby on their sleds, urging the men with their ponies forward to pack the trail.

Gaelin stumbled as he followed Terrek beside his horse. *What if I try to help?* he thought, gripping his staff. *Mornius could strengthen them, but then I'd be slowing them down.*

He grimaced, imagining himself sick and vulnerable again and needing to be carried. Reaching out, he leaned his weight on Duncan's rump as he struggled to walk, feeling under his palm how the horse trembled.

∞ ∞ ∞

AVALAR GRINNED AT Tye Warren's rapt expression while the youngest Talhaidor master evaluated her from the sidelines. She swung her shoulders toward her trainer, Roshar Navaren, tipping her blade at the last moment to parry his thrust.

Because of her size, they trained in the plaza, where the citizens of Tierdon could watch. *This is a good thing, all this noise,* she reminded herself as she feinted with her weapon. *It forces me to focus!*

Seeing Roshar's blue eyes go wide, Avalar's grin faltered. She followed his rigid stare over the heads of her audience. Far in the distance, past the wintry fields and dense pines, she saw a blackness like a cloak appear above the Snarltooths and then fall swiftly to hide the mountains from her view.

Behind the benighted peaks, Avalar beheld an ominous storm rising, a wedge-shaped darkness composed of wings and skull-like faces, needle-sharp teeth, and flashing sabers all aimed like a dagger at Tierdon's heart.

"Dachs!" Roshar yelled. "They're coming! To Battle's Hall, everyone, be quick!"

Ponu, hear me, Avalar thought. She squeezed her eyes shut, concentrating her magic as hard as she could to summon the winged elf. *This is your city they are coming for!*

She recoiled, for the fiery wall her mind struck was perilously alien. Something mighty gripped the elf-mage and held him in thrall. "Sails take you, Ponu!" she cried. "We need you, *now!*"

Avalar, fighting back sobs, whirled to confront the human-made building where Tierdon's citizens fled. There were ten of her trainers to protect the people from an attacking force surpassing her ability to count, and she was but one giant.

Camron! The thought spurred her into motion toward the museum. Raising her sword, she darted forward—one quick stride, two—as a massive swarm of wings and tails swooped under the domes, a horde of screeching blackness, human flesh warped beyond repair.

She fought with abandon, hacking into her unnatural foes' toughened hide, cutting through their elongated bones and poisoned spines. Repeatedly, she swiped at her face to clear her sight, her armor streaming with blood.

Avalar took a step, jabbing with her sword to impale another howling creature flying at her, its clawed, leathery wings open to grab, its toothy mouth grinning. Yanking her blade free from its bony chest, she struggled relentlessly toward the museum's white stairs. It was at this place where, so many times during her short stay at Tierdon, she had met Camron Florne. *My friend*, she thought. *My friend!*

Screams rang from the direction of the hall. The Masterswords had failed. There were too many dachs against too few of the elf-trained humans. All of them were dead: Roshar Navaren, Tye Warren, and Graham Steel. And now innocent people were perishing as a result—women, children, and the fearless little girl who had walked by her knee . . .

With an anguished roar, Avalar charged a black-robed human descending the steps to meet her, hating him for not being the one she wanted to see. He raised the staff he held, aiming its stone at her chest. She screamed as a fiery fist swept her off her feet.

Stretched on her side with her limbs tingling, Avalar caught snatches of Tierdon's people racing past her and falling, many of them dragged aloft by the winged mob. She heard a loud crack when the city's sheltering domes shattered above her, the tinkling crystal morphing into snowflakes to blanket the buildings and streets.

She spotted Camron in his blue uniform jacket with a shortsword in his hand, hurrying stealthily down the stairs behind her attacker. In horror, she saw the amateurish grip he had on his weapon.

Despite her numbness, she clambered to her feet, charging at the black-robe to distract him, smiting any foes that blocked her way.

A flying shape caught her attention, fluttering low over the steps in pursuit of her friend. Avalar stopped in mid-charge, stunned as she saw the dach's knobby knees tucking under its chest, its claws seizing Camron by his shoulders. With furious flaps of its leathery wings, the magic-warped creature hauled him into the air.

"No!" Screaming, she sprang forward.

"Avalar!" yelled Camron, his face strangely calm while he met her shocked stare. "Protect the museum!"

Sobbing, she plunged into the second wave of fire from the mage's staff, her body going numb when she toppled through its heat, her weight crashing into the black-robe's body and pinning him beneath her.

His eyes goggled at her, his fingers tugging at his staff, slamming it hard along her belly. Pushing up despite how her muscles spasmed, she twisted her weapon, setting its keen edge beneath his jaw.

Blinded by her tears, she pressed with all her strength, feeling the sharp steel of her sword grind through the man's tendons and muscles. She heard the soft crunch as the vertebrae parted—then her blade connected with the blood-soaked stone. Repulsed by the corpse's agonal breath from the massive wound, she gagged and rose onto her right elbow, slapping aside the gaping head, far away from its twitching body.

Her nerves still numb, Avalar fought to stumble erect. Again something stretched her flat, knocking the air from her lungs as she hit the slippery steps. She heard a sizzling pop and grabbed at her rib cage under her mail shirt, gawking as she withdrew her palm covered with blood.

Through the stinging of her grief, she spied another human in black robes standing across the courtyard, his thin body rocking from the force of the staff he held, its fiery blasts lancing through the city, cutting down Tierdon's buildings and reducing to rubble its once-proud wall.

"*Protect the museum!*" Camron had said. Dazed and retching, Avalar cast a defiant glare at the wizard's ruddy features through the flashes of his fire and half crawled, half staggered, dragging her sword and her convulsing body up the stairs and under the ornate archway.

Chapter 12

G aelin looked up at the distant sound of Terrek's voice. He struggled to focus far ahead, squinting through the sunlight as his friend, still leading his tired horse, stopped in front of the sleds.

"Another rest. Even the ponies are faltering now," said Wren behind his back, and with a groan of relief, Gaelin sagged to his knees in the frigid powder, hearing the grunts and sighs around him as the warriors still standing did the same. His hand trembling, he unfastened the half-empty flask from his hip and lifted it to take a gulp, closing his eyes when the fire in his throat reached his belly. He passed the container to Wren, who accepted it gravely.

"We're not going to make it," the guard confided under his breath. "This is the third winter that I've made this crossing with Terrek. The last two times it was never this bad so soon."

Bending over his knees, Gaelin rubbed at his numb feet through his boots. "I didn't realize you—" He stopped, his lungs aching as he strained to breathe the chilled air. "You seem so young to have been with him that long."

"I was fifteen when I started," Wren said proudly. "Lucian Florne is a good employer, and everyone who lives around Kideren knows it. So when Vale Horse needed more hands, my grandfather recommended me. I began as a messenger boy. By the end of the first year, I was already riding patrols with Terrek, and now I'm a guard.

"Not many people get along with Florne Senior, as you've probably heard, but I'm quiet, so he tolerates me. '*To judge a man's mettle, consider the companions he keeps.*' That's what my grandfather always said, and that's what I do. I notice the ones who are loyal to him." The young guard nodded at a figure moving among the recumbent men. "Captain Vyergin there is a former Enforcer and Lucian's best friend. And the big Lieutenant Oburne with all the fur, he was accepted by the giants enough to fight with them. He's ridden on a giantship, I hear, and he—"

"Please, Wren," Gaelin interjected. "If I need to know about these people, I'll ask them!"

Wren looked him up and down with a glare and then gestured to his garments. "Fur-lined gloves and boots with heels . . . pretty nice, wouldn't you say? Not to mention the quilted leggings padded for riding and that jacket you're wearing. Florne's your employer, too, whether you realize it or not, and it's wise to know about the men you travel—"

Wren stopped as the shadow of a lean, compact figure fell over them both. Gaelin looked up at Brant Vyergin's craggy face. With his palms braced on his knees, the captain bent and puffed for air, then motioned to the staff lying inert beside Gaelin's leg. "I need your help, Lavahl," Vyergin said.

Wearily, Gaelin reached for Mornius, using it to lever himself upright to face the man who, not so long ago and with Terrek's help, had cut away his matted hair.

"I can see you don't trust me now," said Vyergin, "but Hawk is lame."

As Vyergin guided him around the warriors, Gaelin looked ahead to where the animals were tethered near the sleds.

"Anything you can do," Vyergin murmured. "It's this damn mountain and my stubborn pride. Hawk's not so young anymore. I pushed him too hard and now he's hurt. Will you look at him?"

Gaelin saw the big dappled gray standing still next to Vyergin's gear, the whiteness under his raised foreleg spattered with crimson. Vyergin moved in to hold the gelding's bridle, speaking quietly into his ear to gentle him down. Gaelin lowered his staff and squatted near the lifted foot, supporting it atop his knee. With gentle touches, he probed the horse's heel.

"It's deep," said Gaelin, his fingertips slick with blood. "He stepped on something, but it came back out."

"It was a sliver of granite and I pried it loose," Vyergin said above him. "I kept it in case you'd need it."

"No, he doesn't have to . . ." Gaelin broke off and stared,

bewildered, at his hands. "That's not how it works."

"*He?*" asked Vyergin. "Who are you talking about?" But Gaelin was still, taken aback by his own words.

"Well, it's the heat in the fetlock I'm worried about," Vyergin said. "He jumped and landed wrong." The captain paused. "Will your magic heal a horse?"

Gaelin regarded Vyergin's tight-lipped visage. Aside from the fact mounts were valuable, the captain's attachment to the big and friendly gelding he had reared from a foal had been obvious to them all.

Taking up Mornius, Gaelin positioned its Skystone against the horse's braced foreleg. With a soft sigh, he shut his eyes. He was so tired he reeled, and Vyergin reached quickly to steady his shoulders. Already his mind was floating, the tightness draining from his muscles.

A presence waited for him in the gem's inner fog, a lion's stern face. *I'll be sick again*, Gaelin thought sadly from a faraway place, but still he wrapped mental arms around the shaggy head, the pulsing fire of the entity's mane expanding from within the stone and then from his chest.

Mornius jerked in his grasp, spouting its flames of blue tinged with silver, pouring wave upon wave of crackling power across the snow. Voices yelled in surprise—from his past or present, he could not tell.

The ripples of the warder's magic spread wide, reaching beyond the wounded horse. Gaelin heard his voice murmuring words he did not understand, and yet he spoke them, muttering them under his breath until the squeal from Vyergin's horse and the repeated neighs from the other animals, alerted him. With a start, he scooted back from the gelding's stamping hooves.

Vyergin knelt near, his eyes incredulous. "Staff-Wielder, what have you done?"

Gaelin hesitated as the men around him climbed to their feet. Oburne was standing by Vyergin, his expression unreadable, while the others . . . The warriors sloshed like children through the slush, converging on him with the blood and fatigue gone from their grinning faces. Mornius's fire had healed them, too.

"I don't . . . know." Gaelin stroked the staff lying beside him, its multicolored gem pulsing in its iron claws. With a shudder, he closed his eyes. "Is Hawk healed?"

Gloved fingers clasped his upper arm. "Yes, indeed!" The captain laughed sharply. "Is there anything that *isn't*? But why in Hades's blazes did you wait so long? You could have been relieving us of all this—"

"Enough, Vyergin." Terrek's voice was stern, his approach soundless. At his gesture, the warriors splashed away to fetch their gear.

As the tipping world righted itself, Gaelin drew a long, shaky breath. "Take it slow at first," he counseled Vyergin with a gesture to Hawk. "He lost a lot of blood."

"You bet." Vyergin stood and patted the charger's muscular neck. "You have my thanks, Staff-Wielder."

Gaelin stared. Tendrils of fog were stretching in front of his sight, and he wanted to follow. By degrees, he drooped forward. His body was heavy, his shoulders sagging. Then knuckles were thumping his knee. After a reluctant pause, Gaelin lifted his head.

Terrek knelt before him, his hazel eyes clear and alert, concern deepening the lines around his mouth. "Gaelin?"

"Tired," Gaelin said.

"Understood." Terrek hauled him to his feet. Numbly Gaelin leaned on his staff as Terrek hurried to retrieve his horse. The snow was twirling around him again, the white flakes indistinguishable from the fog.

LULLED BY DUNCAN'S easy strides, Gaelin wandered through a soothing mist. He heard snatches of voices on the wind, the men telling him how the company had reached the summit and had rested farther on. At one point, a dialogue interested him enough to focus his drifting mind. He recognized Vyergin's gruff voice.

"I am grateful for what he did, believe me," the captain said, "but he could be trying harder, don't you think? All that time while we were freezing, what did he do?"

"He followed my instructions," was Terrek's retort. "I told him I wanted him to recover, and he knows if he uses Mornius, he can't. Look what it does, Vyergin. He says it helped him get through his childhood, but do you remember how he was when we found him? You think he got that way just from Lavahl's abuse? I don't. He has become dependent upon that power. I know you see it, too, how much it harms him. So let's make his staff our last resort, shall we? I'd like to get through this without destroying him."

Gaelin frowned as he returned to the mist. The answers he sought were not with these men but in the safety of the Skystone with its realm of inner vapor where the warder dwelled. With care, he sifted through the gem's matrix, struggling to understand what the strange being in Mornius wanted, yet always the answers flitted beyond his reach.

Twice the staff had acted independently of his will, first during the battle at Heartwood and now by healing more than Vyergin's horse. Gaelin frowned at the helpless feeling it gave him.

I am not your tool! he thought to the warder, and then he drifted.

He roused to find himself draped over the saddle, his face against Duncan's lowered neck. With a groan, he straightened on the horse and peered at the twilight through the branches. Pale above the forest, the Companion's crescent winked between the clouds, its light as solitary as he was, circling life without getting too near.

Shivering, he listened to the sounds of camp approaching completion, the removal of tack and gear. He heard a soft crunching; footsteps paused and then briskly resumed.

"Silva and I pitched the shelter," Terrek called. "I had hoped you wouldn't awaken."

Terrek emerged from the trees and stopped in front of the horse, a faint mist rising to swirl around them both. Dismounting, Gaelin reached to untie Mornius from the saddle. "I'm glad I did," he said. "I'm *not* dependent, and I've been babied enough!"

Aware of Terrek's scrutiny, he squared his shoulders and strode toward the tents.

Chapter 13

*A*s Terrek reined in his horse, Gaelin straightened behind him on the gelding's back to peer at Tierdon. He had glimpsed the ruined city through the low-hanging clouds during their arduous descent from the summit. The destruction, viewed from the higher altitude, had not seemed so extensive then, or as final as it did now. Gaelin sighed, his gaze on the sad expressions of the warriors around him.

Gravely the men spread out in the knee-deep snow at the edge of the valley, their bloodshot eyes staring at Tierdon's remains under the flock of carrion birds. Two days earlier the fighters had been angry, Gaelin recalled, or grieving while they walked. But now—

Terrek sat rigid in his saddle as Vyergin, drawing alongside them with a click of his tongue to his horse, broke the silence, swearing from Hawk's dappled back.

"*I know every building and street.*" Gaelin remembered Terrek's words to his men from three nights ago. "*I know the faces, the people.*"

Without a sound, Gaelin lifted his staff, its power tickling his palms while he sought to pass endurance and strength to his friend.

Terrek twisted to scrutinize the terrain, tears brimming in his hazel eyes. "No tracks at all," he observed. His jaw hardened. "If our enemies came through on foot there would be some sign. They must have flown."

Oburne's thin black braids flicked when he turned to study the empty field. "The attack came from above," he agreed. "We have no defense against so many winged dachs, and they know it. Next time we'll be powerless to stop them."

Terrek glowered as he gathered up the reins and motioned to the sleds.

∞ ∞ ∞

GAELIN COVERED HIS ears. The chatter from the scavenging birds was unnerving as the company passed beneath a bent tangle of metal and then picked their way around the scattered debris beyond. Still seated behind Terrek on his sturdy white horse, Gaelin squinted at the brightness of the sun's reflections flaring from Tierdon's splintered glass.

He gripped Terrek's belt in reflex as Duncan sidled beneath him and reared. With a soft curse, Terrek pressed the animal's neck with his hand until the gelding, his ears laid flat, dropped with a thud to paw with his foot.

The six ponies balked between the shafts attached to their sleds, their short legs stamping while several neighed. The restless wind shifted, bringing with it the tang of thawing meat. Gaelin gagged, for the stench brought to mind the cabin on Mount Desheya, the buzzing insects, and Seth Lavahl. He pressed his nose to Terrek's back, the leather scent of the commander's jacket serving to mask the smell.

Corpses littered the streets, their shapes blurred by the recent snowfall. Glancing above him, Gaelin cringed at the sight of even more dead, the frosted protrusions of human limbs poking from the city's wreckage. He focused on the heart of the square where someone had draped children, their motionless bodies grotesque to behold, over the broken outstretched wings of a bird's statue.

Terrek lifted his leg over Duncan's left shoulder and dismounted. For a moment, he pressed his forehead against his horse's muscular neck and then pushed away fiercely.

"Camron!" With a snarl, Terrek sprinted up the stone stairs of an enormous building, his guard, Deravin Silva, leaping to his side as together they charged through the open doorway.

Left alone on the gelding's back, Gaelin nodded his gratitude as Caven Roth guided his stallion in close to snatch Duncan's reins. "What is that?" Gaelin asked, jerking his head at the lofty structure. Hunching under the gray blanket he had shared with Terrek, he hugged the fabric to his chest, watching the warriors dash at the hungry birds.

Roth glared, his brow furrowed as he surveyed the entrance that had swallowed Terrek and Silva. "The museum," he said. "Camron's favorite place to be. It has treasures, or it *did* have. I'm sure they're destroyed now. Erebos's creatures can't stand anything beautiful. I'm surprised the great hall stands at all. I've heard tell from Camron that—"

A roar cut him off, a guttural sound more animal than human. Turning, Gaelin saw Terrek stagger from the museum, his bright sword tipping upward in his grasp while he caught his balance above the stair. Then, with a rapid pounding of footsteps, Silva dashed out a moment later, his torn white sleeve dripping with blood.

Before Silva could dodge, a tall armored figure, her blond braids flying, sprang from the doorway and pounced on him. Clenching a massive sword, she seized the middle-aged guard, howling again as she dragged him off his feet.

"Avalar!" Oburne shouted and bolted up the steps. "Avalar Mistavere!"

The warrior froze, Silva dangling from her fingers, his throat a hairsbreadth from her blade's keen edge. Panting, the imposing creature leveled a scowl at them.

Gaelin, staring at the giant, dropped off Duncan to follow Oburne. He stumbled, awed by the comparative height of the stranger to Terrek standing beside her. Stopping to eye her glittering breastplate and mail, Gaelin found his gaze descending to her fur-wrapped boots, the thin strips dangling at the ends and flapping in the wind.

She's been sleeping, he guessed, discerning lines on her left cheek. *And crying, too*, he thought, taking in the splotches under her eyes when she tipped her head.

"Easy does it, Avalar," Oburne said, and Gaelin, standing in his shadow, heard how soothing he made his voice. "Take a look at the one you hold. He is no dach and he hasn't any magic. He's a warrior. You share a common foe."

The giant regarded Silva, giving him a light shake as she twisted her grip to get a better view. "So he is," she said at last. With sudden care, she placed Silva on the flat stone above the steps and bowed before him. "Pardon me. It seems I have erred."

"An understandable mistake, Giant," said Oburne. He stepped up next to Silva. "Back away," he told the warrior. "Do it *now*!"

"Lieutenant," Terrek asked while the guard complied. "Who is she?"

"Old magic in the flesh," said Oburne. "Her people are filled with it." Oburne halted before the giant, his brown eyes flashing at Gaelin. "Keep that staff away. Stay where you are, Lavahl."

Trembling, stunned by the size of the creature towering above them, Gaelin obeyed. He stood rigid, feeling like an intruder, a spectator the giant strove to ignore. As she examined Oburne, her eyes went wide and she lowered her sword. "Jahn Oburne. You joined my father to defend the Northian tribes. I have seen you on my uncle Kurgenrock's ship."

"Yes, Avalar," Oburne acknowledged. "When the Sundor Khan threatened my village, your father and his warriors helped us. Now we honor his name. Grevelin Mistavere's a legend among my people."

Terrek straightened and sheathed his weapon. "Why did you tell Gaelin to stay back?" he asked Oburne. "What is it about Mornius?"

"Think about the story you told Lavahl after the battle at Heartwood, Commander. How the land was ruined by the warders." Oburne nodded to the giant. "What in all sails are you doing so far from home, my dear? Are you injured? Did Erebos's priests have their staves when they attacked you?"

The giant glared. "Men in black robes blasted the city with their magic," she said. "They tried to enter the museum, for they knew I was here. But then I heard the wind come shrieking from over the mountains, and they could not approach." She wheeled to confront Terrek. "You are his leader?"

Terrek returned her stare. "Yes, I am called that, and I try my best to guide my father's men. That includes my guard, whom you injured." Terrek's voice hardened. "So tell me what you are, friend or foe."

"I'm fine, Terrek!" Silva called out from behind Gaelin. "The tip of her blade caught my sleeve. That's all. Just a scratch."

The giant inclined her head politely to the guard. Then, puffing out her chest, she focused on Terrek. "I am Avalar," she announced, "the only child of Grevelin Mistavere, who is Leader Second to Trentor Govorian. I am no enemy of humans who reject magic. But I *am* very tired."

Terrek frowned. "That much is plain. You have death and battle all over you. But please, can you tell us what happened here?"

Avalar studied her weapon. "They surprised us on the ninth day after I began learning the Talhaidor," she said. "I was training with the Masters in the square when they came, a great wedge of blackness." She motioned to the distant peaks. "Then they were here, swooping in under the domes. I fought with one of their leaders on these steps, but my strength did not suffice. A second man attacked me and drove me back, for I was but one giant!"

Avalar rubbed at her eyes. "I did what I could." Her voice thickened in her throat. "I saved the treasures stored within . . . trinkets and baubles, but none of the hearts who cherished them most."

Reaching out, Oburne caressed her bloodstained knuckles. "Avalar, you're a novice fighter," he said. "For your first battle, you did very well. You claimed your position and held it. But, Giant, you must go home. There is a new kind of magic here. If it touches you, we're dead."

The giant shuddered and drew back her arm. "I know of this new magic," she said, her lips curling with distaste. "I know of Sephrym, and the perilous might of the three warders he struck down. The power I battled on *these* steps, however"—she tipped her head to indicate a glimpse of red under the snow on a nearby step—"was from this world; it was human-tainted, so I smote it with my sword. As I would crush any human with magic. Any humans who would dare . . . What they did to my people, I would gladly slay—"

"If you stay here, you might get the chance," Oburne cut her off, risking a glance at Terrek. "She is old magic in physical form, Commander. The living Circle protected by the elves. We *must* keep her safe."

"You shall do no such thing!" Avalar said. "I am no child. It is my duty to safeguard *you*." With a sigh, she sat heavily on the topmost stair, placing her massive weapon by her outstretched leg.

Gaelin, standing several steps below, felt invisible as the giant looked past him, her blue eyes appraising the warriors in the plaza below. "My leader, Trentor, refused when I begged him to let me voyage here," she said. "And thus, I followed my heart and the demands of the blade that sang to me when I was little. I knew I needed greater skill to offer Redeemer, so I came first to Tierdon for the Talhaidor, the *Swordslore*."

Watching the giant, Gaelin sensed a heaviness upon his heart and the ripples of tension from his staff. An angry heat was mounting under his ribs as the restless wind brought reminders of Tierdon's dead. He pressed his fist to his chest and opened his mouth, struggling not to vomit. Death was everywhere he turned. His distress pricked at the warder in his staff, prodding the sleeping Holram awake.

Gaelin, seeing the giant's gaze shift to him at last, tilted his head to hide his face. *If Holram rouses,* he realized, *she will know I have magic.* He clenched his fists. *If the warder discovers those murdered children—* "Terrek!" Gaelin blurted. "I have to leave!"

Terrek whirled, and with three long strides, reached his side.

"It's Holram," Gaelin said. He reeled when the world slanted to the left, and reaching out, seized Terrek's arm. "He senses the dead! If he wakes, I would lose myself, and if the giant saw . . ."

"Understood, Oburne!" Terrek said over his shoulder. "I'm taking him to that clearing we found in the forest. Stay here and help the men gather the fallen, as many as you can find. We can't leave them like this. And take care of that giant. We owe her. She defended my brother's city."

Gaelin tottered stiff-kneed down the stairs, clutching at his staff to keep its heel from banging the stone. He fixed his gaze on the twisted metal framework atop Tierdon's shattered walls, the blue-white fields beckoning beyond.

Abruptly Terrek released him, pausing to rub his eyes. Gaelin yelped as he tripped and stumbled over the bottom stair, careening into Silva beside the horse. As the guard caught him by his elbow, Gaelin spotted the blood on Silva's sleeve. Before he could think, the warder in his staff yawned mightily, its great mane flaring, and a gentle pulse of healing light encircled the injured guard.

Gaelin heard a howl from above and the chink of steel.

"*Behind* you!" Oburne shouted.

Gaelin whirled to see Terrek leap to his defense, his body braced to deflect the giant's charge. She threw him aside, then plunged at Gaelin as he toppled onto his back, her fingers ready to kill.

"No, *no!*" Oburne rushed down the stairs as Terrek clambered erect and yanked out his sword. "Terrek, no, don't hurt her!"

Looking up, Gaelin met the giant's glare. She was straddling him, her hands poised to rip out his life. Yet she hesitated, her gaze shying from his staff. Beside her, Terrek bent close, his expression grim as his blade pressed against her throat.

"Move away, my dear," Oburne's voice said. "Please, Avalar, or he'll kill you."

"It was my father's," Gaelin told her with a glance toward Mornius. "It's one of the three you mentioned—one of the warders trapped here. He chose me, even though I killed a man." He nodded at her stare. "This is a special place, this city. I . . . don't belong here."

"It's not your kind of magic he wields, Avalar!" Oburne hurried to her opposite side to clasp her wrist. "He doesn't touch the Circle at all. Trust me, he's just a healer. Avalar, *forbear!*"

The giant broke from Oburne's grasp and staggered back, her fingers throttling the empty air. Oburne turned to Terrek. "Get him out of here!"

"Gaelin." Terrek slid his sword into its scabbard and stepped quickly to Gaelin. "Let's go."

Gaelin lurched dizzily to his feet and accepted Terrek's aid, allowing his friend to help him mount the nervous Duncan. Then Terrek, walking in front, led him on the gelding through a patch of sunlight.

"Commander!" Roth hastened over, leading his steel-gray stallion. He tipped up a painting he held and pointed. "See the man's face? I saw this in the gallery and recognized the jacket. That's Camron with the giant!"

Terrek squinted at Avalar standing rigid as she scanned the mountains. "Yes, very nice. Now return it to its place, Caven. Enough has been taken from Tierdon."

Roth grimaced. "But I thought you'd want his picture, since—" He sagged, and Terrek clapped his shoulder, gripping hard until he nodded. "There's something else," Roth whispered. "There's a dead little girl in one of the rooms. The giant fixed a bed for her."

"Was she wounded?" Terrek asked. "Perhaps Avalar was tending her and she—"

"No, I saw her wounds," said Roth. "The child was dead long before she was ever brought there. Terrek—" He drew a sharp breath. "These people have been like this for days. What if the giant's not . . . What if her mind is injured?"

"Then we'll deal with that if or when it becomes a problem," Terrek replied. "People in distress do peculiar things. Now put that artwork back where it belongs, Lieutenant. It isn't yours."

Sighing, Roth moved to obey.

"Get the men to scavenge for wood!" Terrek called to Vyergin. He stopped next to the captain's gelding, peering up at his second-in-command. "Have them check the arena first. It's the one building here that isn't made of stone." As Terrek paused to twist Duncan's reins in his hand, Gaelin glimpsed the damp sheen around his eyes, the shimmer of grief on his face.

Vyergin leaned over with a creaking of his saddle. "Oburne and I will take care of it," he said in a gruff voice.

Terrek grunted. "I'll get the camp set up first, but then I'll need to search for my brother. If you happen to locate Camron's body, send me word."

Gaelin ignored the stifled murmur of sympathy from the scattered men. His attention had followed Roth across the square to find the giant abandoning her study of the mountains. Turning, she stared at Terrek, tears brimming in her eyes at the mention of Camron's name.

Chapter 14

aelin faced Tierdon's distant ruins and shivered as the silence dragged out, as the sky darkened to velvety black and the starlight shimmered a pale blue.

Terrek remained frozen, the vapor from his breath the only indication Gaelin had that his friend still lived. Gaelin frowned at a fiery burst from across the drifts. He saw another flash, yellow glints stabbing through the city's wreckage. Wiping his eyes, he spied flames in the gaps between the shattered buildings, lashing outrage at the sky through the mounting smoke.

"Gaelin." Terrek's voice was very soft. "Please go."

"But, Terrek, I . . ." Gaelin stumbled back. Aching under his ribs, he turned and then hesitated at the sight of a faraway structure through the haze. The edifice sat high atop the cliff beyond Tierdon, its jagged towers resembling teeth behind a section of crumbling wall. Dazed, he rubbed at his chest, sensing the warder from his Skystone move to occupy his body—a pressure tapping urgently beneath his bones.

Opening his mouth at the pressure in his throat, he peered at Mornius's gem above his shoulder, its multicolor flashes matching the rhythm of his heart. "But why can't I help you search?" he asked Terrek. "The giant's here in camp now, so wouldn't I be safer with you?"

Terrek lowered his head, and Gaelin waited. The echo of Terrek's request repeated in his ears until at last he forced himself to cut with his knees through the windblown powder. Directing his gaze to the trees around their tents, he aimed his weary frame at the glimmers of the camp's six fires barely discernable among the clustered men.

His steps quickened when he entered the forest, finding much of the winter's accumulation cradled in the branches overhead. Pausing, he squinted through the fog. Beyond the trees, he saw splotches of light, the perimeter fires marking the camp's border, with the warriors' misty shapes huddled around them.

Gaelin rubbed his beard. He was no fighter, and while the men were polite enough, he sensed how he made them uneasy. Holding himself friendless and apart, he stared at the smallest fire, a cozy blaze just a few strides away. "They'd make room," he whispered, "but I don't think they'd welcome me." His teeth gritted, he wheeled from the light. *I'm not like them and they know it.* He sighed, his attention straying to his staff. *They don't have you.*

Shuddering from the cold, he pushed through the icy brush toward the cooking fire at the center of the camp, and there, by the crackling flames, he glimpsed the giant who wanted him dead. She crouched with Jahn Oburne standing next to her urging her to eat. Her head was up; she was glaring at him through the trees.

He averted his gaze, hugging Mornius to his chest as the cold chilled his bones. Again he surveyed the perimeter fires, hearing the soft murmur of the warriors talking. Torn by indecision, he grimaced at the figures by the closest little blaze. The men were dipping rags into a pot of steamy water—to cleanse away stains from Tierdon's dead.

He flinched when Avalar surged to her feet with her fists clenched—to scowl at him as she edged around the fire. Wavering in the shallow snow, he turned stiffly and watched her come. Gone were the tears and streaks of blood on her face. Her forehead gleamed in the light of the flames, her damp hair pulled back and woven into several blond braids. His body rigid, he stared at the darkness beneath her furrowed brows. *She's beautiful*, he thought before the giant, advancing toward him, moved beyond the firelight.

Her silhouette, blocking the blaze's reassuring glow, parted the fog and grew larger as she came, a tall black figure reminding him of the bear who had reared up before him on Mount Desheya.

As she passed between the trees in front of him, Gaelin heard a hesitation in the crunching of her footsteps—the giant muttering to herself as she exhaled. Struggling to hold his ground, he cast a desperate glance at Jahn Oburne. The lieutenant, watching by the fire where the giant had left him, glowered fiercely as though his trust in her was absolute.

Gaelin toppled backward as the giant neared, his staff tipping from his fingers and flipping sideways. *She's so big!* he realized, his mind registering how, body and shoulders, she was taller even than Oburne. *What's to stop her from killing me?* he thought with a groan.

She halted, looming before him, and he squeezed his eyelids shut, expecting the blade of her great sword to pin him to the ground. When nothing happened, he risked a glance to see her glaring down. He heard the chinking of her mail with her ragged breaths, each one declaring her desire for his death. Yet she hauled him erect, her strength pressing the tendons of his wrist to the bone. "It is as I thought," she said. "You *do* fear me."

Gaelin bent to retrieve his fallen staff, trembling as her magic charged the air at the back of his neck. *What would happen if she touched Mornius?* he wondered as he straightened up. Somehow, he sensed from the wind through the branches that the ground itself would crumble to dust. "Yes, I do," he confessed finally, for he sensed that the giant, too, heard messages in the air. Any deception on his part and the night voice would sing it to her. "Not fair," he murmured, cringing under the weight of her scrutiny. "It's dark so I can't see you, but you have your magic to see me."

He jumped when she tapped his chest. "*Prowlers* hunt after dusk," she said. "Not giants. Our magic enhances our size, not our vision, and only when we become angry and our blood is quickened." She paused. "I would not inflict injury to an ally of a friend. I have faith in Jahn Oburne, who has urged me to trust you."

"Quickened?" he asked.

"That is our word for when our blood heats up for battle. Our males grow large, the ones who are not *laori*."

"I wouldn't harm you," Gaelin said. "Examine my heart if you don't believe me. I know nothing about your magic. Can't you sense I'm telling the truth?"

The giant was silent. Perhaps she did what he had requested and searched his soul. He held his breath. "You are freezing, little human," Avalar said at length, "as am I. Come." She stepped aside, unblocking his path.

Cautiously he preceded her, moving to unite with the men around the cooking fire. The dozen or so fighters were on their feet when he arrived, their faces anxious, Wren Neche straining to break free from Oburne's arms.

"Lavahl," Oburne greeted him, his smug smile made whiter by the darkness of his skin. Several warriors hastened to deposit marker coins on the furry cloak he had tossed by the fire. With a jerk of his head, Oburne released Gaelin's guard. "Join us."

"You made a bet?" Gaelin asked. He glared at Wren as the furious young guard straightened his leather breastplate and then gestured to the collection of silver on Oburne's fur. "On whether she'd kill me?"

"I knew for a fact she wouldn't," Oburne said. "But these others, now, they presume to think they know giants better than I do."

"Your healer requires sustenance," Avalar told him. She leveled a measuring look at Gaelin as she stomped to a boulder by the fire. With a deep sigh, she dropped to the rock and hunched her shoulders, stretching out her hands. Gaelin marveled when the dancing flames sprang tall and leaned toward her.

"That's the old magic," Oburne explained to the curious men. He regarded the giant through the firelight, his white-rimmed eyes glinting red. "You've heard of it, Staff-Wielder?"

"Yes," Gaelin acknowledged before accepting his plated rations, a thick and meaty stew, from Wren. Without thinking, he filled his mouth and then grabbed the nearest cup of melted snow to soothe his tongue. "I've heard of it," he said after taking a drink. "But what is it?" *I don't even know what my staff is*, he thought glumly.

"There's a legend," said Oburne, settling his great bulk on his seat opposite the giant. He motioned to Avalar while Gaelin sat close to him on the rotted wood. "She can tell it better than I can, for the giants remember how things were before we came."

Avalar glanced over the fire at Oburne. "That is sooth," she said. "Though I do not. It is from my father's memories that I glean the older wisdom. You arrived at the rebirth of our sun, with other life, too, such as the great bear, and the leapers that chase our boats. The elves share this tale, not the giants. We have naught to say when it comes to your people on this world. We are the oldest race. There was a time when some of us rode the Azkharren males, or what you humans call dragons, from Skythorn's mighty peaks on Tholuna in the South. That is how we would reach the villages that needed our help."

Oburne fiddled with his spoon, toying with his congealing stew. Gaelin looked away, wincing at the reminder of the scraps he had been fed for so long. *When I was allowed to eat*, he thought bitterly.

"I don't question your people, Avalar," Oburne was saying. "But since you know the legend, won't you tell us?"

She inspected her fingers on her lap. "I will not. Nor," she added, peering over at Gaelin's surprise, "shall I discuss the Azkharren at length, or Stormfuries, as they are called, for the queens carry enough wind on their wings to shift the clouds. Wild magical creatures are not giants or elves. They hide from you humans. You cannot discern their presence on this world. And if you do happen to behold one, you should beware, for it might be that it hunts you."

"That's true, Avalar." Oburne shifted to scan the faces of the men seated or standing near. "If not for the elves, we would not even see the Skimmers in Luen Bay. The elves have trained those serpents to trust us. But in their wild state, they'd be invisible."

Gaelin tapped the big lieutenant's knee with his staff. "Terrek described our arrival to me, or at least some of it. You were there and you heard. What didn't he say?"

Oburne met his stare. In a quiet voice, he replied, "Forget the tale, Lavahl. She does not wish to hear it."

Gaelin sank back. *Everyone knows more than I do*, he thought. *Terrek and Vyergin have educations, and Oburne is familiar with the North. So what can I contribute?* He frowned and, with his spoon, lifted a fragment of bluebark cone from his plate and tossed it into the fire.

He glowered at Mornius propped upright by his knee. It had nothing to do with the giant's old magic, and yet it had power, enough that it had wrested control from him twice. *Even you understand more than I do.*

The giant was studying him. He shut his eyes, feeling the sudden tingle of magic in the air against his skin.

"Northman Oburne speaks truly," she said. "You do not realize what you hold, and now I fear I have wronged you."

Gaelin opened his eyes to meet hers. "Are you testing me now?" he said. "What else can I tell you? I admitted when you attacked me that the staff came from my father, whom I never knew. In fact, I don't know anything about—"

The warmth of her smile shocked his heart. For the first time, he espied the person she was under her stern demeanor, a bright, shining glimpse of compassion and kindness. Her eyes laughed at his reaction.

"I suppose I am testing you," the giant admitted. Once more she surveyed her fingers abraded red from her recent battle. "My people are no longer so willing to trust. Jahn Oburne urged me to let go of my wrath, but I required a sign from you first, which now you have given. You are angry and resentful. Those are honest feelings. Yet you carry a staff of new magic that you are ignorant of, and that makes you a threat, whether you wish to be or not. How can I expect you to refrain from damaging me without comprehending what it is you hold? So, inquire again, little human, and I shall endeavor to not be rude. What do you wish to know?"

Avalar paused, accepting a flask from a warrior behind her. She drained the container with two long gulps and then sat clasping the empty vessel, her expression sad.

As her question sank in, Gaelin leaned to see her through the smoke. "Everything!" he said. "My staff instructed me in my dreams, but never enough. Why does Erebos want me dead? And what is the old magic? And . . . *that?*" He indicated the structure on the distant cliff. "Will you tell me?"

Considering him, Avalar reached toward the fire. The flames flickered again, bowing to her as though in homage. "The castle is a relic from your world; mayhap you should inquire of a human what it is. But this"—she nodded to the campfire—"is the old magic. Do you see? Old magic connects me to this fire, and the flames to the air. We call this the Circle, for it links us to our world and binds this world to us. It is a fragile thing that the elves work to preserve. Talenkai is ancient. Our warder, Sephrym, has the energy and might to restore our dying sun, but he cannot touch nor influence the Circle that binds our magic. Only the strongest of us can do that, from the magic in the flesh of giants to the bloodstones beneath the dirt, we hold Talenkai together and steady its power."

Gaelin sighed, his exhaustion weighing down his bones. Transfixed, he gaped at the blue-orange flames bending flat in the giant's direction.

Satisfied, Avalar sat back. "You hunger for understanding," she said. "Therefore, hear me. Our magic may indeed have a soul of its own; on this the elves and our elders are undecided. Yet either way, it is helpless, a tool for anyone with enough sensitivity to feel it. Some elves have used this power to create cities like Tierdon or to protect my people. But with you humans . . ."

"We corrupt," said Gaelin.

Her eyes softened. "Not all humans do," she said. "This is new information I intend to share with my people when I return home. No." She grunted. "What you are does not make you evil; it makes you vulnerable. Magic dwells everywhere on this world. It is natural for your people to crave it for yourselves."

Avalar cleared her throat. "You are not from here, so the Circle does not include you. Any effort on your part to channel its power would distort it, and it would destroy you. Over time this may change," she added. "You drink our water and consume our food. Mayhap, in cycles to come, you shall be as my people are. Not in your lifetime, but someday."

Gaelin regarded Oburne. The big warrior appraised her through the firelight, his elbows braced on his knees.

"Perhaps," said Oburne, "if you think on this, Lavahl, other knowledge will come to you. But do you not see"—he pointed toward the giant—"how weary she is? Since we can't aid her with your staff, how about we let her rest?"

Gaelin considered Avalar's slumped posture and drooping eyelids. He grimaced as her head sagged.

"Come." Oburne stood and snatched his bearskin cloak from the log before striding around the fire to the giant's side. "Let's get you to bed," he said, reaching to nudge her shoulder.

She jerked, and for a moment, Gaelin caught the readiness for combat in her eyes as she lifted her head, her wide-open glare of hatred. Her confusion faded when she saw their faces. "Sails!" Avalar rubbed at her cheek. "Did I drift off already?"

"Almost," Oburne said. With unexpected tenderness, he patted her hand and helped her to her feet. "Come, my dear. Let's get you settled."

Chapter 15

Gaelin smiled as, trudging beside Avalar, he helped support her tottering weight. Always Oburne had daunted him with his size and booming voice, yet now the lieutenant looked puny next to the giant, his head reaching just past her waist while he walked bracing her opposite elbow.

As they approached the shelter Oburne had prepared, Gaelin observed that it was two tents laced together. The first was Oburne's own from the barren North, a structure so white it glowed in the darkness, while the other tent's gray hues blended with the night.

Gaelin sidled out of Avalar's way as she crouched to untie the canvas flap that served as the shelter's door. Thrusting her arm through the entrance, she patted the bed pad and furs before crawling in at last, the rear wall threatening to burst while she settled. Oburne squatted to help the giant secure the tent's laces from within. Then with a grunt, pushed himself to his feet and turned. "Let's walk," he said, and Gaelin sighed as the big warrior steered him toward the central fire, only to stop him after a few quick strides. "You want to know more?"

Gaelin nodded. "What are you afraid of?" he asked. Wind blasted through the camp, whipping the branches above them, and Oburne shuddered. Slowly his hold relaxed until Gaelin pulled free. "Do you think I would hurt her?"

"Not on purpose," Oburne said. "Maybe your warder cares enough to protect her. But who can say? Staff-Wielder, she is the magic in its purest form. Just . . . stay your power until we know more."

"But if—" Gaelin began. He broke off, seeing Mornius flash abruptly and flicker. Peering into the Skystone, he spied in its foggy depths Terrek sitting hunched on the ground and barely conscious. A wave of sadness reached him from the image in the crystal, a grief–throttled pain beyond what his staff could heal.

Skirting around Oburne, he rushed through the frozen brush toward the cooking fire. There he found his benefactor hunched on his heels close to the blaze with Vyergin standing behind him, his brow smeared with soot. Caven Roth, kneeling beside Terrek, seized the pot abandoned by the flames to scrape up the last bits of stew.

"The giant was hungry," Oburne called to Vyergin. "She cleaned two plates even before Lavahl here showed up. Don't *worry*, I'm sure there's more. Check the other fires. I used the deer Grenner brought down yesterday, plus what I scavenged from Tierdon's stores."

Vyergin nodded vaguely, his gaze lifting from Terrek to Gaelin. "We found him searching for his brother. He hasn't responded to us."

"Terrek!" Gaelin dropped to his knees by his shivering friend. Terrek's lips were blue above his short-cropped beard, his features contorted. On instinct, Gaelin raised his staff.

"No!" shouted Oburne. "I told you, Lavahl, not while the giant is with us!"

Gaelin squeezed Terrek's rigid arm. Groaning, the commander collapsed, and as he pitched toward the fire, only Vyergin's swift grab kept his sandy hair out of the flames.

Shaking his head, Gaelin lifted Mornius and turned toward Terrek, yet before he could blink, angry hands snatched the staff from his grasp.

"I *said* no!" Oburne flung Mornius away, the staff landing upright at an angle in a drift beyond Vyergin. Then Oburne seized Gaelin by the collar and dragged him erect, thrusting his bearded chin close. "Why don't you *listen?*"

Gaelin threw his lighter weight against Oburne's barrel chest, forcing the larger man to stumble back. "I *do* listen! But what you're asking is for me to give up the *one thing* I can do to help, and why? Nothing you said makes any sense!"

Terrek shuddered. Stiffly he lifted himself from the damp ground to settle on a nearby log. "Oburne, both of you, stop it. Gaelin, I'm fine. I don't need your staff."

As Gaelin jerked free from Oburne's hard grasp, a strange elation frayed his wrath. Again, he knelt. "You don't look so good, Terrek. I can help you."

Terrek was silent, staring at the flames. "I feel nothing," he muttered. Growling, he shrugged off Vyergin's grip on his shoulder and stood, his arms locked across his chest, to confront Oburne. Gaelin, with a worried glance at Vyergin, climbed to his feet.

"You forbade him to use his staff?" Terrek asked the lieutenant. "Are you out of your mind?"

Jahn Oburne returned Terrek's stare and Gaelin trembled at the strong man's fierceness—what he imagined had been the last glimpse of life for the Sundor Khan creatures Oburne had fought. "Everything's changed now, Commander," said Oburne. "What do you think will happen if his magic touches the giant? Talenkai would die. All of us would."

"The air is part of the Circle, too, according to Avalar," Gaelin interjected. "Mornius is touching the air right now, and nothing terrible happ—" He stopped as Terrek flicked him a glare.

"Stay out of this, please." Terrek, without missing a beat, rounded on Oburne, his fist thumping hard against the lieutenant's wide chest. "I don't know what you've been telling this boy, but you listen to me. We need Holram's power to defeat Erebos, and Gaelin to give it to us."

"Not anymore, Terrek," Oburne said. "Not if Avalar—"

"*Forget* the giant!" Terrek glowered into Oburne's face. "We don't even know if she'll remain with us. And even if she does, why would the staff be a danger? Mornius interacts with old magic all the time, as Gaelin says. That's why it was made, to keep Holram from hurting the world."

"Are you sure about that?" Oburne challenged, leaning into his leader's fist. "How can you be certain enough to take that risk? We're talking about our extinction!

"The fact is, you can't know," Oburne answered Terrek's silence. "Commander, the Khanal elves have said . . ."

Gaelin frowned when Terrek swayed on his feet. "The Khanal elves are not from Thalus," Terrek told him. "They lack experience when it comes to this power. The Eris elves know more. They shielded Holram in their petrified tree when he arrived. They built Mornius for the warder and chose the Skystone for its crown.

"Oburne." Terrek tottered, scowling as he fought to steady himself. "We've made it this far, haven't we? Let Gaelin be." As his strength continued to ebb, he sagged against the larger man.

Gaelin stepped in, his attention on Oburne's face. The burly lieutenant's eyes were filled with doubt as well as concern, yet he held himself silent, his jaws clenched.

"Go," said Gaelin. "I'll catch up. I need to grab my staff."

Oburne winced. With his strong arm around his commander's shoulders, he guided the shambling Terrek into the darkness toward the tents.

Chapter 16

Clamping his wings behind his back, Ponu accepted the bowl from his host. Despite Grevelin Mistavere's stern demeanor, tears for his wayward daughter wetted his cheeks above his beard. Still, the giant asked again. "Are you well, my friend?"

Ponu ached in his heart, feeling his companion's pain through the involuntary bond linking him to the veteran warrior. He took care to attend to his hands, or his steaming supper, or anything at all but Grevelin's worry and grief. Lowering his head, he inhaled the soup's fishy aroma before managing a grin.

"I am well indeed. Thank you," he said. Turning, he retraced his steps across the octagonal room, his attention drawn to the intimidating sword in its human-sized scabbard by the fire.

Mindful of his wings, he settled on the rug in front of the hearth and cautiously sipped at the broth as he studied his friend.

"Ah, so you came for the sake of my health," Grevelin rumbled. He stood in the cook-room doorway, his sea-gray eyes thoughtful beneath his prominent brows. Barefoot and clad in his tattered white sleep shirt, he looked nothing like the fighter he was.

"Of course I did," Ponu said. He glanced about him at the home's cozy interior—to Avalar's feminine touches here and there, the pile of her quilts and her basket of yarn near the hearth, and her curtains softening the only window. He met the serene gaze of Alaysha, Grevelin's mate, in the painted likeness Avalar had rendered from her many glimpses of her father's memories. Beyond the frosted panes of the window by the portrait, he heard the frigid ocean, the relentless drumming of Hothra's arctic surf.

Raising his head, Ponu met Grevelin's stare. "I know how anxious you get when I am away too long, so I thought I would visit tonight rather than make you wait."

Grevelin, returning his smile, retreated once more into the cook-room, the fringe of his auburn hair sliding about his shoulders. "Tonight, or tomorrow," he called. "You are always welcome, my friend."

Left alone, Ponu peered at his abandoned staff by the front door, with Grevelin's black waders standing upright next to it. Compared to the staff's gleaming crystal, the boots were as unremarkable and homey as the rest of the house. Like Avalar's green-and-blue-striped curtains, they belonged, while his Staff of Time did not.

Reappearing with his own helping of the savory soup, Grevelin grinned at his expression, the apprehension he failed to conceal from the giant. "Go and contemplate your stick if you must," the big warrior said with a sigh. "Mayhap its mysteries will ease you in ways I cannot."

Ponu set down his dinner, climbed to his feet and flexed his white wings. Unable to hide his fears any longer, he hurried to retrieve his staff and grip the heat-sculpted crystal. "I worry about Avalar, too," he said. "Something is wrong. Ever since Tierdon's destruction, I have felt nothing but distress from her."

Grevelin dropped onto his stone seat, hissing when the broth inside his bowl sloshed his palm. "Could she be wounded?" he asked. "My daughter is yet untrained for battle. If she tried to defend your city . . ."

"Will you wait?" Ponu strained to concentrate on his staff. "Please, dear friend, let me see."

He sifted through the crystal's matrix, beholding reflections of the present in its multiple forms, the past hidden behind its elusive curtain of mist, and the tantalizing glimpses of the future. Fixing on Avalar, he directed his thoughts to the lone giant while employing the subtle power from his homeworld, a magic of language, gesture, and nuance of tone.

As he hummed through his teeth, his staff responded, pulsing softly in rhythm. "She sleeps," he said. "They've housed her in . . . a kind of shelter."

"They?" Grevelin placed his bowl on the stone floor by his chair.

"Yes, *they*." Ponu squinted as he sorted through the staff's uneasy layers. "Grevelin, something is amiss. Your daughter tosses in her sleep. Her dreams are haunted by a danger she senses . . . someone she . . ."

Ponu stared at the visions within his staff. He recalled witnessing through his lion familiar how Avalar had rescued the child near Firanth. His interest in her encounter after—the prowler who had answered his magic's call—had made him forget the little human.

"That boy!" He whirled on Grevelin. "She has always loved children, Grev. Kray was in trouble, and she saved him. You know what that means. He is linked to her!"

With three long strides, Grevelin crossed the room. His gray gaze was hooded, dark with suspicion and fear as he glowered at the staff. Before Ponu could reassure him, Grevelin lashed out and seized his wrist. "Speak to me, elf!" the giant demanded. "Who is this Kray? Who has *dared* to confine my daughter?"

Ponu, wincing, struggled to grin at his bearded friend. "Not confined, Master. *Given*," he said. "She rests within a tent they provided for her. They are showing her courtesy and respect. Now ease *up*, Grev! Please! I am not made of stone!"

Grevelin frowned and relaxed his grip, his eyes welling with tears.

"I must leave you," Ponu told him. "I'm sorry, but if I ignore what she feels and something terrible happens to Kray . . ."

Seeing his companion's dawning comprehension, Ponu nodded. "She would never forgive me, as you well know. Do you recall when you fished me out of the sea after I *transferred* into the storm? There was a connection between us even before your heart bonded, and it's because you saved my life." He took a breath and, trying to lighten the giant's mood, waggled his brows at his friend. "Well?"

"Ponu, no!" Grevelin said. "She *cannot* bond with this child. Not with a human. You need to stop her!"

"She won't." Holding his breath, Ponu pulled himself free. "She rescued him, Grevelin; that is all. Therefore, she can sense when he's in trouble. Since his is the only life she has ever preserved, I have to assume *he* is the cause of her unrest. Now—"

He lifted his staff, visualizing in his mind the forested town of Firanth where he knew Kray lived, the abandoned farms and neglected fields surrounded by trees. "Fear not, Grev! I will help Avalar. I swear it!"

Power surged in his palms, a flash of burning followed by an intense cold. The transition was swift enough to make him gasp, the energy propelling him quickened by his misgivings.

Something dire was happening. Within the kaleidoscope of images he plunged through, he saw fire, an orange-red destruction blazing toward the heavens. A seething vapor rose to block his view. Momentarily blinded, he lost control of his staff and landed with a thud on the frozen ground.

Gray smoke billowed in front of him to obscure the stars, the fire below it blistering the shingled rooftops of the clustered buildings that formed the diminutive town. Fueled by the wind from the mountains, the flames raged at the sky.

Ponu choked as he rubbed his stinging eyes. Grabbing at his tunic, he tore off its hem, then pressed the clump of fabric over his nose and mouth. He swayed as he dragged himself erect to peer upward.

Pushing with his mind, he wove his consciousness deep among the strands of Talenkai's magic, visualizing new pathways to guide its currents. Firmly he nudged the Circle's fragile web, compelling it to obey until the clouds clashed and swelled overhead. With a deafening crash, the power released as he lifted his hands, torrents of rain hammering down.

"Kray!" Ponu fought to see past the angry spats of steam. He waded from the town and across a soggy field, the snow dissolving fast into muck and slushy puddles. He spied a blackened house beyond the trees, a fading orange flicker beneath the glow of its flayed roof. *Kray?* he thought, spreading out his fingers. He grimaced, catching no sense of life, only terror, echoes of pain in the scorched wood—the brutal death of the woman, the capture of the man.

"Sails!" With a sharp cry, Ponu slumped to his knees.

"Foolish bird!" A sibilant voice hissed behind him. "Fire, so fly! Or run like diradil do. Flee burning!"

Startled, Ponu scrambled to his feet and turned. A heavily maned prowler squatted low in a refuse ditch and glared back at him, the carnivore's striped head resting on massive forepaws. The creature lifted his ebony lips as their gazes met, his curved fangs glistening. Ponu crouched on his heels. "Did you witness what kindled this?" He pointed to the burning town.

The creature bristled. "Prowler *see* everything," he boasted. He lowered his muzzle between his leg and his dappled belly. "Humans *gone*. Blood take 'em like others. This kitten mews like cubling alone, so I catch!"

Ponu squinted, discerning through the rain the trembling figure the predator guarded. "Kray?" he said.

The prowler snorted. "Little one whimpers, fears big male. I hunt him before when hungry. Toy good sport, but now comes water from eyes. Sick, maybe, notter good hunting. Notter run."

"You must be Shem," said Ponu, standing to shake the water from his hair.

"Ah!" the prowler spat and, grinning, puffed out his chest. "Great male, yes? Big. *Strong!*"

"Indeed, you are," said Ponu. He motioned toward the child. "Is he your dinner or not? Do you claim this prey?"

As Shem rose from the ditch, his movements fluid and graceful, Ponu stared. *He's too big*, he thought. *Is he a hybrid?*

The creature grinned at his reaction. "Grandsire Sherkon Raider," he explained. "See you?" Unsheathing his claws, Shem reared upright, his tufted tail whipping the air as he arched back his neck and roared.

"Help!" a voice cried. Then Kray's head poked into view from the darkness below the ditch. The tow-haired boy scuttled swiftly away from his captor to cower, trembling, behind Ponu's wings.

"Magic favors cubling," Shem observed with a nonchalant yawn. He dropped to all fours in the mud, his green eyes aglitter below his hairy brows. "He mighty friends. Great male notter claim scrawny human."

"Good." Ponu glanced down at the sliver of Kray he managed to glimpse under the drenched arch of his wing. *Such interesting creatures, humans*, he mused. *What candle-flicker lives, and yet they have so much spirit!* "Since you give him up freely," Ponu said aloud, "I will accept this gift from you."

Shem humphed and sank onto his haunches. "I *prowler!*" he spat. "Who say what prowler do?"

Ponu inclined his head, keeping his expression severe. "When it comes to prowlers, one can never say." He grinned at the big male's response, the haughty sneer on Shem's leonine face. Then Ponu seized the boy by the waist, flared wide his wings, and *transferred*.

He felt, rather than heard, the little human screaming against his wrist. Sensing the child's distress, his unfamiliarity with the forces buffeting his small body, Ponu shielded him as best as he could, until his underground home sprang into existence around them both.

As his staff's power dissipated and his cave went dark, Ponu leaned the molded crystal against the protrusion that served as a shelf. With a thought he lit the braziers in their nooks along the walls before placing the youngster on his feet. Stepping back, he bowed to the bewildered child and gestured, giving him leave to explore.

Ponu watched Kray totter across his workroom's granite floor, stopping to examine the stone table Ponu had carved from stalagmites that had once divided the room—complete with its pile of books, its jumbled assortment of dried plants and instruments. When the boy spotted the tangled bedclothes on his unmade cot, Ponu sighed. "I will make another bed for you," he said. "For now, however, you may sleep there."

If Kray heard, he gave no sign. Then, as the child neared the room's only doorway, he hesitated again, this time to stroke the polished black tube Ponu had taken care to set aside in the corner, the cylinder tilted up and mounted on wooden legs.

"That's my stargazer," Ponu told him. "The stone is called obsidian, and the legs are wrought from bottomwood, from trees under the sea. I set a crystal at its core for the light to pass through. It's crude, but with some help from my magic, it lets me view—"

"What will you do to me?" Turning, Kray acknowledged him for the first time. His voice quivered as he spoke.

"*Do?*" Ponu pulled a chair from next to the wall and scooted it at his guest. Then, his chest still burning from the smoke he had inhaled, he moved to sit on his bed. Carefully he smoothed its blankets before emptying out his vest's bulging pockets, arranging the baubles he had collected on the giant-woven fabric beside him.

A few of these I can use, Ponu thought, touching the colorful disks of surf-polished glass scavenged from Hothra's shore, the petrified bark from a tree even older than he was. *These others are trinkets*, he admitted to himself with a smile.

As he had hoped, Kray goggled at the treasure, forgetting his recent trauma and fear. "Are all those *real?*" He pointed to the gems.

"I know humans value these," Ponu said, smiling, stirring with his forefinger the stones he had taken the time to cut, nudging them with magic to make them flash with rainbow colors.

Enchanted, Kray padded over. Ponu studied the child while the boy examined the sparkling rocks, his brown eyes marveling.

"Perhaps we can work a deal," Ponu said. When the boy glanced up, Ponu tapped the stones. "If you agree to feed my ferret and keep my cave tidy, I shall pay you one bauble every ninth day . . . along with food and shelter, of course."

"Really?" The child gaped at the riches spread out before him. "I'd—I'd have to ask my . . ." Kray trembled, tears glistening on his cheeks.

Ponu clasped the boy's shoulders until Kray raised his head. For a long, quiet moment, he held the youngster's gaze. "Your people are gone." Ponu made his voice as gentle as he could. "You must be brave for me now like your mother was for you. As you were the first time that big prowler chased you. Can you do that for me?"

The tiny human was silent, quaking with grief. Ponu wiped the boy's face with the corner of his blanket. At last, not knowing what else to do, he drew the shuddering child to his breast and held him tight.

Chapter 17

Felrina gripped the altar's dead stone, shutting her eyes when the chamber faded to spin around her. Teeth clenched, she inhaled, feigning a dramatic pause. *Stop it, you fool*, she thought. *Don't let them see that you know him.* She chewed her lip and nodded, breathing slowly until her vertigo stopped. *Try not to look at him and it'll be fine. If you give yourself away, they'll force you to torture—*

"Rina?" The sacrifice spoke from the tilted slab, and his familiar voice, so much a part of her old cherished life, shattered her self-control. Biting back a cry, she bent, her knife forgotten as his unfocused gaze found her face. Stiffly she leaned over his chest with a summoning motion to her god, letting her thick brown hair tumble forward.

So much blood, she thought, regarding her friend's shackled arms, his kind mouth and the freckles around his nose.

Camron's muscles flexed under his scraggly beard as he lifted his head to stare at her. "I'm glad it's you," he whispered. "If you find my father or Terrek . . ."

"Hush!" Felrina hissed, sensing the watchful eyes of the young assistant next to her and the Attendant First behind her standing on his wooden stool and holding his torch. Two other clerics also observed her movements, a man and a young woman waiting with their buckets near the wall. *Mens is here, too*, she thought. Glancing up with another ritualistic flourish, she glimpsed her superior scowling beside the chamber's front entrance. "I do this to *spare* you, Camron," she said under her breath. "Be silent."

"Tell them I love them," he responded. "My father, Lucian, needs to know it didn't hurt. He'll blame himself for this. I don't want . . . Tell him your being here helped me."

She made a show of checking his bonds. His wounded wrists extended beyond the stone, his arms bound to the altar above his elbows. "If the others realize I know you," she murmured, "they'll make me hurt you even more. You'll die in terrible pain. Or I'll be forced to make you a dach, and, trust me, death is better."

Camron struggled to move, his hands twitching weakly over the basins positioned on the floor to catch his blood. "Remember when I hit the bottom of the river with my head," he asked, "and you and Terrek had to jump in to save me?"

Felrina rocked, and with theatrical gestures—taking care not to strike the burning torch above her—she called upon Erebos.

"Remember when I wouldn't leave you alone?" Camron was saying. "What a pest I was back then. A silly little boy. I never minded that you loved Terrek. He was older and the best rider in Kideren. Of course you'd love him. I loved him, too."

"Oh, Camron!" She caught his wrist and squeezed it tight. "I know it hurts. But I have to believe it's for the good of us all. You'll come back to me. You'll see. We'll build our houses, the castles Erebos gives us, beside another river someday. And we'll play our water games like we used to."

Felrina paused. "Why did it have to be you? Why did you let them catch you?" Fighting back tears, she caressed his cheek. "*Why? Forgive* me!"

For a moment more, Camron gazed at her. "I love . . . Always have," he said. "Tell Terrek . . . and Father . . . Tell . . ."

She gulped down sobs as she clung to her knife. His eyes were closed, his lips smiling. She bent to kiss his forehead and mouth, her thumb drawing a thin line with his blood from between his brows to his chin. Listening, she heard his last breath, a gentle sighing between his lips. Only then did she open his throat, slicing from ear to ear.

She stumbled back, memories flashing through her brain. *Everything I loved is dead*, she thought, gagging as she clutched at her chest. *Now I am dead, too!*

Her body rigid, she walked from behind the altar and passed the Attendant First on his pedestal. Stopping at the center of the platform where the altar sat, she lifted her hands and confronted her seated congregation. Except for Allastor Mens, the twenty-eight men and women were oblivious now in their hooded robes, their minds immersed in the ecstasy of the ritual.

With reverent care, they passed their bowls of greenberry wine mixed with sacrificial blood, their lips glistening as they each took a sip. She nodded when her turn came and went through the motions expected of her, staining her brow and chin with the liquid before accepting a taste herself. Swallowing hard, the wine helping her to keep it down, she handed the bowl to the waiting junior cleric. On reflex then, she touched her forehead. *I drink to honor and share in the sacrifice*, she thought. She tilted her neck to gape at the ceiling, stretching out her arms as the potent beverage took effect. *I am yours, great Erebos, completely and forever. Do with me as you will!*

Felrina drew a deep breath, glancing at Mens in the front of the room. His glare jolted her to alertness, yet she refused to look away. The fear he instilled quickened swiftly to rage in her heart, enough defiance to endure what she now was forced to hear as the attendants behind her dismembered her friend.

Camron! She shuddered as she pictured him with his crooked, contagious smile. He had been the moody younger brother, weaker in body than Terrek, but gifted with a brilliant mind and a passion to learn. She had always loved his honesty and his open and trusting heart.

He had never uttered a sound while her three gray-robed assistants placed him unresisting before her, binding him naked on the stone. She recalled her horror at seeing him for the first time in over a year, the determined fire in his eyes while he stared at the ceiling, his jaw muscles tensing as she pressed her knife to his flesh.

Now he's gone, she thought, licking her lips with her dry tongue. *And I must continue for the sake of our future. These trials give Erebos the strength to hasten his rebirth. This is what matters, nothing else.* She swiped at her cheek. *I mustn't lose sight of that.*

Felrina grimaced at Mens as he approached, accepting Erebos's ancient staff when he placed it in her grasp. As she turned to the altar, her three assistants hurried down the steps and out of her way. Then Felrina paused, allowing the First enough time to climb down from his low box and follow. With a nod, she lifted her staff and aimed its Blazenstone at Camron's remains. "Great Erebos, accept this life!" she said.

Flames blistered the oval chamber, whirling out from her stone as a second blaze rose from the altar itself—from her god, Erebos, hiding within its obsidian heart. As Camron's bones withered, she heard laughter from the winged shadow rising over the burning slab, a long, mirthless cackle from the Slayer of Suns.

Felrina sank to her knees, feeling the chamber around her creak and rock. The granite crackled beneath her, its sharp repetitive snaps hurting her ears.

She cringed where she knelt, blinded by the inferno that charred the walls beyond the altar and rippled in streamers above her. Any moment and she would feel her eyes melting, her flesh dropping in tatters from her bones.

A hush filled the chamber as the flames slowly died, the air tinged with the smell of sulfur. Felrina opened one eye. The elated priests were staring at her—stunned and holding their breath.

"Erebos is pleased," Felrina said, trembling as she stumbled to her feet. "Our offering was a potent one. The boy has fed Erebos well, and one day we'll see him again in paradise!"

"Praise to the spirit of the sacrifice!" As one, the acolytes exulted, lifting their bloodstone staves as they chanted. "Feast, great Warder, and save us!"

"Now go!" Felrina whirled her staff above her, its flames drawing arcs of glowing crimson across the ceiling. "Go and worship our one true hope!"

"Our *hope!*" Erebos's minions echoed. With a rustle of heavy fabric, they filed out through the chamber's front exit, their voices chanting soft and slow.

"You selfish whore," said Allastor Mens's voice behind her. Then, wearily, Felrina turned.

Her leader leaned toward her, his weight on his staff, as his glare flayed her bones. Camron's blood splotched his chin and neck, with more of it streaked on his balding head.

Ignoring him, she glanced again at the altar. In silence the two attendants with the buckets approached the back of the chamber, the containers they held thudding against their calves.

"Felrina." Mens, grabbing her elbow, pressed the warped heat of his body close. "You were talking to him! You *knew* that young man!

You—"

She threw off his touch. "Yes, he was frightened, so I comforted him. What is the harm in that, Mens? It wasn't that kind of ceremony, anyway. We were to harvest blood, not pain."

"That boy affected you," said Mens, "so his death should have been entrusted to me for the benefit of us all." He shoved at her until she stepped back, his flaring nostrils a hairsbreadth from her own. "Instead you took from our god's table!"

"My pain this night," she said, her voice quivering, "fed Erebos more than any hurts that boy might have felt!"

Allastor Mens's upper lip curled, his reddish eyes flaring beneath his wild black brows. "What makes you think Erebos will spare you?" he demanded. "There's always a price for treachery, Felrina. A *price*, do you hear me? And I guarantee you *will*—"

She cut him off with a brusque gesture, diverting his attention to the attendants waiting beside the altar. "Are you finished? We have other work yet to do, Mens. Arawn's spirit hungers now, and your army of dachs needs replenishment. Have you prepared the prisoners?"

Mens nodded as she left him to join her helpers. When the grim-faced First hefted his torch and started down the granite rear passage that led from the chamber, Felrina followed, descending the stairs with Mens on her heels.

She snarled silently as he darted to flank her. "The last batch you made was flawed, Felrina. Too many of them killed themselves before I could use them." He grunted when the steps ended and then narrowed and resumed a few paces later. "This time, I want warriors with *no* conscience at all and no self-awareness. Give me dachs who'll brave both fire *and* sunlight for me and every—"

"I'm familiar with your *needs*, Mens," she interjected, slowing her pace when the stairway forked before her. Crouching beneath the mountain's dense rock, she veered left, the glow from the First's torch barely visible ahead. "Perhaps they'll be met this time. Who can say? Erebos's ability to work through Arawn's magic increases daily. It isn't just me, you know, who decides the outcome."

She abandoned the steps and padded along the sloping volcanic rock, then hurried up more stairs to enter the place she considered her workroom. The Attendant First's fiery brand illuminated her sunken tarn below where she stood, and the sight of its black, greasy surface steadied her. Once more she summoned fire from Erebos's staff. As she started down the stony shelves surrounding the pool, her attendants passed her by, the two clerics stopping to kneel at the pond's flat edge and flick blood from their buckets across the water.

Felrina moved into position by the female attendant, a girl with a dirty-blond braid down her back. "Hearken and make ready, great Arawn!" Felrina cried. "For we now bring life in exchange for your service, and a heart in trade for your power. Grant us the potency of your magic! Let the old and the new merge as one!"

She motioned, and the two attendants emptied their buckets. Camron's organs vanished beneath the water. Gulping, she watched his head bob toward the pool's oily center, his blank face staring upward as it sank.

Groans of fear rose from the nude men and women hidden in the shadows against the wall. They were the prisoners from Tierdon, the ones deemed sturdy enough to survive her staff. At her command, Mens's clerics drove them forward into the pool, harrying them up to their necks in the slimy water.

"Stay in the shallows close to the edge," one of the acolytes warned while Felrina watched, "or you'll be yanked under for sure, the flesh ripped from your bones."

Felrina nodded. *He saw what happened last summer,* she thought as she raised her staff high. *That woman . . .* She remembered the captive—the feeble thrashing of the prisoner as Arawn's spirit, hungry for life, had devoured her legs. Then Mens, with a vicious grin, had used his staff to prod the woman back into the ghost's merciless grasp after she had struggled so hard to break free.

Clearing her throat, Felrina lifted her gaze to the cavern's vaulted ceiling. "Hail, great Arawn," she intoned, "master and mage, slaver of giants and the wielder of the power which preserves you. Hear me, Lord!" She spread her arms. "Erebos has promised to create a New Earth for us. A world fit for humans alone with *you* as our king. But death must come first, so grant us the power to *destroy* and rebuild, great one! Help Erebos transform this flesh we offer, and construct from these hearts mighty warriors, combatants who would rather *die* than fail. With this, the water that holds your magic, help us, Lord!"

She tapped the stalactite above the immersed prisoners with her

staff, and the Blazenstone crackled with heat, its lurid energy blasting in all directions. It was Erebos's power she held, eager, unfettered, and raw.

Felrina closed her eyes. Gripping her staff, she envisioned the dachs Mens had described to her, for she was the guide Erebos needed, that Arawn's knowledge of magic would then help him form from the captives' living tissue. As Erebos's power struck the pool, he awakened the dead wizard's awareness, Arawn's spirit bound to the water by his final spell. When the great mage absorbed the blood that was offered, his thoughts, fully roused, focused on manipulating Erebos's power, answering the demands of the staff that animated his soul.

Screams filled the chamber. The tarn ignited as the old magic connected with the new, the prisoners shrieking when the flames swept over them, their bodies writhing as their flesh melted like heated wax.

With Camron's name on her lips, Felrina struck the inferno with her staff, and the black water erupted, spouting upward from beneath the fire.

She recoiled, stepping clear of the currents within the pool, the flailing liquid battering the stricken captives against the basin's stony rim and the mountain above it, the force of it crushing their bones.

When at last the magic abated, the water sloshing back and forth, Felrina dropped her robe and slipped naked into the shallows, her toes finding the steps beneath the water. Descending to her waist, she glanced around her at the scattered bodies. Two were dead, with gory pouches of brain and bone swaying above their necks—and already Arawn consumed them, their torsos jerking as his spirit in the water tore them apart. She scanned the remaining prisoners, all floating spread-eagled, their broken bodies pliable now, like clay ready to mold.

Reaching with her staff, Felrina touched one chest after another with the Blazenstone. Again she formed images in her mind, this time of the shattered limbs mending into the shapes she wanted, the skin of the arms widening into wings, the thickening fingers growing talons, and the backs elongating into tails with poisonous spines. She clenched her staff, visualizing the skulls of her creatures growing heavy, their jaws reinforced and bristling with fangs, the skin of their heads and bodies hardening into scales.

"So many with wings," Allastor Mens said from beside the pool, and yet his voice sounded far away. She nodded while she finished her work, adding mottled patterns of gray and green on the skin of her creations, with ebony-colored wings and crimson on the barbs along their tails.

Felrina, pressing her staff to the final dach's widening chest, peered up at Mens. "Erebos and Arawn do all the work, while I just picture what I want from them. If not for my imagination, Mens, I'd be just like you, and someone else would carry my staff."

He grimaced, his dark eyes flaring while his mind rejected her words. "No, Felrina. You've never dared to handle a bloodstone because you're *afraid*. You don't want your teeth to fall out or your precious body to rot. So instead you carry *that*." He motioned to her staff. "And because somebody has to, I approve, but it does make you a coward among us, while every day the rest of us, Erebos's *true* followers, deteriorate."

Felrina frowned, taken aback by Mens's resentment, the utter contempt in his voice. She waded out of the pool's oily water and onto the stone ledge, standing with pinkish rivulets streaming down her legs. She raised her staff, sensing Arawn's mind sink again into the pool's dark depths, while, in the blood-red Blazenstone, Erebos's power crackled and burned, reacting to Mens's anger.

With the warder's strength, she struck the black-robe's groping fingers when he came too close, his yellowed teeth bared as though he meant to bite her. "Don't *touch* me, Mens! How many times must I tell you?"

He continued to stare, quivering as he stooped to the rocky floor and lifted her discarded robe. "Wear it!" he said in a hoarse whisper. He flung the garment at her chest. "Have mercy, Felrina."

She smiled and let the robe fall, laughing when his hungry eyes widened to devour her body. "Why should I cover up for *you*?" she asked. "Why not just blind yourself, Mens? Erebos would like that, too, I'm sure. You've said yourself how much he loves pain, and how it's all for the sake of our future."

He gaped at her, his thin lips fumbling for words.

Felrina glared back. "You promised me that if I joined this order, I'd never have to use the old magic. You swore to me I would never have to torture anyone, either. Now if you have a problem with that, you go talk to your mirror. I have better things to do. *Begone!*"

She trembled with the power of the two great forces that had joined within her. *I am their instrument*, she realized. *I give birth to their magic, and nothing else matters. Not Kideren, where I was born, or Terrek, whom I love.*

A low howl began in Mens's throat. He whirled and bolted up the steps, fleeing from her presence so she would not hear him scream. Still, she did, and smiling at the sound, she bent to retrieve her robe.

Chapter 18

*T*errek wheeled from the golden caress of dawn on Tierdon's ruined walls. As his surveillance shifted to Avalar, he recalled the painting Roth had shown him depicting the giant with his younger brother. The portrait had captured a hint of tenderness in her expression that went beyond friendship. Yet here she stood, having survived what had abducted or destroyed everyone else, including Camron. *What does that tell me?* he wondered.

From the corner of his vision, he watched the giant examine Tierdon, observing how her emotions vied for dominance on her face, her lip and chin quivering between winces of regret. As he stepped closer, she detected his approach and turned, her blue eyes glittering. *If she's an enemy, I'll know it now. I'll wring the truth from her if I have to while Oburne's still asleep!*

"You mistrust me," Avalar said.

He stopped in the giant's shadow. Tilting back his head, he met her gaze. He was surprised at the sheen of tears on her cheeks, her sorrow more profound than he had thought. "The bodachs have a stench," he told her quietly. "They smell of corruption, if that's even possible. So why do I smell that on you?"

"I am not your enemy," she said. "I tried to wash. Jahn Oburne heated water on the fire for me last night—"

"You attacked our healer," he interjected. "You cannot undo that, Giant."

"Yes, I did. I would have killed him if not for you."

"Your presence threatens the one person who gives us a chance." Terrek rested his hand on the pommel of his sword. "Giant, perhaps it is your youth that makes you impulsive, which isn't your fault, I know. But you're a danger to Gaelin, so I must ask you to go."

"Go?" Avalar peered above him at the sparkling trees, the morning sun illuminating her features through her clouding breath. She was old magic personified, yet it was plain to him how vulnerable she was. "Where shall I go? All my trainers are dead."

Terrek studied her armored frame, from the bloodstained mail protecting her lower torso to the intimidating sword at her hip. He scowled, remembering her cries during the night, how her dreams had roused them all. "Go home. You heard what Oburne said. It's dangerous for you here. Return to Hothra and to safety."

She staggered, her face suddenly pale. "I must go away? But I was weary. I would never have lost control if I had not—"

"I ask this for several reasons, not just for that," Terrek cut in. "This area isn't safe and you'd be a target. Plus, my healer shouldn't have to worry about being attacked when he uses his staff. Avalar, please respect my wishes."

She sagged to her knees. "Sails! I cannot!" she said. "My windrunner boat is naught but splinters in the surf. Even if I had strength enough to journey there . . ." Her voice trailed off as she clutched the mail at her waist, fresh blood oozing between her fingers.

Tears blurred her eyes. "Forgive me," she said. "I thought it better your healer not know. If he had tried to succor me . . ."

Terrek hurried to support her injured side and to unfasten her heavy breastplate. Then, with all his strength, he helped her down, easing her onto her back beside a drift at the base of two entwined trees. He shrugged off his cloak, folded it, and tucked it under her head. "Avalar. Who did this to you? Was it the mage you fought on the steps?"

She clenched her fists when, with a grimace, he removed her belt and then heaved her mail up as high as he could to expose her wound.

"The first one failed to damage me . . ." She coughed. "Yet I was unprepared for how *wrong* his magic felt. After I slew him, another mage took his place to strike at me—the one who felled the city. Now, should I go . . ."

Terrek silenced her with a gesture. "You can stay on one condition. You must promise me you will never again attack my healer. Can you swear?"

She snatched a breath. "I shall not harm him. We spoke together last night and much has changed."

"Good," Terrek said. "I believe you. And now I require your trust. If you stay, you must follow my orders even if you don't agree with them. Can you do that?" He waited until she bobbed her head. "Very well, then I command you to let Gaelin help you."

"No!" Her eyes stared up. "You cannot ask that of me! I am the old magic, Leader Terrek!"

"Giant, *listen* to me! Holram had the staff made for occasions like this. You must accept him now, for I do not believe you have a choice."

"Yes, I *do*," Avalar said. "Leave me alone and I will mend. For two days I have endured this pain. Give me shelter and food . . . I vow to you I shall *mend!*"

Terrek gripped her fingers, feeling them quiver as she fell back. *This is more than fright. She loathes the new magic. If I send for Gaelin—*

He winced, picturing the sorely wounded giant bolting away from him through the trees. "Avalar."

He had raised his gelding, Duncan, from a foal and had gentled the animal himself. Now, caressing her wrist, he spoke to the young giant as he had once done to the fractious colt. She turned her face, tracking his every move. "I'm not a healer," he told her. "Neither is Oburne. Captain Vyergin knows some field medicine, but his experience is limited to humans. A giant would—"

"Terrek?" Gaelin's sleepy voice jolted them both. He stood on the drift, blinking down at them, his frayed cloak askew across his shoulders. "What . . . ?" He rubbed his eyes. "How did I get here? I feel . . . Terrek. Are you well?"

"Gaelin." Terrek willed the giant to keep calm. Gaelin's arrival had caught him off guard, but he was glad of it. "I need Holram to answer a question for me. I must know if it's safe for him to help her."

Squinting, Gaelin bent low. A section of the drift's upper crust collapsed under him, skittering in chunks between the tangled trees. Then Gaelin fell, dropping his staff as he slid on his rump with a shower of frigid powder, to land on his stomach by the giant.

"Steady!" Terrek reached to catch his friend.

"She's hurt?" Gaelin asked. He peered past Terrek at Avalar's bloody mail, and her eyes wide with fright. "She is! But I don't . . . She wasn't last night, was she? How did it happen, Terrek? When?"

"Avalar," Terrek said, "will you trust me?" Once more, her frantic gaze found his. Her muscles were unyielding beneath his palm, her entire body tensed for battle.

"Avalar, *no!*" Terrek sat on her arm. In a moment, she would throw him, and he would be powerless to prevent it. "Giant, *listen* to me! Gaelin won't use his magic unless you agree. I promise! And only if the warder assures us it won't hurt you."

Her breathing rasped in her throat as she glared up, her blond hair forming a halo behind her head. Terrek nodded at Gaelin. Then once more he struggled to raise her mail enough to bare her wound. The black-robe had blasted a hole above the giant's hip. The damage, inflicted by old magic, spread noticeably as the warped power absorbed strength from its contact with the air.

Terrek held his breath at the warmth in Gaelin's expression. A hum reverberated in the younger man's throat. "She is *strong,*" Gaelin said, and Terrek started at the strangeness of the voice, how it projected deep and hollow as though from a well. He had heard it before when he had grabbed at Gaelin during the battle above Heartwood.

Staring at Gaelin, Terrek found nothing familiar—no glimmer of humanity in the staff-wielder's darkened eyes. Avalar flinched at Gaelin's touch on her cheek, her breath quickening as Terrek felt heat beneath his fingers, a fire rising from the giant's skin.

"No," Avalar groaned.

"Gaelin." Terrek jostled the young man's arm. "You heard what I promised. Not without her consent!"

"I heard you," Gaelin replied. "But we can restore her. Holram demands that I . . ." Gaelin reached for his staff. "Avalar, let me help. The magic is warped and doesn't care that you're a giant. It is feeding on you!"

"Do *not!*" She wrested her arm free from Terrek's hold and clambered upright, slapping aside their attempts to detain her. "I am a giant! I will *mend!*"

Terrek jumped to seize her hand and, with all his weight, swung her to confront him. "Obviously, you won't! It's not just your life at stake here. It's the world! You're a giant, Avalar. You must stay alive!"

"And you are human," she said. "How can *you* under—" She stopped, gawking openmouthed as a ribbon of light clamped onto her right forearm and then, flicking sideways, looped to ensnare her left wrist. The quicksilver thread rippled to gird both her waist and neck, then descended to manacle her knees.

Terrek spun to Gaelin. The younger man stood with his staff leveled at the giant. Fiery tentacles of power swirled from Mornius's stone, up the giant's legs, and around her body.

Avalar yanked her arms free and drew her sword. "I said *no!*" she howled, hacking at the strands connecting her to the staff.

Terrek recalled the lessons he had learned of the giants, how they retained the memories of their forebears. Her great blade flashed in the morning sunlight. She was blind with fury, yet she was beautiful as she fought, uninhibited and wild.

Terrek snatched out his own sword and, facing the angry giant, leapt to stand in front of his healer. Then a feeling like ice stabbed into him from behind. He glimpsed a flashing below his ribs. His body going numb, he plunged to his knees while the magic from Mornius, striking him in the back, passed through him to hit the giant. With an astonished gasp, Avalar dropped senseless to the snow.

"When she wakes," a powerful voice droned, "she will not remember this, Terrek Florne."

"*Avalar!*" Oburne flung himself down what remained of the drift, skidding on his heels toward the giant. The big man bent to touch her brow as he glared at Gaelin. "You reckless fool! What have you done?"

The staff-wielder's expression was dark, with the same fierce intensity Terrek recalled during the brawl at Kideren when Gaelin had saved his life. "I healed her," Gaelin said in that oddly flat voice. "She would have died."

"*Died?*" Oburne echoed, the angry glint in his brown eyes fading.

Terrek climbed to his feet and sheathed his sword. "She was wounded defending Tierdon. You must have heard her whimpering in her sleep last night. She was in pain."

Oburne laid his hand on Avalar's chest, watching it rise and fall. "She was dreaming," he said. "There was a name she kept calling. Someone she wanted to protect. I think he must be dead now. He must have died in the city."

"Or was taken," said Terrek.

"I'm sorry," Gaelin muttered, and Terrek sighed, for this was the Gaelin he knew. "She was dying. I didn't know what else to do."

"How in this world did humans enslave giants?" Terrek asked. "I can't control even one!"

Oburne twitched his bearskin from his shoulders and spread it over Avalar's chest. "She's young, Commander. It's common for giant children to be difficult."

"You call this a child?" said Terrek. "I thought she was older. Is it because they don't age, or is that a myth?"

"No, it's true," Oburne said. "But first they must reach adulthood, and she hasn't. At a hundred and twenty, Avalar's not stopped growing yet. That won't happen until she reaches her prime—assuming she gets to. We must convince her to go home."

Terrek frowned as he stared at the still-smoking pyres and the ruins of the city his brother had loved. *A human did that*, he thought grimly. *Someone in that cult has a lot of power.*

"Avalar says she can't go home," Terrek informed his warriors standing on the drifts above. Vyergin descended to join Oburne, and before long, both men were struggling to roll the senseless giant onto an oiled swath of canvas. "She can't."

Oburne climbed to his feet. "She *must*! She's not safe here! Thalus is the last place that any giant should be."

"When I asked her to leave," Terrek told him, "she argued that her boat was destroyed, so either we abandon her here, which would endanger her life, or we bring her with us until we can think of something else. You've described how skilled she is with her sword— we can use that. If she wishes to travel with us, we'd be fools to deny her."

To Terrek's surprise, Gaelin pushed between him and his senior lieutenant. "Mornius healed her," Gaelin said. "You have no choice now, but to allow me to protect her."

"You will do *nothing* when it comes to her," Oburne said. "If I catch you anywhere *near* her with that *thing*, I'll rip your head off!"

In a motion too swift to follow, Gaelin seized Oburne by his throat. "*What* did you say?"

"Gaelin!" Terrek gripped the staff-wielder's bony shoulders, subduing him while Oburne pried the smaller man's fingers from around his neck. "No!" Terrek yelled as Gaelin lunged again, and deflected the younger man's momentum, spinning him toward Tierdon. "Nothing will shield her if we meet whoever did this to Camron's city. Not even your warder."

Gaelin was silent, his muscles rigid beneath Terrek's grasp. Then his voice rose quivering above the wind. "He talks to me, Terrek, but now I listen. I still don't know what he is, or what he wants, but I feel . . ."

Terrek retreated. Gaelin's pupils were dilated—twin pools of nothingness, desperate for light. Yet under the surface, Terrek spied a glint of silver, as if another's eyes also appraised him. "You are mistaken," the staff-wielder said, his bearded face stern.

Terrek scowled. "How exactly am I wrong—" he began, but Gaelin cut him off.

"Never presume," the younger man said, his words clipped and very precise as though he had never used his tongue before, "to tell me what I can or cannot do!"

Chapter 19

Vyergin grumbled as he sorted through the staples. Fehley oats filled the iron pot near where the captain knelt, enough for the porridge he prepared for the company's breakfast, yet something eluded him. "Grakan's teeth!" he muttered.

Seated on the length of a fallen tree, Gaelin watched Terrek's second-in-command search for a moment longer, then, smiling, he extended his leg. With the toe of his boot, he prodded the little white pouch of sea salt, nudging it into Vyergin's view from among the pack's scattered contents and closer to the captain's questing hand.

"Ha!" Vyergin, grinning, snatched up the diminutive bag and worked at its knotted ties.

Gaelin winced at the sudden thudding in his ears. The noise had awakened him before dawn. Holram had slipped into his head, had manipulated his pulse to get his attention, and now the intruding warder was back, making his blood thump so hard he had to strain to make out the captain's words.

". . . old age," Vyergin was saying. "I must be going blind. What do you think, Wizardling? Would your—"

Vyergin's lips continued to move, but Gaelin had stopped listening. He glowered at the castle far away atop the cliff. This was the sight Holram wanted him to see, the warder who partially dwelled inside him. So often now he heard the strange being's messages merging with his thoughts, hissing in whispers like falling snow.

Out of the corner of his eye, he saw Terrek straddle the big log he sat on. Caven Roth, stopping beside Terrek, kicked the splintered wood where lightning had struck it, and Gaelin felt the vibration under his thighs. "When Cheron was attacked, we were protecting

Vale Horse," Terrek said. "And after we left Kideren to chase what we thought was an army, that's when *Kideren* fell! We're fighting two forces now, with next to no men!"

Roth pulled off his gloves with his teeth and flexed the swollen fingers of his sword-hand. "We *can't* disband. There's no way I'm going to quit after what they did to my family. What if we hide and wait near the places they travel? We can study their habits and ambush them when they're vulnerable."

Terrek sighed. "And when will that be? No trickery or traps can stop what we saw hit Kideren, and now it's taken Tierdon. It must have flown over us while we were sleep—" He broke off. "We won't disband. But it's plain to me we must alter our tactics, and there's only one left: attack them directly."

"I think," Roth replied, "I'd like nothing more than to . . ."

Gaelin scowled as the voice faded. His blood crackled in his ears, overwhelming Roth's response, as well as the clink of Vyergin's spoon as the captain stirred the boiling grain and the crunching of Grenner's boots when the bowman sauntered near. Then shouting from the warriors beyond the trees reached him, the sound luring his gaze to where the giant practiced among the men, the playful young creature laughing behind her blade. *She doesn't remember I healed her,* he realized with dismay. *Has she forgotten her wound?*

"We're going to fail," he announced to the empty air. His thoughts had become vague beneath the throbbing of his pulse, slipping from his reach when he fought to pin them down. He shifted on the log to face Terrek. "We're missing something vital. Our journey hasn't ended yet."

"Of course it hasn't," Terrek said. "But what makes you say that?"

"I hear words in my head," Gaelin replied with a nod to his staff, "and yet I don't. They're telling me we must go to that castle. There's a task we have to complete before we can hope to defeat Erebos, and . . ." Gaelin frowned at Roth's pursed lips and blazing eyes. "We can't do that unless we go. Someone is trapped there, Terrek. We must set him free."

"What fool would get trapped *there?*" Terrek asked. "Gaelin, we can't just—"

"No, we can't, Commander," Roth interjected. "We just survived the mountains. We burned hundreds of dead! All those children. Now your brother's gone; we need to grieve for him! And the men, what about them? They're exhausted!"

"Roth, stop it!" said Terrek. "How am I supposed to think with you hanging over me like that?"

"The men can stay here," Gaelin told them. "Wren is still breathing too hard. I wanted to heal him this morning, but he won't let me since I helped Avalar. Please," he begged. "I first spotted the castle last night, and now I have thunder in my ears, words telling me we have to go. We must free the trapped warrior, and we can't leave this valley until we do!"

Roth crossed his arms. "You're not going anywhere without me, Terrek. I've lost one good friend already. I won't lose you, too."

Gaelin jumped as a large hand clamped his shoulder. "I shall also be coming," Avalar said in her rumbling voice. "It will take my mind off . . ."

"Off what?" Gaelin asked.

"Off my anger at *you*," she answered with the hint of a smile.

SHELTERED BY DENSE forest, the pathway was clear, the frigid ground drumming beneath the soles of Gaelin's boots as he walked. He lagged behind Terrek and Roth, the giant flanking him as he contended with his vertigo and aching joints, having left the two horses tethered among the frozen greenberry bushes they loved.

Gaelin quickened his pace when Terrek disappeared from sight around a bend in the trail. He followed Avalar's stare as she surveyed the pale cliff past the wintry pines. "Your steps are longer than mine," he said. "If you're angry at me, why not walk ahead with the others?"

Avalar sniffed. "Because they carry swords while you do not. And mayhap I wish to shield you from harm. Or perhaps because the best solution to danger, other than to avoid it, is to keep it close and learn its ways." She grinned. "My uncle Kurgenrock taught me that."

"But I'm not a—" Gaelin stopped when she came at him, her big thumb pressing the center of his chest.

"You *are* a danger!" she said. "As long as you carry that staff, you threaten all the giants on this world."

"No, I don't. Look!" He tipped his staff downward, letting the weight of its Skystone tap the frosted ground. "See? That's old magic touching Mornius, isn't it? Yet there's nothing. So why is it any different with *you*?"

She seized him by the elbow, yanking him up the narrow track. "You fail to understand," she said. "Though our magic is everywhere, how it responds depends on the characteristics of whatever it connects with. When you dig, the dirt yields, does it not? It sinks or crumbles apart under your weight when you step on it. Likewise, when your staff comes in contact with the magic in the soil, it behaves in the same way."

"Everything is white," said Gaelin, pulling at her grasp. "It's winter. *What* dirt?"

She pointed to the sky. "Now consider the air," she said, ignoring his frustration. "We call it animal magic because all living creatures take it in so it becomes a part of them. It is ever moving and difficult to master, which makes it the weakest of the Circle's links."

Her toe sent a small boulder skidding from her path as she walked. "Stone," she said, "is durable, and yet its magic is brittle. Only a skilled elf can make use of it. Even the ground under your feet can be more reliable, if it is dense enough, though not so much as fire."

"Fire's magic is strongest?" Gaelin, aware of the fact she strove to instruct him and anxious to appease her, watched the rock tumble along the trail's edge and into the brush. He grimaced, recalling when the flames had bowed to the giant the night before and how her eyes had laughed at them.

Avalar shrugged back her blond braids. "Fire is eager, yet water defeats it and restores life. Water submits to change and holds little or no consistency. Which is why the slavers of giants preferred it.

"Rare are my people, Staff-Wielder. Because so few of us survived our slavery, the magic in our flesh is stronger.

"Two things anchor the Circle to this world, the bloodstones deep and the giants tall. Though we are less, the same magical currents fill us as they did when we were many. It is a strain on our bodies, so much that the elves suspect if one more of us should perish, those forces might tear us apart. So until we give birth to enough children to regain our numbers, our magic defends us and prevents us from aging. No one can say what will happen to the world if one of us dies. No one wishes to."

Avalar dropped to her knees in front of him. "Here," she said, "mayhap this will help." Gently, she cupped his shoulders and drew him against her, lifting his head to press his cheek to her armored breast.

Gaelin heard the quiet murmur of her breathing near his ear, the slow, steady thumping of her heart, and something else, a soft thrum of power, like the wind through the branches, or an unending sea.

"That sound you hear is my magic," she said. "All living things have it, even plants and trees, which is why the elves require you to build with dead wood. Yet nothing else has as much power as giants. Now do you comprehend?"

She let him go, but something small, aching, and lost rose up in him. He could not recall when he had last felt so protected or had known the feeling of another person holding him tight. A pain throbbed in his chest, the longing of a child who had been denied for so long. With an instinct made blind by tears, he reached out to return her embrace.

"Sails," Avalar whispered. He drew a shuddering breath, focusing his thoughts on the red-yellow finches singing in the branches above and the random plop of ice from the silvery tree limbs behind him. He loosened his grip and the giant let him go.

"Thank you," said Gaelin. "Whatever I did to anger you, I'm sorry."

Her fingers brushed his forehead. "Come," she said.

Chapter 20

Wiping his cheek, Gaelin glanced to where the giant pointed. Ahead of them on the trail, Terrek stood with his arms crossed. If he had witnessed their embrace, he gave no sign. "We've made it to the cliff," he said. "Are you ready to join us?"

Gaelin frowned, his attention on the vertical slash of the hill's craggy bones through the trees. As he and Avalar followed behind Terrek, the path curved to the left and ended, torn asunder where the ground had collapsed.

Caven Roth stood poised on a protrusion above them, his back against the precipice's uneven surface, the toes of his boots jutting beyond a boulder's edge. "This is the way!" he shouted and then gestured to the jumble of rocks and twisted roots over his head. "Just don't step on that loose slab, or more will go!"

Crouching on his heels, Gaelin leaned as far as he dared to examine the rock wall below. The trail had taken them halfway up the steep ascent, and yet even from here, the fall was lethal.

He eyed the giant when she stopped beside him. "This is why my trainer Roshar Navaren would not recommend this climb to me," she said. "See you how the shale is separated? The stone has been depleted of its magic. Power from one of the warders must have touched this place long ago."

"The creatures kill whatever land they come in contact with," Terrek agreed while he stripped off his pack, followed by his furry cloak. "Holram was near death when he arrived here, and that is the only reason this area still has life. As for the castle, it appears as though he placed it here. The relic is not damaged enough to have fallen from the sky."

Gaelin averted his face when Terrek turned toward him. "Feeling better?" he asked.

Gaelin shrugged. "I do if I don't look down."

"My brother went up this at least once," Terrek said. "He wanted to salvage treasures from the castle to display in the museum. I think if he managed it, you can."

Gaelin stared at the cliff's rocky base, the thunder of his blood pulsing again behind his thoughts. From deep within his staff, he heard Holram sing with the storm's massive voice, urging him to climb and free the trapped warrior. Dazed, shifting his weight, Gaelin nodded.

"Enough of this!" Roth complained from the rocks above.

"Hold, Lieutenant!" Terrek paused. "Now, *boys*," he drawled, "there'll be none of that. Roth, remember what we discussed. You have nothing to prove today."

Gaelin tensed as Avalar knelt next to him. "Mount my neck," she bid him in an undertone, "and I shall carry you."

"But what if my staff touches you?" Gaelin said.

Her jaw hardened. "Has it not already? Or do you expect me not to comprehend why you are ill?"

Gaelin flinched. He had done much worse than touch her with magic. He had hoped to erase her memory, and she knew it. "*That's why you're angry,*" he murmured. "You never said."

Her ire faded. "I saw no need," she said. "You made a mistake, and I am grateful the air shielded me. Your magic was diluted by Leader Terrek's body. I still know not what direct exposure would do. It is my hope you never show me."

Her capacity for forgiveness astonished him. Shakily Gaelin rose to his feet. Never in his adult life had he surrendered himself bodily into the care of another person, and here she was asking him to. *But she's also taking a risk*, he reminded himself, *and she's a giant; she has every reason not to.* "I won't let it touch you," he promised.

She smiled and hoisted him up by the hips, placing him astride her warm neck. He rocked back, catching a heart-stopping view of the trees at the foot of the cliff, and grabbed wildly for her head.

"I do have to *see*," she told him, prying his death grip from her face. "Hold on to my braids if you must. You can give your magic to Leader Terrek. Mayhap it will aid him if I cannot."

Trembling, keeping his elbow locked straight to avoid contact with the giant, he inclined his staff, scowling at its darkened Skystone's indifference to his fear.

As Terrek approached, Gaelin spied a glint in his hazel eyes, a glimmer of empathy. With a sigh, Gaelin leaned forward over Avalar's shoulders and surrendered Mornius to his friend. His outstretched hand empty, he watched Terrek turn away clasping what had always been his, the one comfort he had known since losing his mother. Then abruptly Gaelin gasped when the tree trunks dropped around him, the giant lurching to her feet, raising him among the branches.

With determined strides, she followed the humans, her efforts lifting him to where he could see the sharp rocks below. Her back was bent while she climbed. In two powerful surges, her head reached the slab where Terrek and Roth stood.

"Take it slow," said Terrek to Roth. "No showing off."

"I hear you," Roth replied as he ventured higher. When a stone crumbled beneath his boot, Roth kicked out blindly in search of a toehold, Terrek's grip on his waist supporting him until he found one.

"Wait!" Terrek snatched an object that had slid from Roth's pack, unrolling it to reveal an all too familiar image. "What's this you have?" he demanded. "You took this after I told you not to. Where's its frame?"

"I left it at the museum," Roth said. "Terrek, it's *his* picture. What else could I do? This is all that we have left of—"

"He loved that museum, and that's where his likeness belongs." Terrek returned the painting to its place in Roth's weathered bundle. "Now get going," he said, giving the youth's ribs a firm nudge. "We'll discuss it later."

Roth dragged himself up another step. Behind him, Terrek reached over his shoulder to shove the staff he had agreed to carry further under his pack and out of his way.

Groaning, Roth stopped, his fingers clutching at the frosted stone. *Is he afraid?* Gaelin wondered, hearing Terrek's reassuring words to the boy.

Gaelin, grasping Avalar's braids when she leaned backward, waited while she scrutinized the boulders looming above them. He held his breath, awed by her skill as she vaulted to the lip of a slab nearby before continuing on all fours. He remembered the lesson she had imparted to him on the trail. Even without his staff, he sensed the shale's surviving magic lending its strength to her.

The giant's proximity annoyed Terrek, Gaelin noted, seeing him glance at her repeatedly. Smiling, Gaelin rested his chin on her blond head. "Avalar," he murmured into her hair. "I think they *want* this to be dangerous, at least a little."

"I have erred?" she asked. "I mean only to protect them."

"I know. And so does Terrek, but—"

Something sharp struck his scalp as their companions reached the top. Gaelin ducked when Terrek's foot dislodged another barrage of fragments.

Avalar sprang to catch a rim of stone with both hands and then clambered up. Another prodigious effort brought her armored shoulders above the overhang where the two men stood. She hung with her weight on her elbows, her fingers scrabbling at the ice. "Get *off*, Staff-Wielder!" she cried, as she began to slip.

Terrek darted to snag Gaelin's wrist, helping him scramble off Avalar's neck. Giddy with fear, Gaelin stared while Terrek and Roth seized the collar of his cloak, dragging him on his back from the lethal fall.

As Avalar raised herself again to swipe at the ledge with her heel, Gaelin wrung his hands. *If she falls, we can't help her. She's too big. I could use my—* He froze in helpless horror, seeing Mornius wedged out of his reach among Terrek's gear.

Yanking a rope from Roth's pack, Terrek lunged at the giant. She cried out when more ice crumbled, pawing at the slick surface, her eyes wild with fear.

"Avalar!" Terrek crouched in front of her, the heels of his boots catching on a thin patch of granite.

"Do *not!*" Avalar raged. Her fingers slid, gouging furrows into the layers glazing the rock. "I shall *not* be your slayer!"

Terrek knelt, looping the rope under both the giant's arms as she heaved upward. The overhang fell with a sharp crack, huge chunks of ice dropping away to leave Avalar clawing at the stone, her blood staining its surface.

His feet braced, Terrek threw himself back against the pull of

Avalar's weight. Drawn by the urgent demand of his stare, Gaelin hurried behind him to seize the line.

"Fight, Giant!" Terrek shouted. "Holram's balls, *fight!*"

Avalar planted her palms, pushing with all her strength. "I *am in need!*" she cried to the sky. "Help me!"

Wind, sudden and intense, yowled fiercely from the expanse around Tierdon. A tumbling knot of gray-white air surged up from below, lifting Avalar and flinging her to safety above the cliff.

Terrek released the rope and hastened to the giant, supporting her as best he could while she struggled into a seated position. Then, squatting beside her, he cradled her bruised fingers and opened them gently, pressing snow to her lacerated flesh.

"You could have died," she whispered, shuddering. "If I had fallen, you surely would have died."

Terrek patted her hand. "I knew you'd fight harder so I would not. Now come," he said, peering into her eyes. "You're bleeding. Let's get you bandaged up."

Chapter 21

*A*valar, her mail chinking softly, bent to Gaelin's level. "There *is* something here," she said. "I sense a lonesomeness about this place."

Gaelin examined the cornerstone nearest to him, a gray block wider than the span of his arm, then peered at the jagged top of the frosty rampart, its details blurred by the light of the sun setting in crimson beyond the mountains. To his left, below the cliff, he scanned the wintry field they had left behind. Squinting, he made out the disjointed line where their horses had slogged through the drifts. He rubbed his eyes, spying larger splayed-toed tracks that marred the pristine white blanket around the city, imprints that vanished the instant he spotted them. A swirling of snow rose abruptly, and for a blink, the suggestion of wings.

Gaelin tensed when the giant tilted his face toward her. "It is a Stormfury," she whispered. "An Azkhar. Rare to find one this far north. When you looked his way, I fear it made him uneasy. If you can see him, Staff-Wielder, you are the second human I have known who can."

"I can't," Gaelin said as the giant straightened up. "Just a whole lot of winter." He chewed his lip, fingering his staff while he stepped to examine what he could of the castle above, a series of pointed rooftops descending into rows of clouded icicles. He shuddered, his gaze finding the empty slits of the darkened windows, and the chilled winged statues glaring down. "How big are they?" he asked the giant. "These . . . Azkhar."

"There is much on this world you cannot see," she said. "The wings of the largest Azkharren queens stretch as wide as the sky, Staff-Wielder. When the fighting males came to defend us against the slavers, those wizards scorched their wings. Many of the great creatures fell into the sea and perished. Which is why, out of respect, we giants no longer fly them."

Gaelin nodded as Terrek stopped in front of him. The commander was staring at the point where the outer wall of the citadel ended and another, lesser wall angled in adjacent to the castle, a curved roof with an ornate archway joining it to the main structure.

"I wonder if this led to a garden," Terrek murmured, tugging open what remained of the rusted gate.

Avalar frowned while she sniffed at the wind. "The breeze feels *wrong* upon my skin. Corruption has touched it, and not so long ago."

"Keep alert," Terrek urged. Leaning down, he picked up a stick and then stepped forward, sweeping away the dried vegetation to vanish into the sheltered path.

Gaelin heard the thuds of his shoulder colliding with something hard, followed by a slow metallic squeak. Sounds of strangled coughing ensued, and Terrek, red-faced, stumbled back.

Avalar crouched behind Terrek, scowling into the shadows beneath the archway. Uneasily she shifted her feet, clasping her weapon's hilt as Terrek slipped again out of sight. "I would need to crawl to fit through there," she muttered. "After so many cycles of slavery, the bones of this giant's neck shall not be the first glimpse this human place has of my people. Yet mayhap there are other ways in. If not . . . Call if you need my blade, Leader Terrek. I am a giant. I do not fear."

"There's nothing wrong with being afraid," Terrek replied from under the arch, his words punctuated by the scrape of his stick. "It saved you on the cliff, did it not?"

She puffed out her chest. "Nevertheless, I shall come to your aid should you require me. Even if I must *order* this stone to unblock my way!"

"Don't be ridiculous," Terrek said. "These rocks are not of your world and they wouldn't hear you. Even if they did, you will do no such thing." Cobwebs fluttered from the curved piece of wood Terrek held as he reemerged. He tossed the stick into the snow and gestured to the giant. "The main entrance is at the rear facing those trees, according to my brother. It's very tall, so I doubt, my dear, you'll even have to duck."

Avalar swept him a bow over her massive sword. With a humph, she strode past him, drumming her fingers along the contours of the layered stones as she slipped out of sight around a corner.

"Staff-Wielder," said Terrek. "Come and see."

Gaelin hurried to join his friend before the ruined gate. He peered through the dusty shadows, discerning at last the barrier Terrek had opened.

"Be careful," Terrek warned when Gaelin slid forward. Catching himself on the entry's frame, Gaelin stood for a long moment and stared wide-eyed beyond its threshold into a darkened room.

As Mornius crackled abruptly, a tiny globe of light erupted from its Skystone and shot across the doorstep, dashing from candlesticks to lamps to sconces on the walls and igniting them as it went. The rounded chamber brightened as Gaelin watched, the sputtering flames from the lanterns illuminating bookshelves from floor to ceiling along the walls.

With an enormous puff of soot, the blue sphere slammed into a hearth, kindling the husks of ancient logs scattered within. Bouncing back, the little ball hovered above the library's floor, whirled once in a glowing arc, then zigzagged up the castle's marble stairs.

Caven Roth whistled a sharp note of approval as he stopped by the fireplace and leaned on the mantel, running his thumb through the dust.

"What did you do?" Terrek asked, and Gaelin jumped when the commander gripped his shoulder.

"I don't know," said Gaelin. "It just happened. I think it was Holram controlling the staff. Like he did when I was healing Vyergin's horse."

Terrek pulled him farther into the room and set him, dizzy and stumbling, at the edge of a circular black-and-white mosaic that took up half the chamber's floor. "Holram is a warder. He can't do anything without your guidance. What were you thinking?"

Gaelin trembled despite the heat from the fire. "I wasn't thinking anything. I was just . . . wishing I could see. I was about to ask my—"

"There!" said Terrek. "There's our answer. I suspected this might happen after you shared what the Seeker elves said. Holram's responding to your thoughts faster than you can. Do you realize what this means? You and he are becoming one."

149

Terrek's gaze burned with certainty, and yet Gaelin rejected his words. Shaking, tripping over his own feet, he wheeled and blundered toward the entrance.

"That's not true!" The words passed his lips before he could stop them. Hugging his staff to his chest, he pressed against the doorway. *I won't be possessed*, he thought. *This is my life!*

Terrek moved to stand behind him. "Holram responds to you, Staff-Wielder. The more you let yourself accept him, the greater your skill will be."

Gaelin turned. "Should I give up?" he demanded. "What about my hope to live for me? Or is that asking too—" He broke off.

"Until we stop Erebos," Terrek reminded him gently, "none of us will live the way we want. I trained horses to sell. Do you think I like being here? Or that I enjoy killing innocent people? It makes me sick, what we are forced to do!"

Gaelin bowed his head, his cheeks flaming. He studied his feet and the patch of the library's floor he could see in the firelight. Despite its layers of dust, the mosaic still gleamed under the faint pulse of Mornius's gem, its black-and-white marble pattern oddly familiar.

As a child, he had slept with his staff in his hand, ready to fend off his fears. On nights when the Companion's eye was full, its silvery light had spilled through the cracks in the rafters above him. He had pretended its brightness was hope, a place to which he could fly, the radiant Skystone guiding his way.

He smelled the rotted barn where he had slept and heard again the wind whistling through the pines around him, though now, instead of rafters, a midnight sky wheeled overhead. He saw deep within the blackness, the outline of a figure lifting its hand. In its grasp swelled an ancient sun, its brilliance fading to crimson, its six worlds doomed to die with it.

The entity reached to catch a golden star, then contracted its fingers until flames shot out in all directions in a soundless, blinding explosion.

Stop! Gaelin found himself on his knees supported by Terrek. He heard himself speak in a low, flat voice, uttering words that could never be his. Whole sentences tumbled from his lips while the mosaic beneath him stretched out forever.

Gaelin sensed Avalar near. "The front of the castle is ruined," the giant murmured to Terrek. "It is melted. I have never beheld stone so damaged as . . ."

As her comment faded in his ears, Gaelin heard the snapping of the fire in the hearth, the shrieks of the dying flames. He bent, his brow pressed to Terrek's shoulder as the murdered star pleaded from far away. He moaned in response, his sight dimming where the sun had been, as everything would be until he acted to prevent it.

The power of Avalar's touch on his neck brought him back to the mosaic and the echoes of Holram's voice. The warder had climbed from Mornius's hard crystal heart into his warm and beating one. It was a violation worse than anything Seth Lavahl could ever have done.

Groaning, Gaelin pulled away from Terrek and retched. Around him, his watching companions stood mutely. When at last the spasms ebbed, he scrubbed at his mouth, squirming under Terrek's stare. Then, leaning forward, he clasped his staff. He had dropped it, but he could not remember when.

With a grateful nod, he accepted the flask of roy Terrek offered to cleanse his mouth. "He never asked me, Terrek. He never even asked!"

Terrek was silent, waiting for him to sip the sweet ale and regain his composure. Gaelin met the sympathy in Terrek's eyes. The firelight showed him something else lurking there too: hope. The man he admired felt gladness in this thing, a chance for the world's survival.

"I don't have a choice, do I?" Gaelin said bitterly. "I'm the tool, right? What I want for my life doesn't matter."

"Your influence is greater than you think." Terrek gripped his shoulders. "Gaelin, this is why he preserved this castle. The books have knowledge he wants us to keep. And this mosaic, too, had a message he wanted to impart to us. We couldn't understand it, so he used your voice to explain it."

"*Without* my permission!"

Terrek gave him a light shake. "How would you feel right now if he had chosen to speak through Roth or me instead?"

Roth swung from the wall of books at the mention of his name. The dusty tome he held fell open, scattering tiny brownish flakes on the floor. "Terrek," he said. He touched a crumbling page, then set the book on a square wooden table. "I think this is what he meant."

Terrek climbed to his feet to join his lieutenant.

"And this, what *is* it?" Roth asked, taking up a lantern from the little table. "Shouldn't there be a wick right here?"

"It has a wick," said Terrek. "There was a cleaner example at university. Our ancestors put the wicks inside the glass. I have no idea how they got them lit."

Roth tugged at a black cord angling to the floor from the table. "There's a leash, too, connecting it to the wall."

"Wire," Terrek supplied the word. "One of the things elves forbid. We can rediscover some of the lore we had on Earth, but not all, not that. There was a Seeker on campus who acted as an advisor to keep us in—"

Gaelin jerked back when Avalar's feet stopped in front of him. She crouched, her thumb raising his chin.

"You have the same look my father gets when he thinks about freedom too much," she said. Her voice caught, a single tear sliding down her cheek. "My people were slaves. Their magic made them thus after the humans turned it on them, just as yours betrays you now. In the darkness of the mines, giants dreamt of better days. They would envision their farms on Thalus or their ancient southern homes on Tholuna. Many of them met their deaths with their dream of returning home unrealized. Others were born and perished, never once beholding the sun. Even now our freedom is naught but delusion. For the sake of our magic, we must live protected by elves. I say this is not freedom. Sacrifice to save a world seldom allows such things."

His pain forgotten, Gaelin raised his hand to her face. "If the elves want you guarded, why are you here? Why aren't they searching for you?"

"What makes you think they are not?" she asked. She took the flask from his swollen fingers and sealed it. Then she straightened to tower above him. "You fear this presence reaching for you. I understand, for no one wishes to be a slave. Yet consider. This warder is similar to us, is he not? He longs for freedom as we do, and to reach his full potential. You and I wish for these things as well. I yearn to protect this land as a giant should. While you—mayhap you wish for someone to hold you as I did on the trail."

"No," he said. "I want to learn to ride horseback by myself so I'm not a burden. I wish to be fearless like Terrek or loyal like *him*." He jerked his head at Roth, who caught his look and shrugged.

At that, Avalar nodded. She flexed her wide shoulders, her big hand swatting at the dust.

Terrek turned toward him. "If we make it through this, Gaelin, I will bring you to Vale Horse and teach you how to ride horses myself."

Gaelin scrubbed at his eyes. "Holram took me over," he said gruffly. "Why?"

"He wanted to describe to us how Erebos attacked Earth, and he asked us to locate this." Terrek lifted the heavy volume and placed it at an angle in Gaelin's lap so he could see. The tome was thick, with strange letters on the cover, and carried with it a mossy smell.

"He told us where on these shelves to search," Terrek continued, letting the pages fall open. "Take a look, Staff-Wielder. I know you can't read it. But notice the pictures. Do you recognize these?"

While Terrek flipped the pages one by one, Gaelin saw images of horses or cattle of various kinds, sheep, ducks, lizards, and goats. He identified wolves and raccoons, lemurs and lioncats, diradil deer, and partial images of creatures he thought he knew. "Look at the trees," he murmured. "They're all green."

"And the animals," Terrek said. "We've encountered some of these, haven't we? They lived on Earth just as we did. A planet where the magic was smothered by our technology and greed. Talenkai's guardian, Sephrym, brought them here with us when he harvested the power of our sun.

"I found a relic close to Vale Horse," Terrek went on, "made of glass and a rusted kind of metal and some other flexible substance. It had four metal disks supporting it, and skeletons of what appeared to be chairs. Why is it here? Why do we keep finding these . . . remnants from Earth? Because the warders resisted when Sephrym caught them up, and they grabbed at the world they were fighting over. It was a reflex, not intentional, yet it brought us here, with these animals and debris like this castle. Holram told us all this through you, Gaelin. You've become his voice."

"His slave is more like it," Gaelin complained under his breath.

He stroked the book's fragile pages, tracing the symbols on the front. The binding felt like leather, but at the one torn corner, strings of fabric peeked out.

"Gaelin," Terrek said. "You mentioned earlier how you felt called to this place, and you insist someone is trapped here. During your vision, Roth checked in all the rooms he could reach. Most have locked doors or are beyond where the floors have collapsed."

"There's a room filled with masks upstairs," Roth added, "and costumes of all kinds. There are bendable knives and swords, and jewelry with gems that aren't real. I wish we could—"

"The point is, no one's here," Terrek cut in. "Gaelin, there *is* no trapped warrior."

Gaelin gestured to the floor and the mosaic's pattern of stars. "Holram's thoughts drown me out," he said. "Half the time I can't even tell what you're saying, he's so loud. The only reason I still hear at all is that I resist him. What happens if I stop? Will I even exist?"

He hesitated, remembering Avalar's story about her people. The meaning of it became clear to him all at once, and he regretted his petulant words. Talenkai's survival depended on him, on his sacrifice and surrender. "He *is* here," Gaelin said. "There's a room right above us. A chamber filled with swords."

Roth sputtered a protest. "They're all fake, as I said. I checked it already. There's nothing, just cobwebs and blunted weapons."

"Look again," Gaelin insisted. "There's one blade that is very real, and if you find it you'll find him. "He's a warrior—Holram's friend."

"His friend," Terrek muttered while he gave Roth the book. Then he strode to the nearby stairs.

As Terrek started to climb, Gaelin rose to follow. When Avalar sighed, he paused. "But there are swords and shields," he told her. "Even if they aren't real, it might be interesting."

"I would enjoy the adventure, I am sure, but no. Do you hear?" She motioned to the marble steps groaning under Terrek's weight. "The stairs fail. They might support a human, or mayhap even three, but not a giant. No, I am unsuited for this place."

Avalar turned away, the top of her head brushing the ceiling. Her lips curved up, her expression filling with wonder as she moved to examine the shelves of books.

"Behold! she exclaimed. "These writings come from a different world!" Her eyes glinted as she peered over her shoulder at his face. "Be not concerned for me, Staff-Wielder. There is much to occupy me here."

"*Gaelin!*" Terrek thundered. Already Roth was halfway up the twisted staircase, running with his sword drawn. Gripping Mornius like a spear, Gaelin sprinted after the younger man.

Chapter 22

aelin felt the marble fracture beneath him as he pursued Roth up the steps. He halted at the top near the landing to look in both directions, his focus drawn to the candles in their sconces sputtering between the shuttered rooms. *Is every lamp lit?* he wondered, glancing at his staff. *If my thoughts did this, wouldn't I know it?* He started, seeing Roth slip from his sight.

No door, Gaelin observed as he hurried to the entrance Roth had chosen. Snatching a breath, he ventured into the gloomy chamber, its narrow window barely visible through the dust.

He swatted away the cobwebs dragging at his neck. As his eyes adjusted to the darkness, he spotted Terrek at the center of the cramped space, a row of orange-colored bins beyond him along the wall. The containers were packed with items covered with grime, while above them four metal shelves dangled askew, with more treasure—pint-sized daggers and swords—scattered below on the wooden floor.

Gaelin stopped an arm's length from his friend. He could sense Terrek's revulsion, the commander glaring at the moldering scabbard he held. With a feeling of dread, Gaelin met his stare.

"You two," Terrek said. "Pay attention. Tell me what you see when I draw this."

Gaelin touched the sword's moss-colored hilt, the rotted leather flopping around its base. As Terrek yanked the blade free, Gaelin jerked up his staff, seeing a green-gold smoke pour from the exposed steel. The vapor swirled beneath the ceiling, condensing into the shape of a man, its gray head and body obscuring the faded tapestries behind it. The semblance of a bearded face appeared above the hint of a muscular neck. Gaelin shuddered, struggling to speak as the entity rose over him, its ghostly armored torso encircled by streamers of green. "Is that . . . is that a—"

"*Again?*" the apparition thundered.

Gaelin cringed as a pattering of dead insects struck his hair.

"That's *him!*" he said. "The trapped warrior we're supposed to—"

"*Trapped?*" Peering down his spectral nose, the dead knight crossed his arms over the hawk-shaped emblem on his breastplate. "I am *dead*, boy. Or you may call it cursed. I most certainly am that.

Or thwarted, even. Yes, that works, too. *Trying* to decompose with dignity, and now here I am *furious you would wake me twice!*" he howled, his onyx eyes rimmed with white. "Do you have any *idea* who I am?"

"Wait," Terrek said. "Holram's warrior is a *ghost?*"

"*Ghost?*" the specter bellowed.

Gaelin heard a distant pop, and Avalar's voice calling from below: "Leader Terr—"

"Stay where you are, Giant!" Terrek yelled. "We'll be right—"

"I was a *Thalian Knight* when I was alive!" the spirit interrupted. "Lord Nathaniel *Argus*, to be exact. I was Commander Othelion's body-shield, *and* the target of Arawn's final spell, which I . . ."

Argus stopped, registering their blank reactions. "I can accept you don't know my name after so many years, but surely you've heard tell of Othelion's guard, or perhaps a *song?*"

"No," said Terrek. "None that I know of."

"The warder never told me what he was." Gaelin, ignoring the ghost's pink-faced sputters of outrage, uncovered his ears. "I heard a voice in my dreams say 'fighter,' and I saw images, too." He closed his eyes, sifting through his thoughts for an explanation from Holram, but his staff was silent.

Terrek swung the ancient sword, hefting it again to test its weight. Gaelin saw that the metal hilt was carved into the shape of a snake's head, the serpent's open jaws forming the weapon's crossguard. *It's beautiful,* he thought.

"There haven't been any knights," Terrek said.

"Not since the battle at Warder's Fall," said Argus. "How long ago was that? The giants had just been enslaved . . ." He raised his transparent hands, counting on his phantom fingers. "*Five hundred years?* By my shield, has it been that long?"

Gaelin realized Roth was speaking. With the discordant tones of the entity's outburst echoing in his ears, he barely discerned what the lieutenant was trying to say. Roth, his expression distraught, sidled up to Terrek, his elbow poking through the dead knight's flat stomach.

Glancing down, Lord Argus scowled at the younger man.

"Terrek, answer me!" Roth demanded. "What are you talking to?"

"Humph!" Argus floated away from Roth. "I am a *who*, not a

what!" he said. "Do we not educate our youth anymore? We let them run amok? When I was a lad, I treated my elders with respect! And I never—"

"There's a ghost here," said Terrek. "You don't see him? He appears when I draw the sword from its scabbard."

"I see him," Gaelin said. "I also hear him and very little else!"

"Of *course* you do!" Argus stormed. The spirit grimaced when Gaelin plugged his ears, and with a transparent shrug, whispered so Gaelin strained to hear. "*That's how it is with these old-magic curses. The spell makes me visible to magical creatures.*"

"Well, I'm glad I'm not you, Terrek," Roth said. "I don't like ghosts." He knelt to examine the artifacts on the floor. "Commander?" Perplexed, he held up a furry, long-eared object. "What *is* all this stuff?"

"*You*," said Argus, tilting his head at Terrek. "I am within your sight since you hold my sword. But Mister *Elbows* here cannot see me." He pointed at Roth. "Ah, and now he's found the magician's props." His fierce eyes glinting, Argus flitted down to Roth's level. "Why, he's a child. He seems a bit *laori*, too. Is he your son?"

"No!" Terrek shot back. "He is neither *laori* nor my son, and I'm tired of your rudeness. It's clear to me you hoped to be found. Yours is the only real weapon in this room, and how curious that it ended up in plain sight. As for Roth—"

"There was nothing in this room," Roth broke in. He sat cross-legged beside Terrek, a tall hat jiggling above his unruly brown hair. "I'm not blind. I would have noticed a real sword. I—"

"As for Roth," Terrek repeated, "I think seventeen is old enough for him to decide to become a man. He wanted to fight after his family was killed. The towns have few men left. Erebos's cult has taken them all."

Gaelin regarded the hawk emblazoned across the warrior knight's breastplate. The specter's face that was not hidden by his beard was as lean and hungry as the bird on his chest, the suggestion of skin around his eyes creased by the pain he had endured long ago.

"You summoned me here," Argus said. "Tell me why. Is there some point to this? I suspect Holram compelled you to come to this place, didn't he? Still, curse or no, this place is home to me, and I've come to appreciate the peace and quiet. I don't care what Holram says. I am *not* fighting Arawn."

"He wants you to be free," Gaelin said. "He wants—"

"You think I don't know? He hopes I will do what you cannot. Fight the cult's ghost and break the spell holding him here. In my day he was *Lesedi* Arawn. But he grew dark and brooding, his power consuming him until he turned on the giants. Speaking of which, you brought one with you, did you not?" Argus's numinous gaze slid to Terrek. "She hasn't spoken of him?"

"She didn't have to," said Terrek. "We're familiar with the slaver lord. His first cult turned the giants' magic against them. Now his dachs do the same thing to us."

"Oh, '*against* them'?" Argus grunted and rolled his eyes. "Is that what we call it now? It was *abhorrent*, what they did to those great people." Argus coughed, his contempt fading as he caught sight of Gaelin's baffled stare. "Reflex," he explained. "I see dust and I forget I'm dead." He paused to scrutinize Gaelin. "I can't get over how much you resemble my commander, Jaegar Othelion. You must be related. He was a good man. Ruthless and *wicked* with his blade!"

As Gaelin studied the knight, his mother's long-ago words echoed through his thoughts. "*He never fought with this, Gaelin, but your great-grandfather's father did.*"

Gaelin jerked when the dead knight snorted. The ghost floated upward within his green light to hover in front of the encrusted window. "I spent my prime fighting Erebos's cult," Argus said. "Or I did until Arawn cornered me and slew me with the Blazenstone. It's because of *him* my bones are on that cliff. *Yes*, right below those boulders you disturbed! In fact, you would have seen my kneecap if you had turned your head." He nodded to Gaelin. "Your shoulder was right by it."

"You're afraid," Gaelin said. "He murdered you and now you fear him."

Argus growled. "As should *you*, my boy. Or you would if you had any sense. His magecraft turns water to acid and molds living flesh, obliterating minds." The spirit stretched out his wrist, his appendage vanishing through the windowpane. "Did you see the things that attacked Tierdon? Those were *his* abominations, and I enabled that to happen. The curse he put on me holds *him* here as well."

"And Erebos uses him," Terrek muttered. "Arawn's ghost is just another weapon. A tool."

"Precisely," said Argus. "No doubt hoping to live again."

Gaelin licked his chapped lips. "We need to think of a way to destroy both the dead wizard's spirit and the Blazenstone. If we could, we'd blind Erebos. He'd be helpless."

"Helpless?" The specter sneered. "Erebos is a *warder*, boy. You have no idea the kind of power you're—" Argus bit down on his words, his lips drawn back in a silent snarl. "Still, you might be able to diminish him, *if* you can keep him within his mountain. But if you drive him out, he'll connect to the Circle, and that'll be the end of the giants and everything else."

Argus stared out the window. "It takes the dead to fight the dead. Holram knows this. If I did fight Giants' Bane, I'd— That's his *other* name," he added at Gaelin's stare. "He's bound by the same curse I am. If I managed to *destroy* Arawn, Erebos couldn't make his dachs anymore."

"But you told us you won't," Gaelin said.

"Yes, I did, didn't I?" The grimace vanished from Argus's face. A rack of rusted blades in the corner sparkled greenly in patches through his frame, as if even now his foe sought to impale him. "He's connected to Erebos now, and even stronger than before. While I . . ." With a gesture of frustration, the ghost bobbed out of their sight through a wall, coughing as he reemerged in a puff of gray dust. "You *see*? There it is. The extent of the influence I have on this world. Or, if I focus *really* hard, I might move a book."

"Or a sword," Terrek put in, and above him, Argus nodded.

The objects in the room were the color of grass in the ghost's green light. On the floor below the shelves, Roth, his pupils dilated, was goggling at Terrek from under his odd-shaped hat. Gaelin frowned, realizing how much blacker the room would appear to Roth. "But if Holram wants you for something . . ." Gaelin began. He squinted as Mornius flickered to life, the glow of its Skystone brightening the tiny chamber. "He must think you can help."

Terrek sighed, his gaze fixed on the window with its ominous glimpse of night sky. "It's late," he noted. "We'll discuss this later." He nodded to Argus, then brusquely sheathed the ancient blade.

"Is it *gone*?" Roth asked with a shudder. Holding the tall hat on his head, he scrambled to his feet, his right boot grazing the curiosities next to him and knocking several across the floor. Looking down, he swiped with his free hand at his dusty leggings. "Leave that thing in its scabbard, Terrek. Don't ever draw it again!"

"Yes, he's gone," Terrek said. "Don't worry, Roth. The spirit is a good guy, a warrior who fought the slaver cult at Warder's Fall long ago. We have a Thalian Knight at Vale Horse, too, a ghost named Ralen Galadus. I've never met him, but my father has. It was *Ralen* who led us to your location the day your horse, Jack, threw you down the cliff. If not for my father's friendship with him, you'd be dead right now."

"How many ghost knights are there?" Roth asked, looking about at the room's dark shapes under Mornius's light. His face hardened as he bent, still holding the satiny hat's brim, to pick up his sword. With a glance at Gaelin, he slapped it into its scabbard.

Mutely Gaelin followed Terrek as the commander, eyeing the prop atop the lieutenant's curls, clasped the younger man's arm. "That's a chimney hat," Terrek remarked as he propelled Roth from the room. "Your ears will freeze in that thing."

"I know, but it's black," Roth replied. "I like it."

Gaelin parted the cobwebs with his staff, flipping them aside as he returned to the lighted hallway. Hurrying to catch up, he listened while Roth grilled Terrek about his rescue from the cliff. Gaelin sensed that Terrek retold the story to comfort the boy. *He's not mentioning the ghost knight this time,* Gaelin thought, watching as Terrek held Argus's rotted scabbard so Roth would not see.

Chapter 23

aelin, following Roth and Terrek down the stairway, glanced at Mornius's crystal glowing in the darkness above him. Smiling, he tipped the staff, bringing the Skystone closer, the quartz not quite touching his nose. *I found your friend for you*, he thought to the warder as he peered into the gem. He hesitated, hoping to spy a flicker of acknowledgment from Holram within the egg-shaped rock. "But I don't understand."

His voice carried over the sound of his companions' boots on the shattered marble. At Caven Roth's inquisitive stare, he inclined his head. "Lord Argus denied he was trapped," Gaelin said. "If that's true, why would he be here?"

"Find out from Argus when you can," Terrek urged over his shoulder. "Assuming I draw his sword."

Gaelin nodded, hearing the steps groan beneath Terrek's weight. "When do you think you will?" he asked.

As Terrek jerked to a halt, Gaelin, catching sight of his black scowl, tottered backward and raised his staff. Trembling, he sank to his knees as he recalled chairs being flung in the tiny cabin and Seth Lavahl shouting, the big man's fists striking his flesh.

"Is he sick?" Roth queried.

Gaelin tensed as gloved fingers engulfed his wrist. "Enough of this," said Terrek. "It's night. We must hurry for Avalar's sake. I'm quite sure the cult would love to kill a giant."

"Or make her a dach," Roth added.

"I'm sorry," Gaelin said. "Just dizzy."

"Not 'just,'" Terrek responded. "Look." He reached down, and Gaelin shivered when the commander's fingers ran through his hair, drawing with them a cluster of loose strands. "The warder's damaging you." Terrek held up a withered tangle and then let it fall. "I don't want you using your staff anymore. Not unless we are desperate."

"I'll decide what I do," said Gaelin. He thrust his hand out to Roth and let the lieutenant pull him to his feet. "The staff's how I earn my keep. I need to do something!"

"You won't if you injure yourself," Terrek said. "While Holram's still listening and aware, I need you to talk to him. Make sure he knows how much he's hurting you. And, while you're at it"—Terrek brandished Argus's sheathed weapon between them, lifting it into Mornius's light—"tell him I already *have* a sword. I don't need anoth—"

"Ugh!" Gagging, Roth motioned to a bulge in the discolored leather. "I think something dead was there. Terrek!"

"What if *I'm* supposed to carry the sword?" Gaelin asked, his voice louder than he had intended. "Argus mentioned he had a leader who looked like me. If this 'Jaegar Othelion' is the grandfather my mother told me about, he would have wielded both the staff *and* a blade. So maybe that's what Holram wants from me. Except I'd rather not. I—" He broke off, shaking his head.

"I don't understand why the ghost was so loud." Gaelin tilted his staff's crown, extending the Skystone's glowing sphere to reveal the greenish planks of flooring at the bottom of the ruined staircase.

"Imagine shouting at the top of your lungs and never being heard," said Terrek. "My brother is not the only one who has visited here. It could be Lord Argus is insane now, from all those years of not being able to communicate. But he did tone it down, didn't he?"

Roth curled his lip at the rotted scabbard. "Why are you bringing that old thing? If you keep it, we'll be haunted for sure!" He stepped back as Terrek dropped to the floor beside him.

"We'll discuss it later," Terrek said. "There are one and a half leagues standing between us and camp, and now there's the giant to protect, with just two of us carrying—"

"Leader Terrek?" Avalar called.

There was a dull thud, and the giant appeared from out of the darkness, wincing and rubbing her forehead.

"A strange voice was shouting up the stairs," she said. "I was trying to reach you when the steps fell from under me." She shifted her feet. "I meant to stay close to help you down, but . . . there were noises outside the castle. I have been listening, standing guard *there*." She pointed toward the library's outer door.

Gaelin bent, straining to see through the dusty gloom past the glowing red that remained of the fire. He caught a soft rustle, then spied the fluttering pages of the open book Roth had left on the little table.

"Corruption draws near," Avalar said. "It is stinging my skin. I felt this in Tierdon before the attack. It brought the creatures who killed my trainers!"

"The cleric you battled on the steps?" Terrek asked, pulling out his sword. "He's *here*?" Terrek strode past them and into the library, his heels clicking on the mosaic's marble tiles.

"I do not *know* if it is he!" Avalar moaned and swiped at her cheek. "I never fought the second mage. He struck me down and I . . . I *mislike* this feeling. I *see* the slavers in my memories . . . the things they do to giants."

"There's nobody here," Gaelin reassured her. "But the candles are out. Holram wants us to go!"

"No, what did I tell you, Gaelin?" Terrek called from the outer passage. "At least for now, you guide the staff. *You* are the one who wishes to go."

Gaelin heard more footsteps as Terrek strode away over the stone, and then the grainy soft sound of boots crunching snow. "Deravin Silva!" Terrek greeted.

Gaelin pressed against Roth. Eyes shut, he discerned snatches of murmurs, Terrek and Silva talking back and forth.

"Of course I'd follow you," the guard returned. "I've been with you . . . ten years old, Terrek. But do not fear for me. I didn't exhaust myself. I took the longer trail and . . ." The guard's voice faded, overwhelmed by the skitter of ice across the yard and, closer at hand, the creaking of armor as Roth swung his sword. ". . . keeping you in my sights, of course," Silva said.

Gaelin touched Avalar's sleeve. "We're safe," he whispered. "It's just Silva, Terrek's—"

"I'm glad Oburne wasn't along to witness the giant's close call on the cliff," Silva remarked. "She almost fell, didn't she? I can't even imagine how *he* would have reacted to—"

"I told you to rest," Terrek interjected. "Like it or not, that mountain tired you, my friend."

"Which *one*?" Silva laughed.

"You're not so young anymore," said Terrek.

"I'm spry enough to keep up with *you*!"

Gaelin hunched against Roth's back, the chilled air fanning his neck through the open door. Once more there was a snippet of dialogue, a gentle reprimand from Terrek. "Deravin, there was no reason for you—"

Roth snorted abruptly. "He should have stayed put," the lieutenant said to Gaelin. "Terrek gave him an *order*. Silva's *old*. I'm better with a blade than he is. How many times do I have to prove my—"

"There *was* a reason!" Silva exclaimed, his urgency silencing Roth. "At the time, there was. After you left, we saw a shadow crossing the trees. I *had* to follow you. What kind of guard would I be if something happened to y—"

Gaelin started as a large hand clasped him behind his neck. "Shh," Avalar hissed into his ear when he glanced up. She steered him away from Caven Roth, urging him through the blue-lit darkness alongside the stairs and under a rotted archway, the hints of its remaining wood obscured by scales of tattered paint.

"Where are you going? I need your light," Roth called to Gaelin. "Lavahl, where'd you go?"

"Fear not for him," the giant whispered. "He has his sword, and skill to keep him safe."

Avalar guided Gaelin across a faded rug, passing a long table set with utensils, dishes, and mugs, and an ancient carcass on a tray with a myriad of dusty webs between its bones.

"I sense the power in your staff," she said, halting before an undulating curtain of beaded glass strands. "It is much akin to what I feel now on my skin. My hope is that it may defend me from harm, for I cannot perish. The world will not survive if I do, and, Staff-Wielder, you must also endure. So I ask you. As comrades, should we not strive together against this ill?"

Avalar stopped, waiting for her words to register while she drew her sword. "This wrong threatens us both; do you not feel it? If this foe slays me, the world is ended. If it should kill you—"

"The same thing happens," Gaelin answered after a moment. "But it would take them longer. They'd have to carry my staff to Erebos first and break its Skystone. Holram would be exposed. He would die, and . . ."

"Rest easy," Avalar said. "You have a giant to fight for you." Raising her sword, she parted the multicolored curtain. Then, tugging at his wrist, she guided him through.

The alabaster ceiling of the forehall rose into an ornate arch. With a grunt Avalar strode between two white pedestals, coming to a stop before a massive ironclad barrier. She tilted her sword back and cracked the door open.

Gaelin heard the tinkling and swish of the threaded beads behind him, the footsteps of Terrek and the others approaching. "We stay together," Terrek said. "And look. Silva is here."

Gaelin stared into the shadows beyond Mornius's light, finding the guard in his usual place at Terrek's shoulder.

"Avalar," Terrek called. "We checked outside. You were right. There was a shadow earlier. But from what Silva can tell, right now the forest is clear."

With her hand clasping the knob, Avalar grimaced. "It is not," she murmured. The flash of her teeth reminded Gaelin of the gravid wolf he had met on the mountain when he was a child, the intrepid guardian with the scarred face who had kept him from freezing after he had run away.

"You feel warped magic?" Terrek asked, and at her nod, he gestured her behind him. There was a tense pause, after which Avalar complied. *She's sizing him up*, Gaelin realized as Terrek tucked Argus's lumpy scabbard under his belt.

Gaelin shuffled back when Silva cut in front to protect Terrek's flank. The older man glanced up, his features amused as he tipped his balding head to eye Avalar. "There's one thing I've known for many years," he said. "Bigger is not always better."

Avalar frowned. "I would not *presume* to think that."

"*Focus!*" said Terrek. He reached for the weapon that was an extension of his arm, the sword that had so often saved his life. Gaelin lifted his staff in response, the Skystone's brilliance spilling into the darkness beyond the doorway.

No stars, he noted as he exited the castle. Shivering within the folds of his blue-gray cloak, Gaelin pressed close to Roth beside him, his spine tingling at the foreboding in his heart.

As he squinted at the surrounding walls, Mornius sputtered, the staff's agitated light pulsing by his head. Bewildered, Gaelin stared at the Skystone's corona with its upper half hidden from his view—the staff's light overwhelmed by the blackness above him.

Terrek stood with his sword at the ready, confronting the jagged line of trees beyond the citadel. Turning, Gaelin found Avalar between the ancient structure and its ruined rampart. The giant had her back to him, yet he heard her harsh muttering as she lunged with her sword at the shadow oozing down over the castle.

"It is *not* gone!" Avalar shouted over her shoulder. "It is here! I can *feel* it!"

Terrek approached the towers where the nothingness had devoured the stone. *There's no Companion*, Gaelin reasoned. *No moonlight. Please*, he begged Holram. *If it's your enemy, we'll need you.*

Gaelin caught his breath, remembering Argus's words. "*It takes the dead to fight the dead!*" Gaelin froze. "This isn't Erebos," he said. "The warder can't leave his mountain!"

He plunged forward to block Terrek, straining to grasp the ghost's scabbard below the commander's belt. "*Arawn's* doing this! Quick, draw the sword! Let Argus defeat him!"

"Back off, now," said Silva by his ear. The guard seized his elbow, driving him to his knees.

"It's *not* Arawn!" Terrek said, stepping in front of him.

Gaelin surged to his feet. "But according to Argus—"

"*Forget* the ghost," Terrek interrupted. "We've never seen Erebos or Arawn. We battle his priests, that's it. They use their warder's reflection to shield the dachs from the sunlight. That's what the shadow is. It isn't Erebos himself, it's—"

"*Slaver!*" Avalar thundered. She leapt to climb a nearby pine, her weight snapping its branches as she stabbed at the sky. "I am a *giant*! You shall *not*—"

She screamed as scarlet light blasted at her from the woods. Then she fell, crashing through the little tree's bones and hitting the drifts with an explosion of powder. Terrek and his men sprinted to join her, their weapons cutting through the thickening shadows.

Gaelin tried to follow, his vertigo making the castle's parapets spin as the ebony sky descended, the air burning against his skin.

A weight struck him down. Again he was on his knees, a rhythmic cracking in his ears muting everything he needed to hear. He howled as something sharp bit him through the leather and fabric that protected his back, a penetrating pain like multiple daggers digging into his flesh. Gaelin glimpsed elongated arms, still human in shape but stretched to form wings. Dimly, he felt his hands and knees furrowing the snow. A dach was dragging him. He struggled to lift his staff, to cry a command to the slumbering Holram, but now the dach was hitching him to its belly, its wings pounding faster until the land beneath him fell away.

Avalar appeared below his flopping limbs, leaping to grab at his boots. *You're alive!* Gaelin wanted to yell, but pain stole his breath. Below him Roth scaled the giant's back, sword-tip raised as Avalar thrust the lieutenant over her head, yet Gaelin watched them both shrink as the dach carried him higher, far and away from their efforts to save him.

"Gaelin!" Terrek cried, and for a moment, Gaelin saw across the distance his helpless rage, Terrek's weapon dangling powerless in his hand. Then Gaelin spied movement past the dead weight of his limbs, the giant rushing into the forest, slashing her great sword as she plowed among the branches.

He followed her progress for as long as he could until the dach's wings carried him into the clouds. He fought to hold Mornius, feeling his captor's sharp talons shifting to tip his face up. A spiked tail wound around his neck. He gagged as the creature's enlarged head ducked to sniff at him, its jaws straining to reach his throat.

Gaelin yelped when the fangs pierced his skin. With a frenzied snarl, the dach clamped its lips over his seeping blood. He felt more pain—a frenetic suction against his flesh, the dach's throat muscles bunching and sliding while it drank. Darkness descended to numb his body, covering his sight with a tumbling fog. He groaned as the world went black.

Chapter 24

Gaelin floated through a familiar fog. His consciousness had fled to this place when he was a child, to the same sanctuary he had revisited after the battle in the hills above Heartwood. Only now the mist held him within a storm of fire, the heat of it snatching the breath from his lungs.

With an effort, he lifted his head as a molten liquid rushed toward him from out of the vapor, splashing down in a rain of sparks. The lava frothed and churned in front of him, shaping itself into a snarling dragon, then an ember-maned wolf, and at last forming into someone he recognized, a golden semblance of Terrek Florne.

"I hope," the figure boomed, "you will fear me less if I hold to this likeness."

Mutely, Gaelin dropped to his knees.

"You cannot stay here," the entity told him as it approached. Its lurid eyes flared, and yet Gaelin felt sorrow from the warder, a tangible weight of sadness. "If you can feel me, you can be saved. But you must wake and defend yourself!"

Defend myself? The words rebounded through his thoughts. His body ached for the freedom of death, for the chance to turn from Holram's fiery regard. *Terrek's wrong,"* Gaelin realized. *This is a god. But why would it care for me?*

"I am not a deity," Holram asserted. There was another flash, another change, the bottom half of the warder's face and jaw morphing into a lion's muzzle. "I am the caretaker of stars. Time preceded my birth and will continue after my end. I had to wait for a fighting spirit. Now that I have you, you must endure!"

Holram's image dissipated, melting into the currents of the lava, his anger cooled by the fog's return. "Live," he called behind the gathering clouds, "for I have no other. If you fail, I perish, along with everything else."

Gaelin heard a hissing in his ears. He caught a murmur of dialogue—a human speaking close by—before Holram's ominous voice jerked him back. "My creator, Sephrym, will destroy all life," the warder said. "He will shatter this world to find his foe."

"His foe?" Gaelin echoed. "You mean Erebos . . ."

He struggled, choking and tasting blood as he fought to breathe through the pain in his lungs. Lifting his fingers to his chest, he explored his skin and his aching ribs. *Why am I naked?* he wondered. *Where am I?*

"Fool!" a voice mocked him. "Better for you if you had stayed asleep!"

A set of hands dragged him erect. He tottered on his feet, rubbing his eyes while he struggled to focus. He grunted as he was shoved into something solid—*a tree*, he thought, identifying the trunk with his palms. Groaning, he slumped against it, squinting at a gray-robed figure bending over him, a middle-aged man holding a staff aloft, its teardrop-shaped gem blazing silver. Despite the color of its light, the crystal seated upon the iron shaft was opaque red, Gaelin observed, and then felt Holram's presence recoiling in fear under his ribs. "*It is the world's blood!*" said the warder's horrified whisper in his head. "*Keep away from it!*"

Gaelin cringed when his assailant pressed close, the man's blade of a nose a mere finger's length from his. As his captor's body blocked his view of the staff, Gaelin felt Holram's terror unclench within him. The tree bark was digging into his muscles as he shrank from the stranger's cruel stare.

"When I look on you, I see falsehood," a voice intoned, and Gaelin started as he realized that the words had come from his mouth. He lifted his hand to feel his lips still soundlessly moving. *What is . . . what? Stop it!* he thought at Holram. *You cannot use me like I'm—*

"You pretend to be what you are not," Holram said again through his mouth. Gaelin tried to clamp his jaws shut, yet still his lips demanded, "Why are you here?"

"I am Erebos's loyal cleric," the mage replied. "I do my god's bidding; that's why. You should brace yourself, puppet. For you are about to die." Sneering, the stranger gestured to a drift beyond the tree. "Notice how your staff just lies there? You're nothing, and your god is nothing, clearly." With exaggerated care, the mage pulled a knife from a slit in his robe. "I regret your life's been a waste; I really do. But your death will remedy that. I swear it. Already Erebos feasts on you."

Gaelin moaned as the older man shoved him onto his side and then grabbed his ankles, raising his hips until claws from the canopy above seized his feet. The tree came alive overhead as two winged dachs hauled at his legs. Scrabbling, they climbed, dragging his shoulders from the snow until he hung helpless, his head throbbing between his dangling arms.

"This is where Mens steps in," the priest said. "I've watched him work and he's very thorough. He feeds Erebos the victim's pain, while his helpers harvest the blood, and later the dachs are fed the meat. Or Arawn is, depending on the room. Nothing goes to waste. I think it's brilliant how Mens can prolong the ritual; sometimes it lasts several hours. I tend to have a weak stomach. But if I want to get anywhere close to my daughter in the hierarchy, I'll need to toughen up. Mens tells me to practice. If I do, he says I'll get used to it." The priest shrugged. "Well, I guess we'll find out, won't we?"

Gaelin eyed the dagger in his captor's hand. "Now, where do I begin?" the cleric muttered, leaning in. Gaelin screamed as the blade's edge dragged along his skin, slicing slowly from his breastbone to his navel.

"Yeesh, I could have chosen a better tool!" the mage said. "It's more pulling than cutting anyway. Once I get a good grip with my hand. And not so messy as you might think." Gaelin hissed, flinching as the man probed his wound.

"You have a lot of old scars, my friend," his captor observed. "And now all these bite marks, too. Tell me, puppet, do they sting?"

Gaelin shut his eyes. He heard the cleric's warped humans clustering around him, then felt their talons grasp his wrists, stretching his arms from his body.

"Good," the priest said. "We don't want him flopping or I'll cut too—wait, not so hard! I need his hide in one piece when I present it with the staff . . ." The mage chuckled nervously. "No more gray-robes for me!"

Gaelin stared at the eight creatures whining for his blood. Even without Mornius, he sensed their torment. *Yet they endure*, he thought, reading fury and exhaustion in the dachs' red eyes. *And hunger, too. The poor things are starving.*

"I could feed you to my friends right now," the priest said as if perceiving his thoughts. "But I'd have no trophy if I did that, would I? I'd have nothing to prove my worth."

Gaelin screamed as the knife's tip deepened his cut. A trickle of blood ran down into his mouth while the cult leader smiled crookedly above him. "Did you get to see Tierdon?" the cleric asked. "That was Mens; I can't take credit for someone else's work. But I helped to expand his power. I am Nithra Vlyn. My daughter is Erebos's favorite *and* the wielder of the Blazenstone. Rest assured, puppet, he hears me. And he will hear your screams tonight."

The gray-robe dug in with the knife, grinding its edge between Gaelin's ribs and making him jerk with every cut. Around him and his torturer, the huddled dachs licked their lips, fighting each other for a taste of his blood.

"I'm sorry you missed the first part; you were unconscious, I'm afraid," Nithra told him. "The dach wasn't supposed to drain you, but they're almost mindless once they're changed, and difficult to command." Slowly, Nithra withdrew a short wooden club from his cloak and held it out. "In case you're wondering where you got those bruises. I've gotten handy with this, too. I use it in the dungeons where I work. In fact ..." Gaelin winced as the mage's knuckles pressed his ribs. "You're dead already; you just don't realize it. I could take your staff now and be done, let the dachs finish you, but then Erebos would lose his meal, and I'd be punished. Mens would get all the credit for finding the staff, of course."

Gaelin choked, tasting blood on his tongue. "I don't believe you," he said, relieved to discover he could control his mouth once more. He coughed as his vision blurred red. "They put you in the dungeons because you're nothing to them. Even Erebos doesn't know you."

"*Boy!*" Nithra's black eyes flared within the depths of his hood. Gaelin screamed when the club descended, shattering his right knee. "Do not mock me! I do this for our *future!* You can't fathom it yet; you're among the unenlightened. But one day you will, after you're resurrected and New Earth is born, a world meant for humans alone, where *we* decide the rules!"

Gaelin writhed, with more groans escaping his lips as his tormentor returned to his knife.

"You did that on purpose!" his captor raged. "Clever boy, but I'm on to you now. You're trying to get me to kill you. Well, I—"

The hissing sound was back. Gaelin tasted vomit, the contents of his stomach mixed with blood. The upside-down forest was spinning, and the motion was making him sick. He spied his staff lying abandoned on a hillock beyond the dachs, its shaft and Skystone coated with ice. *Please*, he implored Holram, yearning for oblivion to take him, to sink him into a place without fear. A flash responded, the flicker of Mornius's gem coming to life. Someone was near, he sensed, and very angry.

Light burst from the Skystone, and out of the surrounding trees, Avalar sprang. She stormed toward Nithra, her great sword raised above her head.

In a movement too fast for Gaelin to follow, her blade struck the first dach, the power of her stroke driving the steel straight through the creature's skull and ribs to its groin. The body slid free, the giant's blade streaming with gore.

Gaelin let out a yelp as his torso flopped askew and the dachs in the branches above him took wing. Avalar leapt with a furious howl. Gone was the graceful dance of the Talhaidor that she had learned in Tierdon. Here was one of the greatest and last of the ancient warrior races, the long-ago protectors of Talenkai. Like a scythe, Avalar's sword swept bodies off their feet, flinging jagged, gory pieces over the snow.

Abandoning her sword, the giant charged the two remaining dachs, the rippling white fur of her heavy cloak glistening with blood. She seized the first and ripped the wing from its shoulder. As the magic-warped human collapsed, Avalar pounced with fists flailing.

Gaelin turned away. In the quiet of the forest, he caught the rhythmic cracking of bones. Her blows were precise and calculated. He nodded as he recalled how she had been trained to fight the Sundor Khan beasts threatening the North. Her bare hands knew how to kill.

Nithra Vlyn hunched staring behind the tree, with indecision on his wrinkled brow.

"You better run," Gaelin said, his words slurred by waves of fatigue. "She destroys them to get to you."

Nithra glared, his staff brandished over his head.

"Liar," Gaelin murmured. "You were never at Tierdon."

The gray-robe retreated with mincing steps, and as Avalar stalked the terrified priest, it seemed to Gaelin from her snarling expression she felt every chain her ancestors had borne.

With a despairing groan, Nithra Vlyn fled.

Avalar jerked to a wavering halt. Shivering with the force of her restraint, she moved backward into the furrow her boots had made.

"Staff-Wielder?" The giant's voice was harsh. *How far had she run?* Gaelin wondered, eyeing her reddened features, her torn leggings slicked with blood, the bear hide unraveled, dangling free from her knees and calves.

Avalar sank beside him, gingerly touching his neck. "Sails, you're frozen!" she said and then crawled forward to snatch his cloak, his deer-hide leggings, and his gray jerkin. He gasped in pain when she cradled his shattered body. Covering him as best she could, she wiped the blood from his face with her furry cloak.

"Help me, Gaelin! You must not sleep!" She inspected the burning cut below his ribs. "This, at least, is not a threat," she said. "It is shallow. The little man was timid with his blade."

Gaelin moaned as Avalar dressed him. He was well beyond obeying her words, his head lolling over her elbow.

"Stay awake," Avalar urged. Her fingers shook as she caressed his hair. Squinting, he saw that her skin was streaked with sweat as well as blood. A cut at the base of her throat wept a sickly brownish fluid. He recognized its acrid smell. *Oh no!* he thought. *Poison!* He trembled as Avalar, unaware of her injury, pressed him to her chest. Groaning, she hauled herself upright and limped in the direction from which she had come.

He struggled to make himself heard, his hand pulling at her furry cloak. "Wait! My staff. Avalar, please. Let me . . ."

"I cannot touch it," she said.

"I don't . . . need you to." Gaelin fought to stay alert. His strength was failing, with winter gnawing in his heart. Holram could restore him—and save her as well, for the young giant, too, was dying, the puncture in her neck darkening as he watched.

He visualized Mornius. So often, he had ignored Holram's thoughts, had mistaken them for his own, or had rejected and resisted them. Now, by choice, he would surrender, as Avalar's people had sacrificed their freedom to save the world.

Gaelin pulled in a breath that tasted of blood. The staff was his— Holram's. His mind gripped it, held it, embracing the heat that leapt to seize his heart.

Desire knifed through him, the need to make recompense, to drive Erebos from hiding, to escape the magic of Talenkai's sky that held him trapped.

Gaelin sighed. He would endure as Holram had bidden him. He heard the song of the vanquished warder, understood for an instant the language of the stars. Pulling free, he emerged unscathed from the bonding to wrap a mental hug around his abandoned staff. He summoned fire and renewal, power and health. His crushed knee tingled in response, the fiery jolts of healing lancing throughout his body.

"Staff-Wielder!" Avalar, cursing, threw him into the snow. He landed with a grunt by his staff.

Howling, she lunged at the scattered dead, stamping them to a gory pulp as she hacked and chopped with her sword. Then abruptly she whirled, her massive blade spattering blood when she flung it away. Hunched over, gasping for breath, she lurched toward him. "*Why am I doing this?*" She pummeled the air with her fists. "So I will not destroy *you!*"

Seizing his staff, Gaelin clambered upright. He had seen this kind of rage before on his stepbrothers' faces, the mindless violence taking them over, making both Delbert and Jax cruel copies of their father, oblivious to his cries.

As he struggled to flee despite the trees spinning around his head, his legs gave way beneath him.

The giant bared her teeth. "You *touched* me, with *magic!* After *everything* I have said!"

Gaelin crouched at her feet, loathing his body's responses—the parched mouth and throat, the flinching of his limbs. *Please don't shout*, he wanted to protest, but his tongue was immobile, locked behind his teeth.

"You know what it did to my people!" Avalar spat. She, too, was reliving a memory, her abhorrence of it reflected in the rolling of her eyes, the clenching of her chin.

"Yes," said Gaelin, finding his voice at last. Though his wounds were gone, sickness roiled in his gut and tasted sour on his tongue. He sucked in air, hating how pitiful he was, his exhausted body sagging over his folded knees. "You were dying. We both were. I had to do *something*!"

He paused, keenly aware that his rescuer deserved more than his excuses. "When you almost fell from the cliff," he said, "you were frightened and I wanted to help. But I couldn't. So Terrek did—he had my staff—and the wind raised you up, or . . . whatever that was, because I was afraid I'd make it worse.

"You were *poisoned*!" he shouted, pressing his fists to the knot of frustration in his chest. "Your only hope was my staff, and I'm sorry if it upsets you, but I will *not* be sorry for saving you! I'm tired of doing nothing while everyone suffers!"

Avalar loomed over him as he fumbled for words. "It had to be me this time, taking the risk," he said. "Me. *Finally*! Terrek wasn't here. On the cliff, he had my staff and you had the wind—magic—that you *called* to because you were afraid. Well, so was I, when I thought you would die. So I called! I *did* something! And I will not be sorry for not failing you *twice*!"

Avalar was silent, a tall black shape blotting out the stars. Her breath plumed as she swung away. "We must get back," she said severely. "Leader Terrek is hunting for you."

Bracing himself, Gaelin tried to stand. His body felt dead from the waist down. His legs moved, yet they had no strength.

Avalar watched in silence. Nothing would soften her iron heart now, he realized. *She's a giant*, he thought, and ruefully shook his head.

He started when Avalar knelt, her big palms light on his shoulders, cupping them gently. "This is a fell place, little mage," she said. "It pits us against ourselves. Come."

She lifted him up, bracing him on his feet. Bemused, Gaelin registered her compassion, her reassuring touch that moments ago had yearned for his death.

"I see," Avalar said. "You mistrust the violence of my quickened blood. Should I try now to explain to you the whys and hows of giants, I fear we would both freeze ere the telling is done. Still, we must away. Let me carry you from this place."

Gaelin motioned to his staff at his feet. "You want me to trust you?" he asked.

He pulled free and bent, prying Mornius from its icy sheath, and then lifted its Skystone to the giant. "Touch it," he insisted. "I won't go anywhere with you until you do."

Her body suddenly rigid, Avalar glared down.

Chapter 25

G aelin confronted the young giant who had run so far to risk her life for him. She glared at Mornius in his hands, her body flinching as if it were a serpent with its head reared to bite.

"Why do you wish the world harm?" Avalar said. "I cannot touch your magic. You know this!"

"The elves created Mornius so you could," he told her. "There's a stone tree somewhere in the forest around Tierdon. That was the temple where the Eris elves shielded Holram until they could make him the staff." Gaelin paused. "The warder speaks to me. He wants you to know he won't hurt you as long as he has Mornius. But neither of you consider how *I* might feel!"

He gestured at the bloodstained snow and shuddered. "These dachs were human once, yet you tore them apart with your bare hands, and now you expect me to *trust* you? How do I know you won't turn on me if I use my staff? Please," he urged, "we need to get past this. On the cliff, it made sense for me to give my staff to Terrek. If Mornius had touched you then, you could have fallen and killed us both. But here there's no such danger. We can find out the truth. Or"—he shrugged—"we can both go on being afraid. Is that what you want?"

She scowled. "I am not 'afraid' of any—"

"You are and you have reason to be, from what you've told me. But when Holram healed you through the Skystone, there was no harm." Gaelin glowered at the staff. *Light*, he willed its lusterless gem. *Just—* "And Terrek," he said to the giant. "He agrees Mornius is not a threat to you. Why can't you believe him?"

"You know not how that stone jangles my nerves," Avalar replied.

"Everything in me recoils when I am near it. My magic is in my flesh. It is a part of me. I have no choice but to heed it more than I do Leader Terrek. And it is telling me—"

"So go home!" Gaelin stared at his chilled arms as the wind ruffled his sleeves. "Where's my jacket and cloak?" he muttered.

The giant strode through the trampled dachs to gather his things. He wriggled into the leather and wool garments she gave him, his gaze on the tracks she had left in the snow. "Your path is clear enough even for me," he said. "I can follow it by myself."

"Are you certain you can walk?" she asked. "You are wobbling where you stand."

"I will manage," said Gaelin. "If you're gone, at least I won't have to worry about being torn limb from limb the next time I try to— Oh!"

A blue light sprang above him, crackling with bolts of violet, brighter than any fire Mornius had emitted before. He gaped at the staff in his grasp, and at Avalar's white knuckles engulfing his. She had reached out despite her fear, to wrap her strong fingers over his own. Her head was thrown back, her teeth bared at the sky, and in her face was terror, as if she braced for the clouds to tumble down and the ground to crack asunder.

"Avalar!" He extricated his fingers from hers and seized her wrists. "Look! You're doing it!"

"I *cannot be*! I—" She goggled at the staff's expanding power, Mornius's pulses flaring more radiantly with every convulsion. The woods around them came to life, the dachs' spilled blood absorbing into the thawing soil. New leaves poked like springtime into their view, and moss shed its ice to grow green among the gnarled bark of the trees.

Avalar gasped, and as Mornius toppled from her hands, Gaelin caught its shaft. Then the ground lurched beneath him, the trees creaking as they bent and swayed. A soundless brilliance lit the heavy clouds, the shaking of the forest knocking him flat and stretching the giant beside him.

"Was that my—" He focused on the quartz glowing in the mud above his hair, feeling the weight of Mornius's iron heel skitter down his neck from where it had landed across his throat. *No, it isn't*, he thought, eyeing the Skystone's quiet flicker. *That flash came from the city*!

Avalar struggled to her feet and lifted her head, tracking something outside his vision. "I must go," she announced abruptly, hastening to penetrate the underwood between the dense trees.

Gaelin, clambering to his feet, tried to follow. "Wait!" he called. He lost his balance and tripped, pitching onto his chest. "Avalar!" Arms quivering, he pushed himself erect. "You can't just leave! What if Nithra's still out there?"

She turned, holding out her hands as she wheeled in a circle. Something invisible was colliding with her body, the force of it making her stumble. "He summons my magic!" Avalar howled, her face red. "The air and the rocks! The flesh of animals and *giants* must answer!"

"*Who* wants your magic?" Gaelin shouted. "Avalar, don't go!"

She swooped down on him, scooping him up in the crook of her elbow. "An elf!" she answered. She was sprinting with him flopping in her grasp, her body crashing through the brush. Gaelin, glimpsing creatures racing by, spied a bird larger than he was leaping through the lower branches over his head.

"Where are we going?" he cried. "What elf?"

"Does it matter? I *must*—"

"Avalar, *hold*!" a familiar voice roared.

A white horse appeared with a spray of bitter cold powder, its haunches bunching as its hind feet skidded. Terrek was astride Duncan, Gaelin realized, accompanied by Silva riding behind him. Then Roth pushed from the trees on his dark gray stallion, Jack nervously stomping to a halt beside Terrek's mount.

"Let Gaelin go," Terrek told the giant. "He's in no condition to be thrown around like that. Put him—"

Gaelin grunted as his body hit the ground. "Done!" Avalar replied curtly. Growling, she shouldered aside the two horses. "Now I must go! I am summoned!"

"An elf calls her!" Gaelin explained to the bewildered Terrek.

Silva slid from Terrek's gelding and hastened over, reaching to pull Gaelin up. "What was that fire in the sky? Did you see it?" Gaelin asked him. Receiving no answer, he opened his mouth to inquire again but stopped when Terrek threaded his horse between the clustered pines to head off the giant.

181

"Avalar, *think!*" Terrek maneuvered Duncan to block her path, then leaned to grab her arm. "No elf would summon one of your people for magic. The giants are too few for them to—" Terrek stopped. "Holram's *balls!*" he howled as Avalar pushed past him into the shadows.

As Terrek glared at the swaying branches that had swallowed the giant, Silva boosted Gaelin onto Duncan's back.

"Jack won't carry two," Roth said dourly to Silva. "You'll have to ride him." With a grunt, he jumped to the ground. "Don't worry, I'm fast. I'll run in front. Just get on my horse!"

"It's not *you* I'm worried about," the guard grumbled, moving to stand by Roth's jittery mount.

Roth waited, holding his stallion's reins while Silva swung onto the gray's back to sit quietly as Jack bucked. Crooning to his horse to calm him down, Roth patted the animal's neck and then darted into the trees.

"You're pale, Staff-Wielder," observed Terrek. "You used Mornius, didn't you?"

"Avalar was sick and I was . . ." Gaelin shook his head. "The mage who captured me told me a dach drained my blood. Holram couldn't replace that, but . . . I'm well enough. Let's go!"

As Duncan's muscles surged beneath him, Gaelin pressed his knees in tight to the gelding, the branches clawing at his legs, threatening to rip him from the animal's back. A salty odor assailed his nostrils; for a moment he felt as if he was plunging in terror to flee the dilapidated cabin, his threadbare tunic covered with his stepfather's blood.

"Gods, what a beast!" Silva complained. "High withers, green broke . . . And his mouth! Hard as leather!"

"He's the finest racer in Kideren," Terrek said. "You should be in front by now. Come on, old friend! Get him moving!"

Raising his head, Gaelin peered at the hint of golden dawn between the trees. As the two horses clattered over the frozen dirt, Gaelin felt magic prickling his skin. He yelped at a second fiery burst, the power of it hitting him again a moment later, its vibrations rippling through his hair as it rocked the ground. *This is bigger than Avalar's magic,* he thought. *It's just so—*

The leggy young Jack bounded by, his black tail flagging above his back. It was as if he had caught his master's scent and was galloping to find him while Silva, swaying in the saddle, bared his teeth and fought for control.

Gaelin shuddered at the sensation of magic on his skin. *So effortless*, he marveled, clenching his staff. *This elf is mighty! The power he calls begs to answer!*

Terrek and Silva loosened their reins as the trees thinned out, letting their mounts plunge into the snow. "It's attacking Tierdon!" Terrek shouted as Gaelin spotted Roth standing red-faced and still at the edge of the open field.

When Jack stopped in his tracks to neigh at Roth, Silva quickly dismounted. Beyond them, Avalar crouched among the drifts with her left knee lifted. A halo of white framed the shattered city past her shoulders, the same blinding fire Gaelin had witnessed over the forest.

Dazed, he raised his staff.

Chapter 26

*G*aelin screamed as another wave struck. The blast of power slammed against his chest, jolting him from Duncan's back. His cry cut off as he landed on his belly with his head turned sideways, the ground heaving beneath him. Duncan stood motionless in a nearby drift, the gelding's ears pricked toward the city, while Terrek lay sprawled at the animal's feet, his body partially concealed by the snow.

"Commander!" Roth cried. "I can't move!"

"Neither can I!" Terrek shouted.

Resting on his stomach, Gaelin squinted when another flash engulfed Tierdon.

"What is it, Staff-Wielder?" demanded Terrek. "Can you tell if—"

"Somebody's by the ruins!" Silva cut in. "What is . . . he's got feathers. He's . . . Wait, what is he doing?"

Summoning Avalar, Gaelin thought, straining in vain to see the elf. *But why?* His gaze settled on Mornius's shaft lying near him, its orb half-buried, with just a sliver of the gem visible. His image peered back at him sadly, his face reflected in the crystal's rounded surface. He stared past the stone to Roth's stallion held immobile in mid-canter, the horse's long black tail flipped up, his hooves suspended.

Gaelin focused beyond Jack, finding Avalar still squatting with her back turned. A distortion rippled between her midriff and the city, a ribbon of shimmering light connecting her to Tierdon.

Shadows were darkening the distant wreckage, cast by a pair of hovering, semitransparent beasts. The immense creatures sparkled as they flew, their blue hides resembling liquid glass, and the force of their wingbeats stirred up whirlwinds of powdery white, stripping the ice around the city bare. Gaelin strained to make out their forms, their dragonesque heads reared back. Two glimmering tendrils held the monsters in place, the elf's strange power tethering them as surely as it had ensnared Avalar.

"The wings of the largest Azkharren queens stretch as wide as the sky," he recalled the giant describing her Stormfuries, and it was true. Clouds tumbled overhead, disrupted by the creatures' flight. He glimpsed in his mind Holram's perceptions through the Skystone—of countless magical animals frozen on the outskirts of the field. Like Avalar, they had been drawn to contribute their strength, and now an untold number of glowing gossamer threads reached from their bodies to converge at the city's heart.

Gaelin felt a surge from beneath the drifts, molten stone thrusting through layers of ancient sediment toward the surface. The steaming air was pressing him flat, the wings above him quickening their tempo.

Avalar groaned, and through Holram's senses, Gaelin felt her strength ebbing, the magic linking her to the elf growing fainter. *She's going to die,* he realized. Another flash brought tears to his eyes as the clouds revolved atop the wind. He gasped when Mornius found his hand, the Skystone crackling to form a sphere around his body, a multicolored shield allowing him, at last, to stumble to his feet.

"No, Staff-Wielder, do not!" Avalar cried out weakly. "That is Ponu, do you hear? Leader Terrek, stop him! I know you named this Camron's city. In sooth, it is not! Ponu created it, and he will—"

As thunder muffled her words, Gaelin hefted his staff and sprinted toward the elven intruder. He discerned the figure now, the mage at the eye of the storm springing astride an Azkhar suspended above him and close to the ground, the creature lifting Ponu up and out of the way of the gale's hot fury.

The winged elf clambered to his feet between the queen's translucent shoulders. Standing indomitable, his silvery hair flying wild in the blast, he raised his bare arms, ensnaring the threads of magic from the myriad of beasts surrounding him, forming the strands into a flashing ball. With a fierce cry, Ponu hurled the mass into the wind, lighting it afire using an object he snatched from one of his many pockets. The power blasted Tierdon, shattering what remained of its buildings and domes.

Gaelin tottered below his staff's protective arch, his hearing muted, his legs threatening to topple him to the ashy slush. Tears stung his eyes as the great city melted, slumping like wax into a glowing lake of scalding vapor, magma bursting forth from the riven terrain. A huge slab of granite, streaming with water, tore through the ice to his left, and another sprang before him, and another to his right, columns of rock jutting up in every direction. A forest of stone, massive spires of jagged granite, erupted around the city's sagging walls, driven to the surface by the pressures underneath, merging Tierdon with the bones of the world.

Dropping his staff, Gaelin gagged at the stench of the air. The soil sank beneath his weight, his dizziness making the valley whirl, knocking him flat onto his stomach. His mouth was full of blood, smearing his hand. He stared as the city rose anew from the steam and fire, leaping ribbons of lava adhering to form buildings and walls. The storm flayed the rising granite, grinding the stones into glass and crystal, the diamond-paned surface of overlapping domes climbing skyward.

The outline of the Azkhar queen lowered itself, the field trembling when her clawed feet hit the ground. In a flutter of white pinions, the elf leapt from her back—to land with a splash below the beast as the great creature sprang aloft. The mage faced Tierdon with his wings unfurled, his hand holding up a pale-blue crystal that shaped the fire and molded the stone.

Stop! Gaelin wanted to shout, but he was fading, his breaths ripping agony through his chest. He coughed, spraying blood. "You're hurting her!" he shouted as he struggled to rise, his voice frayed into nothingness by the howling wind. "You're—"

The flames beneath the clouds receded, the currents from the Azkharrens' wings hardening the city. The elf made a sweeping gesture and a lump of molten rock thrashed upward in the new plaza—to form itself into the statue of a gaunt giant, the obsidian figure poised with his battle braids flying, a broken shackle and chain in his upraised fist.

A bolt of emerald whizzed past Gaelin to dive at the winged elf. It rounded into a ball of green light as it halted in front of the mage, then darkened at its center as the image of a knight filled it, a phantom warrior stretching tall with his arms crossed. "End this, you fool!" Nathaniel Argus bellowed, his voice cracking above the thunder. "Or is it your *wish* to slay a giant?"

When the elf waved his hand, Argus vanished and everything stopped, the crimson storm dissipating from the sky. Gaelin waited for the granite studding the field to sink back into the loosened dirt, but the smoothed ebony spires remained, whitening under the freezing mist. He struggled to move as the elf approached him, as the water hardened around him and held him still. He could no longer feel his fingers, and his bones ached as the numbness extended into his wrists.

Ice crunched beside him. "Child of Othelion," a voice said quietly, a pleased note of discovery in its lyrical tone. Calves clad in laced leather boots stepped into his sight, followed by knees as the stranger knelt. The elf reached out; then Gaelin felt a touch at the base of his throat, a tingle spreading through his body as the frozen slush melted and let him go. "You are a mess, Staff-Wielder," the elf observed.

Gaelin jerked his gaze up to see the elf leaning over him. *Ponu*, Gaelin thought, surprised by the strength of the fingers that flipped him onto his back, Ponu sliding him up until his head rested on the elf's lap. Gaelin stretched out his arm, groping for his staff.

"Mornius is here," Ponu reassured him. "But right now, we need to think about *you*. You are dying, Staff-Wielder. Your flesh was not made for such power. Even the elves on this world would not withstand it for long. Behold!" Gaelin shuddered when Ponu touched his scalp and lifted from it a clump of snarled hair.

"I *know*," Gaelin rasped. "Terrek showed me already."

"This kind of energy is deadly, and yet you squander it recklessly," scolded the elf. "Crossing the field with Mornius blazing, when you could have sent the ghost. You need to think before you act. Or you will never survive. You must learn—" Wearily Gaelin closed his eyes, and the voice above him stopped.

"Avalar is well," Ponu told him after a pause. "She's on her way to your encampment. You were right to warn me. But she survived. I did not realize she was so near. Her sire, Grevelin, is also; perhaps now she is preparing herself to meet him, for where I go, he often goes as well. I left him where my magic would not hurt him, sheltered by the walls of the sacrificed tree that housed Holram after the warders arrived." There was a moment of silence.

"What Avalar suffered this day is only a taste of what her father endured from the slavers," Ponu went on. "Many giants died because of humans touching magic, and not so long ago. Yet Grevelin insisted on coming to this place of humans. 'To protect *me*,' he said." Ponu chuckled, a sparkle of amusement in his eyes. "Such is the stubbornness of giants, I suppose."

"Am I really dying?" Gaelin whispered.

Ponu regarded him sadly. "Indeed, you are, my friend. We must act soon. Now wait, let me . . ." Ponu delved into one of two pouches affixed to his belt. He nodded, noting Gaelin's expression. "What is it about you humans fearing death?" he asked, withdrawing from the pouch a tiny parcel tied with string. Carefully he unknotted the twine with his teeth and set the paper beside him. "Death . . ." He pointed at his upturned hand and then made a quick spooning motion. "Yes, you are dying. And one day you will be gone. Do you think endless life is better? Bethink you, as giants would say. It is not so easy, being immortal."

Curls of steam wafted from Ponu's palm. The winged elf lifted the little packet, tipping a dried yellow powder into what he held before stirring it with his thumb. "The *cure*," Ponu explained, grinning down. "There. That should be enough, I think. Now, drink this."

"Medicine?" Gaelin queried. He wriggled his shoulders, struggling to prop himself higher. "But I thought—"

Ponu shrugged. "Not everything can be remedied with a flick of a wrist. Sometimes magic needs help. Your drained body craves fluids, young human. This power of yours is not magic, though the elves and giants call it that. It is energy. The fuel of stars. Human flesh cannot . . ."

The elf hesitated. "I wonder how your Terrek Florne found strength enough to confound my magic to move and free the ghost. I am called Ponu," he added. "Pardon my lack of courtesy, but when you live as long as I have, names become irrelevant. I am *me*. I had a longer name once, but I don't recall what it was. Now drink." He held his cupped hand under Gaelin's lips and tipped the steamy liquid toward him.

Gaelin took a sip, swallowing quickly, then gulping when the mage forced more fluid into his mouth. He stared at the falling snow, a taste like berries on his tongue. "You saved Tierdon," he murmured.

Ponu grunted and retied the string around the diminutive parcel. "I saved *nothing*," he replied, returning the packet to his pouch. "A city reborn does not replace the lives lost. And now I sense you resisting Holram's control. Our one hope is finally rousing, and you refuse him." Ponu scowled. "Do you realize the damage you cause yourself? You force Holram to ravage your entire body when all he needs is a window in your mind. Now that he wakes, you must surrender, Gaelin. I know the Seeker elves warned you of this. Did you not listen? No wonder you are dying."

"No one asks me what I want," Gaelin said. "I was a captive my whole life. I will not . . ." He clenched his teeth. "When I lose control, I *kill* people. I become as bad as my stepfather was." Gaelin yawned, and Ponu lowered him until he lay supine again. Memories rose, rushing to consume him. He shut his eyes against the return of his vertigo.

"Tell me," Ponu urged. "Why are you so reluctant to tear down this fortress you hide behind? You can talk to me. There is nothing I have not encountered in my life, Gaelin Othelion. I will not think ill of you no matter what you say."

"*Lavahl*," Gaelin corrected. "My name is—"

"The Seeker elves may have tolerated that nonsense, but I am not so gentle," Ponu said. "You harm yourself by clinging to that false identity, and you will refrain from doing so in my presence. Do you understand me, young human?"

"I'm . . . not supposed to talk about it," Gaelin said as the elf laid a staff of twisted crystal across his chest.

"So *think* whatever it is, and my magic will show me," said Ponu. "Meanwhile, let me tend to this." Gaelin yelped when the winged elf lifted his reddened hands to examine them. "Don't you have gloves?"

"I don't know where they are!" Gaelin cried.

"That sensation you feel is a good thing," Ponu said. "It means you can keep your fingers. Fear not, for the discomfort will pass. Now look to my staff and visualize what you're forbidden to say."

Gaelin focused on the lumpy crystal, following the twist of its clear matrix within, the hints of fiery bubbles underneath its glossy exterior. He tensed as the sculpted quartz clouded, an image of trees taking shape around the likeness of a cabin he knew. He moaned when familiar hands dragged at him. Then he thrashed, the strength of his stepbrother Delbert pressing him onto the seat of a wobbly chair.

Gaelin saw the memory he had tried to block—Seth Lavahl standing red-faced and intoxicated across the kitchen floor, stains of oil and liquor spattered on his journeyman's vest. The big man had bound Gaelin's mother naked to the table; now once more Gaelin spotted Sareh Lavahl lying with her limbs outstretched, her wrists and ankles tied. "No!" Gaelin writhed, striking with his fists at the hands that squeezed his throat. In helpless rage, he watched Sareh's efforts to move, her head rolling on her bruised neck, blood streaming from her shattered cheekbone and jaw.

He froze, spying the long dagger in his stepfather's fist as Seth Lavahl mashed his fat belly against the table. Grinning mirthlessly, the drunk leaned his weight upon his knife's antler haft—to drive the blade deep under his victim's breastbone. Gaelin sobbed at the sight, grieving for the parent who had sung to him in the tumbledown barn, who had comforted him at night when he had cried.

Yet now she was no more than meat to the one who had forced her into servitude, just a deer for her captor to gut. The smith, panting with bloodlust, rubbed the sweat from his palms. Clasping the knife's hilt two-handed, he jerked the embedded blade down through his victim's navel to her hips. Gaelin whimpered when his mother's scream cut off, replaced by a rattling cough as his stepfather cast the knife skittering across the floor. Laughing then, Lavahl sank his fingers into his victim's gaping wound and ripped Gaelin's world apart.

"Bring it here!" the smith shouted.

Gaelin's stepbrothers leapt to obey, and now as an observer, Gaelin recognized their fear of the brutal man. They dragged him up kicking and screaming, Gaelin howling his terror as the smith snatched him from the older boys' grasp. "Hold her open!" Lavahl gestured to the wound, and then Gaelin was fighting for his life, gasping for breath when the drunkard smashed him atop his mother, shoving him into a wet and salty warmth until the top of his head felt the thrum of her heart.

"Take it back!" Lavahl roared. "Take it back, you bitch! Take your stinking runt *back!*"

"No!" Frantic, Gaelin struggled to escape. The grip he battled was impossibly strong, holding him still though he fought with all his might. "She died. She died because of *me!*"

"Hush now," Ponu soothed. "It is a *memory*, Gaelin, one no child could ever deserve. I understand how you view Holram as another bully seeking to erase you. Yet what you just showed me is what Holram must endure every day, Staff-Wielder. Erebos kills in the same cruel way. Only *he* does so repeatedly, while all the warders are forced to bear witness through the power that joins them. Do you comprehend now why his evil must be stopped?"

Gaelin barely heard the elf over his mother's echoing screams in his head, her look of agony and revulsion he would never forget.

"You are wise to keep silent," Ponu murmured abruptly. "This is what Gaelin needs. Did you see what was in my staff?"

"I saw," Terrek replied from somewhere near. "What have you done to him, elf?"

"I hope something akin to what I did to Tierdon," said Ponu. "His life needs restoring, but his fears hold him back."

"Don't talk about me like I'm not here," Gaelin called from the mist around him, the dizzy whirling where the cabin had been. "I hear what you're—" He stopped at another memory, the odor of rot as his mother's corpse lay moldering on the woodpile. Trembling, he saw again her staring skull as every day he had been forced to fetch the wood. "I was eight," he whispered.

Ponu's eyes glittered above him. "I never knew. Through my crystal, which is much like your Skystone, Gaelin, I checked on you," he said. "I was waiting for you to discover Holram. I could tell your life was difficult. But I never realized . . ." His expression uneasy, he flicked back his silvery hair. "I caught flashes. I knew you slept in the relic of an old barn. Or you would stay in a gloomy place below a . . ."

"That was the cellar," Gaelin provided. "He locked me there when he took his sons to town."

"I will find him," said Ponu. "You needn't worry about that, Terrek Florne. He and his offspring shall be brought to justice, I assure you. Humans are a part of this world now. On Talenkai, such things are not tolerated.

"As for you, child of Othelion," Ponu advised Gaelin, "you must reject your stepfather's name, for titles held too tightly can become wounds that never heal. Spurn the label as I have; Lavahl is a cruel drunkard. *Othelion* is your proper surname. Garrick Othelion was the name of your father. Othelion: of the lion—or one who is noble. It is a giantkin word for a creature from your Earth."

He flicked his white wings, staring over Gaelin's head at the distant trees. "Your people lacked both names and memories when they first arrived. Most of you were dead. Sephrym was intent on saving his star, and you were in his way, so he threw you down. The few of you who survived it were the foundlings, the children the elves cared for at Heartwood. The Seekers researched your world in books like the one you examined in the castle. Adhering to your traditions, they gave you two names, and some of them were taken from those books.

"You owe them everything." Ponu grimaced. "Yet you humans resent them and reject their language. They give you the simplest rules, the laws of the Seekers, to protect the magic. And you chafe under that. Always you must be superior. On the Earth, you considered yourselves *entitled*," said Ponu with disgust, "much to the detriment of your world, and now some of you intend to repeat those behaviors here."

Gaelin scowled as he struggled to find his bearings; he failed to comprehend the elf's anger or his words. "But I'm used to Lavahl," he said finally. "That's the only name I know!"

"Not all humans are the same," Terrek put in. "We have classes at our university. We instruct our young people to learn your rules as you wish us to."

"Not *wish*," Ponu said. "It is what the elves demand. And you are correct when you say 'not all.' Gaelin has been respectful. I saw him as a child, a feral little animal in the woods. He possessed no pride or lofty ambitions. He slept with wolves, and one even helped him when no human would. But *you*, Terrek Florne. You hesitated when the time came to dispose of the louse-ridden hair you cut from his head, even though the elves were clear about the importance of burying or burning. I heard you through my staff."

Terrek shifted, troubled. "Feel any better?" he asked Gaelin quietly.

"I'm *hungry*," Gaelin complained.

Terrek nodded. "We had already frightened and humiliated him . . ."

As Terrek explained his actions to the winged mage, Gaelin shuddered, recalling the two men holding him down his first night in camp—to cut away his matted hair and splash alcohol on his scalp. "I thought burying the clippings might add to that," Terrek continued. "But still I covered them, didn't I? I have assumed my whole life there's some logic behind these laws the elves give us, and so I do try to follow them."

Ponu snorted. "You strengthen the world when you give back. The more of yourselves you bury in the soil or burn clean for the air to breathe, the sooner this planet will recognize you. Do you wish to stop being an outsider and have magic of your own? Then respect the rules," said Ponu with a grin.

"Now . . ." Gesturing to Terrek, Ponu reached down, then together the man and the elf helped Gaelin to his feet. "I think our young Master Othelion requires *food!*"

Chapter 27

G aelin glared at Ponu across the cooking fire. "I did *not* sleep with wolves! There was just *a* wolf, and she kept me warm in the woods one night after she . . . freed me from my mother. I had released the wolf's pup from a snare once, so sometimes Beauty would visit and bring me small animals. I'd eat them raw because I couldn't cook and I was hungry!"

"Freed you?" Vyergin asked. The captain crouched before two large pots of stew, the ladle in his grasp dripping broth. "From your *mother*? Why would anyone need to be—" Vyergin grunted when Terrek shook his head.

"You saw in his staff, you said," Gaelin muttered to Terrek. "You know what my stepfather made me do."

"You didn't 'do' anything," Ponu told him. The elf sniffed curiously at the bowl Vyergin proffered him, the scent of leaves, roots, and rabbit wafting through tendrils of steam. "Seth Lavahl did that to you. You were a child; he was a man grown."

"He stitched her up," Gaelin remembered. "He made Delbert hold me while my head was inside. He wanted her to take me back, but I was too big. So he left me like that to suffocate; that's what he said. But Beauty came. I was screaming and knocking wood off the pile he dumped us on when Beauty heard me and got to me with her teeth. He had me strapped to my mother, and my legs were bound, too, so I couldn't get free." Gaelin shuddered. "Somehow the wolf knew where to bite and . . . next thing I knew she was licking my cheek."

"Well, that's no surprise!" Oburne said. "She was drawn to the blood. You're lucky she didn't gobble up your mother!"

"Come now, gentlemen!" Vyergin lifted his hand to get their attention. "Eat now while it's hot. That storm blasted away whatever dead branches we could have used. We have the wood we brought from the ruined sled and that's all." He paused to gesture at a passing swordsman. "Abithane Tayert!" Vyergin waited until the man stopped beside him to sniff at the stew, then slid his fire stick under the nearest cauldron's bail to heft it above the flames. "This one's ready. Be a good lad and carry it over to the others, would you? Be careful," he cautioned the black-haired warrior. "It's hot!"

Ponu smiled while Abithane crab-walked the swaying vessel toward the huddle of men by a second blaze among the trees. Then, sighing, the elf flicked his wings and sipped carefully at Vyergin's concoction.

"Elves don't eat meat," Roth protested behind him. "*Do they?*"

Shifting on the rock he had chosen for his seat, Ponu grinned. "I suppose that depends on the elf. This one *does*."

Ponu turned to Vyergin. "I can help your fire to hold," he said. "Here, Captain." Extracting a small vial from a pocket of his tunic, Ponu handed it over. "Be mindful when using this. Just a few drops when the flames are low. If you look again you will find many felled trees in the forest now. The saplings are no match for the downstrokes of an Azkhar queen trying to rise.

"This you may have also," Ponu added, passing to Vyergin several flat crusts of what resembled moldy bread. "It is bark from the fungi tree, Orthayli, that grows in the southlands of Tholuna. Just a smidgen can thicken up your broth. It will keep your hunger at bay as well."

Fungi? Gaelin grimaced in disgust as he surveyed his own plate of stew. He picked up his spoon and filled his mouth with tender rabbit and bits of potato. Washing it down with a sip of the ice water in his mug, he frowned at the bitter aftertaste. "I already *had* medicine," he grumbled.

"It is not the same kind," Ponu said. "This is tagwort; it will help you rest. I gave the remainder of the yellow powder you had before to Captain Vyergin here. He has promised to keep it for when you use your staff needlessly again. Which you will. You are human, so you have *no* idea—"

"You're an apothecary, I take it," Terrek interjected. "This medicine you gave to the captain for Gaelin. Is it a cure?"

"No," Ponu said. "What Gaelin has is no illness. A fire burns within him. It is my hope the Seeker elves may reverse some of the harm to his body, assuming he survives." The elf-mage reached between his knees. Raising up his crystal staff, he tilted it toward the fire, the quartz casting prisms of gold upon the sunlit tents. "I am curious, Leader Florne." Ponu stared at Terrek. "Where did you find the strength to break my hold on you out on the field? How did you free the ghost to alert me of Avalar's plight?"

"Free the . . . ?" Terrek's brow knitted. "I don't know what you're talking about. I didn't break any hold. Thanks to you, I couldn't even move. I don't know—"

"He means the scabbard," Roth said. "It dropped from the sword when we were trying to find the giant. One of the brambles you cut through tore it right off. I didn't see any ghost come out of the blade, though." Hugging his chest, Roth kicked at the ground. "I *hate* ghosts!"

"Ah." Terrek nodded.

"You will see the ghost only if he lets you," Ponu said.

Terrek wiped at his mouth. "So that's it. Well, good for Argus. Now he's free and I don't have to carry that rusty weapon of his around. I hope he behaves himself out there."

"But you *do* have his sword," Roth said. "It was caught beneath the straps of your pack. I wrapped it in a blanket for you."

"Which means you also have the ghost," Ponu told Terrek. He rounded on Roth, feathers flaring. "*You're* the one, aren't you? You took something of mine, and I want it back."

Roth blanched. "I *did*?"

"The painting, Lieutenant," Terrek said with a grin. "The one with my brother and Avalar. You still have it, I hope."

"Oh, that! Of course I do. B-but it's wrinkled now," Roth said sadly.

"That's easy enough to fix," Ponu assured him. "Bring it here to me, won't you?"

Roth edged reluctantly to one of the tents and crawled in.

"He's lying," Terrek informed the elf in an undertone. "It's not damaged. Roth has been fretting over that thing for the last day and a half."

"I am teasing him," Ponu whispered back. "He's *laori*, isn't he? They're always fun to meddle with. I don't envy you, though, managing him and Avalar both. Stop me if you think I'm being cruel, or if he starts to be—"

"*Laori?*" Gaelin echoed. "What's that?"

"It means great-hearted," Ponu said. "A passionate or empathic spirit. *Laori* giants are more apt to friend-bond. In fact, I—" The elf broke off. "Grevelin! I forgot about him! He must be frantic with worry for me! I need to contact him and let him know I am well." Ponu closed his eyes.

"I think the boy can cope with whatever you—" Terrek stopped when Roth reappeared from the tent. "Shh!" Terrek hissed at him and then motioned to Ponu. "Just bring it here. Let the elf see it."

Ponu opened his eyes as Roth stopped before him and held out the painting. "It's creased *and* filthy," Ponu observed. "What have you to say for yourself? A prized possession like that—ruined!"

"I'm sorry!" Roth gasped. Trembling, he hastily began to unroll the canvas.

"*Stop* that!" Ponu cried. "Are your fingers clean, boy? How careless of you. You put another splotch on that beautiful sky!"

Roth froze, and to Gaelin's horror, he began to cry. "I'm sorry." Roth fell to his knees and thrust the tube in Ponu's direction. "Please. Take it!"

Ponu, crossing his forearms, glanced over Roth toward the tents. "I do not want it now," he said severely. "You have soiled it. Therefore, you must give me something else in exchange."

Roth sniffed. "But I don't *have* anything. You said you could fix the wrinkles! Why can't you clean it, too?"

"Aha!" Ponu said. "How typically human of you to say that, and to think magic can resolve anything. Now, I do not have all day. Go quickly and fetch me something valuable. Make sure it's unique like the picture."

Terrek clasped Roth's shoulder. "I believe he's asking for your hat," he whispered.

Ponu turned his back on Roth's look of horror. "I have no need for a human's sleight-of-hand prop," he said with a haughty sneer. "There's something else. What is that bulge in your pocket, boy?"

Relief flooded visibly through Roth, his expression relaxing as he returned the hat to his tangled mop of curls. Ducking his head, he probed inside the breast pocket of his moss-green coat.

"I thought there was something odd," Terrek said. "From this angle, you resemble a *girl* I used to know."

"*Funny*," Roth muttered under his breath. "I don't remember why I took it. I just—" As he pulled his hand free, Gaelin glimpsed a puff of white fur between his fingers and thumb. Two large padded feet flipped out next, followed by dangling fuzzy ears with snips of satiny pink in their middles.

"A floppy bunny!" Ponu exclaimed. "And one with whiskers, too!"

Roth gasped. "Is it valuable? I liked it because it . . . well . . ." His face reddened. "I do know what *floppy* is," he added at Oburne's snort.

"At your age?" Vyergin said. "Oh dear. How sad for such a vibrant young man!" The captain took a swig from the flask Oburne offered him.

Roth shot him a glare. "But what's a *bunny*?"

Terrek harrumphed. "It's a technical term, Roth. We used it in our advanced classes at university," he said, the corners of his lips twitching. "I could explain, but the concept might be a bit beyond you."

"Indeed," Ponu agreed. "He is just a boy."

"You'd have to study for several years the way I did," Terrek teased Roth. "What do you think, Elf?"

"I believe," Ponu said, a note of reproof in his voice, "you are even harder on *laoris* than I am, Terrek Florne."

"Good." Terrek snapped his fingers in front of Roth's startled eyes. "Now hand that thing over, Lieuten—" He stopped and made a face as he fanned the air. "Wasn't it *you* who had a problem with smells?"

Roth raised the stuffed rabbit to his nostrils and shrugged. "It reminds me of flowers."

"*Flowers?*" Terrek laughed. "It's the same stench the scabbard had!"

Ponu huffed down his nose at Terrek. "That 'thing,' as you call it, is a treasure," the elf chided. "You have *no* taste when it comes to the finer things, Terrek Florne. This will do nicely to make a little boy I know very happy." He coughed. "Or it will after I use my *amazing magical powers* to neutralize that smell!"

Roth, sniffling, swiped at his cheek. "It's *not* valuable? But you said it was."

Ponu grinned and pointed to the painting Roth held. "I lied. It is no more valuable than that canvas of yours is dirty. Look again. Where are the spots and wrinkles? Why did you not trust your own perceptions of reality? The picture is pristine; anyone can see that. You have done a fine job taking care of it. Well done!"

"But I thought . . ."

"I have decided the painting belongs with you," Ponu announced. He joined Gaelin by the fire, jouncing the toy to make its ears flip. "Now tuck it away! I give it to you with an added gift, young man. Henceforth the portrait shall not wrinkle or get stained. *Ever.*"

"That was kind of you," Terrek remarked as Roth, covering his face to hide his tears, bolted to the refuge of his tent.

"He lost too much too soon," Terrek told the elf-mage after a strained silence. "His family . . . and if not for that racer of his, *he* would have died that day as well. Now my brother, his best friend, is gone. We've all lost people. In Kideren, Chalse, or Shethea . . ." He sighed. "In our haste to reach Tierdon, none of us have managed to grieve."

"I am to blame for the loss of your brother," Ponu said bitterly. "I could have stopped the whole thing from happening, but I was indisposed. I am my warder's vessel on this world. While Tierdon was being attacked I was present physically, but my senses were not. I believe"—he squinted at Gaelin—"soon you will know what I mean."

Gaelin tensed before the power of the elf's stare. "Do you have something to confess before I go?" Ponu asked. "Grevelin is waiting where I left him at the stone tree, with no cozy fire to ease his bones."

"I—" Gaelin bit his lip, his hands tingling. "I don't know what you mean."

"I saw how you both reacted," Ponu said with an oblique glance at Terrek. "After Tierdon's restoration, when I promised to bring to justice the drunkard, Seth Lavahl." He waited a beat to let his words sink in. "Your abuser is already dead, is he not? You have been wanting to reveal this fact to me since that moment. So now I am wondering. Why haven't you?"

Gaelin felt his flesh go cold. As much as he wanted to turn away, he could only stand like a stature as Ponu peered into his eyes.

"I see," Ponu responded, and Gaelin felt his muscles unclench, his ability to move return. Angrily, he averted his face, glaring at the flames.

"He was trying to kill me!" Gaelin muttered.

"You were defending yourself," Ponu said quietly. "And yet you have worried this bone ever since, fearing you are just as bad as he. *Do* you deserve punishment, child of Othelion? You were there, and I was not. You tell me."

"I wanted to live," replied Gaelin. "He had no right to do what he did. He had no *right!*"

"So let it go," Ponu advised. Gaelin released his breath slowly, feeling the mage's strong grip on his shoulder.

Chapter 28

*P*onu sprang to his feet beside Vyergin's fire and stumbled, his white wings spreading to catch his balance. "Grevelin!" the mage cried. "Oh *Hades*, no!" He hopped forward and pointed to Tierdon. "See there? Because of my carelessness, now my friend searches for me!"

"Another giant?" Terrek asked, standing. "I'm still wondering where the first one is. Why would Avalar want to hide from you?"

"Giants do not 'hide,'" said Ponu. "No doubt she is preparing to confront her father and will join soon."

Gaelin smiled when Ponu stepped to clasp his shoulder. "Cover the Skystone, Gaelin!" the elf spoke into his ear. "My friend Grevelin mustn't know you carry magic."

"Now *that* is a giant!" Vyergin said, dropping his ladle with a clatter. "Blazes, look at his sword!"

"He is Avalar's father," Ponu said, staring at Gaelin. "What did I tell you, Staff-Wielder? Stow Mornius now and be quick! This warrior is not Avalar. He has been tortured. Magic from humans has made him resentful of your—"

"*Stow?*" Gaelin gaped through his stupor at Ponu's face and at Roth emerging from the tent to peer westward into the sun. "*What?*" he demanded. "What is everyone looking at? Oh!"

Gaelin yelped as his back spasmed, a jangling pain in his muscles from the nape of his neck to his tailbone. He snatched Mornius from the ground and clambered upright, vibrations of power thrumming along his arms as he turned.

An armor-clad figure, his features indistinct, strode long-legged past the stony spires Ponu had left exposed on the field. The giant broke from the darkness cast by the city, his shadow stretching ahead of him, aiming itself at their camp.

"Terrek, you can't fight him!" Oburne said when Terrek reached for his weapon. "I *know* this giant. I fought with him! He is—"

"If you do not hide the Skystone," Ponu enunciated beside Gaelin, "Grevelin will attack you. If the giant's blood quickens fully, he can grow large and very fierce. I will not be able to stop him."

Gaelin swallowed to keep down his breakfast, the thunder in his head drowning out the elf-mage's words. Fog rose before him that he alone could see, the tree-trunks becoming translucent, the substance of the world he knew fraying. Only the giant remained solid within his sight, the big warrior's size becoming apparent as he reached the trees.

"Brace yourself, child of Othelion." Ponu raised his voice over the throbbing of blood in Gaelin's ears. "I shall do what I can for you. But I am not his keeper. I do not hold his leash."

The giant jerked to a halt and bent, his eyes scanning the forest, his right fist on the pommel of his sword. He glared through fern-stalks and the skeletons of tansy, the twisted vines of greenberry and the trunks of white saplings. A finch exploded from the brush in front of him in a tiny cloud of sparkling powder.

Gaelin felt his face go cold when the warrior's gaze, drawn by the bird, fastened on him.

"I suggest you let this thing play out, Terrek Florne," Ponu said over his shoulder. "Or I will be forced to stay your hand. And *you*, Wren Neche. You are Gaelin's guard, are you not? You must also—"

"I don't know what you are!" Wren retorted. "But you're correct; I am his guard, and I will not stay *my*—"

Gaelin risked a furtive glance back at the abrupt silence, seeing Wren crouched to spring with his weapon half-drawn, and Terrek, his elbow raised to block him. Both were motionless, as were Vyergin and Oburne, and Caven Roth poised beside the tent. Gaelin tensed, sweat trickling down his neck, the mysterious pain growing inside him.

"Ponu?" A rough voice coughed.

Stop hurting me! Gaelin wanted to shout to the giant. He froze when the burly fighter recaptured his stare. "*Humans*, Ponu?" Grevelin roared, the wind through the trees whipping back his black cloak. "You consort with *slavers*?"

Gaelin goggled at the giant's taut strength ready to rip him apart. The thunderous scowl he received in return was enough to drive him into the catatonic depths he had fled to after his mother's murder. A time when he had whimpered and whined under the she-wolf's tongue. But here he had his staff—Holram's reassuring strength pouring into him from the stone.

Gaelin stood rooted to the ground, eyeing the powerful warrior. *He's huge,* he thought, struggling to breathe despite his cramped muscles. *Avalar's head would only reach his chest!*

"Deep breaths," Ponu instructed. "You are experiencing undiluted old magic, Gaelin. The feeling will pass as your body adjusts."

"*No!*" the elf boomed at the giant. "I stand among *friends.* Come and see, Master Grevelin! The fire here is enough to thaw even *your* stubborn bones."

"*Friends?*" Grevelin stamped his feet as he prowled from side to side in front of the trees. His brawny arms were bare, crisscrossed with old scars. The black quilted leather of the giant's jerkin below his mail was hardly visible, and yet it proved to Gaelin the imposing fighter was mortal, as susceptible to the chill air as he was. Turning, Grevelin stopped and leaned over, staring into the forest, his lips drawn back in hate.

"I'm sorry," Gaelin whispered as, in his hands, Mornius flickered to life.

Ponu grunted in response. "Sails, no! Darken the stone, Staff-Wielder! If he sees—"

A bellow drowned out the mage's words. Terrified, Gaelin dropped his staff when Grevelin charged.

He shut his eyes, hearing the cracking of tree limbs and brush as the massive warrior thrashed toward him. *Death's better than pretending I'm Othelion when I'm not,* Gaelin thought. *I'd fight for them if I had to. But I can't be someone I'm—*

A hand swept him up, smashing him hard against a tree trunk. Gaelin choked as the giant's fingers constricted, forcing open his jaws. As if from a great distance, Ponu yelled. "Grev, *stop* it!"

Through a blur of tears, Gaelin saw a face resembling Avalar's before him, the same wide-spaced eyes and strong chin. He strained for air, his heart aching at the scars he glimpsed carved into the giant's flesh, so much like those marking his own.

"What did they do?" Gaelin asked as the blade's bright edge fell swiftly to nip at his throat. "What did those bastards do?"

The giant's eyes bored into him. *They're gray*, Gaelin realized, like the storm-heavy clouds he had seen over the mountains.

"Please, Father, *stop*!" called a familiar voice. A filthy apparition stepped around a tree to take hold of Grevelin's cloak. It was Avalar, Gaelin realized, her clothing and skin coated with freezing mud. "Father, no! Behold his scars. Are they not familiar?"

"I look upon *you*!" Grevelin Mistavere returned, his teeth bared. He nodded at the dead ivy Avalar had wound around her neck and wrists, the intertwining links she had woven to resemble chains.

"And what do you *see*?" Avalar challenged. "If I am your slave to drag home against my will, should I not appear as one? Will you compel me by force, as you do to my friend? *Behold*, Father! There are bruises under your fingers. Is *this* what giants do? He was enslaved as you were!"

Gaelin doubled his fists in helpless shame as his captor flipped back his sleeve to examine his scars. "How can this be?" Grevelin asked. "Held against his will?"

"Yes, Gaelin was held, Father!" Avalar replied. "His mother was butchered, and he was enslaved. By *humans*! Now please let him go. Twice his power has healed me. I would not be alive if it were not for him."

"A human enslaved by humans?" The warrior glanced down at Ponu. "This is sooth?"

Gaelin sucked in air as the giant's grip loosened around his throat. "If you are not ..." Grevelin began. His body slumped, weighed down by sadness. "Pardon me, for I am not who I was. Have I harmed you?"

"I'm used to it." Gaelin smiled at Avalar. "Your daughter has attacked me twice, though *she* never held a blade at my throat."

Grevelin set him on his feet. "Ah, well," he said, a glimmer of humor softening his eyes. "She has the kindly heart of her mother, the healer Alaysha. I fear for her now because of it. How will she fare in combat?"

Gaelin's legs folded beneath him until he sat on the ground, his knees splayed. "Last night she battled to save me," he informed the worried giant. "She is my friend."

"You are injured," said Grevelin.

Gaelin glanced up. "No, just tired."

"I hear fondness for my daughter in your voice. Is this not a danger?" Grevelin demanded of Ponu. "If the young one bonds with this human, indeed, it would shorten her life!"

Ponu sniffed. "I considered that, Master. She came very close to it with a different man, but sadly, he has died. I do not think she will allow herself such weakness again."

"She cannot choose," Grevelin said. "She is *laori*, as I am; her wild heart will do as it will!"

Ponu stepped in front of Terrek, peering into the immobile commander's raging eyes. "You are angry I took control from you and your men," he observed. "Like a slaver. Do you understand how attacking a giant would threaten us all? Perhaps Talenkai would endure it if Avalar were to perish. But Grevelin Mistavere is fully grown. The world could not survive his loss. None of us would."

"That little warrior would never harm me," Grevelin said with a snort and a gesture to Wren. "With one hand tied, I could rend him limb from limb and scatter his bones!"

"Yes, you're *very* strong," Ponu said. He glowered at Terrek. "He is Avalar's father. See his scars? Humans with magic did that. Now Avalar is back and no one is hurt. You need to relax, Terrek Florne."

Gaelin felt himself falling. *I can't sleep yet*, he thought when his cheek hit the ground. *I want to hear this.*

"Your Staff-Wielder is reacting to the tagwort I gave him," Ponu said above him. "He is undamaged. Now you—"

"I'm fine, Terrek," Gaelin muttered. He frowned at the loudness of his words in his ears. "My neck's a little sore. My tongue is—"

"You and your men will put away your weapons," Ponu said, ignoring him. "And you will *control* Wren Neche."

Terrek stumbled when the elf released him with a flick of the fingers. Turning, he swung his arm at his bewildered men. "Back to the fires," he ordered. "Go and get yourselves warm!"

Gaelin shut his eyes, listening to the activity around him. Then someone touched his hair.

"Leave us, Elf," Terrek said sharply. "Take your friend—I don't care if he *is* Avalar's father, he has threatened my man—and go. We are done here."

"Terrek, you can't!" Jahn Oburne protested. "That is Grevelin Mistavere!"

Terrek faced Ponu. "I ask you to depart, or we *will* defend ourselves," he said. "Twice now, Elf, you've put my men in danger. If the dach forces had come, we would have all been captured or killed."

"No, I would have revived you to fight them, of course," Ponu replied. "Yet I shall do as you wish, Terrek Florne. Master Grevelin, there is a little boy I know who must want his breakfast. Shall we withdraw?"

"My daughter—" Grevelin began.

"I am not *yours*," Avalar cut him off. "Do these chains I bear teach you nothing, Father? Or does it suit you to see me as your slave?"

Gaelin moaned. *Don't go, Ponu*, his heart ached to say. *There's so much I still need to—*

"Gaelin is sleeping," Avalar announced above his ear. "I shall bear my *friend* now to his blankets. For, indeed, he is my friend until you decide to take him away from me, Father. If you do so, it will not help me."

Gaelin smiled, feeling a strong hand slip beneath him and raise him up. He was little again, cradled to his mother's chest. A palm caressed his cheek; he heard the soft rustle of the tent's flap being folded back.

"What have I done for you to hate me so much, my daughter?"

"*Hate?*" Avalar retorted. "I *love* you, Father. Do you think I wish to hurt you? I do not!"

"Here," she crooned to Gaelin as she ducked into the tent. "Be at rest, my gallant friend. I saw what you did. You braved Ponu's fire as he was rebuilding Tierdon, and you tried to get him to stop. I shall not forget!"

Gaelin rolled onto his side on the comfortable pad that served as his bed. He reached out his arm as she drew up his blankets. "Don't go away," he begged. "I need you."

"He is my father," Avalar responded, bending to kiss his forehead. "If he commands me, I must go. But I dressed this way so mayhap he will not. Soon we shall know. My father has a good heart, Staff-Wielder."

Gaelin drifted, spinning like a twig in a powerful current. Somewhere outside the tent's sun-dappled walls, he could hear Avalar defending her right to remain on Thalus—to answer the song of a sword she called Redeemer.

How is it that staves or swords can sing? Gaelin wondered. *I hear it everywhere now. Mornius's song is in me.*

"No, Terrek Florne is my leader and I intend to shield him against harm," Avalar insisted. "I do not burden him or anyone else! I strive to protect my world as a giant should!"

"We safeguard each other," Terrek agreed quietly.

"I want her here, too," Gaelin, alone in his tent, muttered to himself.

"*Fear not,*" Holram's voice reassured in his head. "*Your friend will prevail and she will stay.*" Gaelin nodded and turned onto his stomach, the black velvet of slumber covering his sight.

∞ ∞ ∞

GAELIN JERKED AS a hand patted his cheek. Groaning softly, he opened his eyes wide at the sight of Ponu's face.

"Shh!" the elf-mage hissed. "I am not supposed to be here. I took Grevelin home, but I returned, for I sense you still have questions for me."

Gaelin smiled when he caught the sound of Avalar's bubbling laugh. "She's still here! I was so afraid . . ."

Ponu grunted. "Of *that* one leaving? It broke her father's heart to see her like that, as she knew it would. No, she is here. Nothing will make her go until she is ready."

"What *are* you?" Gaelin asked. "You're not like the Seekers I met. Are you immortal?"

"I am an alien, just as you are," Ponu told him. "I came from a different place, arriving here fifty some years before the giants broke free. My homeworld, Chorahn, was a time portal, and my people were the first elves. We explored other worlds. During our travels, we achieved great things, and we left our seed behind. Talenkai's elves, the Seekers and the Khanal, the Eris and Starians . . . I am like their father. They sense this and fear me.

"We dabbled on your world also, Gaelin," he confessed. "For a time, you made us your gods, but it was tiresome for us and damaging to you, so we stopped. That was when you began to make your own crueler gods in your image."

Gaelin stared at the elf. "Does that mean I am . . . ?"

"Indeed it does," Ponu said. "We tampered with your species as well. Not all humans, but enough. Which is why your people are conflicted. Some of you behave in ways that seem alien or primitive to others of your kind. Seth Lavahl, for example. If not for the blood of my people, humans would have perished long ago. You would have destroyed each other."

"Why can't *you* save the world?" Gaelin whispered. "I'm not powerful. I don't know . . . I can't even . . ." He closed his eyes.

"It isn't what you know. It's what you have right here," Ponu said. Then Gaelin felt Ponu's hand on his chest, its weight pressing firmly at his heart.

Chapter 29

elrina peered into the depths of her father's frightened eyes. She covered his fumbling fingers with her own, cradling them in her lap. "You cannot be serious," she said. "You had Mornius and *lost* it? Such a failure as that would warrant immediate—"

"You think I don't know it?" Nithra snuffled back blood, the pinched lines deepening on his brow. "I tried to use my staff. I waited for Erebos to smite the giant through it, but he did nothing, so I *ran*. What else could I do?"

"Erebos requires the *Blazenstone* to focus through, Father," Felrina reminded him. "The bloodstone on your staff would only expand his power; that's all. I would have needed to be there with Erebos's crystal for him to help. Why didn't you tell us you were going?"

"I watched Mens attack Kideren, and all he used was the world's blood, the same red gem my staff has. I was there, Rina. He destroyed our city with that staff. It's identical to mine, so why couldn't I . . . ?"

"That wasn't Erebos's power," she said. "Father, we've been over this before. Mens uses the old magic from this world, not Erebos, remember? That's why he's damaged now."

Sitting back in her chair by his bed, Felrina regarded the low ceiling, the damp, inward-slanting walls around them. Nithra's tiny chamber was colder and closer to the mountain's exterior than the other rooms she was used to. "Father, if what you're saying is true, you have little time left. Erebos will hunt for you. He'll want you punished. That he hasn't already . . ."

Nithra pressed a rag to his bloody nose. "Of course, I'll be slain, my daughter, and it'll be slow. Unless you kill me now, beautiful one. Can you—" He stopped at her groan. "Shame on me for asking such a thing!" he chided himself. "No, Mens will drag it out as long as he can; he's always hated me. There's nothing we can do. Erebos listens to Mens. You, little Rina, he'll force you to watch, I'm sure. Or he'll have you do the deed. That would be like him."

Felrina clung to his hand. "Why did you go? You had nothing to prove. You—"

"A father gets tired of humiliating his child," Nithra answered gruffly. "I wanted you to be proud of me like you used to be. I'd come home and you'd run out to welcome me. I never see that look from you anymore, not since this whole thing started."

"If anyone should be ashamed, it should be me! I got you into this, Father. You didn't want to be here. You did it for *me!*" she cried. "I can't let him kill you!"

"Shh, Felrina!" Nithra sprang from his straw mattress and rushed to his staff, covering its bloodstone crystal with the soiled cloth. Then he froze, glancing sidelong at her Blazenstone. "Oh, what's the use? I'm as good as dead right now."

"Father, I . . ."

"No." Nithra sank to his knees in front of her. "Listen to me. *This* is the reality of our beliefs. It is a test. A burden we must bear. You still believe, don't you, my child? You're the one who convinced me!"

"I try to," she admitted. "But every day I catch myself doubting more."

"*Never* question!" Her father bent near, his red-stained nose a finger's length from her own. "Erebos hears what you say. Maybe that's why he wouldn't help me with the giant. If he senses *your* doubts, our great lord may have been—" Nithra grunted at her expression. "No, that's not right, either. I'm a fool. What can I say? But do try to have faith, Felrina. Think of it this way; our god needs blood to create our new world, and I will give him that. I will die and he will feed. What better death is there for an old man like me?"

Felrina stroked his hand. "In that other world you go to, will you build us a place like the home we used to have? Make it so the Florne boys can visit, too, when all is done, and we can be young together like we used to be before . . . before I betrayed them *and* you."

"You betrayed no one!" he insisted. "They're lost; that's all. And

211

none of that's your fault. There's so much promise, so much beauty in the wake of death, but they cannot see it, for they are blind. Felrina!" She shut her eyes as his calloused hand stroked her cheek. "For your sake, you must abandon that dream. The man you love is doomed. Terrek Florne will never believe until it stares him in the face. Erebos came to Earth to free us. If not for the . . . enemy opposing him, we'd already *be* in our forever home!"

"You mean Holram!" Felrina coughed, a sour taste like venom on her tongue. "I hate him, Father! It's his fault Terrek despises me. And now I'm going to lose *you*, too. And soon I'll have no—"

Felrina broke off at a light tap on the door. A timid voice called, "Nithra Vlyn?"

As her father straightened, Felrina extricated herself from his grasp and moved to the doorway. With dread, she drew back the bolt.

Her gray-robed apprentice stood in the tunnel, his gaze darting to her father. "Erebos summons Nithra. And you also, Mistress Vlyn, to the chamber above the pool."

"We hear you." Felrina took her father's hand. "And we come."

$$\infty \quad \infty \quad \infty$$

"STAFF-WIELDER!" WREN'S voice shouted.

Gaelin stirred where he lay on his back, licking his lips and frowning at the drug's taste in his mouth. "*It will help you rest,*" Ponu's words echoed in his mind and Gaelin grimaced, recalling how in his greedy hunger he had emptied his bowl.

"*Wake up, Gaelin!*" Holram alerted him, the warder's thoughts filling his head from the staff.

Raucous cries and the clanging of metal drew closer. Gaelin flung off his covers. Seeing combatants wrestling outside the door, he struggled to sit up. When one of them fell against the tent, Gaelin scuttled from the pad he had slept on, the canvas sagging above him. Choking down vomit, he gripped his belly at the wet sound of steel carving flesh, the plink of blades against bone. Pressure mounted in his throat. His arm was moving against his will to seize his staff. It was Holram, reaching to possess his body. "*Walk!*" the being commanded. "*Rouse yourself so I may help . . .*"

Gaelin started. His feet were shuffling along beneath him, his arm using his staff for support. *How did I get here?* he wondered, taking in the sight of his spattered and dripping tunic, the gory snow freezing his unshod feet. *When did I leave the—*

"*I brought you out,*" Holram informed him inwardly. "*You would have been pinned under your shelter. Now you must surrender to me, Gaelin! The time has come!*"

The world canted as Gaelin strove to keep his balance, gawking at Terrek's fighters battling among the camp's ruins, the carnage between the tents, and the warriors and ponies already torn apart. The dachs were swooping in to snatch the men and carry them off. Then a second wave of wings crashed down, so many of the warped humans he could no longer see the snow.

He spotted Terrek cut off from his men, his right arm dangling useless, Roth and Silva at his side struggling to defend him. "Terrek, I'm coming!" Gaelin cried. He lurched forward, desperate to join his friend. He howled when his legs buckled, pitching him onto his chest.

"Lavahl!" Wren Neche burst out of a tattered shelter to his left. Gaelin rolled onto his knees as the young fighter chopped and flailed his way over to him to help him stand.

"You didn't wake me!" Gaelin accused. With a furious shout, Wren sprang past him, hacking at a gray rush of bodies wielding swords.

"I tried!" Wren grunted as he parried a blow. "When your tent collapsed under all those dachs, I thought you were dead!"

Gaelin held his breath, dazzled by a sudden flash, Holram's crackling sphere of power springing into existence around him. Through it he spied an enormous dach landing in front of Terrek, its falchion poised above its misshapen skull. As the hulking creature swung its weapon, Gaelin yelled to Silva and Roth guarding Terrek's back, "Behind you!" He sobbed as the big dach's saber shattered Terrek's lifted sword, then swept to hew through his mail and ribs.

Silva, lunging at Terrek's attacker, tottered to a stop and sank down, blood spurting from his neck.

"No! Let me *go*!" Gaelin cried as Holram slowed his movements. He scrambled toward an ax buried in a drift, a warrior's severed hand still clinging to its haft. Mornius grew heavier, demanding both his arms to keep it from dragging on the muddy ground. He wanted to run, to grab the nearby weapon and use it, but the staff held him back. He saw Terrek clutching at his midriff, calling out even as a howling mob of creatures threw themselves upon him, hiding him from Gaelin's view.

"No!" Gaelin heaved his weighty staff up, stumbling forward as the oversized dach stabbed Roth in the back. The young man's face turned ashen, his eyes unseeing above the falchion's protruding tip. His muscles slack, he dropped from the blade, vanishing as Terrek had beneath the horde.

More dachs hastened down out of the branches, their sharp claws gouging the rough bark, their weapons biting flesh as they swarmed at the few men struggling to battle on.

"*Holram, help!*" Gaelin shouted mentally to his warder. He slumped onto his haunches. "*I need you. Why haven't you healed them?*"

"*Stop resisting me!*" Holram thundered back.

Beside him Wren, still trying to protect him, crashed to his knees, holding up his blade to shield his face.

"Wren, get under my magic!" Gaelin yelled and at the sound of his voice, the dachs by the ruined tents pivoted as one, their attention shifting to him at last inside the shimmer of Mornius's fire.

Gaelin stared toward the trees past his enemies. Avalar's angry cries had stopped, he realized. Then Wren slipped as he came near. The guard's head was yanked back by a winged figure landing behind him, the creature's saber flashing down to cleave his skull.

Gaelin closed his eyes as Wren fell. *It's over*, he grieved. *They're dead. All my friends . . .*

"*Now, will you surrender?*" Holram, exasperated, spoke through his thoughts. "*Death and murder. Without fail, it seems the human solution; in that way you are not unlike my foe.*"

Gaelin sighed, his body quivering. The same power that had rescued him from his trampled tent was waiting to take him, as it had been all along. The warder's changing shape appeared to him in the fog as he transitioned without effort, his consciousness drifting into the Skystone's inner realm, his despairing mind unable to resist.

Impressions of teeth filled his vision. The horde of scaly dachs surrounded him and raised him up, flinging his body like a rag doll above their heads. He felt himself smiling, for Holram's lion's shape filled his sight, pulling him into its gaze of gold.

His staff dropped from his hand. He had lost it, or the creatures had taken it from his grasp—he did not know or care. There was only the hissing wind in his ears and Holram's triumphant roar when the lion possessed him fully—to draw a first breath through him as a living being.

Everywhere Gaelin looked, fire blasted, lashing silver at the frozen land. It came from himself as well as from his staff lying inert by the trees—from his own chest and his screaming mouth.

His sight was the lion's, perceiving everything, his mortal heart burning with Holram's rage. Squealing, his assailants tumbled away in all directions, their limbs writhing in the heatless inferno the warder made. Gaelin nodded. No longer did he feel pain or fear. Time as he knew it stopped, as healing streamed across Tierdon's valley.

Men were climbing to their feet out of the bloody slush. He saw Terrek approaching him, whole in body and stretching out his hands.

Gaelin's pulse resumed its steady rhythm in his throat. He remembered to breathe when his lungs craved air; Holram allowed him that much—involuntary movements to keep his flesh alive. Yet now the lion's fierceness crouched in him, the memory of its roar echoing through his head. Gaelin accepted the warder's embrace, slipping with ease into the background of himself.

Chapter 30

*A*valar, sweat stinging in her eyes, penetrated deep through the press of dach bodies, her blade skewering two before she yanked her arm back. Her father's words echoed in her head: "*Even breaths, child! Aim true and never flail—there! Now, again!*"

She set aside her anger as he had so often urged. *This is what I was born to do*, she thought, and parried swiftly to deflect a strike. *Defending the vulnerable. That is why giants exist!*

A saber's tip nicked her thigh between the straps of her cuisse. With a howl, she whirled to protect her injured leg, dragging her heavy weapon around for more.

These creatures feel nothing, she realized, seeing her attacker's confused expression as it slumped over her hilt, the weight of its body sliding slowly from her blade.

She stabbed through a winged dach's belly, then chopped off its leg below the knee, the frail bone splitting beneath her blow. The throb of her heart and the heat of her blood spurred her on, her limbs growing strong and sure. Onward she fought, her sword cleaving the skull of one creature, the momentum of her strike opening the abdomen of yet another.

As she sprang past the gore, she caught an image in her head of a figure behind the trees, his cruel face leering at her, his features from her very worst dreams. It was her magic, she realized, warning her of danger.

She searched for him among her enemies even as more magic-warped humans scrabbled from the branches, their primitive sabers gleaming. A chill at the nape of her neck alerted her. Turning, she froze, staring as the familiar black-robed wizard strode confidently toward her.

Meeting her gaze, he placed himself between two trees, his cloak billowing back as he raised up his staff, aiming its teardrop-shaped gem straight at her.

She groaned, doubling over in sudden pain. Then, with a flick of a gesture, he sent her stumbling. She tripped on a corpse and fell.

"*Avalar!*" Oburne's furry cloak rippled as he floundered to her aid. "Sails take you!" he cursed when he came up short, a knot of flightless dachs cutting across his path and shoving him back.

Cowering, Avalar glanced up, repulsed by the sense of wrong the human brought with him, the fully mastered bloodstone mounted on his staff. She screamed when the power-hungry gem seemed to swell within its prongs, the crystal humming as it fed, gorging on the life force in her flesh.

Blood filled her mouth as she clawed at her chest, helplessly falling onto her side.

"Now you die!" her enemy said from behind her shoulders. "And after that, my god, Erebos, will be forced to act, won't he? He'll have no choice; your world will be shattered to its core.

"Do you know who I am?" he drawled. "I am the slayer of Tierdon. Allastor Mens!"

Groaning, Avalar kicked desperately as blood sprayed from her throat. The mage was harvesting her magic with his stone, the pressure of it stretching her bones apart. She was being turned inside out like so many of her people before her, and it was agony.

"*Mine!*"

Avalar glimpsed a tawny blur leaping over her, the lean, gray-dappled prowler springing from the forest to knock the wizard flat. Still moaning, Avalar rolled onto her back as the she-prowler crouched next to her, the predator unhinging her jaws to fasten on the black-robe's scrawny neck. Allastor Mens let out a gurgling wail.

The stone of his staff erupted, a rising sheet of midnight shadow blotting out the dawn. The breath whooshed out of Shetra's lungs, and as her burnt body thudded to the ground, Avalar gagged at the stench of charred fur.

Terrek shouted from beyond the trees, and looking toward him, Avalar saw more creatures flitting from the branches with their sabers flashing, driving her leader and two other men before them. Then a swirl of ebony robes blocked Terrek from her sight. Allastor

Mens stopped in front of her with his eyes afire, blood streaming from his wounds. She screamed when he touched his staff's gem to her forehead, the stone adhering to her skin, greedily devouring her strength.

"Avalar!"

It was Terrek's voice, so much like his brother's, calling for her aid. Angrily, she slapped aside the bloodstone and scrambled to her knees. *You already killed Camron*, she raged silently at her attacker. *You will not slay his brother, too*!

Allastor Mens regarded her with a smug smile, his hooked nose level with her own. Glowering back in utter contempt, Avalar hauled herself erect and brandished her sword. "Govorian *take* you!" she howled.

The mage stopped her with a gesture. Avalar glanced where he pointed, seeing Terrek, her leader's face bone white, clutching at his injured arm.

"So dies the fool, Terrek Florne," the black-robe mocked.

Lunging with her weapon, her fury compensating for the weakness of her muscles, Avalar slashed at the mage's hated face. She struck a blow for Camron and Terrek, and for her people long dead—to find empty air, her blade whistling unimpeded through the place where Mens had stood.

She wept as Terrek sank from her view among the horde, his two companions along with him. *Too late*! she thought in despair. *Oh, Terrek*!

A groan drew her to the side of the dying prowler.

Shetra's amber eyes met hers, the predator's nose wrinkling as she coughed in pain. "Giant . . . well?" she asked.

"No." Avalar stayed the creature's wrist. *It is better this way*, she thought, *kinder for Shetra*. Below the she-prowler's chest, an oily liquid sizzled and popped, the warped magic dissolving Shetra's flesh and bone beneath the blackened skin.

Shetra sniffed. "Yeesh!" she spat. "Smell she-prowler?"

"You saved my life," Avalar said thickly. "You were so brave to fight for me."

The prowler's lips curled back. "Sephrym . . . command," she gritted. "Watch giant. Defend! Give ball with fish, so I follow. I protect! Is . . . good?"

"Yes." Avalar's voice broke. "It was very kind of you. You saved me as . . . as any *giant* would!"

"Prowler follow," Shetra whispered. "Protect . . ." She went rigid, her spine arching. With a sigh, she fell limp, her fierce, golden eyes growing dull.

Holding the prowler close, Avalar stroked Shetra's lifeless cheek, this friend who had so discreetly watched over her. At any moment the wedge of dachs would complete their work. *They think the wizard finished me.* Avalar shook her head. *When they realize I am alive . . . I cannot hope to fight so many!*

Through the dripping tangle of her hair, she spied a figure among the trees. Power streamed from his slight form, vibrating through the air to tingle on her skin. *No,* she decided. Calmly she leaned forward to settle the prowler's dead weight. Here and now, it would end. She would kill this menace, this mage who had destroyed Tierdon!

Allastor Mens! Now that she knew it, her heart pounded with the rhythm of his name. *Slayer!*

She crouched as the human advanced toward the site of Terrek's fall. She identified the staff gleaming in his hands, Mornius's multicolored stone flashing as his voice slurred out two words: "Holram, *come!*"

"*Gaelin!*" Avalar whispered.

A rush of dachs swarmed at her as another horde surrounded him. The staff-wielder's eyes were open, and yet he flopped like a dead thing when the mob lifted him up, the creatures tossing his body above their heads. *Why is he not fighting?* Avalar wondered. *Great Sephrym, has he surrendered?*

She jumped as a rope settled around her neck, jerking her off her feet. Reaching up, Avalar tugged back hard—to haul the three dachs lifting her within the reach of her sword.

Blood soaked her hair. She landed in the mud and stumbled, the contorted bodies of her winged assailants thudding down dead beside her. Another dach, running full tilt, rammed her in the belly with its knobby skull. She collapsed, retching. Then the ground heaved beneath her. A silent detonation followed, sharp granules from the trees flaying her skin.

Steam filled the air. A white fire blasted, surging in wave after crackling wave between the tents. She dropped her sword, her arms shielding her face. In a slow kind of amazement, she peered through a protective haze that reached her from the staff, watching as her foes toppled away from her, their wings and tails thrashing.

A second eruption drowned out the first. She saw writhing dachs everywhere she looked, the creatures huddled in groups struggling onto their knees, crawling together through a swath of icy flame.

The sheets of energy crackled upward, a brightness as fierce as a sun. Within the glare, she beheld a lone figure.

Gaelin Lavahl.

She stared at the transforming dachs wading through his magic toward him. Their bodies shrank under his power, their wings, spines, and tails melting into their flesh, the angry lines of their hardened scales softening back to skin.

How can this be? Avalar thought. *They are humans again, healthy and . . .* She gasped as she recognized a face, a young man climbing to his feet, his eyes bewildered. *The artist who painted my picture!*

Close by her, the prowler was moving, coming alive in shudders and starts. As Avalar watched in awe, Shetra batted with a tentative paw at the vapor lingering where her wound had been.

Avalar held her breath as the world stopped trembling, as the power's lurid radiance faded within the camp and among the splintered trees. The former dachs, naked and confused, blundered past her through the clammy mud. As she watched, the people pressed together shivering in the merciless cold, their glad cries changing to wails as they desperately fought to get warm.

"Gaelin?" someone called.

Avalar rubbed at her eyes and looked up. Terrek, his sleeve stained with blood, stooped over his friend. Below him Gaelin sat unresponsive in the ooze, his legs splayed.

"Can you help these people?" Terrek was asking the staff-wielder to no avail. "Gaelin?" Terrek shook him. "*Gaelin!*"

Terrek stepped back and straightened his shoulders. "*Roth!*" he rapped out. "The Eris village isn't far. Ride south and west of the trail that brought us here! The elves live at the foot of Mount Alianth. You'll make out their fires once you cross. Tell them we need blankets, food, and clothing. Ask if they have shelters or anything they can spare!"

As Roth sprinted toward the two remaining horses tethered by the trampled tents, Terrek hastened to Avalar. "All that magic!" he exclaimed, sliding to a stop before her. "How did you endure it, Giant? Are you hurt?"

Avalar peered at her bloody mail and her mended thigh the dach had cut. "I am healed," she said. Dazed, she probed beneath her jerkin. "I do not understand. Gaelin's magic never touched me."

"*Good.*" Terrek gestured to Shetra. "What about . . . ? That's a magical creature. Is it a danger?" He frowned at Shetra's toothy smile. "Oh, never mind," he said. "Avalar, we must do what we can for these people. *Now,* before they freeze! I must find Vyergin.

"*Oburne!*" he called as the warrior stomped by them. "Form a crew from those who are able. Get those shelters up fast!"

"There are at least a hundred people," Oburne protested. "And only—"

"We'll have to pack them in," said Terrek. "Getting them warm; that's our priority. Vyergin has a crate of blankets and clothing on one of the sleds. Dig through the packs of our men who are missing. Distribute their bedding and provisions. Have Silva forage while you rekindle those fires. *Look* at them, Jahn. These are victims now; they deserve our compassion."

"Vyergin's better at this. Where is he? *Silva!*" Oburne bellowed to a distant black-armored figure. "Find Wren Neche!"

Avalar met Shetra's curious regard while Terrek crouched at Gaelin's side. The prowler huffed between her teeth, her whiskers flaring. "Heem *bossy,*" she said. "Human leader?"

"Yes, beautiful one," Avalar affirmed, watching Terrek position Gaelin at the base of a tree and try to rouse him. Then, getting no response, Terrek straightened Gaelin's legs.

Shetra yawned, flicking her long red tail. "Heem sick?" she asked.

"I know not," Avalar said. She strode to the tent she shared with Jahn Oburne and groped within until she grasped her Sundor Khan cloak. Carrying it to Gaelin, she went to work, tucking its folds behind him and covering his legs.

"I don't understand," Terrek told her. "He doesn't answer me."

Avalar rolled to her knees. Gaelin slumped, his features slack, his dull stare directed past her.

"Maybe it was too much for him," said Terrek. "He was already ill. He didn't kill them this time. He *restored* them!"

She caught Gaelin's chin and raised it, forcing his eyes into the light. "Sails," she whispered. She turned, leaning her forehead on Terrek's shoulder until he pulled away.

"Giant, what is it?"

"Nothing . . ." The word fluttered in her throat like a wounded bird. "He is gone. Gaelin is gone!"

"*No!*" The cry issued from Gaelin's lips.

Avalar jerked back as Terrek stood to grip the staff-wielder's shoulders. "What?" he demanded. "Talk to me. I've heard your voice before. Who are you?"

"I am the music!" Gaelin's mouth twitched oddly as the words boomed from his throat, reminding Avalar of a puppet she had seen at solstice fair. "The singer of Mornius remains with you, and you know him," the speaker said. "But the time has come for you to meet another. I am Holram, the *song*."

Chapter 31

*H*olram grimaced at the bitter taste of the medicine in Gaelin's mouth as he compelled his young host to smile. He peered across the valley where Roth had galloped his stallion. Now, as Roth returned, his steel-gray horse dancing nervously, he brought behind him a procession of elves.

Holram scowled. *I did not expect this*, he thought upon seeing the Eris. *I have missed these elves.* He straightened Gaelin's shoulders, recalling how the forest's defenders had once served him, helping him to endure his separation from the stars.

The Eris came riding with stoic stiffness on their wide-backed beasts, the bells tied to the creatures' manes jingling softly.

The little shan the Eris chose to ride were as colorful as he remembered, with splotches of orange or crimson on their withers and shaggy chests and horizontal brown or red stripes down their stumpy legs. Each broad head was hooded with black, matching the ends of their tufted tails.

The animals squealed and fretted, their rounded ears swiveling and their yellowed teeth bared, their upright manes rippling in the wind.

Terrek intercepted Roth as the lieutenant reined in his lathered horse. With his hand on the stallion's shoulder, Terrek greeted the elves.

Holram struggled to shuffle Gaelin's feet, to manipulate his borrowed body to the place where Avalar stood, her expression wary as she surveyed the approaching strangers.

The giant searched his face. "*Gaelin?*"

"He is sleeping," Holram said. "I, alone, control this body. It is a difficult task. Creatures of flesh make motion seem so effortless, but it is not."

"Shetra is gone," Avalar said bitterly, speaking to the frigid air above him. "The prowler defended you when I could not. She knew I would falter. Now bid Gaelin to wake up!"

Holram sensed his lips curling. "I regret I cannot," he said.

"I need my friend," Avalar responded, knuckling away her tears. "And he is *not* you!"

She whirled and stormed off.

I did that, he realized sadly, watching her slip among the trees. *I am responsible.*

Holram shivered. Though Gaelin's mind was slumbering, his flesh was awake and aware, the winter's chill creeping into his bones. Holram, unaccustomed to his host's vulnerability to cold, stood in the icy wind. *I want to move like humans do*, he thought. *Without dragging my feet.*

The directions from his brain raced through his nerves to his lower appendages. *Foot out! Out and push!*

Holram started as Gaelin's left leg jerked parallel to the ground. His torso reared back when his right foot followed, and then he was falling, landing hard on his rump.

He gaped as a tangled thatch of red hair rose from the wedge of white between his splayed legs. A furrowed brow climbed next into his view, followed by two piercing eyes.

"Interesting," remarked Argus, his crooked mouth half-hidden by the snow. He wriggled his phantom mustache and sniffed.

Holram tried to glare, which widened the dead knight's grin. His full lips twitching, the specter looked Gaelin over. "Troubles?" he queried at last. "You've escaped the Skystone; well done! But I must say, I am not impressed by this new mode of transportation."

"Lord Argus," Holram addressed the ghostly head. "How did you convey yourself when you were alive?"

Argus smirked. "'*Convey*'?" He snorted. "You mean walk? I thought you gods knew everything."

"No 'god' would get itself in this position." Holram shifted Gaelin's hips, marveling that he managed to do so. "Please instruct me, old friend. I do not know how to stand up."

Flashing him a toothy grin, Argus sank down again until just the mop of his hair remained above the snow.

"*This is ridiculous,*" Holram thought to his drowsy human. "*Gaelin, please wake.*"

Then hands gripped Gaelin's body and hauled it erect. Holram swayed for a moment, focusing on his knee joints that threatened to buckle. From the corner of his sight, he spotted a face, a man in black armor scowling fiercely. "Wren Neche," he acknowledged. "On Earth, your surname meant 'friend.'"

"I lost track of you," Wren said.

Concentrating hard, Holram turned Gaelin's head. "Which fighters have been lost?" he asked.

"Captain Vyergin's missing, and Terrek fears the worst," Wren said. "Of the few we had to begin with, ten remain, myself included. The rest—"

"Have joined the dance," Holram finished, addressing the pain in Wren's voice. "And one day their ashes will help birth new stars. I regret I cannot restore life to bodies torn to pieces. I have limitations, as all mortals do."

Wren seized him by the neck, clasping him hard. "Whatever you are," he hissed, "give some thought to what we've done here. How many of us have died for you? Too many, if you ask me."

Holram frowned, concerned by Gaelin's quickened respiration. His host's consciousness was stirring at last, flinching away as if stung.

"*Vyergin's lost?*" Gaelin's grief bubbled from his dreams.

"Now *that* voice, I recognize," said Wren. "He sounds hurt. What have you done to him?"

"I have 'done' nothing except save his life, *and* yours," Holram said. "Your companion requires rest after his ordeal. I am giving him that. I comfort him, Wren Neche."

Wren glowered. "I don't trust you!"

Lord Argus floated up from the base of a tree, laughing and spreading his arms. "Turn around, O supreme exalted one," he boomed. "Your doubters are coming. Time to prove who you are!"

Holram glanced at the apparition with what he hoped was a quizzical expression. He continued to eye the ghost until Wren, with a cough, gripped Gaelin's shoulders and spun him around.

The forest elves drew near, a formation of five elders with someone Holram recognized at their head. It was Kildoren, the same skinny boy who had frequented his temple prior to his transference into the staff. After six hundred cycles, the elven imp was not so young. Gray strands cut through his long black hair, matching the ruffled fur of his parka. Fine lines crinkled his temples, enhancing his stern expression.

"I tried to change his mind," Terrek said from behind the solemn group. "But he insisted. He wanted to see you for himself."

The small company of elves stopped and stared.

"It is true, then?" Kildoren asked. He lifted his arms with his palms turned upward—and Holram recalled how the elves could connect to the air with their nerves to read its magic, the Circle's vibrations allowing them to feel beyond the range of their other senses.

Holram nodded. It was how the elves had recognized when he first arrived that he was unlike his foe. Smiling, he inhaled Kideren's spicy scent. For the first time, he understood smell as humans experienced it. It reminded him of fire, the birthing place of stars. He gestured to the elf's parted fingers. "What does the wind tell you?"

Kildoren's green eyes went wide below his glistening hair as he mouthed, "*Tiava*," the elven word for father, and stumbled forward.

Holram embraced the onetime orphan until Kildoren shuddered and pulled away. With dignity, the elf stepped back to rejoin his people. Placing one hand over the small of his back, he bent from his waist.

The other elves bowed low beside their chieftain, their faces placid beneath their furry hoods.

Holram strained to tilt Gaelin's body forward as well to show his respect, but his host would not bend at the middle. Abruptly the snow came rushing to meet him, the cold engulfing his human face. Kicking hard, he shuddered at the chill, grainy whiteness against his skin.

"You're doing it!" said Argus's voice, and Holram spied a greenish glow in the snow beside his head. "Now, do the same thing standing up, and you'll be walking!"

A firm grasp seized Gaelin's hips and yanked, and then Holram was upright again, teetering in front of Terrek, frigid water dripping from his nose as he sneezed. "What did I do wrong?" he asked.

"Great Warder," Kildoren said, "are you well?"

Holram nodded. "These others need rest, Leader Kildoren. Will your people shelter them?"

"Of course," the elf responded, beaming with pride while he went on to describe how his village had prospered. Holram half listened as he tried to read Terrek's expression. The commander had turned away, his attention fixed on the trampled space where so many of his men had lost their lives.

"You will come?" Kildoren gestured to his unseen village to the south. "Please, great Warder. This flesh you inhabit requires rest and sustenance. Give us this honor. Let us provide for you once more."

"We need a way around Alianth peak," Terrek said. "Is there anyone in your village who could guide us?"

"The Shukaia River will lead you," Kildoren replied. "It runs through the gorge near our village that you can follow down the mountain. But alas, it is too dangerous now. You must wait until spring. The river crosses a valley more than thrice the size of this one. It will bring you close to the city of Shattan, which I caution you is also dead. After which you will reach an immense forest and beyond it the Skywhite Peaks, and Mount Chesna, where Erebos dwells."

As Terrek appraised the elf, Holram sensed him gathering himself to protest, his anger and exhaustion rising to the surface.

With a soft mental touch through his Skystone, Holram bid Terrek not to speak. "Have you visited Warder's Fall where I first landed?" Holram asked Kildoren. "It is forever dead now, for makers of stars are poison to this world. You know this, Kildoren, for your father is the elf who called me to your honored tree to shield me. He witnessed how, even at my weakest, I gutted that ancient wood, forcing him to turn it to stone. No. We cannot wait until the spring."

"We have become fond of you, Warder," Kildoren said. "*Tiava*, if you fail in this, Talenkai will die. You are our hope for life, our one chance to defeat this evil. Still, we will not join you in this fight. We wish to, but we . . ."

"Cannot," finished Holram. "The Seekers have said this as well."

Kildoren's eyes narrowed. "And they were correct," he said. "The magic of old would resist you, yes, even against our will. The Circle would be undone, and our world would fall to ruin. The Seekers have shown us this, and we believe it. We wish to help you as best we may, however. Your horses are weary and in sore need of food and water;

they are ill-equipped for such a journey. I offer you our shan, the very best we have." Kildoren motioned to the shaggy little creatures. "They will bear you where your horses cannot."

Holram smiled as the elves retreated to confer with their waiting companions. He shivered, and when Terrek stepped near to offer him his cloak, he managed a gracious nod. Then, kicking his way through the snow, he followed behind the two humans.

"Wait," he called after a few prancing steps. When Terrek glanced back, Holram nodded at the trampled camp. "Avalar," he said. "She went there, toward the fire. I believe she might require a friend."

∞ ∞ ∞

AVALAR RAN THE soft, dry cloth along the blade of her sword, the central fire burning low with no attentive Captain Vyergin to fetch more wood. Already she missed his gentle wit, the steaming chimara tea he would press her to drink from the polished bowl that was her cup.

"Avalar?" Terrek stopped next to her. "You must be cold sitting here." He snatched up several broken branches and placed them on the embers.

Bowing her head, she leaned over her weapon. "I cannot make them *stop*," she said, gesturing to her tears. "Again I have disappointed a companion of mine. I did not protect you as a giant should. I . . . I knew your brother, Leader Terrek, and I failed him, too! Camron was my *friend*!"

Terrek nodded. "Go on," he said.

"Camron showed me the truth about humans," she told him. "I felt such fear when I entered the city, but he was kind to me. When Tierdon was attacked, I wanted to save him. I could have stayed and helped my trainers defend the hall, but Camron—I needed to try— yet *still* they took him from me. And you! I saw you wounded during the battle. I could not come to your aid and you *died*!"

"I sometimes forget how young you are," said Terrek. "You haven't failed anyone. Not Camron, not your trainers, and certainly not me."

"So many are lost. Your wranglers and warriors. Captain Vyergin . . ." Her voice broke. "I am a giant, Leader Terrek. *We* are the protectors of this world, not prowlers!"

"I see," Terrek said. "You're upset the magical creature defended you. Avalar, the prowler was being a friend."

She wiped her tears from her sword's shining blade. "If that is sooth, why would she leave me without a farewell? I could not thank her properly for her—"

"She's a *prowler*!" Terrek grinned. "Maybe I'm wrong, and it had nothing to do with friendship. As a fellow magical creature, perhaps she understands your importance to the world. Maybe that's it. But you're not a failure. You are flesh and blood, like everyone else. Besides, *who* you are shouldn't be determined by *what* you are." He waited, nodding as she yawned. "Come, Giant," he said. "A little rest will help you see things clearly. Let's get you to bed."

Chapter 32

*P*onu stared into the shadows of his cave, listening to the little human's skittering retreat. "Kray?" he called after the boy. Then wincing, he glanced at the giant.

Grevelin, standing behind him, shifted from foot to foot. "I have frightened a child!" he moaned.

"I will go after him, Grev, and explain who you are," said Ponu. "You stay out here. I will not have you below ground reliving your memories."

"You wanted us to meet," the giant protested. "If he is important to you, we should be introduced!"

"Another time, perhaps. The young one is frightened, as you say. Which is something I can remedy."

Grevelin kicked at the crusted snow at the mouth of the cave, rubbing his bare palm over his weapon's hilt. "Hurry, and I shall wait for you," he said. Hunching his shoulders, he stumbled to the cliff overlooking Tierdon, drawing his blade as he neared the edge. With a howl, he attacked the wall of ice Ponu had formed to keep Kray from falling, slivers of white flying through the air like snow.

Ponu recalled Gaelin's dismay when he had confronted the giant for the first time: *What did those bastards do?*

"Oh, Grev," Ponu whispered. Reluctantly, he turned and hastened down the tunnel, allowing the giant his space. *If only I could undo it all so you wouldn't have these dreams!*

Entering his workroom, Ponu nudged magic into a single wick, coaxing out a flame. As the soft light spilled across the little chamber, he propped his staff against the table, casting about through the room's shadows for the boy. "Kray?" He smiled as the lithe body of his ferret, Saemson, darted under a chair. "I'm here."

"I couldn't make it light," came a frightened whimper. "Mother never showed me. She said I wasn't old enough to touch fire."

"I know." Ponu approached the cot and the small shape buried among its blankets. "But that's not why you're hiding, is it? My friend spooked you."

Kray flipped back his covers. "I saw something big!"

Smiling, Ponu moved around the cot and sat on his bed. "Yes, Grevelin is very tall."

"Is he a bear?" Kray asked.

"A *bear*?" Ponu grinned. "Grev would be flattered! No, the bears are enjoying their winter sleep down below, little Kray, but come spring you might catch sight of a sow with her cub by the river. That's where they go for fish." As Ponu brushed the blond wisps from the child's brow, he wondered at the heat of the boy's skin. *Perhaps this is why humans are short-lived*, he mused. *They burn themselves out.*

"I brought the father of the giant who rescued you," he told the child. "He's my friend Grevelin Mistavere, and he would like to meet you, Kray. Soon I may need to leave for several days, and Grevelin will want to care for you on Hothra. Not many of your people have visited the isle of giants. But you will!"

"Ponu?" Kray wriggled near and looked up, his sad eyes luminous.

Ponu smiled. *I will never sire children*, he thought. *This is the closest I'll come.* "Yes?"

"I want magic, too!" Kray said. "I want to build cities and make statues. Can you teach me?"

Ponu's heart sank. He stared across the room at his stalagmite table with its depiction of stars. Stacked on it were his spell books, along with his assorted tools, vials, and pouches. Magically potent rocks were piled at one end, while his Staff of Time leaned upon the other. "There are different kinds of magic," he said finally. "The old magic that I used to restore Tierdon is the only true form on this world. Warders like Sephrym are energy, not magic."

Kray focused on his face. "Could you have stopped him?" the child asked. "The bad man who destroyed the city?"

Ponu nodded. "Yes, but I was not aware of the attack until it was too late. Perhaps that's why Sephrym took hold of me in that moment. I am not here to play god, Kray. We were talking about *magic*, were we not?" He waited until the boy nodded. "Then know this. Talenkai's magic spreads from the core of this world, from its bloodstone veins that bind all life together. That is the first link, and the other elements carry it on. Weaken just one, and the Circle is broken. Destroy the anchors, which are the giants, who bind the whole, and the Circle is gone."

"Will you teach me?" Kray asked.

Ponu pursed his lips. "I *cannot*," he said. "Only creatures who originate from this world have this magic. They don't *wield* it, per se. It's just part of them, Kray, like breathing is a part of you. There's nothing to teach!"

"But you learned it," the human pointed out. "You *use* it, too, and you're not from here."

Ponu sat back. "The magic on your Earth was next to nonexistent. Yes, some unique individuals were able to influence it to some degree. But your species never depended on it for survival the way Talenkai's creatures do. Here, the magic is crucial to everything. On my world, Chorahn, our planet's force was stronger still. Do you understand? You cannot compare yourself to me. My flesh is used to potent magic, and yours is not. The old magic hurts humans who try to master it. It would make you very sick, little Kray."

"Isn't there something I can do?" Kray begged. "If anyone can teach me, it's you, Ponu. You built a whole city!"

Ponu stared at his grimoires piled high among the clutter, the patterns he had drawn on parchment of the shapes he planned to weave, the precious stones he would command. Like his staff, the books were from his homeworld.

I still have Chorahn's magic, he thought. Though his planet was gone, its magic lived on in him and through him, memorized in such a way that his heart knew when his brain did not. Never could he forget all his trials and many failures, the lessons he had pounded into himself.

"Here." Ponu drew from one of his pouches the floppy-eared toy he had accepted from Roth. He prodded its pink whisker nose and plopped it onto the boy's lap. "This is a magical bunny," he told the child. "We will begin with this. It is called a familiar. You can sleep with it, or hold it when you are afraid or feeling alone, and it will give you courage."

"But how is—" Kray began.

"The rest I will have to ponder," said Ponu. "I do have the magic from my homeworld, which I only ever use as a buffer between Sephrym and the old magic. My crystal staff's internal environment is Chorahn's; nothing of its power connects with or threatens this world. But everything else . . ." He shrugged. "On Earth, Sephrym's power, or even Holram's, could strengthen its weak magic. But here, a warder's touch would kill."

"Is Sephrym—"

"He dwells above the sky," Ponu cut in. "Your ancestors from Earth viewed the warders as mindless phenomena, just nebulas or black holes without consciousness or spirit. What humans don't know as fact, they *assume*. They considered their homeworld a lifeless rock and did everything in their power to make it so. But they never completely depleted its magic. Earth still had a few blue trees, the last time I was there." Gently he thumped the child's knee. "Now I need to get Grevelin home. He must be freezing."

Kray slumped in defeat on his mattress of straw, rolling into a ball. Ponu pulled the blankets up over the boy's shoulders and tucked them in tight, nodding as he spied the stuffed rabbit nestled beneath the child's chin.

"I will give it some thought," Ponu said. "The Seekers forbid humans to use magic, so I'm afraid that is all I can promise you, Kray Middleton."

As the boy looked up, his hopeful eyes glinting, Ponu patted the child's hair. "Sleep, little one, and dream easy. I will leave the light burning, and I will return soon."

With a glance at the flickering candle flame, Ponu padded toward the table for his staff.

Chapter 33

Felrina trembled as she walked. She had traversed this route often enough, but never like this. Now she noticed the contours of the smoothed and polished floor, and how every echoing step brought her closer to the mountain's dead core.

The light of a sconce flamed on her father's features, the walls of the tunnel amplifying his harsh breathing. Beads of sweat sheened his brow as his frightened eyes met hers. Her finger to her lips, she pushed him into the shadows, feeling the hammering of his heart against her arm. "Father." She wrinkled her nose. "Smell."

His face was ashen. "I know," he replied. "I expected this. He's brewing hazel-thorn to double my pain. I told you, my death will be slow."

Chanting filled the nearby chamber. She knew the words by rote. "They mean to sacrifice you," she hissed into his ear. "Father, come. I know a way out, a cleft in the rock not far from here!"

Nithra patted her hair awkwardly. His head was up, his thin lips taut. "Erebos would know of it, too, my daughter, through you, and he'd find us. You can't hide from him. No matter what we do, or where I go, I'll be dead by the end of this day. I had *Mornius*, my daughter. The enemy was in my grasp and I lost him. Whatever they do, I deserve it!"

Felrina clutched his shoulders. "No! You followed Erebos for me! I can't let them kill you!"

"Child," Nithra said, "be silent. Even without your staff in your possession, Erebos hears you. Do you want to be next? Let me go!" He shoved past her toward the chamber's lighted entrance.

She hastened to block his path. "*No!*"

He touched her cheek and the curve of her jaw. "I tortured Gaelin Lavahl," he admitted softly. "And what did he ever do to me? Nothing! This place has changed me, Felrina. Even if they let me live, I can't be a part of this anymore." He reached to hold her tight. "It's not too late for you, my daughter. Listen to me. I see what the Destroyer is doing to you. You must resist him."

Felrina stared. "You said I *shouldn't* doubt. You—"

"Because I wasn't thinking clearly! That staff of yours was in the room and I didn't want Erebos hearing us. I forgot he knows our *thoughts*, too." He bared his teeth. "Anything that tells you it's wrong to question should *absolutely* be questioned! Don't wait until it's too late! You're young and strong! You can break free and reclaim your life and never again have to—"

He grabbed at his throat. Gurgling, his expression contorted, he stumbled back, his mouth working as he collapsed into the arms that seized him from the darkness. "Erebos *awaits*," crooned Allastor Mens. "You lost the staff—our one chance to end this. For that, you die!"

"Mens!" Felrina cried. "Please! No, Mens, he's my *father*!"

"All of this would be over if not for *him*!" Mens spat. "He must pay!"

"He made a mistake!" Felrina sank to her knees. A swirl of gray-robes jostled past her to take hold of her father, immobilizing him with touches of their staves and murmured words. Nithra's face went rigid when they raised him up, his head turning as he searched the tunnel for her.

"Father!" She stumbled through the chamber's rounded doorway. Already the attendants had lifted Nithra to the altar. They caught his flailing limbs, stretching him out along the tilted stone. Above them, the shadowy shape of a dragon hovered, its ebony wings unfurled.

"You see Erebos," Mens said. At any other time, she would have reacted to his proximity, to the toxic heat emanating from his skin, but not now. Though he was so close his arm touched hers, she saw only her father.

Nithra bucked and twisted as the clerics stripped him. Then swiftly the dragon shape fell, wrapping its arms like black smoke around him. Nithra stiffened in his god's embrace, his cry rising to a scream.

"Erebos wants it his way." Mens caught her wrists, restraining her as she fought to escape. Across the chamber, her father pleaded and sobbed. Rhythmically, Erebos's darkness flexed against his body, until at last the shadow relaxed, settling to the floor.

Nithra yelped as the Attendant First's knife pierced the back of his head, his blood trickling into the bowl set below him.

"There," said Mens beside her. "Erebos has liquified the connective tissue under his skin. It should slide right off now, with a few cuts and pulls."

Felrina strained to turn, to shut her eyes and not see the clerics raising her father's head or the grim-faced First pouring the hazel-thorn down his throat.

"Erebos no longer trusts you, Felrina," Mens said. "He's observing you now. Your turn is next if you dare to look away."

She had no choice, for invisible shackles held her fast. In silence, she watched the dragon shadow transform into a tar-like mass, a tendril of it lifting from the floor to touch the balls of Nithra's feet.

Her father cried out, the skin of his heels stretching from his bones while Erebos tugged. Nithra thrashed upon the altar, his mouth gaping as all along the length of his body his skin sprang taut, creeping relentlessly toward his feet. By degrees, the cut yawned open at the back of his head, his patches of short-cropped hair sliding toward his eyes and down along his neck, baring the bloody dome of his skull.

Felrina sobbed. From what seemed like far away, she heard Mens's demented chuckle. "It's fascinating, really," he said. "In much the same way, our god consumes the stars."

Her cries catching in her throat, Felrina stared while Nithra's hairline crept over his nose. Repeatedly he screamed, the outline of his teeth visible through the skin that had covered his forehead.

"I've supervised this before," Mens was saying. "Over the span of a few days, Erebos strips the bones. He creates a membrane first, protecting the internal organs while the rest of the body is digested. He was absorbing five of our captives yesterday when Nithra came barging in. By that time there was nothing left, yet the prisoners were still breathing, and your father saw it. He didn't take it well."

Felrina sank to her knees and retched. She remembered her father as he used to be when she was little, his happy grin as he swept her up and swung her around. She was his one child, his single remaining joy after her mother's death, and she had loved him, trailing like a puppy behind him over the piece of land he worked.

Now he lay writhing, his heels pressed to the stone. A crossing of veins and muscle had replaced his face, his lipless mouth stretched in an unending wail. Clambering upright, Felrina threw herself at Mens. "*Kill* him!" she screamed. "*Finish it!*"

He pushed her back. "I wish I could," he said with feigned sadness. "But this is all he's good for now. Do you want him to go to waste? Don't you want his death to count?"

Gasping, she focused on the altar. She had no choice but to fix her gaze forward, and yet her merciful mind spiraled, taking her back to her days of romping by the river or in its current up to her knees. How many times had she searched the slimy reeds for leapers, with Terrek splashing nearby and Camron, his book in hand, spectating from the bank? Her father was there, too, chopping the wood the elves had brought, keeping watch on her from the cabin as he always did.

A scream jerked her to the present. Nithra's spine was twisted, his body glistening like a silk bug ripped prematurely from its cocoon. A black-haired tendril of scalp still clung to one bloody toe, stretching thin as Erebos devoured it.

Mens bent forward eagerly as he surveyed the ritual, his eyes aglitter and his fingers clawed. "*Now!*" he whispered.

Felrina bowed her head. She wanted it to end. Trembling, she watched Erebos's shadow shape spreading itself over her father once more, the warder's oily threads working their way through his muscles and bones.

Convulsing, Nithra screamed.

FELRINA ROUSED TO find her pillow was wet, her eyelids sore from crying. Across from her bed sat Mens, his bloodstone staff between his knees.

"Not fair, my dear," he drawled. "You weren't supposed to faint."

Groaning, she gripped her stomach. "How could you do that to me after all I have done? Why did Erebos turn on me?"

"Shh," Mens hissed. "Our god can only tolerate so much, Felrina. You are his eyes and ears, remember? You wanted Nithra to escape. You even encouraged it! Erebos heard you, and so did I."

"Let him hear *this*!" Lifting her head, she glared at the ceiling. "You lied to me, Dark Warder! You took my mind and my control from me and you *lied*!"

Mens seized her shoulders, shaking her. "Stop it!" He leaned close, his sweaty palm on her brow, pressing her back onto her pillow. "Fool! Do you want to be dead, too? He'd do it, you know. What he did to your father satisfies him more than any other torture we've found. Once he's through with Nithra, we have three others prepared. You could be the fourth if you're not careful."

"He's not supposed to touch the world, Mens!" She struggled to sit up, and then collapsed, trembling. "I'm going to be sick. Why does my stomach hurt? Why do I *hurt*, Mens?"

He tapped her wrists with his staff, rendering them limp and lifeless with a soft word of magic. "Erebos is displeased with your behavior," he said. "Now, if you don't accept your punishment, he'll allow me to do much worse." He slid his arm up within the generous sleeve of her robe. "I could, you know." Savagely, he twisted her nipple. "Erebos would enjoy it, too." He paused for effect, grinding his knuckles against her breast. "I had no idea you were a virgin."

"*Bastard!*" The contents of her stomach filled her mouth, and with an effort, she choked it down. "You *took* me!"

Mens grinned. "Indeed, I did. *Several* times." Sitting back, he separated and paralyzed her legs. "Just like that. This is the old magic, Priestess. If you had the courage to learn the bloodstones, you'd have this power, too."

Felrina flinched from his touch. "I don't want it," she snarled. "It's made you a monster!" Sobbing, she tossed her head. "I can't believe I listened to you. I talked my father into following Erebos for *you*, abandoned the man I loved and my home for *you*! Erebos has taken everyone now, and I *helped* him!"

"We've never beheld our god as he truly is," Mens said sternly. "On this world, his power is limited, so he needs us. Even the old magic is stronger if you have the courage to use it. Which you don't. You have never—"

"I don't want to! Look at what it's done to you! You were so kind to me! I left *everything*. I gave up my *life* for your cursed lies!"

Closing her eyes, Felrina buried her head in the pillow, her stomach clenching at the sudden chill air on her skin as he folded back her robe, then pulled her arms from its sleeves.

"There now," Mens whispered. She gagged, feeling his fingers between her legs. "*So* much better."

Felrina struggled to think without Erebos hearing her. The warder's mind was feeding on *her* now, on her humiliation and anguish. There was no way she could keep it from him.

She ground her teeth as Mens bent her knees, his arm raising her hips while he tore her robe from under her and tossed it to the floor. She would find a way.

Chapter 34

valar stared at the massive tree with its pink-and-silver trunk. The proud sentinel's magic was potent on her skin, its consciousness reaching across the Eris village to connect with her. Behind its purple mantle of blanket-sized leaves, she made contact, her mind caressing the tree's knotted heart. Gently the Nada borrowed her strength and granted her a boon in return, a glimpse of its growth from seedling to sapling as it stretched its branches to the sun. In time its roots had formed burrows in the ground, providing shelter to the elves who kept it fed, the strong young tree grown mighty with power.

She recalled Kildoren's story as they had entered the little town, of how bloodstones embedded deep in the ground had decided the location of their new temple, the power of the buried gems stimulating the tree to grow to a massive size. In their youth, the Eris elders had raised the Nada to replace the one Holram's arrival had destroyed. After eight cycles they were able to relocate their hearths to the lodges formed by the tree, adding exterior homes within and below the shelter of its erupted roots. Now, hundreds of cycles later, their dwellings endured, the oldest tucked within the Nada's iron core. As the world's blood leeched magic from the Nada's rings and bark to heat the ground and warm the homes, so did the roots drink hungrily from the nourishing soil the bloodstones provided.

They benefit each other, Avalar thought. *It is different for me. The stones only take my magic. I feel it even now.*

Frowning, she watched the sun set beyond the mountains and the elves retire into their homes. Since her arrival with Terrek's remaining men, the village had swarmed with activity, with many of the elves riding off to Tierdon on their shan to lend their aid to the

former dachs. Her scowl had deepened whenever she saw Gaelin among them, his perplexity obvious in his soft brown eyes during the moments when Holram possessed him.

Raising her head, she scoured the camp for her leader. *Does Terrek see Gaelin's plight? Does he care?*

She hissed as pain clenched her belly. Whatever Gaelin had done with her magic during the battle had depleted her. Allastor Mens had ripped at her guts in his attempt to extract her magic, but her flesh had fought back, her power surging to renew itself. This draining by a friend to heal the dachs had caught her unaware. Without the help of her blood heated in rage or battle, it would take time for her tissues to compensate.

"Avalar?"

Gaelin halted in front of her, his skin glowing in the gathering dusk. "Which one are you?" she asked. "The human or the god? Your countenance bespeaks Gaelin. And the way you hold your body."

Unflinching, he peered back. So often before, his eyes had shied away from any direct stare. She had sensed shame in him, a terrible guilt he longed to hide. Yet now his regard was steady and bright— filled with worry for her. "Not a god," he said. "Avalar, it's *me*."

"What of Holram?" Doubtfully, she gazed into his eyes. "Are you both?"

"The elves told Terrek the transition is complete, or as much as it can be for a human," he said. "But I'm not so sure. Look!" He lifted his arm. "I did that. *Me*! If he's a part of me, why don't I feel him?"

Avalar cocked her head. "Mayhap he has released you?"

"I don't think so," Gaelin said. "Through me, he can walk and speak his mind. He won't give that up. Not when he is so close. I think he's letting me rest. He must realize his magic weakens me."

Avalar studied the lodges around her, the dwellings built within the trunks of the many smaller trees that had sprouted from the roots of their looming parent. "It is so easy for ones of power to wave their hands and say who goes where and does what," she muttered.

He clasped her wrist. "I feel things now," he said. "You're in pain because of me. Holram didn't plan to take your magic as he did. But the dachs had to be restored, and you were there."

She sank to her haunches beside him. All day she had tolerated the looks from the elves, their disapproval of her proximity to the humans. *If they see my distress*, she thought, *there is naught I can do, for I am weary.* She looked down into Gaelin's troubled face. "Holram *used* me?" she asked.

"Listen," said Gaelin. "Your presence made it possible to revive those people. I didn't have that before. The warder could heal Terrek's men, but never the dachs."

"We are a pair, are we not?" she murmured wryly. "Freedom. It is an elusive thing."

He sighed. "You need to know why you're hurting. It's my fault. When Terrek fell beneath the dachs' swords, I gave up. I couldn't move, but at the same time, I felt this power. All I had to do was let it take me. I was still afraid, but I surrendered to it. I had no choice. Terrek needed me!"

"You did well," she reassured him. "You saved your friend when I could not, and Erebos's dachs. You aided *them*, too."

"No, you did," he said. "*You* changed them back. When Holram took me over, I lost control, freeing him to touch the world. He connected with *you*, Avalar. Only your power, combined with his, could so unravel the warped old magic."

She drew a quick breath and he grimaced. "It took the strength of giants to undo the harm," he told her. "Warped water made the dachs, and you said it yourself: magic of flesh is stronger."

Biting her lip, Avalar nodded.

"I'm sorry," he added.

"No." She scrambled to her feet. "There is no call for regret. Those humans are free. My pain is naught by comparison. It is but an annoyance, and it will pass. But the good that results from my discomfort shall endure."

Gaelin smiled.

Avalar gestured toward the tree. "I dare not venture there. That warren is magic-fed. It holds bloodstones beneath it. I sense its roots growing tight around them. Its sap weaves a mighty spell."

"The inside of the tree is hollow and warm," he said. "Terrek is waiting for me to bring you. The leader of the Eris has concerns, and Terrek won't discuss them without you."

Avalar snarled. "Kildoren wants me to stay here. He will wish to see me home—have one of his elves march me eastward to Luen or Foss Bay and put me on one of their Skimmers. No. This is *my* life. He will *not* have his way!"

"Avalar!" Gaelin trotted at her hip as she approached the tree. "I'll have them come out to you instead! That way you won't have to—"

"Oh, but I *do*," she cut him off. "I am Grevelin's daughter! My uncle Kurg says *Mistaveres* are always the first forward and the very last to fall!" She ducked, charging through the rounded doorway, her skin prickling as the tree's inner light replaced the dusk, the slant of rich red wood above her forcing her into a crouch. The air was humid, heated by the breaths of Terrek with his men, along with Kildoren and the elders.

Her human leader rose as he caught sight of her, his brow smoothing when their gazes met. "Good," he said. "Come, Giant. It's a tight crawl for you, I know. But it opens up; I promise. Come. We have much we need to discuss."

She dropped to her knees and pushed her shoulders into the cleft, squeezing sideways to make room for Gaelin. She could feel the slight ridges of the tree's rings tingle under her fingers as she climbed. The wood was bestowing on her its strength.

She caught its nutty scent, and then she was sliding down, landing on her knees and calloused palms in the basin beyond the gap.

Terrek sat in front of a recess on a raised formation of roots. The elves reclined with him in the circular hollow, eight on each side of him along the walls. Darkness hovered where the ceiling ended, the lines denoting the tree's age stretching out of her sight to form a vertical cavity, the largest of many pockets within the Nada's core. Swaying threads of gossamer descended from the shadows, each holding a lantern over her head. She counted sixteen little lamps, illuminating the upturned faces inspecting her.

Carefully she stood. "This temple has strong magic," she warned Terrek. "These elves planted this tree on top of a cache of bloodstones. That is why this place, this whole village, is not frozen like everything else. The stones are the life of this world, and their power gives the elves their tree-lore. As a giant I am naught but magic for the stones to drain. But I fear in time the spell of this wood might put you and your men to sleep."

Kildoren's green eyes glimmered as he shifted on his seat to address Terrek. "The giant speaks truly of our temple," he said. "Our tree feeds the bloodstones the power they crave, heating the stones to warm our homes for us, which nourishes the Nada as well. You are human and you have no magic. There is no power here to threaten you."

"You admit the stones are draining her?" Terrek asked. "She's been through enough."

Kildoren turned, studying her again as he and his kind had done all day. Bristling, Avalar glared back. *Just try to send me home,* she thought fiercely. *I dare you!*

"The world's blood is mindless," said Kildoren. "It must feed on power in order to pass it on. As we speak, it savors her strength, yet it will not inflict serious harm. Only when humans warp the magic do these stones become dangerous. You call our trees 'warrens,' but to the elves, they are Nada, a word that means *hope*. Our tree is a haven. It would never harm a giant, Leader Florne, and neither would the stones."

"*Enough* of this," Oburne growled from the recess behind Terrek. "I am your third and you need me. With Vyergin gone, you'll be requiring my strength and my sword. Why would you ask me to stay here?"

Avalar followed Gaelin to where Oburne and the other humans huddled beneath the low ceiling. She knelt in front of the crevice, positioning herself like a guard next to her leader. She recognized Grenner, the young bowman who wielded his sword left-handed, standing with Silva at Terrek's back. Behind Gaelin and Roth, and Oburne with the two guards, she spotted three more familiar faces: the surviving wranglers who had tended to the animals.

"What I *want* has nothing to do with it," Terrek said. "These people need our help. The city can shelter them, but it can't show them how to care for themselves and you can. They need a leader, Lieutenant. You can be that for them. Help them to survive until spring."

"Assuming there *is* one!" Oburne shook his braided hair. "That's the problem, isn't it? You can't guarantee any of us will be here in a nineday. So let me stay with you. Let the strength of my blade make a difference in this thing. The elves can aid the humans. You made me third in command. Without Vyergin, you need me!"

Frowning, Terrek shook his head. "You and Grenner will stay," he said. "If we fail, and Talenkai survives, I'll want to die knowing there's someone behind me to take my place. Perhaps you can find a way to get through to the ones in the Destroyer's cult. If they refused to serve him, Erebos would starve."

Avalar glanced at Gaelin. The staff-wielder sat in the cleft, his forearms wrapped around his knees as he assessed the elves. Across the room, Kildoren returned his gaze with a look of deep affection.

Not for the human, Avalar realized. The chieftain's love was for the warder in Gaelin's eyes.

"Bad idea," said a reverberating voice. From the tree's flickering shadows, Argus descended slowly, his emerald outline wavering dramatically back and forth against the ruddy heartwood. He smiled at the uplifted faces of his audience as he lowered himself, enjoying their stunned reactions. Then, floating between the humans and the seated elves, he bowed low, his phantom legs skimming the floor.

With a gasp, Roth went for his sword. Gaelin stopped him with a firm rap on his knuckles. "That's Terrek's ghost," he whispered. "The one from the castle."

"Oh *no!*" Roth groaned.

"Oh, *yes!*" said Argus. "In this warren, everyone gets to appreciate my *wondrous* transparency, including *you*, bunny thief, which is why I have come. Lord Terrek here was kind enough to dispose of my scabbard, thus freeing me to flit aimlessly about the countryside. Yet still, I remain chained by Arawn's curse to my blade."

"I didn't *steal* that bunny! I'm getting tired of hearing about—" Roth broke off at Terrek's look.

One of the elders leaned forward, his gaze intense below his silver fall of hair. "Would you prefer to inhabit a lantern, respected one?" He nodded to the suspended lamps. "We Eris use ordinary flame, while on Tholuna, the Starian elves put spirits to work to light their homes. The Eris denounce this practice. We do not imprison—"

"You speak as though our southern kindred are slavers," another elder cut in. "If you researched further, you would know they are not. The indentured souls are returned to life after a brief period of servitude. They are permitted the honor of joining the Circle, living on as a spirit companion inside whichever magical animal they choose."

"Oh, *goodie!*" sneered Argus.

"One of the Azkharren," Gaelin whispered softly. "I would like that. To be able to fly would be my—"

"Sir Knight," Terrek said, silencing Gaelin with a frown. "What did you wish to say?"

"Always in a rush are the living!" the specter snapped. "Fine. I'll be brief. Deconverting Erebos's priests so they stop feeding him is a waste of time. The knights tried that after the giants escaped. My brothers purged the catacombs of Mount Chesna, and for years, that husk stood empty, or so we thought. Little did we know Erebos lingered on in Chesna's crannies, and over time, he and his dead priest, Arawn, formed this new cult."

"So we can't starve him," Terrek said, "but there must be other things we can try. We can't let them win, Jahn."

"Understood," said Oburne. "This isn't how I imagined giving your father my service, but if it will help . . ." His voice trailed off as he glanced up, a sliver of lantern-light sheening on his dark skin. "I could spend the winter training those people. I could teach them to fight . . . like men this time."

Terrek nodded. "Exactly."

Avalar glared at her leader. "Mayhap there are also women with brave hearts among you. Have you thought of that? Why do they not battle for their families and homes? Do you deny them? Or do you fear to behold how *females* fight?"

"Avalar," Terrek said, his lips twitching. "We humans are few. The women we have left must be protected."

"This is all very well, Leader Florne," Kildoren said. "I am pleased to hear your homeless will not be abandoned. We will give them our aid as well. But what of the giant? You have agreed to entrust your horses with us and take our shan instead, but Avalar cannot ride them."

"Nor could I ride the horses," Avalar responded. "What of it?"

"We think it best if she remains with us," Kildoren went on. "This route along the Shukaia River is stained by the death of giants. For her, it will rouse memories that will tear her from herself, break her grip on reality. She could become savage and endanger you all."

"The sky could also fall," Avalar said. "Or at dawn this tree might burst into flames. Do not trouble me with things that *may* happen. I have endured my father's memories all my life. I do not fear their torment, nor will I ever harm Terrek or his men!"

"You have no idea what that valley will do," Kildoren argued. "You have only experienced the mental strife of your surviving people. In the valley there is nothing but death. You would see and feel how those giants died, just as though you were experiencing it yourself. Your people are driven by strong emotions, kindled by your blood. You have little understanding of what, under duress, you might become. For the sake of these men you claim to care about, we must ward you. You shall remain in our village and allow us to preserve your life."

"Long ere your race crawled from the brine of the sea," Avalar said, glaring, "my people defended this world, yet when has what *giants* desire ever been a consideration? Why should it be now? No! I will not stay here! Leader Terrek, do you hear me? Thresher Govorian's sword called to *me*! It spoke of the importance of freedom, and it bid me come here to play my part! All my life these elves have hindered me! *No more!*"

"You needn't yell," Terrek said. He nodded as Silva hurried across the Nada's sunken floor, the guard hoisting himself up onto the temple's inner ridge to slide from their sight.

Avalar stared at Kildoren. *You have no right!* she raged in silence. She stood, fists clenched, while the other humans filed past her. As Terrek walked by without a glance, his mouth clamped shut, her eyes filled with tears.

"Avalar!" Gaelin gripped her arm. She saw the empathy in his gaze. "The Eris want you to stay," he said. "But I need you with me, and so does Holram. There could be other dachs to heal, if you are willing, that is."

"Of course," she said, trembling.

"Terrek plans to depart at dawn," Gaelin informed her. "He wants this over. The longer we delay in this village, the stronger our enemy gets."

"I know," she said. "I see it in the way he carries himself. His ghosts are troubling him."

"Yes, Vyergin's now, too," Gaelin concurred. As he touched her forearm, her nerves tingled. Dazed, she allowed him to guide her from the Nada's warmth.

Terrek, Roth, and Wren stood waiting under the inky sky. Avalar took in their grim expressions as she stopped beside Terrek. "You agree with the elf?" she demanded. "You wish to leave me here?"

Terrek flicked her a glance. Out of the darkness, a small procession appeared. She saw two elves leading six of the striped-legged shan, with Silva bringing up the rear.

Avalar bristled as Terrek stepped away from her to greet the elves.

Squealing, the shan shook their manes at his approach. Flipping its ebon-tufted tail, the largest of the six bared its yellowed teeth.

"Respect them," Kildoren rumbled behind her, "and they will serve you well." He emerged from the glow of the great tree, a blanket draped over his shoulder.

"Right now," Terrek replied, "we must prepare for tomorrow." He accepted the leads from the shans' young handlers and tugged firmly. The largest shan, a bronze-colored beast with flecks of white along its withers, loosed a fierce bellow.

Kildoren crossed his arms. "Either learn respect now, or they will teach it to you. Shan will not tolerate the kind of brutality your people inflict upon nonhuman animals. Drag at their heads like that again, and you may not live to see the morning."

Avalar rounded on the elf. "He is grieving! Why must you—"

"Avalar!" Terrek passed the leads to Roth and hastened to her side. "Kildoren is kind enough to loan us these creatures, and he's right. I *should* show respect. Though"—Terrek glared at Kildoren—"we do *not* brutalize our horses at Vale Horse."

The elf glowered back. "I suspect your human notion of gentleness differs greatly from my own. I am cautioning you now; our shan will abandon you to this winter if you do anything more to—"

"We won't," Terrek interjected. "I am tired, Leader Kildoren. I will not mistreat your animals again!"

Her throat suddenly tight, Avalar averted her face, for the sight of Terrek's starlit eyes reminded her forcibly of Camron.

"I have no plans to forsake you," Terrek told her.

Avalar sniffed. "You would rather not bring me. You would prefer that I stay *here*!"

"And be safe, yes," he said. "You heard Kildoren describe what awaits us. It will make you miserable. It could even destroy you, which is the last thing I want."

"That is sooth," Avalar spoke bitterly. "My death would shatter the Circle."

"To blackest *blazes* with the Circle! Get it through your thick skull! I value *you*, Giant! You befriended my brother and have given me your trust! Is it wrong for me to want to keep you from danger?"

Avalar inhaled sharply. "No, but if I wanted *protection*, I would never have voyaged here!"

"Was Hothra so terrible," asked Terrek, "that you would give up everything you care about?"

"I love my home and my family," Avalar said. "I am here to fight for them. Still, Govorian's sword spoke to *me*. There must be a reason."

Terrek smiled. "I feel the same way," he said. "My father and Vale Horse are all I have left."

Avalar sighed as he turned to instruct his remaining men, listening to his stern and quiet voice. He was human, yet she would never fear him. He was the brother Camron had loved.

Chapter 35

When her turn came, Avalar bathed as the others had done. Weeks of travel made her desperate to be clean, enough to endure her father's memories of his slavery underground. Summoning her courage, she wriggled through the cave's steamy entrance, scraping her elbow on the dampened stone.

She hurried to undress, placing her armor, sword, boots, and belt to one side, her jerkin, leggings, and fur in a pile next to them.

Quick elven hands snatched away her clothing as she lowered herself into the tiny pool. A lithe figure shimmered in the mist like a creature of dreams. The she-elf smiled and bent to place a green woolen blanket where Avalar's garments had been, the girl's long black mane floating about her shoulders.

"I thank you," Avalar murmured politely as the elf left the chamber. She shut her eyes, savoring the warmth of the spring as it sank into her bones. With her knees to her chest, she sat still and inhaled deeply, filling her lungs with the comforting steam. From a small wooden vessel at the water's edge, she scooped out a fistful of pellets, sniffing their soapy scent as they dissolved into bubbles in her palm.

She hummed a dirge as she washed—for Terrek's lost fighters and for Captain Vyergin, tears trickling over her breasts into the water.

Climbing from the pool, she leaned over, dunking her head and scrubbing, her fingers combing through the tangled mass until her skin and scalp burned. Hastily she dried herself and wrapped the blanket snugly around her torso and hips.

Squeezing out into the frigid night air, she trotted along the snowy path to the heated village.

In an empty structure set apart from the massive warren, a candle flickered in a window frame. Avalar smiled as she slipped within the ball of roots that formed the little house. It was her candle and her refuge for the night, a place that, for the moment, she could call her own.

$$\infty \quad \infty \quad \infty$$

AS THE SILVERY dawn brightened the sky, Avalar stood close to Gaelin and studied the shan. With their forelegs splayed, their short necks stretched to their fullest extent, the six pampered creatures munched contentedly, lipping at the moss and tree-cones their caretakers had fed them.

Kildoren led the smallest beast to the side and coaxed it to raise its shaggy head, slipping the bridle on over its blunt upper lip and behind its hairy ears. "You position the strap that high on his nose?" Terrek asked. He stood by the elf, leaning with his hands on his knees.

Kildoren nodded. "Any lower and it would cut off his air," he said. "In truth, the shan have no need for such trappings. Nor do your horses for that matter. Which you would know if you bothered to learn their language. These 'hackamores,' as your wranglers called them, were constructed during the night for your benefit—just something familiar to hold in your hands. But you will guide the shan with your legs. Lower your tailbone when you want to stop, and"— the chieftain prodded the point where the shan's neck dipped between its rounded shoulders—"nudge here at the withers when you want them to go.

"*Never* kick! The shan react like prey animals when they are struck. They would change, and, trust me, you would *not* like what they become! Follow my instructions, and all will be well." The elf leader stood beside the shan and lifted its reins, gripping them lightly. "Keep the straps loose like this and let them do the work."

Kildoren demonstrated how to mount the wide-backed little beast, and Terrek gave it a try once the elf jumped off.

Avalar nudged Gaelin. "I wonder how the magic changes them they need to protect themselves. Have you heard?"

"Holram could tell you," Gaelin answered. "But he's being quiet this morning."

"Gaelin," Terrek called when the other men had taken a turn. "Come and try. This little one is for you. You should practice now, while you have the elves here to assist."

As Gaelin shook his head, Kildoren moved to embrace him warmly. Avalar stared at the odd mingling of affection and fear on the elf's hard face. When at last Gaelin relaxed enough to respond to the chieftain's clasp, Kildoren released him and hurried off to help with the shan. Gaelin rubbed at his eyes.

"Holram?" Avalar queried.

He grimaced. "No, it's just me. Holram can't understand why people say farewell. When I realized Kildoren needed him to, I . . . pretended."

"Ah." Avalar reached for her pack when he moved to accept the reins of the beast Terrek gave him.

As the six shan plodded from the village in single file, Avalar examined the cumbersome bundle of the extra tent left abandoned in the snow, deemed by the elves to be too weighty for the single calico pack-shan to bear. Sighing, Avalar squatted by the canvas and poles, then heaved them onto her shoulders.

Chapter 36

*I*ce gleamed high on the river's banks where the water had splashed, while lower down the current moved swiftly in the places it could still be seen—a rushing cataract beneath a wintry sheath of gray.

Gaelin trudged along the narrow ledge between the water and the gorge's stony base. On this path, the shan had journeyed before. He saw the creatures' splayed-toed tracks, the frozen lumps of dung beneath the snow.

He fiddled with his cloak, pulling the blue wool around his chest. Already he longed to rejoin the Eris village, to rest and feel safe even for a little while.

"*Sails!*" Avalar gasped nearby as the ice cracked under her weight. Gaelin jumped back and pressed against his shan to steady himself, turning to embrace the beast's muscular neck.

"Gaelin," Terrek said.

With a reluctant nod, Gaelin struggled to mount at last as Kildoren had shown them, lifting his right leg over and easing into the saddle. The shan, unimpressed by his efforts, rubbed its bony cheek along the granite wall. Its tufted tail lashed his calf.

Guided by Argus, Terrek prodded his beast atop the river's steep border. Silva trailed him, followed by Roth, and then Wren Neche leading the calico shan.

Gaelin clicked his tongue, willing the animal beneath him to catch up with the others. He frowned after several failed attempts. *Don't kick*, he thought. *Whatever you do, you are not supposed to—*

The giant next to him slapped the shan's rump. He grunted as it scrambled forward, throwing his arms around its stumpy neck.

"Sit up straight," Terrek called back, his tone amused. "He's only *walking,* Staff-Wielder."

Gaelin nodded and complied. He tensed as the ice beneath him snapped and crackled, yet still, unconcernedly, his mount shuffled on, swinging each hairy leg before taking a step. *It's like he measures where to put his feet,* Gaelin thought, as his little beast tucked one cloven hoof under its belly and hopped across a fractured patch.

". . . smarter than horses," Terrek said from down the path. "I can't say . . . agreement on that one."

Gaelin fought to make out the words, for the voices of his companions kept his mind from the dizzy fall to his left and the water far below.

"Fear not," said Avalar behind him as she patted his shoulder. He shut his eyes. The shan's wide back swayed from side to side while the conversation ahead of him droned on. Gaelin let himself drift, his anxiety melting away.

He was hovering between the stars, in a void of absolute cold and breathless beauty. Within his protection, Earth's sun flared.

Then he was plunging like a comet, a fiery fury blazing through the darkness. His weakness drew him down against his will, imprisoning him beneath Talenkai's sky, surrounded by magic he could not touch.

I do not slay, Holram thought, recalling Warder's Fall and the desolation his landing had caused—the Erises' homewarren destroyed and so many innocent elves and animals murdered. *Hurting, killing. These are the works of my foe.*

Holram let himself drift, feeling his host's body rocking back and forth. He marveled at how at ease he felt now in this soft and yielding prison. Yet the sensation was short-lived; a shan's sudden bugle jolted Gaelin from his slumber, and once more Holram fell into the background of human thoughts.

Gaelin clutched at his shan's ebony mane and forced his eyes to focus as his beast stopped.

The five creatures in front of him stood riderless, their bodies barring his way. An ancient flood had crumpled the wall of the gorge, allowing the path to widen above the Shukaia's icy bank. Here his companions had dismounted. Huddled together along the ledge, they peered at the river below.

Gaelin shivered as Avalar moved close again, her big hand

extending to help him. He caught at her wrist and slid from his saddle.

"What is it?" Fearfully he surveyed the slanted ice. Any misstep could send him careening to the edge.

Avalar shrugged and positioned herself behind him, gripping him securely. "I know not," she said in his ear. "Shall we go and see?"

He shuffled his feet, his heels sliding as he neared the others. Yet through it all, the giant held him up.

"Terrek?" Gaelin halted beside Roth. A gray shape sprawled below, its head and neck immersed in the slushy water under a freezing swirl of mist, its legs twisted and encased in white.

"It's Hawk," Terrek said in a husky voice. "Vyergin's horse."

Vyergin's—

"No!" Gaelin pulled against Avalar's hold. "No, I've got to help him! Vyergin would *want* me to!"

Avalar's arms dragged at him. All around him, the world was spinning. Though voices shouted above, all he knew was the power swelling in his chest, the fire kindling from his bones, crackling tendrils of it stabbing through the coldness beneath him. For this, he existed—to heal and not destroy!

"Hawk is *dead*, Gaelin!" Straddling him, Terrek sat on his chest. "Listen to me! There's *nothing we can do!*"

Gaelin stared at his friend through an angry blur of tears. "No. I *healed* him, Terrek! He can't be dead. I won't let him be dead!"

"Don't be ridiculous." Terrek eased off him and rolled to his knees. "Avalar," he called.

Gaelin surrendered, allowing the giant to draw him to his feet and help him to his shan. "He needs rest, Leader Terrek," Avalar said as she waited for Gaelin to mount. "This . . . presence in his staff is draining him."

"It is," Terrek replied. "And we will set up camp as soon as it's safe, but not now."

Gaelin caught the worry on Terrek's face as he glanced at the walls penning them in. "Come," said Terrek.

Already half drowsing on his shan's shaggy back, Gaelin focused beyond Avalar on Argus's green light, and the ghost's angry scowl as he floated over her head.

∞ ∞ ∞

FELRINA GROANED AS the insistent knock came again, the force of it rattling the hinges. She flinched on the mattress she had come to despise, glaring into the shadows. *"What?"* she demanded.

"Priestess?" called a young man's voice, after which there was a click as slowly the latch raised up and the door squeaked open.

She snorted, recognizing the intruder's countenance behind the candle. "Leave me alone!" she snarled at her apprentice. "Can't you see I'm sick? Go away!"

"But ..." Gulgrin squeezed through the little doorway. "What's he doing? You've been locked in here all day, and Mens wouldn't let me in."

"He's punishing me," she rasped. "Erebos wants this, so you better go!"

"But he's angry you're not d-down there, Priestess," Gulgrin stammered. "He's begun the ritual without you."

"What?" She started up. "Who is? *Mens?*"

"Y-yes, Mistress!" Gulgrin answered. "Oh, my lady, it's terrible! I know it's a necessary thing, but I . . ."

"Yes, it is," she drawled. "Everything we do is important for our future!" She slipped from the bed and gestured to her lantern. "Light that thing, Gulgrin. I must get dressed!"

He leapt to obey, his scrawny arms shaking as he touched his candle's flame to the lantern's charred wick.

Quickly she donned her tunic and her black robe. Choking on vomit, she fumbled for her leggings. "What has you so upset?" she asked with a glance at the boy. "None of these ceremonies are enjoyable. What are you—"

Felrina broke off, cocking her head at a distant shriek. She turned to her Blazenstone staff propped by the wall, reaching to stroke its crimson gem. "Without *you*," she said to it, "Erebos is being cheated. He can't fully absorb the pain unless you're there."

"Mens doesn't care," said Gulgrin. "He wants Erebos to be angry.

He's using *four* attendants, Priestess."

She stared. "Four?"

The youth bobbed his head.

"He's a fool!" She stomped on her boots. "No method should ever require so many. What's he trying to do? Stop the heart? He knows very well it takes *slow* death to satisfy Erebos!"

Grabbing her staff, she bolted from her chamber and raced along the sloping tunnel. Gulgrin struggled to keep up. "He's not thinking about that," he panted. "They had another battle, and Mens lost fighters to Holram's staff! And *you* haven't made him replacements!"

"He had me paralyzed!" Felrina raged. "*Bastard!*" She halted to crouch in front of a hole in the stone floor and gripped its edge, then swung to the tunnel below her own. Louder and more stridently the agonized howling assailed her ears. "That's too much!" she yelled. "*Mens!*"

The black-robe stepped from the darkness, smiling smugly. He arched his brows. "Yes?"

Felrina stumbled. "What in blazes do you think you're doing, Mens? I could hear it from my room! You don't even have my staff!"

"It doesn't matter. Erebos is enjoying himself." Mens lifted his hand into the torchlight, brandishing a tiny saw. "The attendants are having a contest to find out who can cut through first. Come and see for yourself." Seizing her arm, Mens dragged her, struggling, around the bend and into the chamber. The high-pitched screams were frantic now—the mindless wails of a tortured animal.

The acolytes who were her peers turned their troubled faces toward her. Steeling herself, she forced her gaze to the raised platform beyond them and to the altar, where attendants held an older man stretched between them. The sacrifice's back was arched, his face contorted.

She jerked from Mens's grip, rushing between the wooden benches to stop below the altar. She lifted her staff. "*Finish* him!" she screeched at the Attendant First. "Do it *now!*"

He glanced up, the sacrifice's half-severed ankle flopping in his grasp. By force of will, she lighted the gem in her staff's crown. "Do it, or I'll fry the poor man myself!" she spat as the Blazenstone cast arcs of scarlet above her head. "Until there's nothing left of any of you!"

"'*Poor* man'?" Mens snapped behind her. "On the contrary, he is *honored* by this!"

Felrina whirled and blasted her fire at Mens, reducing the floor in front of him to rubble. "It's *all a lie!*" she roared. "Every word you have said! Erebos has promised us a new world, yes? For humans alone, isn't that right? Well, what about *him?*" Wildly she gestured at the dying man. "Where is *his* promised paradise, Mens?

"Or what about the others we've killed? How do we *know* they'll be reborn? What about my *father*, Mens? When will *he* share in our fortune? Will I ever see him again? No!" She wheeled to confront them all at once—the blur of gray and midnight robes, the attendants, and Allastor Mens. "This is *wrong!*"

Unsheathing the little knife at her belt, she sprang behind the altar. The four attendants abandoned their positions, their bloody arms outstretched, pleading with her to stop.

She paused, choking with revulsion as she probed the sacrifice's chest. She slammed her blade in at an angle, ramming it under the ribs.

"*No!*"

The rock overhead splintered from Erebos's cry, and Mens howled.

Felrina gawked at her knife's quivering hilt, a chill of icy fear tingling down her spine. The man beneath her went rigid and convulsed.

Someone seized her from behind, throwing her hard to the floor.

"*Take* her!" Mens barked. He shoved at the attendants, striking them repeatedly across their backs with his staff. "I don't care what you do!"

The Attendant First knelt beside her. Felrina rose with him, his bloody hands steadying her. "I'm going to be sick," she whispered against his shoulder. "Get me out of here!"

"That's right," Allastor Mens snapped. "Take her to her room! I have the staff now! The Blazenstone is mine! *She* will feed Erebos next. You will prepare her at once. Understand?"

"Priestess, come," The First urged sadly.

Chapter 37

errek shifted near the flames. The sun's warmth penetrated his back but left untouched the ice that numbed his heart. Idly he regarded the foraging shan. After another half day of travel, the gorge had widened, allowing them at last to camp by a small stand of trees.

Among the hardy bluebark, the six shan rose on their hind legs. With grunts and squeals, the little creatures threw their shoulders against the gnarled trunks and shook them, a hail of dead cones pattering from the frozen branches. As one of them bounced off his sleepy guard's head, Terrek smiled.

He savored the feeling. The death of his brother still tormented him, and now there was Vyergin, too, and the men who had given him their trust.

Sighing, Terrek glanced over the drop-off at the chill water moving swiftly under the ice below. It reminded him of the stream in the woods next to their old manor, and of playing in the water as a child with Felrina, the friend he had grown to love more dearly than his own life. How he loathed the cult she had joined despite his attempts to dissuade her.

Where are you now? Terrek thought. *What has happened to you, Rina?*

Silva groaned fitfully and swatted at the air. Like Wren Neche, he dozed as though a part of him yearned to stay awake.

Terek nodded. "Exhausted," he whispered, stifling a yawn. He straightened and surveyed the snowy clearing. Beyond the trees, the slab of gray rock loomed. Above the cliff's stone face climbed the roots of the glacier, its blue ice glistening with streaks of white.

When a bare-armed figure appeared from the empty air between the trees, Terrek sprang to his feet and drew his sword. "*Ponu,*" he murmured. Sheathing his weapon, he made his way around the flames and his recumbent companions.

The small winged creature knelt behind a tree and watched him come. Terrek scowled as he remembered Tierdon and the restoration of Camron's city. Nodding at a mage Terrek suspected was the mightiest on Talenkai, he crouched beside him.

Shaking back his long white hair, Ponu ground the crystal heel of his staff into the ice by his knee. "Welcome to my mountain, Terrek Florne," the elf said. "You and your men have accomplished much by depleting Erebos's forces."

"Certainly more than you have," Terrek snapped. He paused, taken aback by the unexpected hostility of his words. "Pardon me. I guess I'm tired, too."

The mage's violet eyes met his. "I do what I can," Ponu said. "I am as alien to this world as you are. In sooth, I should not be here at all. I am too dangerous."

"Why are you here?" Terrek asked.

"My own curiosity, I suppose," Ponu said. "It is a rare thing when a planet has magic, and rarer still when it lives longer than it should. This is Sephrym's doing, Talenkai's warder. All stars must die, Terrek Florne, but this one never does."

"So you came here to investigate? How?"

A knowing smile curved Ponu's lips. He flexed his wings and lifted his crystal staff. "With *this*," he said. "My Staff of Time."

Terrek jumped as a bluebark cone struck his neck. He flicked a glare at the tree beside him and at the shan foraging at its base.

"Now I am trapped here, just like Holram," Ponu said. "My homeworld is long dead. I will never see it again."

Terrek caught the slight tremor of sadness in the mage's lyrical tone. "You do have the elves here," he ventured. "Don't you? The Khanal elves?"

Ponu snorted. "The Khanal are children compared to me. In truth I love the giants more, for, to them, I am an equal. Whereas whenever I try to bond with the elves . . ." He shrugged. "I blame myself entirely. I enjoyed showing off when I arrived on Talenkai. I assumed the Eris elves shared my skills when first we met one hundred and eighty years ago. I built Tierdon, and in doing so, I frightened them. I may look like them. With the exception of my wings, of course. But I am *not* them, Terrek Florne, and how well they know it. So, truly, I have no people other than the giants on this world."

Terrek was moved by the ache in the winged elf's voice. "It must be hard for you to feel so helpless and yet be so powerful. Why do you say your home is dead?"

"Because that is what comes of the temptation that was my world," Ponu answered. "My people loved to explore, and Chorahn was a time-portal. We used up its magic. One day when I tried to return, I found my planet a lifeless shell. Perhaps there are others like me, but Sephrym will not let me search. Warders are intelligent beings. They get bored. Now that Sephrym has me, he can observe the people here and be entertained. He will not let that go."

Terrek peered at the little blaze and his slumbering friends around it. "I wish you could help us," he said, frowning. "Why *did* you come here today, if not to give us your aid? Surely it wasn't to welcome me to your mountain. Do you mean to take Avalar home?"

Ponu gazed into his staff's clear crystal. "Avalar would not wish it. She is the daughter of a former slave. You met him. You know he is dear to me. Avalar's is the first generation in four hundred cycles not to know what bondage feels like. She will *not* learn that lesson from me. However, I am concerned, Terrek Florne. Kildoren was correct. The valley you plan to enter may indeed destroy her. I do not mean physically. In her distress, she might not remember to call out for my help, so I am asking you to."

"You want me to call you?" Terrek glanced at the camp and Avalar's larger bulk beside the others. Wind lashed the fire he had built, sending a line of sparks skittering over the snow.

"Yes, call my name," said Ponu, "if ever a time comes when you cannot control her." He rapped Terrek's shin, demanding his attention. "You *must.* If she loses herself, she might not hear your words. A giant fully enraged, her blood running hot in her veins, cannot stop fighting without help."

Sitting back, Ponu flared his wings for emphasis. "*I* can restrain her," he said. "Should her memories take hold, there might be no other way to get her back. Speak my name, and I will come."

Stiffly Terrek stood. Then once more the wind gusted, snuffing out the little blaze.

∞ ∞ ∞

FOLLOWING WREN'S EXAMPLE, Gaelin guided his shan closer to the wall, positioning himself as far from the steep bank as possible. Beneath his thighs, even his little beast was trembling.

The river seemed endless. As it continued its twisting, downward course, the ice loosened, the rapids roaring through the narrow gorge, frothing white over boulders and trapped debris. The crusty trail cracked under the hooves of the six shan, chips of it splashing among the churning leaves and bits of dirt.

Gaelin shut his eyes as freezing droplets splashed his brow. Clenching Mornius, he leaned against the granite wall close beside him. This was better, he decided. The pain kept him alert, and the rock bruising his skin through his jacket felt solid and secure, so near to the raging beast the river had become.

"We have to keep going!" Terrek called out. "It's too dangerous to stop here!"

Vaguely, Gaelin nodded. A part of him was drifting again, floating unencumbered among the stars. So much of him yearned for the freedom he missed, to live again as a servant of the universe. He had tried too hard to protect his beautiful sun, reducing himself, failing to destroy his foe . . .

Gaelin screamed as the bank collapsed under his shan. The beast bugled, its powerful hind legs slipping off the edge, its cloven feet kicking wildly. "*Help!*" Gaelin cried. Reaching with his staff, he leaned over the creature's straining neck. Then the shan's front hooves broke through the ice, shattering the surface down its length.

With a terrified warble, the little beast fell.

Gripping Mornius, Gaelin hit the frigid water. His vision went black. He tumbled through thunder and mind-numbing cold. His knees slammed rock, twin jolts of pain.

He caught a quick glimpse of sunlight, the frozen bank flashing by above his head. Someone else was in the river, sprinting fast, large feet thumping through the churning sediment. Desperate for air, Gaelin opened his mouth, choking as gritty water filled his lungs.

Something jerked at his wrist, pulling him hard from the current. Breathless, Gaelin gaped at the world. He was being lifted and carried and then passed to someone else.

"Here. Stretch him here, Wren!" yelled Terrek. "No, not like that, on his *side*."

Slowly Gaelin blinked. Liquid dribbled from his mouth over his cheek. His body jerked as a hand struck him between his shoulders— once, and again. He gagged and coughed hard.

Fingers tugged off his clothes, shifting him this way and that. A thick fur was tucked around his arms and under his chin. Someone was holding him, cradling him.

"You saved his life," said Terrek. "Thank you, Giant."

"And *you*," Avalar said.

Gaelin lay limp, too cold to move. From in front and behind came voices he knew. His shan lay dead, dispatched by Silva after breaking its back. Avalar had leapt to stop his fall, and Wren Neche had grabbed for his staff a moment later but had missed.

His staff. His body swaying gently, Gaelin frowned up at the giant bearing him. Avalar was losing her fear of his magic. Because of him, she trusted too much.

"Where is his staff?" she queried as if she discerned his thoughts.

"Here," answered Terrek, slapping his gloved palm against leather. "Wren found it on the ice."

Avalar plodded on in silence. Gaelin, shivering hard beneath the giant's furry cloak, pressed his face to her neck. His whole body ached; his knees were on fire, his calves and feet tingling.

"What do you know of his past?" Avalar inquired. She slowed her stride to match Terrek's shan. "How did you find him?"

Terrek cleared his throat. "I know you wish to be supportive. But you should ask him that question, not me."

"I mislike this place," she said. "Here, we would be trapped, should the dach army find us. How far did Kildoren say this trench goes?"

"To the base of the mountain," said Terrek. "This wall at our flank becomes the river's high bank. In the spring, when the snow melts, the river swells, and according to the elves . . ."

Through Gaelin's drowsing, Holram listened, his thoughts on

Mornius, his ancient tool. No longer did the staff bind him. He was awake, aware, and able to communicate through his host. Never again would he be helpless. "*I am the song,*" he whispered.

Chapter 38

elrina faced the Attendant First, her arms crossed over her chest to quell her trembling. Beyond him stood the open doorway of her chamber, a glimpse of freedom she knew she would never have. "*Why* is Mens doing this?" she cried. "He rapes me and takes my staff? Why? I make his *dachs*!"

A slight frown wrinkled the gray-robe's forehead. He peered past her at Gulgrin scurrying back and forth. Frantic with fear, her apprentice was lighting every candle in the room. "Steady, Gulgrin," the boy muttered to himself. "*Focus!*"

Felrina planted her hands on her hips. "Why here in my room?" she demanded. "If Mens intends to sacrifice me, there must be a ritual, isn't that right? We'll need an altar with . . . troughs to catch my blood. And the others to . . . partake!"

She shuddered as the First's calm gaze met hers. "This is all very untoward, Priestess," he replied. "None of us know what the leader's plans entail. The communion will take place as usual; Mens has assured me of that much at least. It will be performed in the chamber below, where you will be transferred once you are ready. He'll have a runner send us word."

Her mouth went dry. "What does he plan to do to me?"

"I am not him. I cannot say what he has in mind," said the First, his attention sliding to the bed behind her. "I suspect he'll flay you for the ceremony, or at least the parts he likes. He enjoys that with women.

"Your clothing," he said. "Remove it."

"Gulgrin," she whispered, "please go." Her apprentice's face blanched beneath his wavy black hair. Despite her fear, she went to him, gripping his bony shoulders. "Go!" She lowered her voice.

"Listen, get *away* from these people if you can! Whatever he plans, it will be bad, and I don't want you to see. Just *go*!"

Gulgrin groaned with indecision. Releasing him, she stepped aside as he skirted the First and stumbled out. With shaking fingers, she began to disrobe.

"Now what?" she asked when she was done. She turned, covering herself as best she could with her arms.

Mens stood behind the Attendant First, his grin widening as he hefted her staff. Crimson power blasted from the Blazenstone, striking her full across the chest. She flew back, her body going numb, her right elbow shattering as she struck the wall and flopped onto the bed.

"You may leave," Mens told the First, his tone pleasant yet firm. Felrina, eyes frozen shut, heard the rustle of Mens's robes as he crossed her little room, followed by the grunt when he heaved something heavy onto the table.

Desperately she fought to unclench her teeth, to manipulate her tongue enough to speak.

"I thought I told you to *get out*!" Mens snapped.

"You will require an assistant," the First protested. "No ritual is done without at least one—"

"This is not the ceremony," said Mens. His tools clattered onto the table beside her pillow. "I have some techniques I want to try out to *prepare* her."

"There will be no rite to go with this?" the First queried.

Felrina held her breath. *Please*, *Fin*, she thought to the man. *Stop him!*

"You'll get your blood," Mens drawled. "But not tonight. Now go. This one's going to take a while!"

Felrina struggled for air while the Attendant First, after a lengthy pause, shuffled out. Then the bed creaked as Mens settled next to her. "Yes," he breathed into her hair. "We're going to be very quiet, aren't we? No more cries, and no sounds from *this*"—Mens touched her throat—"at all. In fact . . ." There was a low scraping as he pulled a chair close, followed by the soft squeak of wood. "I think you'll be far too busy trying to hold your breath."

He seized her shoulders and flattened her on the mattress. "Nice and relaxed," he murmured. "Felrina, if nothing else, you are predictable. I have the staff, and the rest has played out just as I hoped. Your flesh is now *mine* to carve up and kill. I *knew* you'd try to stop that ritual. Still, I enjoyed our moments together earlier very much. I see no reason to be done with that yet. Only this time, let's make it a game, shall we?"

His ragged panting filled the room, and in the sliver of light beneath her eyelids, Felrina spied the little saw beside her left breast. "You, my dear, get to control how quickly we do this. Each time you're forced to inhale, I get to cut you a little more."

GAELIN STOOD WHERE Avalar had left him, gazing up at Mount Alianth's white slopes, which Avalar had named *Ponu's Peak.* Beside him, the Shukaia cut a vicious gash in the mountain's wide flank, a cut that bled copiously despite the clogging ice, its black currents descending to cross the curve of the landscape below.

"I feel so small," he whispered, gazing at the immense valley, at the darkened hills and clusters of frozen trees between him and the forest beyond. Through this they would need to travel, staying under cover as best they could.

He turned to the pony-sized beast next to him, the calico pack-shan splaying its forelegs to lip at the snow. Wren Neche sat beside Silva nearby, feigning alertness. Not far from the two warriors, Avalar hunched over her sword, cleaning the blade with a tattered cloth.

Terrek moved among the four other shan, his breath pluming in the air. With him strode Roth, unconsciously mimicking his posture and stride.

"You have changed much, Warder," a voice said.

Argus hovered above him within his cloud of emerald light, his phantom wrists crossed over the emblazoned hawk on his breastplate. Slowly the ghost reached out, tapping Gaelin's brow with a fleshless finger. "Are you *in* there, my friend?"

Holram smiled as his weary human host retreated among his thoughts. "I am here," he said. "And in the staff, also."

"Ah," murmured Argus. Bobbing gently, he reclined on his back, eyeing the moonless sky.

"I will miss our talks," Holram told him. "There is beauty where I go, but isolation as well. Warders create and protect. That is all. There are no friends."

"You'll still have me." Argus grinned. "I like to think I'll be able to visit you. I am a *ghost*, you know."

"I do hope, after I am free at last from this world, I may retain some contact with young Gaelin through my stone," Holram said. "The boy might have difficulty at first, living without me."

"Hmm," said Argus. "You mean *this* little mortal would become our one connection?"

Gaelin blinked to clear his vision, finding himself nodding at the ghost. His face went hot when Argus, watching him, grunted. "Home again, gone again," the specter sang. "Jiggity jig."

Slowly Argus rose above the treetops, his arms spread wide as if to hug the stars. His visage, when at last Gaelin saw it, gleamed silver with phantom tears.

Chapter 39

Avalar raised her hand, shielding her eyes from the glare of sunlight on the drifts as she ventured into the open where the river entered the valley. After a moment, she turned back to peer below the branches at her companions.

"*Then* what do I do?" Gaelin was asking. The staff-wielder sat on a stump by the fire while Terrek fastened snow-paddles to his boots. He wriggled his leg until Terrek gripped his ankle to hold it still. "How am I supposed to walk in these?"

"You're in my light," Terrek complained, his swollen fingers fumbling with the straps.

Avalar crouched beside him. "This is a new pair," she pointed out. "They have never been used so the hide is stiff. Here." She yanked off her gloves with her teeth and folded Terrek's hands gently between her own. For a long moment she massaged them, blowing her warm breath through her fingers.

Abruptly, she released him. "Now it should be easier," she said.

"Oh, I see," said Gaelin, watching Roth and the two guards try out their Eris footgear. The men were already beyond the trees, struggling to walk on the tops of the drifts.

We use paddles, too, Avalar thought. *Not like these, but similar. An oval of wood lashed with leather.* She smiled as Terrek hooked the last buckle. "I wish now I had remembered to bring mine," she told him.

"If only the Eris had a pair in your size," Terrek grumbled. He gestured to Gaelin. "Walk around and get used to them. You'll figure it out." He claimed the seat Gaelin vacated, and as the staff-wielder went floundering toward the other men, he bent to attach the devices to his own boots.

"Let me," Avalar said, staying his hand.

She sniffed as she worked. In the corner of her eye she saw Mount Alianth through the trees. Somewhere, high above the peak's wintry slopes, Ponu would be gazing from his cave at the same cloudy sky.

Or observing me in his mirror, she thought. *Even on Thalus, I am not free.*

Standing to help her leader to his feet, she glanced at the shifting haze above the river. The wisps coalesced into streamers as she watched, a graceful line of dancers swaying to and fro. *Not so unlike the colored lights we see in the sky north from Hothra.* She smiled despite herself. The fog stretched into forms she fancied were faery people, the elves' distant cousins on Tholuna. *Or mayhap they are the giants from long ago;* her mouth went dry as the thought intruded. Shivering, she heaved her pack onto her shoulders and stamped out the fire.

"KEEP GOING!" AVALAR laughed as Gaelin tripped and almost fell. He had been demonstrating his newfound skill, grinning as he lurched in a tight circle in his ungainly footwear. "The others are leaving you behind!"

She froze as the mist solidified above the riverbank, a giant taking on form at its edge. The figure's shimmering skin was the inky black of the royal and long-extinct bloodline. Unseen by her companions, the specter passed through their bodies, his muscular arms outstretched as he shambled toward her, his torn, short-sleeved tunic covered with blood and his transparent jaw stretched in a howl.

Avalar sagged to the snow. The arrival of the ghost sparked a burning along her nerves, the memory of heat the phantom carried from happier moments in his life, a time when he had roamed under Tholuna's searing sun.

She strained to focus through the fog accompanying the ghost. *Who am I?* she wondered, gazing blankly at flashes of darkness, of dank, smelly stone pressing close to her neck and hunched back. She was cringing on her bloody knees, her back stinging under the rhythmic fall of the lash. Weak from hunger, she quaked as she tried to raise her scraper and work so that her pain might stop.

She moaned as the apparition touched her face. Then it softened to vapor and blew apart.

"Giant?" Terrek said. He had been speaking to her for some time, calling her name repeatedly as he hastened to join her. "What is it?"

"I . . . know not, Leader Terrek." Avalar staggered to her feet as Roth, Silva, and Wren plodded by, each of them leading a lightly burdened shan and carrying what the lazy beasts had refused. Bugling joyfully, the little creatures burrowed and breast-stroked through the deep snow, their tufted tails sticking straight up.

She fell in behind the peculiar procession, sinking to her knees in the icy whiteness. Stubbornly she waded past Terrek. While he walked unencumbered with his back straight, she flailed and panted. Glancing to her left, she spotted random blades of grass jutting above the snow by the river. Turning, she plowed toward them.

"Good idea!" Terrek approved, "but not too far, Giant! And watch that ice!"

Avalar grunted and trudged, sinking and thrashing, her dread mounting as the steam gathered thick above the water's currents. She gasped when her ankle twisted, her calf muscle spasming painfully, and as she kneaded her aching limb through her boot, a blanket of fog rolled in.

A memory weaved itself around her from the sun's flickering rays, from the gray lines of shadow below the Shukaia's frigid banks, and 8from the mist's unending skeins. A vision of giants rose, surrounding her on all sides. Her people were chained together in a circle with their bloody wrists connected, both children and adults, their features pale as wax, the grooves on their cheeks carved deep by unfathomable agony.

In horror and rage, Avalar's mouth stretched in a silent scream. Four mottled grakan snarled as she sank beneath the weight of her chains. She was to be devoured, along with her friends and family. A rough voice shouted beyond the mist, a human slaver urging the bearlike creatures on.

As one, the great beasts sprang. She lay supine, the shaggy

monster above her tearing out her throat, her blood spraying crimson while she pushed in vain at its bony chest. Yet still she witnessed her people falling, their bodies torn apart. Malnourished and sick as they were, her people died mute, leaving their corpses to nourish the grass.

With a jolt, she remembered who she was and where she stood. Forgotten was the pain in her calf. *River's end*, she thought. *The land of 'final journey' where the injured slaves were taken to be killed.* She stuck out her arms to keep her balance, for the world was spinning, a kaleidoscope of haggard faces, tortured bodies, and wounded hearts. *These are memories, not ghosts. They cannot be real!*

Across the cloudy sky, she spied leathery bat-like wings, the gray body of a lone dach winging her way. She growled as voices clamored behind her, her human companions struggling to reach her in their clumsy gear. Then the snow field erupted into steam, a fretwork of fire zigzagging through the drifts.

High overhead, the enemy hovered, howling its frustration. It tilted its wings into a dive.

As she yanked out her sword, a powerful hand snatched her wrist. Turning, she saw Gaelin beside her, his staff aimed at the creature.

"*Now!*" said Holram's voice through her friend, and a painful tearing sensation seized her chest.

The fog seethed around her hips, and Mornius's flames rebounded to vanish within Gaelin. His staff dropped away, and he exploded with light, sheets of lurid power blasting from his body.

The dach reeled, tumbling backward through the air. Avalar crashed to her knees near the fallen staff and fought to pull away from Gaelin's grasp, aware of Terrek thrusting toward her, and Holram's spirit tearing her apart, his power gripping hers, manipulating it against her will.

She remembered the staff-wielder's words, how the magic of giants could heal such as this, but that had been Gaelin. Now, in his place, a god stood blazing, barely resembling the little human she knew.

With all her force of will, try as she might, she could not stop him. *Nor can the dach*, she thought, seeing how the multicolored flames bound the creature, their tendrils mirroring the fingers of Gaelin's lifted hand. Pulsing, the magic transformed her stricken foe.

The dach's wings and tail melted, the unnatural flesh merging with its body. As the warped human's legs shrank and thickened, the spikes folded and slumped, vanishing into its spine.

Avalar screamed for it to end, yet the hiss of vapor muted her cry. The edges of her vision darkened, blurring everything but the sky and the magic, and the dach, now a man, being lowered to the slushy ground.

She gasped in pain when Gaelin let her go, the staff-wielder collapsing in a boneless heap. Her friends were shouting above the shan's anxious warbles. Avalar sheathed her sword and then dragged Gaelin from the icy water, propping him against her.

Dazed, she scanned the melted field. A short distance in front of her, Terrek knelt and shrugged off his woolen cloak to cover the stranger's shivering form.

"Captain Vyergin's not dead," Gaelin murmured.

"Vyergin?" she echoed. She scooped the staff-wielder into her lap.

Terrek and Roth approached, supporting the man between them. While Silva and Roth lifted Vyergin onto the bronze shan's wide back, Terrek hastened to the other smaller beasts, jostling the first to get at the one behind it.

"Clothes!" Vyergin burst out. "Boots, *blazes* yes! What a lousy morning! Is there no hot tea? Who put *you* in charge, anyway?"

"I think that was my father," Terrek answered with a grin.

The men were converging around the captain, hiding him as best they could from her view. Terrek returned with a bundle of woolens and leathers: his beaver-fur cloak, a dangling sock, gloves, a gray woven shirt. There were leggings, too, and something else—a tan pair of torn underjohns.

"You can have these!" Roth offered, hurrying over with a charcoal pair of riding boots. "I bought them at Westermore, but they pinch my toes, and I think your feet are smaller."

Terrek prodded Vyergin gently. "We'll find clothing that fits you later," he said in a hearty voice. "There are the supplies we foraged from your crate. From the one you had on your sled, remember? Plus, Oburne did some scavenging after the battle. We lost most of our men."

While Wren and Roth helped Vyergin dress, Terrek met his glare. "Oburne didn't strip the dead," said Terrek. "He only took what he thought we could use from the tents."

"Lucky for them that they died." Vyergin winced. "I need armor!"

"Later!" Terrek said. "Once we reach those trees." With a vigorous snap, Terrek cleared the snow from his beaver cloak and handed it over. "What in the blackest blazes happened to you, Captain?"

Vyergin shuddered. "Not my favorite thing. That's for damn sure." He wrapped the cloak about his shoulders. "I shouldn't remember. Oh, but I do. That black-robe had no idea what he was doing with that staff! So many of us died terribly—a great shadowy fist crushing men into pulp. They were slaughtered, butchered by that *thing*! All because that idiot black-robe couldn't make dachs right."

"He made *you*," Terrek pointed out.

"True, but I was among the last, and even I was flawed. I retained my self-awareness. He took everything else from me, but he couldn't take that! So yours truly knew enough to escape the moment I spied the open sky!"

Gaelin moaned as Avalar shook him. "Wake *up*," she hissed into his ear. "You must rouse yourself! It is too cold to sit here, Gaelin. Keep moving."

"Staff-Wielder!" Vyergin dropped from the shan's back, teetering as Wren Neche attached the Eris's paddles to his boots.

"You'll need them, my friend," Terrek said. "When we reach the deeper drifts, you'll understand what I—"

Vyergin snorted. "You think I've never worn snowshoes? What am I? A greenhorn?" With confident strides, he approached Gaelin.

"He has been taken by his warder," Avalar warned Vyergin, smiling despite herself at the welcome sight of the man's familiar face. "I cannot promise he is himself."

Vyergin's eyes narrowed. The lines in his face had deepened from his ordeal, yet his skin was still firm, his muscles lean and hard.

"I'm me," Gaelin reassured them. "Just tired."

Vyergin gestured to Mornius lying in the slush by Avalar's leg. "I've never wanted to be on the receiving end of *that*," he said. "But today I find myself grateful you carry it. Once more you have my thanks, little mage. But what in the North's white blazes is *that* ugly thing?"

The calico shan thrust past Avalar, stretching out its flat muzzle inquisitively to nibble Vyergin's graying hair. "Ugh!" he gasped, pinching his nostrils as he batted at the snuffling nose. "What drop-house has this fellow been in?"

"That's my Vyergin." Terrek grinned.

"Please," said Gaelin in a choked voice, "you need to know about Hawk. When we came upon him up on the mountain, he was dead. He had fallen into the river."

"Ah, *blazes*." Vyergin scratched at the stubble of his beard.

"I would have saved him," Gaelin continued sadly. "But we were too late. I . . ."

"I *know* you would have. But I think you'll learn in time that you can't fix everything, Lavahl, be it you or . . . whatever that thing is inside you," Vyergin said. "Hawk did well for me. I just hope his ending was quick."

"I believe it was," Terrek told him quietly.

Avalar gulped, eyeing the river's haunted mist with suspicion. She shivered at her weakness, remembering her proud defiance in the tree of the Eris Temple, her declaration of fealty despite the naked fear the elves had shown.

Abruptly Gaelin pulled away from her and stood, stepping with care through the slush to retrieve his staff. As Avalar prepared to rise also, Terrek's touch on her arm stopped her.

"How are you?" he asked. "I saw what Holram did. And I know it drained you, too. I can tell how this place is hurting you, Avalar. Tell me what we can do."

"I am a giant, Leader Terrek." Grimly she nodded toward the mist. "Others of my kind have endured far worse."

Chapter 40

Gaelin frowned as he surveyed the giant's progress along the river. Often, she blundered into the silvery mist, as if seeking a union with the tendrils of fog. At intervals she stopped to mutter to herself, gesturing to urge the wispy shapes around her to flee.

Gripping Mornius, Gaelin lurched at Vyergin's side toward Terrek, his calves and hips aching.

"Why aren't you resting?" Terrek demanded. He straightened from cleaning his shan's splayed hoof. "Isn't that herb supposed to make you sleepy?"

"That was the tagwort," said Gaelin, drawing near to rub the forehead of Terrek's shan. "The yellow powder Ponu gave to Vyergin doesn't do a thing."

"Apparently it does," Terrek said. "You're on your feet, aren't you?"

Gaelin shrugged. "At least there's no wind." He buried his fingers in the shan's bristled mane. Beyond the animals, Wren and Deravin Silva were guarding the packs and gear, their soft conversation inaudible above the fall of snow.

"Do you see the giant?" asked Terrek. Then he pointed. "Look at her. By the river again, even though something about it hurts her. Why would she do that? She hasn't been right since you used her to heal Vyergin. How could you risk jeopardizing her, *Warder*?" He emphasized the word. Glancing at his men, he lowered his voice. "You joined with her magic. You couldn't do it alone, could you? You needed her help."

Gaelin felt the shifting inside as Holram, roused by the direct question, stepped to the front, pushing him back in his haste to answer. With a certainty Gaelin did not share, Holram said, "She was never in danger. Indeed, I do need her. Just as Erebos requires water to manipulate strong magic, so do I utilize her flesh, for she is Talenkai. It is because of my need to connect with this world that my staff was made. If you want me to be of use to you, this is what I must do."

Terrek sighed. "I thank you for restoring Captain Vyergin," he said. "He has been a staunch friend to my father for many years, and a great asset to me."

Holram shrugged. "I am a caretaker of suns, Terrek Florne," he said. "Perhaps your gratitude holds significance for others of your kind, but I am not human."

"Good, then know this," Terrek snapped. "Avalar suffered trying to save my brother's life. That makes her family. But even if that wasn't the case, she is my responsibility. Next time you wish to indulge in reckless behavior, *consult* me first. Not because I'm a commander. This has never been an army; our titles are nothing but my father's ridiculous whim. But with the single exception of Gaelin here, these men who are left are employees. My father put me in charge of them, and I vowed I'd try to lead them well."

"At this moment, the giant is with her people," Holram said. "Not yours. She possesses the memories of her forebears, recorded within her magic. Her present turmoil has nothing to do with me or with how I used her to heal your captain. This land torments her, Terrek Florne. On this ground, many giants perished, and now she is forced to experience those deaths. You must escape this valley. Stop picking at these animals and wasting your time. They are not horses, so there is no need. If you really wish to help her, you must flee!"

"So that's her problem?" Vyergin asked with a glance at the giant. "Terrek, did you know about this?"

"You weren't there. And yes, I knew. The elves told us as much. But we can't sprout wings and fly," Terrek said to Holram. "That drug in Gaelin helps him recover, but not completely. If he doesn't have rest, he will sicken and—"

"He will never wholly mend," Holram cut in. "The boy is dying, Terrek Florne, and he will die. There is no remedy for what you humans call aging, but *time* is not to be the cause of Gaelin's demise. His exposure to my power will be. Much like the sacrifices on my enemy's altar, he is the lamb upon mine."

Terrek drew a sharp breath. "You're telling me you've killed him? After all he's been through, now he has no hope?"

Holram scanned the river. "I do not delight in the death of innocents as Erebos does. I am fond of Gaelin and will do my best to save him. But for now, you must find a way to coax the giant from this valley. If you fail in this or delay much longer, Avalar's tortured mind could be split in two."

"I could ask her to leave," Terrek mused, "like I did after her first night."

"Be still," urged Holram. "She is coming!"

With massive strides, the giant plowed through the drifts, her face flushed, her fists clenched at her sides.

"Leader Terrek!" Avalar slammed to a halt, her fury sending the shan into a panic, a milling of cloven hooves, of shaggy manes and tails flying.

"Easy," Terrek soothed her. "Remember what Kildoren said. These creatures the forest elves ride have protective magic that will change them into something terrible. I'd rather not deal with that right now."

Bending to catch her breath, Avalar swiped back her dripping hair. "Pardon," she said, forcing a semblance of calm into her voice. "Your ghost, Leader Terrek. I desire his counsel. He will comprehend what I see. Mayhap he can interpret what I cannot! Leader Terrek, aid me, for I cannot find him. Have you sheathed his weapon? Have you cast away his sword?"

"No!" Terrek caught her wrist, tugging at her as he spoke. "I freed the ghost, remember? I must wield his blade now because mine was destroyed! I lost the scabbard, Giant. Not his sword!"

She broke loose with a snarl. "So *where*? Where did he *go*?"

"Avalar, if I knew, I would tell you," said Terrek.

"He will return soon!" Holram said, meeting her fiery glower beneath her unkempt blond hair. "He must, for he is bound to that steel."

"Avalar, walk in front of us, will you?" Terrek motioned toward the trees. "Head that way, and stay away from the river. Break trail in the snow so we can ride. Gaelin is tired and he needs to rest. Can you do that for me?"

Good, Holram thought. *Give her something to do.*

"I am a giant," Avalar replied. "If I may aid you, I will."

Holram saw the conflict on the giant's face as she glanced again at the narrowing river, her eyes wincing at the sight. He yearned to enter her mind to help her understand. The terror assailing her was a memory; the reality of it had occurred long ago. Even a prowler would fight now to the death—*and had done*, he realized as he remembered Shetra—to keep a giant safe.

"I will do as you bid me," Avalar answered. She thrust herself forward, plowing toward the distant trees.

Holram met Terrek's grim gaze. "Gaelin is dozing," he answered the question in the human's eyes. "Until he wakes, I cannot return to the staff."

"Send her home," Vyergin said. "I've seen what's ahead, and it only gets worse. You're asking her to go where her people were slaughtered."

"You think I don't know?" said Terrek. "I'm not asking anything from her! She's here because she wants to be. It's what she is. How would you feel if I ordered *you* home?"

"Oh, *would* you?" Grinning, Vyergin placed a saddle on the largest shan. "One good meal and a bath, that's all I ask. And before you know it, I'd be running right back to you like the homeless cur I am, to fight with Lucian Florne's son! Believe it or not, I still think we can win this."

"Erebos has wanted the giants' extinction," Holram said. "The one threat to him other than myself would be the defenders of this world. Now they no longer ride their Azkhar males to battle. Rather they hide at the elves' behest. In this way, Erebos has already won."

"Well, this is one giant he will not get to kill," Terrek vowed. "Not while I live and breathe."

Holram nodded. As the others readied the shan to follow the giant, he limped toward the calico. "*Gaelin, for the sake of your health, you must stop sleeping*," he thought to his host. "*I do not wish to harm you.*" He fumbled to remove the paddles from his boots, then tucked them into the pack behind the saddle. Sighing at the fever mounting in his flesh, he considered the shan's wide back.

The wet leather of Gaelin's leggings abraded his thigh when he raised his foot. The sensation was unpleasant, he discovered while the shan, turning its head, lashed at his hip with its tail.

"I do not like you, either," Holram told the beast. He scrambled up at last and, clinging to the creature's mane, settled awkwardly in the saddle. Remembering Kildoren's words, he tipped his heels down, tilting his toes away from the animal's ribs. He sat for a moment, gasping for breath while Terrek hurried on foot after the giant.

Vyergin, sitting astride Terrek's shan, hung back. When Holram rode abreast of him, he snatched the calico's reins. "*You* aren't ready for this, and you know it," Vyergin growled. "I have watched Erebos work. You are no match for him."

"As my enemy has gained power extinguishing life," Holram told him, "so I have grown stronger by restoring it. I have not been idle, Brant Vyergin. Perhaps I am mightier now than you know."

Vyergin nudged his shan into a fast walk. "You don't care what you're doing to this boy," he said. "He is sick, and still here you are, making him worse. You won't let him be. You're a parasite. You're as toxic as Erebos."

With a hard yank, Holram reclaimed his reins from Vyergin's grasp. "Indeed, warders are lethal to creatures of flesh and blood. To save yourselves, you must be rid of us both."

Vyergin snorted and wheeled his beast, Terrek's beaver cloak flaring as he rode at a shambling lope after his companions. Trailing him, Holram let his calico dawdle. He rode with his thoughts directed inward, mulling over the captain's concern.

"Friends," Holram whispered at last, savoring the feel of the word on his tongue. A low thunder rumbled above him. He squinted at the whorls of fog obscuring the treetops, blinking at the granules needling his face. He rode with his head tipped back, his spirit reaching from the confines of Gaelin's flesh. Up and out he stretched with his mental arms, longing for the void that was his home. He knew the empty coldness—for the whole of his long life he had dwelled within that realm. Above all else, it had taught him patience.

Beneath the thickening snow, he was willing to wait, rocking drowsily on his little beast.

Hands caught at his shan's reins. He was lifted from the animal and set on his feet, then guided toward a fire below the trees.

Wren Neche knelt to wrap him in a blanket. Holram, nodding to the guard, gripped the scratchy wool with fingers that burned, hugging it to himself as he peered into the flames.

Beyond the blaze, Avalar crouched on her heels. "My father says giants are free," she said. "Staying on Hothra is our way now to protect the world, but this is a lie, the falsehood the elves teach to our children. The sword has told me this, and I believe it. No one is free in a burning house. We either flee or we fight its destruction. To survive to see it whole again, we *must*."

Holram shivered under his blanket, inclining his shoulders toward the fire's heat. "To flee is not an option for you. Your only choice is to fight. Erebos has grown. The closer I get, the more I feel it. He is fully mature, and I am not."

The giant sat on her cloak with its white fur over her legs, her quiet gaze meeting his. Vyergin stepped into view, an iron pot swinging from his gloved hand, heavy with broth for a stew. He bent to prod at the glowing brands with a stick before positioning the blackened vessel among them.

"Like old times," Terrek remarked, smiling. "Welcome back, Captain."

"Brant Vyergin understands," Holram said. "He witnessed the perversion that is Erebos, and his heart bears the scars. Inquire of *him*, Terrek Florne. You should comprehend what it is you align yourself with. I am poison to you. I belong among the stars."

Quiet fell upon the camp, punctuated by the snap of the flames. Finally, Terrek looked up. "You're telling us we shouldn't trust you?"

Avalar exploded to her feet. By the time Holram started to contemplate dodging her, she was on him, seizing him by the front of his tunic and hauling him to her level. She shook him hard, rattling his teeth. "*Hear me!*" she snarled. "You are a *warder*! And I am a *giant*! We do what we must, which is *all* we can do! You will *not* threaten the Circle! I have beheld it and I trust you. So, too, does Leader Terrek. Now you"—she gave him another hard shake—"must trust yourself!"

Roughly she set him back on his feet, but at once clasped his arm, steadying him.

Holram swayed under the weight of her glare. Terrek, his mouth stern, pulled at the giant's fingers. "Easy does it, Avalar. He is *Gaelin*, too, remember? Don't hurt him!"

"I do not question myself," Holram reassured her. "I only seek to make it clear what you must—" Quaking, he sank to his knees. The salty smell of Vyergin's broth triggered a rolling response, a rhythmic clenching in Gaelin's stomach that he could not stop. Helplessly, Holram gagged as a vile taste flooded his mouth. Then he was heaving, spewing the meager contents of Gaelin's stomach over the ground. "What?" he gasped. "What . . . is wrong?"

"Nothing is wrong," said Terrek. "You're just ill, *Gaelin*." Deliberately he invoked the name, his meaning clear, and Holram, relieved to be relinquishing his hold at last, returned to his staff with a sigh.

"Gaelin?" Terrek crouched, offering him a fistful of snow to cleanse his mouth.

Gaelin gathered himself and stood, wiping his lips. "I need to sleep," he mumbled. "I'm so tired. When I helped Vyergin, Holram kindled all his power in me and through me. Not Mornius. He focused with the staff, but he directed . . . *all* his power . . ."

With a sigh he let himself go, tumbling back into Terrek's strong grasp.

Chapter 41

elrina started awake on her soggy mattress. Through the rattle and catch of her breathing, she heard a faint knock. "Priestess?" called a familiar voice as her door creaked open, spilling light across the room. Gulgrin, his lamp held high, ventured in, liquid sloshing in the vessel he carried against his chest. He cursed softly as the fluid splashed the front of his tunic and his gray robe.

She shifted limply at the sound. Her wrists were tied, her arms bound loosely to the post above her head. With one eye swollen and the other sealed shut, she strained to make out her apprentice as he shuffled through the shadows toward her.

"What's he *done*?" Gulgrin asked in a strangled voice. "Why's it taking so long?" He stiffened as the glow from his lantern found her. "Oh!" He staggered back to crash into the little table. It toppled over, its bloody implements clattering to the floor.

She struggled to breathe as Gulgrin hastened to right the table and replace Mens's tools.

Briefly he touched her wrists while he loosened the coarse rope binding them. "He . . . told us you were ready," Gulgrin stammered. "The others are gathering in the chamber below. It's true? You're . . . dying?"

She wanted to answer, to curl up in a ball, to gouge Mens's eyes out with her fingers, but again the mental shield she had created blocked him, cradling her in gentle oblivion. From far away she had experienced the pain, from a refuge to which her abuser's leering face could not go.

"It *is* true," he whispered.

She groaned as his arms slid under her bruised ribs and eased her from the fouled mattress onto the floor. The soothing coldness of the bare stone pressed upon her skin. He lifted her mattress, bits of its damp straw landing on her cheek as he carried its sagging bulk from her room.

"This is better, I think. See?" Gulgrin, talking mostly to himself, dragged the heavy replacement across the stone and dropped the woven straw into the frame. His robes rustled by her ear as he knelt.

"I must prepare you for the communion," he told her, his voice both gentle and sad. "That's what he said. The others might not want to partake if you smell."

She tensed when water dribbled across her skin, Gulgrin's soft cloth dabbing at her tender scabs.

"You're so hurt," he whispered. She held herself rigid while the rag did its work, drawing blood from injuries she had almost forgotten. "I know the suffering part is necessary to strengthen Erebos. But *this . . .*" He choked.

She winced at the reek of corruption from her various wounds, the painful ruin that remained of her burned chest. "*You, my dear, get to control how quickly we do this,*" Mens's voice echoed in her head. "*Each time you're forced to inhale, I get to cut you a little more!*"

A sudden, stabbing pain jerked her back to the present. Writhing, she screamed. "I'm sorry!" Gulgrin gasped, jumping to his feet. "I didn't mean to— Oh, *Felrina!*"

Once more he raised her up, laying her back on the bed. "I won't retie you," he told her. "There's no need anymore. They're coming for you, Priestess. I promise, all this will end soon!"

For a moment more, he clutched at her, grinding the splinters of her broken wrist. "I'm sorry," he breathed into the silence as she twisted in pain. "I must *go!*"

Felrina shivered at the chill air on her skin. Gulgrin backed away. She sighed as the dancing flame went out. Dazed, she absorbed the novice's words. Shortly the door would reopen, and her attendants would be there, ready and willing to finish their work.

Her chamber was becloaked by night. *This is better*, she thought. *Mens works in the light.*

"*Move!*" a voice cracked.

Felrina struggled to focus. The resonating quality of the speaker's scorn seemed familiar somehow, yet it was neither Arawn's spirit in her mind nor Erebos's roar of thunder. She lifted her head from her pillow, blindly scanning the blackness.

"He's left you *untied*," snarled the voice. "It's your one opportunity. Don't waste it!"

She fought to move, to drag herself up on the mattress until her bare feet touched the stone. She gasped when a vision appeared in front of her, the gray figure of a warrior knight, its outline ablaze with green fire. The grim specter pointed imperiously at her wadded-up clothing. "Cover yourself!" he commanded. "I am here as your guide."

"What?" She gagged at the sour taste in her mouth. A wave of dizziness took her, and then with a shudder, she reached with her shattered fingers for her leggings.

"Argus," said the ghost. "You are nigh unto death, and so I am visible to you. Your condition has forced me to be aware of you. Perhaps with your help, I may save a friend. If I can lead you out of this dung-hole you're in, that is."

Felrina cried at the pain as she wriggled into the sleeves of her tunic, shaking the fabric down over her mangled skin.

"Quickly!" Argus said. "I feel it. Death is coming!"

She shakily slid her mangled toes into her boots and paused, staring at her crumpled leggings. "I d-don't believe I can!"

"You must!" spat the ghost. The specter drifted to the door. "*Hurry!*"

Doubled over, she staggered toward it. Beyond the door, the narrow passage was empty, the uneven floor littered with bits of straw. The image of the knight bobbed near the ceiling, his beady eyes glinting red. Felrina sagged in the doorway and wiped at her mouth. She froze, staring at the smear of crusted crimson it left on her hand.

"Do you *want* to be flayed alive?" The ghost hovered, his eyes blazing in the darkness—twin fiery furnaces of contemptuous heat. "I've seen how he works. Humiliation will be his final triumph. Think of the *joy* you'll bring to his face as he peels off your skin, or what's left of it, in front of all your peers!"

She ventured into the tunnel on her sore and bloody feet, hissing when the drag of her garments tore at the cauterized flesh where her breasts had been. Already fresh blood saturated the front of her tunic and coursed in warm trickles down her skin.

"Faster!" The ghost gestured. "Trust me!"

She tottered, taking one painful step and then another. She groped after his light as it ducked into a hole in the tunnel's wall, a low opening opposite her chamber. "I know this cleft." Felrina sank to her knees, peering through cobwebs at his elusive light. "It collapsed years ago. There's one that's still intact below. I could get there if I dropped through the floor."

"No, *this* way!" the specter commanded. "Hurry!"

She squirmed into the dusty shaft, using her wrists to lift the cobwebs out of her way, letting them flop back into place behind her. "I tell you, it goes nowhere. I'll be t-trapped in here."

The top of her head bumped a jumble of roots, dislodging the soil to patter onto her neck. With difficulty, she raised herself, lying aslant over a slab of smooth boulder. As her vision adjusted to the darkness, she spotted a cranny in the wall, a jagged, weeping fissure. Poking her head inside, she glimpsed a flicker on high, a tiny green speck the size of a pea.

"I hate tight spaces." She twisted her shoulders in, taking care to keep her weight on her knees and the heels of her hands. Painfully, she hitched her way up the damp stone, the angle of the gap thrusting her onto the shards of her fingers, compounding the damage as she smashed against the slimy moss coating the rocks. She hunched and quietly sobbed. "Let me die."

"Or do you want *revenge*?" The ghost's verdant light flashed brightly in front of her. "*Do* you?"

Hiccupping, she lifted her head, spying high above her the faint sliver of a starry sky.

"Hear me," the ghost said. "You cannot survive the cold up there. Not for long. I needed to get you away from *him*, but now you must hide and be silent while I fetch my friend to finish this."

Felrina thrashed upward with her elbows, straining toward freedom. "Erebos dwells within this rock. He'll sense I'm here!"

"No," said Argus. With a flash of green, he darted past her. "Consider your bare legs, my dear. You'd freeze up there long before I could bring any help." He flitted up swiftly, leaving her far out of reach of his trailing light. "I'll hurry back," he called as he shrank to a speck in the inky sliver of the open sky. "Empty your brain. If you don't think, Erebos can't hear you!"

Covering her face, Felrina ground out words. "How can you know that?"

"Because I am *dead*!" His voice was rapidly fading. "That makes me painfully aware of the Destroyer's ways. Now be *still*!"

Felrina drew into a tight ball of misery, imagining herself just as hard, cold, and unyielding as the stone.

Chapter 42

Avalar glared at the Thalian Knight's disembodied face. Argus, the rest of him glowing faintly outside her double-sized tent, poked only the front half of his head through the canvas wall to see her. She burrowed deep into her pillow of folded furs. "Go away!" Her mat was cozy and warm beneath her; blissful sleep pulled her down. "Why are you *here*?"

"Your leader is worried about you," Argus said, his green radiance hurting her eyes. "You must leave this valley behind, for it torments you."

She scowled. "I do not abandon my friends!" His grayish visage bobbed gently as he stared unblinking. "Stop *watching* me!" she complained, then rolled away from him and onto her side. "Let me be!" She thumped her pillow, glaring into the shadows.

"Time to run to the mountain," he sang. "You know you will, oh yes you will! For thou art mighty, a warrior brave and true!"

"You do not frighten me, Ghost," she told him. "Every day I endure much worse." She shuddered as the intensity of his light gradually brightened the floor in front of her. He was floating over her tent now, his glimmering face—the only part of him she could see—protruding as it traversed the ceiling.

"Those are old memories you speak of, not ghosts," he remarked, his mustached grin lowering to her level once more. "I am the *real* thing. You know, dead but, *ooh so spooky*, still *here*?"

She sighed and sat up, flopping her elbows over her furs. "What are you saying? Make haste so I may *sleep*!"

"I've located the slaver who killed Camron," he said. "Does that interest you? Finally you have a chance to avenge his death, but you must hurry, as fast as you can! At present, she has no staff for you to contend with. It's just *her*, the bitch who slew your friend!"

Avalar pulled back as Argus pressed in close. "If you do this," she warned him sternly, "quicken my blood so I lust for battle, I may not be able to stop. Some males of my kind grow immense when their blood is hot. They believe they must kill when this happens lest they die."

"This is your heart's desire, is it not?" he asked. "She is on the mountain, the same one Terrek is trying to get to. There's no need for bloodlust. You'll be scouting ahead to make sure the way is clear! I can always return in the morning to fill Terrek in so he knows."

Avalar hugged her knees. "Are you a soothsayer now, Spirit? No one knows my heart's desire. Mayhap not even I."

Argus shrugged. "Camron's slayer," he said. "The woman who slit his throat. If you do not come now . . ." His voice trailed off.

Still groggy, Avalar reached across her leather pad for her sword and gear.

∞ ∞ ∞

THE RHYTHMS THROBBED in Avalar's ears, the thumping of her feet over the fields and the crack of ice on the streams she crossed. The rocking motion of her body, the sink and surge of her strides, were all that mattered as she trailed Argus's light. She ran through a darkness tinged crimson, a taste like steel in her mouth, and always Camron's smile beckoning.

Wails rose from the faraway river. Still the slaves were calling to her, for she had abandoned them. *I must go back*, she realized. But then she glimpsed her friend shimmering faintly in the specter's green light. It was Camron's ghost she wanted to avenge—his spirit she wept for.

"Hold up, now!" Argus cried, swooping from the treetops. He stretched out his arms, his sleeves rippling. "Giant, *wait!*"

She slammed to a stop. "How much farther, Ghost?" she panted.

"How long must I run?"

"I won't lie to you," Argus said. "You are too slow. The woman will be gone by the time you get there."

"Gone?" Avalar echoed. "What? But my blood craves battle! I told you before, I *cannot* stop! Not before I reach my enemy! Show me where, Ghost! You must!"

Argus floated before her, shaking his head sadly. "This was wrong of me. I plotted this thing to lure you from the valley. But I see now you are too young to control your passions. I have hurt you. I'm sorry!"

"You say this is falsehood?" Infuriated, Avalar flailed her fists. "There *is* no foe?"

"No, there *is*!" he yelled back. "But in your tent, you dawdled, didn't you? I had to sing and practically dance to get you to move. Now this is the price you pay!"

"Wait!" Avalar blinked, staring up at the Skywhite mountains, their silhouettes black beneath the first frail glints of dawn. "There *is* a way I can reach her! Mayhap not fast enough, but we can try!"

The dead knight flitted toward her. "Is there? Do tell!"

"*Yes.*" Avalar snatched a breath. "Ponu," she whispered. She concentrated, visualizing with all her might the winged elf in his sleeveless tunic. "I think he will come if I say I am ready."

Argus frowned. "Ready for *what*?"

"They all want me home," she said. "Even you, it seems, want me somewhere I am not! If this is what it takes for me to strike a blow for Camron, I will do it! Even this I will do! Hear you, Ponu? I am *ready*!"

An oval of brightness struck the snowbank. Avalar covered her dazzled eyes. His magic arrived first, a portal of incandescent strands woven from his staff, from which Ponu stepped forth, smiling crookedly. He flared his wings and bowed.

"I am at your service, my dear," he said as the magical door dissipated behind him. "What is your need?"

"I have decided I will go with you to Hothra," she announced. "But only if you will aid me now."

Ponu's smile held. "All these cycles, Grevelin's daughter," he said, "and still you see not what is in my heart. We are friends; no exchange of favors is necessary. Show me where you wish to go."

Avalar glanced at his staff. "But . . . your magic."

Ponu grinned. "It is wise to be wary of strange forces," he agreed. "But do you truly fear I would ever hurt *you*?"

Avalar grasped his hand. Ponu smiled at her fingers engulfing his and lifted his staff. "Now, Spirit," he said to Argus, "you must guide both my sight and my magic. Think of the place you require this giant to be."

As the Thalian Knight moved to hover above the elf, Ponu shut his eyes and bowed his head. He stiffened as horror crossed his face, his body shaking with anger at what he saw. He glared at the ghost. "It isn't far," he gritted. "Avalar, *now!*"

The forest slipped from her sight. A jumble of images flipped past her like pages in the wind, the places that were or could possibly be, the times to come or the times that had passed. For the span of one breath, Freedom Hall loomed above the sea, the stars mirrored in the crystalline sweep of its roof.

For an instant she saw the boats bobbing in Hothra's harbor, guarded by the greater ships anchored beyond. She saw a landscape from her memories—a place of sunshine and fertile fields. She gasped at the sight of the mines, a brief, terrifying impression that Ponu dispelled with the flick of a gesture. Then he mastered his staff, his powerful mind bending its patterns to his will.

Rock dominated her vision, layers of red-brown slabs forming a high, craggy hill. Gnarled skeletons of bluebark thrust in every direction, their roots entwined in small clefts and fissures.

Avalar staggered on the uneven ground, setting off a slide of tiny stones until Ponu caught her. When she had regained her balance, he released her and descended a short distance to where the ground flattened out.

Confused, she started to follow. "Ponu?"

He faced her with his wings furling along his back. "I will not be a part of this. Do what you came to do, Giant, but I do not approve!"

"Here." Argus motioned to a cranny by her feet and vanished inside. Avalar knelt to look. The crevice shone emerald deep within, its damp walls flickering where the dead knight bobbed.

"That's it," he said. "Now try again!" As Argus ascended slowly, a soft groan came to Avalar's ears, followed by a scuffle of heels scraping stone.

She comes! Avalar thought. Drawing her sword, she clambered erect. Gradually the noises increased, the rasp of the woman's breathing amplified by the fissure's cramped space.

"Almost there," Argus cajoled. "You can do it!"

"Why is she underground?" Avalar asked him. "This is not what you—"

She broke off when a clawlike shape appeared out of the cleft, barely recognizable as a hand. It batted feebly, groping at the empty air. Even in the dawn's light, Avalar saw how damaged the fingers were, how twisted and terribly broken.

She sheathed her sword as the woman emerged by painful inches from the cleft, her bruised and shattered body covered with blood.

The human began to roll as her hips exited the hole, and Avalar caught her. Dazed, she carried her enemy down to where Ponu crouched.

The winged elf rustled his wings. "This is what you came to fight?"

"I did not *know!*" Avalar snapped, laying the woman at his feet. "The ghost did not mention—"

"Help me," the human rasped. "Is somebody there?"

Avalar shuddered, her magic in her blood aching to kill. Here, at last, was her hated foe. *But helpless*, she was quick to remind herself. *Sorely hurt. I am a giant. We protect!*

She waited for Ponu to take charge. Instead, he stood motionless, his gaze on her face.

Blood sank into the snow beneath the tortured body between them. The bare skin of the woman's knees was horribly burned. Argus floated into view, and as he approached, Avalar saw through him to Warder's Fall, the leagues of shattered hills that would never be whole again.

"You sure you don't want to dillydally a bit longer?" The spirit pointed imperiously. "There she is! *Kill* her!"

"This is not what you promised!" Avalar snarled. "There is no worthy battle here. This woman is *dying!*"

"When exactly did I promise you that?" Argus flitted near, his hawk-like features stiff with rage, hacking at the human's neck with a make-believe sword. "This is Felrina Vlyn, the bitch who slit Camron's throat! Now finish her! For I cannot! All her victims call to me. They don't just cry for justice, they *demand* it!"

Avalar struggled for calm. "My blood is up; I must do battle. I followed you to wage combat! I cannot smite the helpless! I am a *giant*! This is not what we do!"

Strike her anyway!" roared Argus. "Hear *me*, since you can't hear her victims! Her dead are haunting you as we speak, and they are begging for retribution! You must slay her, Giant!"

Avalar glared down, her hot blood seething, her forearm an extension of her sword's hilt. The branches glinted pink above her, touched by the first light of dawn, and yet still she waited, an avatar of ghostly justice. "Rise," she said at last. "Stand and let us finish this, Felrina Vlyn."

The woman lay in a heap, her mangled hands twitching weakly. Avalar stooped, doubled her fist in the cowl of the human's robe and hauled her up. "Stand!" Avalar commanded. "You must try! Defend yourself!"

Head lolling, the black-robe dangled in her clasp. "Help me," she moaned. "He's trying to k-kill me."

"No," said Avalar darkly. "That task has befallen me. You have the scent of death already, Felrina Vlyn. The stink of old blood and corruption. This whole mountain reeks of it. Tell me this, Slaver. What manner of creature attacks its own kind?"

The woman's tangled brown hair fell forward over her damaged face as she wailed, the frantic cries of a stricken animal. Stunned, Avalar lowered her sword. She whirled toward Ponu, pleading for his guidance and counsel. She held in her grasp a creature both desperate and dying. *And I am a giant, born to defend and not to kill!*

Against her will, the desire rose to protect, to render aid and give comfort—yearnings completely at odds with her heated blood, her body primed for battle.

Throwing back her head, Avalar howled.

Ponu sprang to her side. "Giant, what will you do?"

She stared at the ghost. The furrows by Argus's mouth emphasized his haggard expression. It was as if by suffering the torments from newer deaths, he was being forced to relive his own final pain. His fist clenched over the phantom belt at his waist, yearning for a blade he could never wield.

"I know *not*!" She shivered as Ponu's touch cooled her body's fire.

"Oh, Ponu! *Hear* her!"

"Hush." Ponu extricated her sword from her clasp and placed it next to her. Gently he cradled the human, stroking the black-robe's forehead as he laid her on the snow.

"Burned," said Ponu grimly, holding his palm flat above the woman's blistered legs. He slipped his hand up her sleeve. "Broken. Arm, wrist, and fingers ... She bleeds in her stomach. Her lung ... her organs fail her. Her eye ..." Ponu flinched as he reached her chest.

"Giant, this trial was never meant for you," he said. "Camron Florne was Terrek's brother. It is *he* who must decide this woman's fate."

With a soft sigh, Avalar bent to retrieve her sword. She winced when her hand brushed the snow, sensing the mountain's grief below its wintry mantle. *If this slaver must perish*, she thought, *let it not be here!*

Stiffly she stood, her gaze drifting once more to the pitted, dead landscape of Warder's Fall beneath the purple dawn.

Ponu lifted the woman. Nodding slowly, Avalar stepped to grip his winged shoulder, and as he raised his staff, she smiled through her tears at the sight of a distant bird.

Chapter 43

elrina writhed, resisting the strength of the winged creature holding her still. Unfamiliar currents buffeted her, an ancient wisdom beyond old magic or new. The elf's staff mastered the tempest, and bore her and the giant through the present, across the past and possible futures.

She sensed the flex of the time crystal's power, how it established the destination the elf-mage visualized and took him *there*. She glimpsed a flash, and then he was striding among the trees.

Snow-clad branches swiped at her arms. Ahead she spotted the giant's furry cloak, the big warrior's heavy blond braid swaying back and forth.

Felrina pressed her cheek to the elf's chest. Soon Terrek would know it was she who had killed his brother, and then it would be as it had been with the giant. She would see loathing on his face and desire for her blood.

This is fitting, she decided, quelling her whimpers as she closed her eyes. *Terrek warned me from the start this could happen, and what did I do? Everything he predicted and worse!*

Her captor quickened his pace as the trees thinned out, the wind pulling at her mud-caked hair. From a distance, a voice yelled: "Avalar!"

"I will do what I can," the winged elf murmured over her head. "You have suffered enough. But I regret I cannot promise you anything."

The giant shouted, breaking into a run. The mage followed at a walk, as if he, like Felrina, dreaded the coming ordeal. She breathed in his spicy elven scent, at once familiar and alien.

Warder's magic permeated his bones, she realized, stronger even than Erebos's presence within her own. Somehow, he kept it shielded from the world, surrounded by the same foreign power she had felt in his staff.

A fire crackled somewhere close. Frozen twigs snagged her robe, threatening to tear the fabric. Then warm bodies closed in around her.

Felrina listened with all her might, both waiting for and dreading the voice of the one she knew.

Softly the giant spoke.

"Camron's killer?" Terrek's response cut like a whip across the sudden silence. "*This?*"

Felrina forced her eye open. Still the elf held her, offering what protection he could. Reluctantly he placed her beside the blaze, surrendering her with a sigh into the hands of human justice. Felrina savored the fire's heat caressing her cheek, taking in the homey sight of the frying pan by the flames, its crisped grillcakes going cold.

A young man, his face pale and drawn, studied her through the smoke. Despite her crippled vision, she knew him, recognizing his features from the hours she had fretted over the waters of Arawn's pool.

"Avalar, are you sure?" Terrek asked.

Steel hissed as the giant drew her sword. "Yes," she rumbled. "The ghost came to me in the night. He urged me to follow him, for he had found Camron's killer. This woman . . . I beg your pardon, my leader, but I was compelled for Camron's sake. I had to strike a blow. I did not know she was injured."

Felrina held her breath. The young giant's conflicted passions had spared her life on Mount Chesna's slopes. Perhaps they might aid her now.

The sharp heel of a boot pressed her jaw. Felrina groaned as Terrek rolled her head, exposing her ruined right eye. He crouched, tugging back her soiled hair.

"She's a black-robe," he observed. "This makes no sense. Why wouldn't Erebos defend her? Who would do this?"

"I care not," Avalar said. "She took Camron's life, and her victims are many. Their souls cry for her blood!"

Felrina gasped at a touch on her belly, slipping cool and soothing beneath her tunic's folds. An older man stood over her, wincing as his gentle fingers found her wounds.

The man sat back to snatch a breath. "She's badly hurt," he said. "Someone has . . ."

"Leader Florne," the elf interjected. "Her life or death is up to you now. Decide quickly, please. I cannot bear this woman's pain."

With an effort, Felrina turned her head, struggling to catch sight of the person she loved. "Terrek?"

He was on her in an instant, seizing her tunic and robes and dragging her up. "*How* is it you know my name?" he demanded. "Do you know what you've done? What you've taken from me?"

"Y-yes," she sobbed. "Oh, Terrek, I'm *sorry*!"

Stunned, he mouthed her name. Then his grip lost its strength, and she struck the icy ground by the fire.

Felrina screamed as she landed on the shards of her fingers. Sobbing, she flipped onto her side, pressing her shattered hands to her stomach.

Terrek stood above her, his hazel eyes filling with tears. A howl ripped from his throat as he savagely hacked with his sword at a log beside him.

"Commander, let me!" a younger warrior pleaded. "I want—"

"Terrek Florne," the elf-mage said. "You must decide!"

"Camron *loved* her!" Terrek shouted. "He loved her all his life! That's how he was and how he loved! And she *murdered* him!"

Across the flames, Felrina saw the haggard man regarding her in silence. He was Gaelin Lavahl, she knew, the Skystone's wielder, but there was more to him, something ancient, a power in him she knew. He was Holram, her foe, no longer lodged in a staff, but in living human flesh.

He stood as if he mistook her fear for an invitation. Glistening with sweat, he stumbled toward her.

Hard hands seized her arms. Bright steel flashed as her captor swung his sword. It was Terrek, Felrina realized. *At least it's a friend who ends my life!*

"Camron loved her," the mage said. "What would *he* want?"

"I want it!" Terrek snapped. "My brother isn't here to tell me what he wants, and whose fault is that?" He shoved his knee into the small of her back and thrust her forward, grinding her bloody chest against the log. "She *killed* my brother!"

"Erebos deceived her," countered the elf. "He *manipulated* her mind; that is what he does, Terrek Florne, and then his cult takes care of the rest. He *interfered* with her. You have no idea what warder's fire can do."

Felrina blinked painfully as she struggled to focus. The winged elf stood with his back to her, steam pouring from his wings and shoulders. Power coiled in him from a god above the sky, a being who perceived the world through him. Pressure climbed in her throat as the remnant of Erebos within her pulled back and thrashed in fear.

"There are punishments worse than death," Ponu said. "And I suspect she has experienced every one. Think on *that*, Leader Florne! If you slay her now in the heat of your rage, it will be *you* in the end who suffers the most. She will be gone and free of her pain when tomorrow you must judge yourself. Or is this how Kideren treats its prisoners? Did your Enforcers make it their practice to slay people on sight? Were not the Seeker elves clear on this? They alone are to judge violent criminals."

Terrek growled. "The Enforcers of Kideren are all *dead*! Murdered by the *thing* she serves! As for the Seekers, her cult rejects their rules, doesn't it?"

"The warder who enslaved her must destroy in order to live," the winged mage said. "He has to deceive the ignorant to get what he wants. I suspect she rebelled. It might behoove you to discover why before you take her life."

Felrina groaned, longing for Terrek's rusty blade to fall.

She flinched as his boot released her. With a sweep of his leg, he stretched her flat.

"Fine, Ponu," Terrek gritted. "I'll do as you ask and wait until I'm calm and *reasonable*. And then I will slay her *myself*!"

He scowled down at her. "There *are* no judges anymore. I'm what you get, and it's a Hades's shade more than you deserve!"

Felrina stiffened when Gaelin Lavahl knelt next to her. "No!" she gasped. She cringed as he drew her onto his lap, cradling her head.

"It is not a kindness to heal you," Holram's strange, flat voice intoned from his mouth. "Not when your future is so uncertain, but one of my kind did this to you. Darkness cannot dwell where light exists. Whenever a candle is lifted in defiance, always there will be shadows to fight against it. *You* are that candle, Felrina Vlyn."

302

She whimpered, flinching at his touch. He was a warder, a maker of stars, caressing her hair. He was Holram, no longer vanquished in the staff but freed by the one Mens had once considered a weakling.

She clung to him as she had always yearned to embrace her god. Unlike the cold granite of Erebos's bones, Holram's mortal flesh yielded. Vulnerable now, and human, he accepted her aching need to be held, his borrowed fingers stroking her face.

Power rose from within him, his spirit fully entwined with Gaelin Lavahl, drawing from the staff left abandoned by the fire, the Skystone that was no longer his prison.

Pain like a thousand needles stabbed through her flesh, mending her burned limbs and knitting her bones. His healing lanced through her body, cleansing, straightening, and restoring what was lost.

Felrina drew a deep breath, marveling that she could do so, but still she hugged the healer's neck. Some hurts still pained her, and she knew they always would. Curled with her knees to her chest on the warder's lap, she lay grieving for the woman she had been.

Terrek stood above her, breathing hard. "Avalar," he said. As the giant stepped near, he gestured down. "Take her out of my sight. If she tries anything, just . . . *kill* her. Understood?"

Avalar sheathed her great sword and bent. Felrina flinched, gasping as the giant seized her upper arm. Before she could blink, she was torn from the healer's embrace. "Sails," the giant swore, hauling her onto her feet. "Will you *walk?*"

Felrina struggled to obey, to coax her legs into motion, half dangling from the giant's angry grasp. "My shoulder!" she cried. "Please . . . stop!"

"Then *walk!*" Avalar snarled.

The giant yanked her to a halt in front of the largest of three tents. "Please!" Felrina begged, struggling to loosen the powerful grip. "You're *hurting* me!"

Avalar tore open the door's flap. Felrina staggered as the giant released her. "You hurt my *friends*," Avalar spat. "First you kill Camron, the gentlest spirit I have ever met, and now you wound him more through his brother! *Inside!*"

Felrina sprawled on the softness of a bed. At once she thrashed away from it and into a corner, curling into a ball.

"Gaelin was *already* ill," Avalar said behind her. "Now . . ."

Slowly Felrina unclenched. The smell of mildew from the tent, the soft feel of the furs beneath her, and the comfortable crackle of the fire unraveled what strength she had left. Exhausted, she let go, slumping along the shelter's taut wall, her long legs unfolding. Tears trickled down her cheeks. Tentatively she lifted her hand, probing the new bruises the giant had left on her skin.

"Are you injured?" asked Avalar.

Felrina nodded. Shuddering as the pressure broke in her heart, she hid her face in her arms and sobbed.

Activity picked up beyond the tent. Contented munching sounds filled the little clearing, the grunts and bugles of creatures she did not know.

Avalar waited, stern as a judge. After a time there came a rustling at the door. "Get her ready," the older man said. "We're heading out."

Felrina snatched a shaky breath and held it. The man's gentle voice soothed her in the same way her father often had. It gave her hope where she thought she had none.

"Felrina Vlyn," said the giant. "These leggings are for you. Will you rise?"

Sniffling, Felrina dragged herself to her knees and pushed back her hair.

"You have suffered," Avalar said. "Like Ponu the mage, I do not relish the sight. Yet now I must know *why*. For the sake of my heart, and the friendship I shared with the one you so coldly dispatched, I *must* comprehend. Why would this power you serve turn on you?"

The tent's walls closed in on her, the space within them going airless and chill. "I stopped believing his promises," she said. "When he k-killed my father, I . . . and after that he—"

"Ah. That explains much," Avalar said. "The death of others is desirable. In the name of your beliefs, you would gladly torture and slay. But when it is *your* father . . ."

"No!" Felrina sat trembling. Any delusions she once had were gone. *I know what I am,* she thought. *And what I was.* "Yes." Her voice was a whisper as she cringed at what she saw within herself. "I'm a monster. I wish he had k-killed me."

"He *may,*" Avalar said. She fell silent, the shadows beyond the shelter moving back and forth. Wood clicked as the two other tents were being dismantled. There came a sudden hiss of steam from the little fire, and through the canvas, Felrina caught the stench of the drenched wood.

"You c–could have saved him the trouble," she stammered, her face suddenly hot. "B–back on the mountain when you had the chance."

Avalar abandoned her place on the mat, setting a pile of folded black fabric and leather where Felrina could reach it. "Put these on," she said. Scooping up her blankets and furs, the giant shoved them into her pack. Then she knelt, rolling her mat and tying it with laces to her bundle of gear. "Come now." She frowned. "You cannot travel in this cold with your legs exposed, Felrina Vlyn, and if you continue ignoring my instructions, you only give my leader more reasons to slay you. Do you understand?"

Felrina seized the leggings and lurched to her feet, drawing them on and then wriggling into a second pair.

As the giant reached for her, Felrina recoiled. "No, I'll go with you! Just please don't hurt me!"

Avalar nodded. "Very well." She punched the door's flap open, smacking it with her fist.

Felrina went first, stepping out through the narrow doorway. She stiffened when Avalar clasped her from behind—her uninjured arm this time. With a groan, Felrina straightened her back, blinking at the glare of the sky.

Chapter 44

Felrina ducked as the overhang of branches, glistening bright under the sun, dripped water on her head. Her thoughts wandered, her gurgling belly making it difficult for her to track the little camp's activity. The two men clad in similar black armor were loading the tents and gear, while the young warrior in his tall stovepipe hat sat by the remains of the fire picking with his knife at the last fragments of meat from a diradil's bones.

She saw Captain Vyergin seated next to the boy, pushing with his spoon at something he held in a bowl on his lap. When the utensil jerked up abruptly, she spied a flattened lump beneath it—the leftover griddle cakes he had folded together with the meat.

Felrina studied the warrior with the knife, his eyes intense below his odd tippy hat. She recalled him wanting, even more than Terrek, to see her dead. *He'll kill me if he gets the chance,* she realized. *As long as he's here, I'm not safe.*

Does it matter? No, because soon I'll be dead. She visualized her demise, the man she loved slitting her throat or hanging her from a tree. She imagined Terrek laughing with Erebos's voice.

Sighing, Felrina settled her gaze on a third figure close to where the fire had been, the young man who carried Holram in his flesh. Gaelin dozed with his chin on his chest, his hands limp over the staff across his knees. For some inexplicable reason, she yearned to embrace him, to hold him to her heart, and never let go.

"He was already ill," Avalar remarked beside her. "He was forced to heal Vyergin after your *cult* made the captain a dach. I know not where he gained strength enough to succor you."

Felrina, her lip between her teeth, hung her head. She flinched when the giant, reaching out, dropped a cloth-wrapped parcel into her pocket. "Vyergin makes these for when we get hungry on the trail," Avalar explained. "He urges you to eat one ere we go, for it is clear to him you have not taken food for several days."

"You shouldn't feed a corpse," Felrina muttered.

"We who are not in your cult," the giant retorted, "*despise* suffering. We gain neither pleasure nor strength from it. You killed my friend and my leader's brother, yet no one here wishes more hardship for you. Not even Leader Terrek, who has yet to decide your fate."

Felrina retrieved the parcel from her pocket and uncovered the greasy cake with its flecks of meat. The sight and the smell of it . . . She pictured herself with her father in the cottage by the river where they had lived, his smile from across the table while he broke apart their morning bread. Choking back a sob, Felrina dropped the food.

Hard fingers seized her wrist. Felrina looked up, expecting Avalar's wrathful glare, but found Terrek beside her instead. He bent to grasp the cake, brushing the snow from it with his gloved fingers. "You *will* eat this," he said.

Felrina stared at the crumbs he held. Nervously, averting her gaze from his angry face, she gathered them into her palm. Cringing, she turned from her captors, thrusting one large section into her mouth and swallowing hard.

"No, don't wolf your—" He drew a sharp breath. "Take smaller bites. *Chew* first, so it doesn't make you sick."

Felrina blinked, fighting back tears at the unfamiliarity of his scathing tone. She squinted at the sun's bright rays, forcing herself to eat.

Terrek motioned to the giant. "Gaelin will need you to carry him again, so this one can ride. Put her on his calico. Vyergin can show you how to tie her. He was an Enforcer; he would know."

Felrina listened while she fed herself, measuring each mouthful. As she swallowed the last little piece, the giant unshouldered her weighty pack.

"Ponu has left?" Avalar asked. She caught Felrina by her robe and then snagged her hands. Felrina stood where she was put, her legs braced to keep her balance while the giant positioned her arms behind her, wrapping a cloth around and between her crossed wrists.

Terrek stopped at Gaelin's side. "Yes, the elf's gone," he answered. "He told me he 'trusts that I will decide rightly,' whatever *that* means. She's only alive now because I still feel rage."

"Mayhap you always will," Avalar said. Terrek nodded somberly.

Felrina shrank from the giant's stare. The shan were being mounted; the warrior in his peculiar hat was already on the move. Felrina submitted without a struggle as Avalar scooped her up and placed her behind the neck of one of the creatures—a colorful beast splotched orange, brown, and black. It tipped its shaggy head, eyeing her as if to check if she was worthy.

Kneeling, the giant grasped Felrina's ankles under the animal's round belly, drawing a rope through the stirrups to bind them together. Then she straightened and, gripping the little beast's lead rope firmly, turned to retrieve Gaelin from Vyergin.

Terrek was riding in front of his companions into the dense forest, but Captain Vyergin held back. Coaxing his ruddy-tan creature alongside the giant, he stretched to pass Gaelin a small flask.

"How long will it be before he k-kills me?" Felrina blurted. Her voice cut through the calm beneath the trees, startling the finches in the boughs overhead. Both the captain and the scowling giant glanced back.

With a grunt, Vyergin nudged his beast into a shambling lope over the frosty, uneven ground. Felrina shivered at the giant's glower. "I'm sorry," she choked out. "I'll be quiet."

Avalar nodded and began to turn back.

"You say you d-despise suffering," Felrina said, "but isn't *this* a kind of torture? Making me sit here and w-wonder just when he might c-come back here and—"

"Did you not take prisoners?" Avalar interjected. "Did you not put them to *death*, Felrina Vlyn?"

Felrina swallowed at the sudden sour taste in her mouth. She recalled her dungeon strolls, how she had kept her eyes forward, never letting herself acknowledge the sad, beseeching looks from the men and women caged and awaiting slaughter. They were the ones deemed unfit for Mens's army, the crippled or the young or very old, but all with lives they cherished as much as she valued her own, lives she had ripped horribly away to placate a monster.

"Could your prisoners hear the executions?" Avalar went on, her words grinding ruthlessly in Felrina's ears. "Were they perchance forced to sit and to wonder when they might be next?"

"Yes," Felrina mumbled. "And y-yes."

For a long tense moment, Avalar stood silent. Felrina waited for the giant's judgment, for more harsh words to flay her alive. But mercifully, Avalar turned away. Clicking softly to the shan, the giant hurried after Vyergin.

GAELIN, SEATED ON his cloak beside the fire, hugged his knees, pressing them to his chest as he peered through the young and hungry flames. He gripped the little flask Wren had given him, shaking it to hear the liquid within, water from the snow he had stuffed in its throat. Uncorking the vessel, he drained it with a gulp, setting it by his leg as a reminder to refill it.

Again he swallowed. He could see his friends clearly now, the men squeezing the tents in among the trees. Roth crouched nearby, grunting with effort as he pried cones from the ice with his boot knife, tossing them into a pile to feed the shan.

The trees were dense, allowing no snow to reach the ground—and no shan to fit between the trunks to shake their branches.

Avalar, standing by his calico, untied their prisoner, the black-robe tumbling from the beast's back. Gaelin followed the woman's progress from the corner of his vision, her legs quivering as she walked small and frightened next to a warrior more than twice her height. Felrina's wrists were bound, and her eyelids, when at last she lifted her head, were swollen and raw.

Gaelin shifted quickly when Avalar stopped by the fire, spreading his cloak to give the prisoner a place to rest. "Sometimes we bring over rocks or wood to sit on, but here there's just that," he said, nodding toward a lone stump. "You'd need a ladder to get up *there*." He grinned at her, hoping to brighten her mood.

"We're c-close," Felrina said, staring into the flames while Avalar, having released her hands, secured them in front of her body instead. "I *feel* him."

As she finished with her work, Avalar grimaced. "I sense *other* things," she said darkly, "but not as often as I did. The river flows pure where we are now. No giants died here."

Gaelin shivered. He had forgotten how every step brought Avalar nearer to the atrocities inflicted upon her people. The giant, squatting behind him, clasped his shoulders and squeezed, her strong fingers kneading gently. He forced himself to relax and lean forward, sighing as the tension eased from his muscles.

Felrina tugged at a snarl in her hair. "Why do you get sick when you use your staff?" she asked. "I had a staff, too. It never depleted me the way yours does."

"Holram's power burns me inside," he confessed. "I try not to use it so I can recover."

Gaelin glanced up, catching Terrek's disapproving frown, his quick head-shake as he approached. "Why are you confiding in her?" Terrek demanded. "As far as we know, she could still be *his*! Perhaps that god of hers hears our every word."

Her back hunched, Felrina closed her eyes. Gaelin, taking the full brunt of the commander's smoldering glare, spied glints of reluctant pity lurking there as well.

"You killed my brother," Terrek snapped. "Little Camron. How do you live with that, Felrina? Yet here you are! Alive and well and chatting with Gaelin as if you're one of us. When you *haven't* been for nearly two years! You've been far too busy, haven't you? Betraying your own kind!

"It's not just Camron." Terrek stepped closer, glowering down. "You've committed heinous crimes. You remember the term for that? You went to Braymore, the same university I did. My father's marker helped you get there. And what did they call mass murder back on Earth? Crimes against humanity! And here you are, not denying it. So you tell me, Felrina Vlyn! Do you deserve death?"

"Yes," she moaned.

"I agree," said Terrek. "And so does Lord Argus, as he's been harping at me all day. And Lieutenant Roth over there—he wants to do the deed himself! Should I let him? Or is that too lenient? Perhaps we should do to you whatever it was *you* did to my brother?"

Terrek drew a shuddering breath. He seized her hair and yanked up her head, forcing her to look at him. She hung with her chin tipped up and her throat exposed, the contours of her neck glowing pale in the firelight as her eyes rolled back in fear.

"No, look at *me!*" Terrek insisted.

Trembling, she raised her bound hands, desperate to hide his rage from her sight. "I . . . I c-*can't*," she sobbed. "Oh, Terrek!"

Releasing her hair, Terrek caught Felrina under her arms and dragged her bodily around the little blaze—to set her firmly on the stump's high seat. "Do as I say, Felrina Vlyn. Or I swear I will kill you right now on the spot and be done! *Look* at me!"

She complied, shuddering, choking back sobs.

"You talk to *me* now." Terrek leaned in, his voice deathly calm. "Not to Gaelin. Not these other people—to *me!* You're going to talk to *me* now, and you're going to describe to me *exactly* what you did to my brother!"

"I—" Felrina rocked where she sat, her hands gripping the edges of the stump. "I was called to the sacrificial chamber." She paused, groaning softly. "I didn't know who it was to be. I saw his face and I . . ."

Gaelin closed his eyes and let his mind wander as Felrina struggled to force out the words, recounting a story she clearly loathed. He listened to the soft sounds of his breathing, the low, comforting crackle of the fire. Over his head, the wind whispered through the low-hanging branches, making the boughs creak in a slow and gentle rhythm.

Behind him, Avalar began to cry, and even that sound belonged in this moment somehow. It meant Camron Florne had known love in his brief chance to exist. He had touched lives and had made a difference.

"You *bitch!*" Roth screamed. "If you don't kill her *now*, Terrek, I will! You heard what she did! They did that to my *family*, too!"

"Will that give them back their lives?" Terrek asked. "Would it bring Camron back?"

"I'm sorry!" Felrina slipped to the ground below the stump. "I *do* deserve to die, Terrek! I *want* to die. Please! Everything you've said is true, and there's n-nothing for me here. My father . . . and you . . . everything I loved is gone!"

"Free her wrists, Vyergin, so she can eat," Terrek said, and Gaelin sighed, for this was the friend he knew. "Avalar, tie her again when she's through. Be gentle with her for now. I need a moment to think."

Chapter 45

aelin sighed as their prisoner picked at her food. When Vyergin came to squat in front of her, Gaelin shifted back to give him room, watching while the captain straightened her forgotten dish on her lap. "You'll get through this, my dear, but you must eat something or you will—" He broke off as she flinched from his hand. "That's all right," Vyergin reassured her.

As he withdrew to give Felrina her space, Gaelin clambered to his feet and retreated with him to the other side of the fire. "I hate this!" he whispered. "Every time I look at her I feel such . . ."

"I know what you mean," said Vyergin.

"She's still hurting. I thought Holram healed her." Seeing the captain wince, Gaelin asked, "You know something, don't you?"

Vyergin shrugged. "Perhaps Terrek's right and she deserves all this. Maybe she does need to die, and perhaps she will. But I cannot abide rape, Staff-Wielder."

"Rape?" Gaelin met the captain's angry eyes. "I'm sorry. I've never . . . Holram doesn't know that word."

"Roth's twin, Gindle, was attacked first," Vyergin told him. "A few days later the same man went after my sister, Elahne. He came past our border and found her by the river checking her snares. He took her at knifepoint—I suppose he believed he had the right. He didn't know the lay of the land, and I did, so he wasn't hard to catch." Vyergin grunted. "He broke his damn ankle trying to cross the river, and that's when I took him down. Right there on the rocks.

"I trussed him up and eviscerated him first," the captain drawled. "Just a nick in the hollow below the belly. Enough to snag his gut and loop it around Hawk's saddle. Hawk wanted to get at the greenberry bushes nearby, so I freed the bit from his mouth and let him wander into the brambles while I enjoyed my lunch. A short while later, seeing that the villain was still alive, I pinched his nose like *this*." Vyergin demonstrated. "And then I fed him his balls in little pieces. I wouldn't let him breathe until he swallowed.

"That's when I heard the dog pack closing in," he said. "They were attracted to the blood, you see. So I opened the man a bit more for them and left. I just cleaned off my saddle, climbed onto Hawk and rode away." He drew a long shaky breath. "The last thing I heard was the screaming."

Gaelin gaped at him. "I can't believe you'd kill like that."

"I was no longer fit to be Captain of the Enforcers, so I quit. What that cult did, though . . . It wasn't just how they murdered our men. It was when they tossed the pieces into the water—as if they were nothing but dead branches cleared from a field.

"I was an Enforcer. I've witnessed some very brutal things in my life, but *that* was the worst." Vyergin turned his head to look him up and down. "*You* slew someone, too, or so I've been told, and you're not so terrible. Even ironwood snaps in a gale, Staff-Wielder, if the wind hits it long enough. The same is true for people. I hear you're handy with an ax."

Gaelin swayed on his feet. "Chopping wood is all I used to do. I . . ."

"Stop!" Vyergin scolded him. "I know all about it, Lavahl. Terrek confided in me. He visited your old haunt the day after you met him. You wanted to know where he had gone to, remember? He took his horse, left camp, and went straight up that mountain to see for himself. I do believe he buried what he found there—your mother's bones that were on the woodpile, too."

"I was the ironwood in the wind," said Gaelin.

"Yes, you were," Vyergin concurred. "So you're human; good for you. I hope it was nice and messy. If you're going to feel guilty about something for the rest of your life, you may as well be thorough about it."

Gaelin nodded as he surveyed Felrina through the smoke. The woman was ignoring the giant's attempts to get her to eat. "I do feel guilty," he muttered. "I know what it's like to be hurt."

"Well, I do not! And if I could catch the miserable bastard who mutilated *her*"—Vyergin motioned toward their prisoner—"I would do it all again!"

Sighing, Gaelin joined the captain at the base of a crooked tree, leaning his tired shoulders against its trunk.

"Now that I'm older and wiser," Vyergin said, "I generally prefer to express my ghoulish inclinations in less violent ways. I just gut innocent animals and make them into stew. Speaking of which," he added with a glance past Gaelin, "here comes Roth with another diradil."

Gaelin sank back as the captain trudged across the little camp to assist the lieutenant with the meat. His gaze settled on Felrina as once more she jerked her head away from the plate Avalar held. The woman blanched, covering her mouth. Following her stare, Gaelin peered at Vyergin, who had hung the diradil by its antlers from the crook of a branch and begun to skin it.

"Felrina?" Avalar called out in alarm. Gaelin scrambled to his feet, his heart pounding as he retrieved his staff, then hastened toward the prisoner passed out cold beside the fire.

FELRINA WATCHED THE flicker of firelight through the canvas. Nighttime shadows kept her company in the tent, crouching low and ominously dark in the corners. Catching the scent of roasting meat, she curled beneath her furry covers, sucking in breaths at the churning in her stomach.

Sounds reached her from beyond the taut fabric. A shadow stretched tall outside by the doorway, its owner, who could only be the giant, rising from where she had been squatting as a steady crunch of footsteps approached.

"She has roused," said Avalar, and Felrina grimaced at what the giant represented to her now—the freedom she no longer had. *But I haven't been free*, she reminded herself. *Not since I left home.*

The tent's door-flap folded back. Felrina squeezed her eyes shut as someone entered, burying her face in her dampened pillow.

"Vyergin described your injuries to me," Terrek's quiet voice said. "Ponu was right. You became Erebos's victim, didn't you, Felrina? You were being deceived; I knew it right from the beginning. You've paid quite a terrible price for it, haven't you?"

Felrina drew a quivering breath, grateful for the gloom that spared her the sight of his loathing.

"I'm no executioner," he continued. He bent over her, his hands brushing her shoulders, and she felt a soft weight—more furs being laid across her back. "My heart aches for my brother. Camron loved you. You were like his big sister, Felrina, and right now I can't imagine killing anything he loved.

"But I must consider Roth. He's the boy who wants you dead. He tried to reach us after your cult butchered his family. He came home to find his mother and his sister, Gindleyn, hanging dead from one of the branches his old treehouse rested on. The men were gone—his father and his brothers. No doubt taken to be dachs. Since then, he's been staying with us at Vale Horse. Now he is begging me to let him kill you, and I understand how he feels."

Felrina rolled her head, listening hard. His breath was catching in his throat. *Is he crying?* she wondered. More than anything, she yearned to sit up and beg his forgiveness.

"I could let him," Terrek rasped. "But he is just a boy. It would be the same as if I did it myself. No, if I made this choice, it would have to be me, *my* sword!"

Holding her breath, Felrina extended her arm along her body to find his leg by her hip. "Give me your knife, Terrek," she quavered. "I'll do it myself. You shouldn't have to. P-please. I d–don't deserve to live."

"No, you don't," Terrek agreed. "But now, thanks to that *thing* you call a god, we're close to extinction, aren't we? If humanity is going to survive, we can't keep killing each other. Therefore, *you* will henceforth dedicate yourself to our cause. You have the knowledge we lack of Erebos's domain so you will help Argus guide us to the place where the Destroyer keeps his power."

She gasped. "I c–*cannot* go back there! They . . . he . . ."

"You can, and you will," said Terrek. "You owe it to Camron. It's the least you can do. Tomorrow you will walk unfettered, and Avalar will keep watch. If you try to run, we'll revisit the topic of Roth and his sword, and I don't think that's something you want."

With an effort, Felrina forced back her terror as she thought of Mens. "I can't go b-back there, Terrek, after . . . what I . . ."

There was a tense pause, a shiver of rage in the air. Felrina held her breath, regretting her words.

"You won't be alone this time," Terrek answered at last. "You're my prisoner and my responsibility. As long as you are with me, I won't let him touch you. The others know. I've instructed them not to discuss this with you, not even Roth, who might try. And *you*. If you want to live, you are not to speak my brother's name in my presence. *Understood?*"

"Yes," she said. "Anything! Terrek, I . . ."

"Good," he said. "If we get through all this, I promise there will be no mob lying in wait for you when we get home. I'll get you to Heartwood, where you'll be treated fairly. Perhaps Ponu is right and Erebos did affect your mind. If that's the case, the Seekers will heal you."

"That wouldn't be fair," Felrina protested. "I deserve to be—"

He wheeled toward the door.

"Terrek?" she spoke softly into the darkness he left behind. He caught his breath as he stopped. "Do you . . . *hate* me?"

She heard his slow breathing while he mulled it over. All his life he had pondered things first. *Too bad I couldn't have—*

"Don't you think you're suffering enough?" his response broke through her thoughts. Again he paused. "Hate and rage are two separate things. What I *hate* is Erebos. For you, Felrina, I feel . . . pity, among other things. I know what you hoped for at the start because you shared it with me. I know it wasn't *this*.

"Don't use *my* name anymore, either," he said. "You're a stranger to me now; you have forfeited the right to be familiar."

Felrina shoved her fist between her teeth, sobs racking her body as, with a whisper of fabric, the door-flap fell shut.

Chapter 46

G aelin roused at the sound of battle, the sight of a dach tearing through the door-flap of the tent he shared with Vyergin and Terrek, its saber raised to strike at his throat. He blinked upward, dismayed as the entire front wall of the shelter caved in abruptly behind his assailant. A wide, scaly muzzle jutted into view, its nearest tusk skewering the warped human. Lifting the dach and the ceiling high, the creature whipped its enormous head, flipping the canvas back and forth.

Gaelin, cowering on his mat, stared at the beast's massive shoulders and neck. He recoiled as the creature's clawed forefeet straddled his bed. The canvas tore from its leather floor as the animal reared, flinging the fabric over its shaggy back. The impaled dach dropped like a stone, the severed halves of its body landing with bloody splats on his bed.

He sprang to his feet and seized his staff, striking the beast sharply across its flank. Screaming, the behemoth bolted, the tent covering its head and upper body flapping in rhythm with its lumbering strides as it crashed among the trees.

"Terrek!" Gaelin staggered. The camp was in chaos, with one beast catching a winged dach in midair between its fangs—to dash it to pieces against a tree. Four other monsters wheeled and collided in a frenzy of slashing tusks and teeth, lashing whiplike tails that coiled around bodies and ripped them apart.

A wing protruded from a branch above Gaelin, its vaguely human hand still twitching. A creature loped past, its withers higher than Avalar, taller even than the giant who was her father. The monstrous beast dragged a tent cut in half, with a body caught inside. Gaelin stumbled out of her way as Avalar stepped past him; with a sweep of her sword, she cut the fabric loose.

"Ward my back!" the giant shouted. She whirled as he leapt to obey. He spied his companions standing frozen behind the trees, their faces anxious as they watched.

"What are these—" he started to ask.

"*Shh!*" she hissed, yanking him close as another monster charged. The tents were gone, he realized, the fire scattered.

"The shan!" Avalar whispered. Carefully she crouched, pulling the form tangled in the fabric beneath the protection of her sword.

There was silence, punctuated by distant bugles as the shan pursued their prey. Bits of fabric and gore pattered down through the branches.

Vyergin ventured from the refuge of a tree. "The dachs woke them up," he said. "The shan—"

"You're not supposed to rouse them until dawn," Roth explained matter-of-factly, poking his head out from behind a second trunk. "That's what the elves said."

"What in Hades's blazes?" Vyergin exclaimed. "You mean they throw fits if you wake them early?" He scowled at the ruins of his fire, his cooking pot broken in half.

"*Or* if you kick them, or pull on their reins!" said Roth.

"That is absurd!" Vyergin glowered.

"They chased off the dachs," Terrek was quick to point out. "I am pretty sure they saved our lives, Captain. He approached the place where the tents had been, inspecting the debris. "At least we still have the spare shelter Avalar brought. "Though I have *no* idea how six humans and a giant will all fit inside."

"We'll make do, Commander," Vyergin said. "I have my twine. I can piece together something. But the rest of you will need to help."

Avalar unrolled the canvas at her feet, uncovering Felrina's limp form. "Still asleep," Avalar muttered in amazement. "How can this be?"

"They ate my deer!" Roth picked up the broken spit and shook it. "But I thought—"

"Apparently," drawled Vyergin, "these creatures become carnivorous when they change."

"Among other things," Terrek agreed, eyeing a leg severed at the thigh lying in a pool of blood. "Where are all the dachs who attacked the camp? Did the shan eat *them*, too?"

"Some of the dachs ran away." Gaelin clenched his jaw, feeling Holram stir inside him, outraged at so much death. "*It's too late,*" he thought to the warder. "*There's nothing you can do.*"

Terrek whistled as he glanced at the cracked and blighted trees marking the place where the shan had gone. "I finally see why the Eris value these creatures so much. When they shift, they really—"

"*Shift?*" echoed Vyergin. "Is *that* what you call this?"

Gaelin struggled to visualize the pampered little beasts with their stout, long-haired bodies and finicky habits.

"They'll be back," Roth said. He kicked at the charred pieces of wood near Vycrgin, drawing the ashes together to attempt to revive the little blaze. "The Eris told me it takes a while. Their blood heats up; that's all."

"That is *all*," Avalar repeated, rolling her eyes. "The same thing happens to male giants who are not *laori*." Sighing, she squatted by Felrina. "How is it possible for this woman to stay asleep through all this? Could she be ill?"

Kneeling by the woman, Gaelin touched her brow, feeling Holram's interest bubbling to the surface. The warder probed with his fingers. "Something," Holram said, taking control of his mouth. "Terrek Florne, you must know there is—"

"Here they come," Silva exclaimed, holding his sword at the ready. Wren Neche stepped in quickly to follow his lead. A shout came from the trees where Roth had gone in search of his deer. Then a line of five shapes shuffled toward them, the colorful creatures dripping gore from their woolly fur, bits of fabric clinging to their manes as they bugled and huffed. They were shrinking as they strutted, their razor-like tails shortening, the tufts at the ends jutting straight up. The tusks shriveled to large, flat teeth, and the elongated claws were hooves again, cloven and harmless.

Vyergin grunted as the creatures stopped where their tethers had been. He poked at the campfire's remains, coaxing a small curl of flame to grow.

"There's no point in that, Captain," Terrek said. "We're leaving. They know we're here." He glared at the sleeping Felrina. "And I suspect I know how. We must locate those mines!"

"Good," said Roth. "I'll be glad to get away from this snow."

Terrek motioned to Felrina. "Avalar, wake her."

Gaelin jostled him to get his attention. "Terrek, there is something Holram needs to tell—"

"Enough!" Terrek said, watching as Avalar lifted the prisoner and then held a sliver of ice to her cheek. Moaning, Felrina thrashed.

"I don't blame her," Vyergin said. "I wouldn't want to wake up either if I were her."

Terrek raised his hand. "Forget it, Giant," he said gruffly. "Leave her be. If she's that exhausted, let her sleep."

Gaelin shivered. Whatever Holram had wanted to say was gone from his thoughts—the warder had retreated again so that his flesh might recover. Resolutely he gripped his staff as Vyergin sorted through the foodstuffs they had left, and Terrek and Roth saddled the shan. The guards hurried to salvage what useable items they could find.

Avalar, still holding Felrina, stood beside Gaelin. As the prisoner's guard, she had new responsibilities now, and so she waited as Gaelin did, watching while her gear was being stowed. "The mines must be near," he told her.

She nodded. "They are close."

Gaelin held out his hand, displaying his tremor for the giant to see. "I'm not getting better," he whispered. "I'm trying to rest, but this thing is . . . I think we need to hurry before—" He broke off at her stare.

"When my stepfather slew my mother," he ventured, "I felt like you do. I knew what it was to hate. It's happening to you with your memories. All the things they did. Like you're reliving it. And you *despise* what you're forced to watch. You're burning with that hate all the time. I can *feel* it."

Frowning, Avalar turned toward him, her blue eyes intense below her tangled blond hair. "You beheld your own mother's—" She bent to regard his face. "Why have you never told me?"

Gaelin hugged his staff to his chest. "It was a long time ago," he said. "Seth Lavahl had discovered that I wasn't his. So he killed my mother, and he—"

"Hush." Avalar pressed a finger to his lips.

"Gaelin!" Terrek called. Both Roth and Vyergin had mounted, while everyone else remained on foot with their swords drawn. At the commander's firm gesture, Gaelin hastened to his calico.

For a time, he rode in silence with his staff across his lap, his grasp even looser on the reins than before. Avalar walked beside him with Felrina's limp body in her arms, flinching as though something dived at her from above, or perhaps, he guessed from her posture, she moved beneath a ceiling as she babbled softly in her native tongue. Only the prisoner she held linked her to the present, he realized. As long as Felrina tossed and fretted, Avalar stayed connected with her surroundings.

Gaelin squinted as the new sun, a tapestry of pink and violet streaks giving way to a sliver of gold, rose from behind the mountains. The branches above him glittered silver. Beyond them, he caught glimpses of Chesna's gray rock through the fog. To the north sprawled a shattered expanse of hills. It was a scar that would never heal, the slash of destruction that marked Erebos's frenetic dash from where he and Holram had landed on the world to his refuge within Mount Chesna.

Fire mountain. That was what Avalar had called it. Filled with darkness and water, its flames snuffed out long ago by the currents of the Shukaia cutting through it. He saw the collapsed peak clearly now under the newborn sun, small and misshapen amid the splendor of the Skywhites. The mountain was warped, like everything else Erebos had touched.

He leaned back, and his calico stopped, while his companions rode on, oblivious to the fact that Avalar was laying Felrina at her feet. The woman flailed in childlike protest, her eyelids fluttering. Ignoring her, Avalar stood with her legs braced, her glare fixed on the glimpse of a meadow through the trees.

"Avalar?" Gaelin dismounted. Terrek looked back and shouted, commanding the others to stop.

"Sails," Avalar whispered. Drawing her sword, she charged forward. Her voice rose to a yell. "Redeemer, *slay them!*"

"Avalar!" Terrek's voice cracked, but deep in the giant's troubled gaze Gaelin saw something break—a flash like steel severing her awareness. With Holram's perceptions rising swiftly to heighten his own, Gaelin experienced it, too—the here and now shattering like glass. The memories, rising out of the wounded ground, crowded around her. She saw her ghosts' peril as they did, and knew the agony of their deaths, each and every one.

"Avalar, *no!*" Gaelin cried as she stumbled into a run. She invoked the names of the dead as she plunged through the snowy branches, identifying the ghosts who gathered around her to urge her on. The specters pleaded with her to flee before the whips and the magic burned her skin, to run from the slavers, always the slavers, their hateful hands ready and eager to deliver pain.

She won't hear you, Terrek, Gaelin thought when the larger man roared at her to stop. Leaving his shan, Gaelin followed the giant, panting while he struggled to step where she did, his legs too short to reach—tipping him onto his face. "*Sails!*" he shouted. It was a giantkin curse, one she had uttered so many times, and he would thunder it now, for the giant who was his friend. He scrambled back up. *They can't have her!* He tried to run, pumping his arms as hard as he could.

The giant raised her blade when she reached the little clearing and then abruptly vanished from his sight.

"No!" He sobbed in frustration, holding his staff like a spear while he thrashed on. Terrek raced past him, his stronger legs surging through the snow. Silva and Roth floundered by as well, followed quickly by Wren, their expressions grim as they braced for combat.

When Avalar began to scream, Gaelin howled. He would never reach her. Holram's fire had weakened him. All the progress he had made on Mount Desheya to build up his strength was gone. He was useless, powerless to save his friend. Gasping hoarsely, he pulled to a stop where the giant had gone, an impenetrable patch of midnight surrounded by white.

Deep in the pit, the giant was wailing as she clawed at the dirt. He could almost see through her eyes as she struck at her unseen foes. With each passing moment, she unraveled more, her identity fraying, her sanity along with it.

"Avalar!" Gaelin shouted. Unfocused power tore from his fingers, flashing quicksilver swift across the snow. Terrek seized his shoulders, shaking him until he stopped.

"No!" said Terrek. "If we're going to regain her trust, she must not feel your magic!"

"Govorian, *wait!*" Avalar shrieked from the blackness below.

"Great Leader, do not leave us!"

Gaelin pulled himself free. "But that leader she speaks of, Terrek! If she goes with him, I don't know how I know this, but that will be the end! We'll never get her back!"

"Summon Ponu!" Vyergin called from behind them. He approached through the trees, the still-groggy Felrina stumbling at his side. "Remember what the winged elf said. We won't get her back if she loses herself! Well, I'm pretty sure she's *lost*, Commander!"

"Not yet, she isn't." Terrek knelt next to Gaelin beside the pit and peered into a tunnel's murky depths. "And we're not going to let her." He unbuckled his sword.

"Terrek, you can't!" Gaelin cried. "She'll mistake you as a slaver from the past! She'll tear you apart!"

"She will not," Terrek said. "You underestimate her." Deliberately he laid his weapon in the snow.

Chapter 47

Screaming, she whirled as the tide of her desperate people surged around her, buffeting her before continuing at a run down the tunnel. In rags and filth, she crouched over her sword as they pounded from her sight around a bend. Her chest aching, she struggled for breath, clutching at her wounded side.

Tangled roots hung from the ceiling, their gray cobwebby tendrils speckled with blue mold. On the floor insects crawled, scuttling from nests wedged deep in the crevices along the walls of stone.

A light shone from above, scattering droplets of water on her head. She glimpsed through her fingers a dazzling view of open sky—the first slice of freedom she had ever beheld.

She flinched at a gentle touch on her leg and glanced down. "Mother," moaned a little girl's voice.

Her daughter and son sat beside her. She had battled for them, fatally injuring herself in her desire to rip apart the ones who had taken her babies at birth. Now they squatted next to her, gazing at her face imploringly.

"Govorian, *wait!*" she shrieked into the empty passage. "Great Leader, do not leave us!"

The echo of her plea rebounded, emphasizing her abandonment, for she knew Thresher Govorian would not return. To keep the Bloodsword singing—kindling newfound courage in the slaves' crippled hearts—her leader was obliged to obey the blade's commands.

She crouched low, embracing her babes with her free arm as she gripped her weapon. *This temptation of sky is a trick*, she thought. *They are baiting me; it is naught but delusion!* She had suffered this cruel game of the slavers before. Somewhere close and out of her sight, the cowards were laughing at her, spying on her through the ravenous bloodstones in their staves.

This sword feels real, she thought. The heft of it was familiar, yet she could not recall ever possessing such a weapon. With care, she lifted its tip to the light, eyeing the trickle of water along its edge.

"Mother, let us go," her son said as he fretfully clasped her knee. "Come, Mother, we need to catch *up*!"

"No," she said. "Something is wrong!" She gasped, seeing the child's hand on her thigh turn to mist. Two tiny skeletons slumped against the wall beside her, their empty sockets staring, yearning for the lives they had lost. Unending child-tears fell glistening down their cheeks of pitted bone.

She screamed and staggered back. "What is my *name*?" she cried hoarsely. "Who am I now?"

"Avalar," said a stern, quiet voice.

She spun toward it with a snarl, for the sound came from the level of her hip, and the accent was human. She charged into the light by the intruder and slammed against the wall.

A man stepped from the brightness, unlike any she had ever beheld. Instead of robes, he wore armor on his breast and thighs, with a cloak of fur across his shoulders and back. Smiling kindly, he spread his hands so that she could see he wielded no magic, nor did he carry staff or sword.

She crouched low, snarling, her fingers digging long furrows in the mud by her feet. "This time, I shall not miss!" she spat, and driven by instinct, she raised the blade.

"Avalar Mistavere," he said. With slow measured steps, he advanced. "That is your name, Giant. Avalar Mistavere. Your father is Grevelin Mistavere. You were a friend to my brother, Camron Florne."

She backed away, the weapon clattering to the floor. This, too, was a delusion, more magic toying with her mind. "My name is . . ."

He nodded. "You see? You *do* know yourself. You dropped your sword so you wouldn't hurt me. Giants from *your* time never attack defenseless people. Avalar, you found the mines for us. Good girl! But Gaelin needs your help. We all do. To *help*," he repeated. "Isn't that the chosen purpose of your people?"

Avalar listened as he spoke, his voice oddly comforting to her heart.

"I need you, Giant," he told her. "You couldn't save Camron, but you tried, remember? That means something to me. *You* mean something to me. Avalar, now you're giving me your aid like you couldn't for Camron. And I *need* you. Please stay."

Tears blurred her vision. "They slew my children," she moaned, "my *babies*!"

"Avalar," he said. "You don't have children." He grimaced as he glanced toward the bones. "Somebody else must have lost her young ones. Perhaps that lonely mother's memory stirs in you now, but this is *your* life to live, not hers. The Bloodsword spoke to *you*, remember? You live on Hothra with your father, Grevelin. You sailed here to fight for freedom for your people."

Shifting on her heels, she peered through her tears into the tunnel. "Camron?" she whispered. "*He . . .*"

"That's right." The man urged her to her knees. She realized from his touch what he was—a human free, unwarped by magic.

"Leader . . . *Terrek?*"

"Yes, Leader Terrek, and I would never hurt you," he reassured her. "Nor have I given you my permission to leave me just yet." He smiled ruefully as he leaned to examine her fingers. "You're bleeding. We'll get Vyergin to fix that."

Peering up, Terrek squinted at his men kneeling above. "She's all right for now. Vyergin and Gaelin, climb down. It's not far. Just grab on to the edge and . . ." He paused. "Or perhaps our friend here can lift you." At her puzzled glance, he patted her wrist. "It may help you stay in the present. Roth, you and the guards gather what supplies we can use in the tunnels. We won't need much. Just water and food and some blankets. According to Kildoren, we needn't worry about the shan. They'll know when it's time to go home."

Shakily, Avalar stood. "I will assist," she said. Moving into the light, she extended her hands, catching a pair of legs as an older human—Vyergin, she recalled—lowered a smaller man into her embrace. She blinked at him as she set him on his feet. "You are Gaelin Lavahl," she said softly. Then she reached for the woman she remembered was their prisoner.

Gaelin stayed her arm. "Terrek Florne," Holram's voice intoned. "Before you proceed, I must warn you. You need to know Erebos is joined to this human, Felrina Vlyn. He linked with her to savor her death, but she never perished, so his connection endures."

Holram paused, and Gaelin's human eyes filled with sorrow. "Erebos sent the dachs because, through her, he learned of our location. Here within his mountain, this ceases to matter; he will perceive where we are through *me*. Yet he can still benefit from this link with her in other ways. He will hear us and gain knowledge of our plans."

"Does *she* know?" Terrek asked sharply. "Is she working for him?"

"I discerned Erebos's essence within her when I healed her," Holram said. "I presumed it was nothing more than an imprint of her lengthy exposure to him. Yet when the dachs attacked she never woke. Not even when we began traveling . . . ah, I see you noticed that as well. She is a window; that is my word for it. As Ponu is a window for Sephrym, and Gaelin is for me, so Erebos is using Felrina Vlyn. By inducing deep sleep in her, he has left her with no way to resist him, and no way to know."

Terrek growled. Glancing up, he met Avalar's stare. "You may receive her now, Giant. And if you would, help Vyergin, too."

Avalar, gesturing to the captain to bring their prisoner within her reach, listened hard as the warder conversed with Terrek.

"You must slay her," said Holram. The warder's soft, alien voice, heavy with regret, floated across the shaft. "She is a danger to all of you."

"But I promised her leniency," Terrek protested. "I can't just . . . That would be beyond cruel."

"It would be," Holram agreed. "Yet here in Erebos's mountain, he could possess her physically. She could lose herself and slit your throats the moment you try to sleep. Terrek Florne, the future of your species could be decided should you fail to act."

"I'm little more than a ranch hand," Terrek said. "For the sake of my father and my city, I've endeavored to be more by leading patrols and defending Kideren. But I cannot kill an unarmed wo—"

He broke off as Avalar swung both the still-groggy Felrina and Brant Vyergin to the floor. Then Avalar stiffened, beholding the tunnel around her as it actually was. The crawling insects were gone. Even the mud she had gouged with her fingers was frozen hard. She winced at the bloody ruin she had made of her nails.

The packs were being dropped from above, landing with tiny explosions of dust. Again Avalar reached up, this time to deliver Roth in his tall black hat to his commander, followed by the two guards, a grunt escaping her as she placed the wide-girthed Silva on his feet. Then she paused, detecting the conflict in her leader's gaze as he focused on Gaelin.

"It occurs to me," Terrek said loudly, "we've been traveling in the wrong direction. This isn't the mountain we want."

"It *isn't?*" Roth slanted a questioning look at Terrek. "But the . . ."

Avalar stood. Terrek's stare bored into her, demanding something from her. Abruptly she started, remembering Holram's warning to Terrek. "Felrina Vlyn," she said firmly. "Come here."

Felrina, by reflex, raised and crossed her wrists as though expecting to be retied, just as Terrek lunged for her head. With one fluid motion, he seized her jaw. There was a dull, wet splinter of bone as he brutally twisted, and she slumped to the ground.

"*Terrek!*" Vyergin stumbled; appalled, he sank to his knees.

Roth goggled at the crumpled, twitching form. Terrek nodded. "*Happy* now? She's paid the price you wanted her to pay, hasn't she? Sorry if it wasn't messy enough for you."

"She deserved a trial, Terrek!" said Vyergin thickly. "We don't just . . . What have you done?"

"The last thing I wanted to do," Terrek said bitterly. "But it had to be done, Brant."

At their feet, Felrina's chest heaved with agonal breathing. Her body, reaved of life, was shutting down.

Terrek knelt beside her, gently pulling the hair from her mouth. "You've never seen someone killed outright before, have you, Roth? It's not quite the way you imagined, is it? One moment she's alive, breathing and feeling, perhaps even cherishing some hopes for herself, and *then* . . ." Terrek snapped his fingers.

Sinking to his knees, Roth sagged toward the wall and quietly retched.

Avalar staggered dizzily. The tunnel seemed to slant all at once and begin to close in. Numbly she bent to inspect her pack, her mind reeling while she fought with the straps. Around her, the guards and Vyergin followed her example, feigning a sudden obsession with their provisions.

Terrek reached out to grip Gaelin's shoulder. "*Holram*," he said, deliberately emphasizing the warder's name, "are you still here with me?"

Gaelin, his eyes glazed and groggy, bobbed his head in response, padding softly toward the woman on the floor. Woodenly he sank to his knees, his hand dropping to her brow. With a soft sigh, he closed his eyes.

"Is he gone?" Terrek questioned.

"Gone," said Holram without looking up. "Shall I restore her?"

"Yes, please do," said Terrek.

The warder bent, and Mornius flickered and flashed, the Skystone's radiance filling the tunnel. Felrina jerked, coughing as she thrashed with the animal instinct to flee danger.

With a touch, the warder soothed her. Climbing to his feet, he drew Felrina up with him, supporting her while she wobbled and lurched. She pressed against his arm, her frantic gaze darting from Avalar to Terrek and then back to Holram.

Terrek cleared his throat in the shocked silence. "Felrina Vlyn," he scolded gently. "That's twice now you have fainted. What have you to say for yourself?"

As Felrina turned to face him, Lord Argus's scowl appeared in Avalar's peripheral vision. Bending down, she squinted into the shaft's murky depths until she spotted the ghost, his visage shrinking to the size of a pea as it wavered and vanished.

"I fainted?" Felrina rubbed her brow.

"Yes, you did," Terrek lied. "Didn't I tell you to keep up your strength?" When Argus reappeared, grinning slyly as he materialized directly over their heads, Terrek gestured at Roth to follow the ghost. The young man complied, his complexion pale as he hurried into the passage after the dead knight's emerald light.

"You didn't wake during the battle, either," Terrek went on, "and that could have gotten you killed. From now on, you *eat* what you are given, Felrina, and no sneaking off by yourself to purge it, either. Yes, Avalar has also reported *that* to me."

Dazed, Felrina blinked at her feet.

"Can you walk?" Vyergin inquired abruptly.

Avalar shot a questioning glance at Gaelin. He was himself again, she realized, for the heat she had sensed from his bones was gone—the fierce burning of Holram's fire.

"Everyone walks." Terrek moved to the packs and hefted the largest. "And everyone carries something, too."

"I can't believe you did that," Vyergin whispered.

"I'll explain it to you later," Terrek said. He turned toward his prisoner. "*Can* you walk?" he asked.

Trembling, Felrina nodded. As timidly she regarded the mine's depths, Avalar guessed at her thoughts. Somewhere down the tunnel, a madman awaited her, ready and eager to deliver more hurt.

"Come." Stepping close, Terrek clasped the woman's arm.

Chapter 48

Avalar followed at a crouch behind her human companions, slowing when the tangled roots that clogged the narrowed shaft forced her onto her knees.

The air was musty, heavy with the stench of moldering roots and soil. In her memory, this passage had been maintained, its threads of gildstone motivating the cult to drive her enslaved people—primarily the children in this cramped section—to cripple their bodies harvesting the garish metal. Over time, pressure from the ceaselessly dripping moisture had eroded the rock, bringing with it fungi and dirt, and a slimy substance that squished beneath her hands.

She ducked low, her gaze on Argus's distant light. Far up the tunnel, she heard the ringing of Roth's machete while he labored to clear their path. Argus reclined in the air above the lieutenant and the guards, his phantom arms behind his head, his verdant glow sheening off the roots Roth hacked with his club-shaped sword.

"It's so dark," Gaelin said. "Like when I was in the cellar."

"Put it out of your thoughts, Gaelin," urged Terrek.

"Argus is too far ahead. Why can't he stay in the middle so we can see?"

"You're in front and you get to see a great deal more than we do," said Terrek. "Avalar can't catch up if she's blind. I think now would be a good time to ask Holram . . ." He paused. "I know very little when it comes to warders. But from what I understand, they guide the creation of suns, do they not?"

"Only mature warders do that," Gaelin corrected. "Holram was too young. He could protect his star; that's all. He warded the sun and Earth and—"

"Well then!" Terrek cut in. "If Holram can do all that, perhaps he might like to do a little *wardering* here for us? You're holding his Skystone. Why not kindle it so Avalar can see?"

"I've been trying to reserve my strength," Gaelin protested. "We're expecting a battle, aren't we?"

"Gaelin Lavahl," Avalar said. "This foul air pains my chest. If I were to see what lies before me, mayhap I could travel more swiftly away from—"

"It could get worse," Felrina interjected. "Some of these b-burrows have collapsed. If this is one, you will have to d-d-dig through it, and the air beyond would be stale, w-worse than if you had brought that torch. The disruption of air could excite the spores they planted here to keep out intruders. They are *poison*."

Gaelin, moving faster now, thumped his staff on the soggy ground between the twisted roots. Avalar sighed as she crawled on all fours behind Terrek, seeing no hint of light from the staff's lifeless crown. Resignedly, she felt with her hands as she went, squirming over the slimy obstacles in her way as gunk collected beneath her shredded nails. *Now I shall be reeking*, she thought morosely, *when at last I am led to fulfill my destiny. I will—*

"*Blazes!*" Gaelin cried. There was a scrambling noise, followed by a soft groan.

"If *you*'re tripping in the darkness," Terrek said sharply, "try to imagine how it might be for a giant!"

Avalar grinned despite herself at a sudden sputter from the Skystone, the staff in Gaelin's hand rousing at last.

She studied the dirt at her feet, observing the patterns of fungi clearly now, the pea-green caps of tiny mushrooms glowing blue beneath Mornius. As the two humans surged to shorten the distance between them and the others, Avalar held back, plucking the wrinkled tops of the mushrooms from their stems and stuffing them into her pocket. It was instinct, some inner compulsion she could not fathom. *Mayhap a memory?* she thought with a shudder.

The humans were huddled in a group as she approached, with Gaelin holding his staff aloft. Terrek shifted closer to Vyergin as if to deliberately block her view.

She nodded at his concern, at the nervous tension of the men. The prisoner, Felrina, was even paler than she had been before. "You fear for me," Avalar said. "Have you discovered another dead child?"

"This one's a bit older, I think," Terrek murmured. "But not by much. It's bad enough they would enslave your people, Avalar. But your children, too?"

"The littlest ones were called 'sniffers,'" she said. "The slavers would take the babies at birth to train them to hunt for magic, and through them our captors found powers within this mountain. They uncovered the bloodstones, the life of this world that absorbs all magic, and learned how to use them. They did not care that the stones drained the children to death. Each child was trained to withstand the loss of their magic long enough to retrieve one stone apiece before they died."

Felrina stared up. "Are you telling us that every stone . . . *every* stone in those staves the black-robes carry, represents a child's death?"

Recognizing pain on the woman's earnest face, Avalar bit down on her retort. "Yes," she answered softly.

Terrek took her hand, his brow furrowed with worry. "Avalar, perhaps the time has come for you to go. Giant, I don't want you to be—"

"No!" Avalar ground out the word. "The time has *not* come! The world was birthed on the shoulders of giants. Mayhap it will end for the failure of mine. Still I must try, Leader Terrek. When I was yet a child, the bloodstone sword, Redeemer, roused something in my heart. I remembered what giants are supposed to be! I have borne this all my life, right *here*." She pressed her fist to her breastplate. "I will not falter, or turn on you a second time. I swear it. Nor will I be dissuaded from my path!"

Terrek chewed his lip. "I have no idea what's coming next. What if we can't protect you and you die? What happens to the world?"

"I am not here for your protection." Avalar gestured toward Gaelin and lowered her voice. "If he fails, our lives will mean naught. All of us will perish."

Gaelin squatted among the men, his staff glowing ominously bright. The others stepped back, leery of the warder's power. As they did, Avalar saw the reason for their desire to shield her.

The child's skeleton lay in pieces, the fragile bone of its orbits and upper skull punctured and torn away. "Grakan," Avalar said. "The slavers always brought two."

She gasped as the boy's image materialized in a sparkling mist only she could see, his gray eyes luminous as he returned her gaze. "He is too old to be a sniffer," she said to the humans. "He must have displeased his captors."

Swift as a blink, the two grakan tore the legs out from under the youngster. Her eyes welling, she watched him fall. He lay silent, his stare fixed on the ceiling, his blood spreading across the stone as the great bears ripped him apart.

"Avalar?" The vision frayed as Terrek tugged at her wrist, merging with the dust motes in Argus's light. Avalar strained to focus past Terrek—to see the bones and not the child, the fragile remains on the floor.

She faced the wall, letting its tilted contours guide her consciousness beyond her friends. A painful groaning reached from her memories, the unending grind of her people's toil.

"Avalar," Terrek cautioned. "What you see is not real."

She nodded. Evil existed in this time, in the form of real human beings serving a monster in these tunnels, hunting and killing their own kind to please their god.

Avalar glanced at the prisoner clinging to Terrek and then past them at Argus. Quietly, she accompanied the ghost away from her companions and from the warder cremating the child's bones.

"You *hear* them, too," Avalar murmured to the Thalian Knight. "You endure your ghosts, as I do my memories."

Argus snorted. "I *am* them." He glared at her from a rounded corner of the ceiling, hugging himself with limbs he could no longer feel. Unable to find comfort in the gesture, he dropped his arms. "You experience the past. Echoes of torment from long ago. Yet the giants themselves are at peace."

He motioned to the empty air above his head. "Her victims *cannot* rest. They cling to their lost lives, screaming for her death while we speak. Yet always, *he* stands in their way. I hear him speaking to his brother, calling into Terrek's ear! He loves her still! After everything she's done!"

"*Who* does?" she asked. "Who stands in the way?"

Argus held up his hand, forestalling her rising flood of words and emotions. "His brother," he said, nodding at Terrek. "Who else?"

"*Camron!*" Frantic for a glimpse of her friend, she scanned the tunnel. "Is he here? Does he know how I fought? How hard I tried to save him, and how I . . ."

"Hush, Giant." Argus's scowl softened, empathy pulsing from his green-limned image. For the briefest of moments, the pain retreated from his expression, replaced by concern for her. "He knows, dear one. Of course he knows!" Argus paused. Then his eyes glinted, as if he had spied something profound within her that moved him.

"Never doubt it, Giant. Camron knows!"

Chapter 49

Obeying the pressure of Terrek's grip on her arm, Felrina shambled to a halt behind the ghost's unnerving light. Next to her, the neighbor she had known all her life—the man who was now her captor—signaled a stop.

"We rest here," Terrek announced. He unshouldered his pack, letting it drop with a thud on a drier patch of dirt. As he released her, Felrina stumbled toward the side of the tunnel. They were venturing under the mountain now. The ceiling, high enough for the giant to stand straight, was fringed with tiny roots, while the floor was sunken through the middle and grooved where the carts had been.

Across from her, Gaelin Lavahl struggled to keep his feet. Terrek spoke to him, and he settled on his heels, his Skystone winking out.

An elbow jostled Felrina.

"How's the neck?" Lieutenant Roth sniggered, glaring under his curly mass of brown hair, his thin lips twisted with hate.

She probed her aching muscles with tentative fingers. "It's sore," she said. "How did you know?"

"I wish he had left you *dead*!" Roth hissed. "My mother didn't get to come back alive. My sister, Gindle, didn't either, nor did Terrek's brother."

"Left me dead? What are you talking about? When was I d–dead?"

Roth made a brutal, twisting motion with his hands. "Just like *that*!" he said. "I loved the sound it made: snap! Terrek did it *himself*, bitch. I'm pretty sure he enjoyed it, too! *I* did!"

Felrina jerked away from his naked contempt. Above him, the ghost knight sneered, his gaze rife with malice.

She moaned as she sank to her haunches. The features of her companions blurred. The rocky wall at her back reminded her of

Erebos, its merciless cold snuffing out her will to live.

With a snort of disgust, Roth stomped off, but his words remained to haunt and to hurt, piercing like a lance through her heart. Somehow, she knew when Terrek gestured his companions on. The ghost's departing illumination left her sitting in the darkness; the footsteps of the men drew away. Yet still, she sat, frozen beyond caring or tears.

Avalar tapped her shoulder. "Come," the giant urged.

Felrina pressed her palms to her face and sagged.

"Now what?" Terrek asked sharply.

Lowering her arms, Felrina focused on a discolored speck on his leather breastplate as he crouched down, her fingers twitching on the floor. "You . . . k–killed me. He says you b–b–broke my neck."

Terrek glowered at Roth, who hovered behind him. "You said this *why?*" he demanded.

"I thought . . . she ought to know," Roth muttered. "She . . ."

"Well, you thought wrong!" Terrek lurched to his feet. "We don't torture people."

"*Torture?*" Roth echoed. "Terrek, I only meant . . ."

"You meant to cause her misery; *that's* what you meant," said Terrek. "I call that torture. You're bullying her, Roth, and this stops now!"

Roth blinked and looked away. "I . . ."

"If you can't show compassion, then let her be." Terrek stared at the younger man. "*Yes*, she slew Camron. And no, I haven't forgotten. I've also known Felrina Vlyn my entire life. Kindly accept that perhaps I have insights here that you do not! Now go. Follow Argus." Terrek gestured toward the knight. "Not you, Gaelin," he added. "If you would, I could still use your light. But the rest of you, go. We'll be right behind you."

Felrina held her breath while the silence stretched out, filled with the soft sound of the two men breathing, the quiet scuffle of Gaelin's heels when, holding Mornius high, he stepped out of earshot.

Once more Terrek squatted before her. Fearing his reprimand, she bowed her head, her gaze averted.

"I had no choice," he told her. "I learned you and Erebos were linked. That made you a threat. Your death, Felrina, was the one way to sever his connection."

338

She shook her head. Her eyes were dry again, her heart a wasteland. "I'm sorry," she whispered. "I wish you had left me d- dead."

"No, you don't," he murmured. As he took her hand, she stiffened at his touch, the subtle reminder of Mens. She thrust with all her might at his chest.

"No," he said. "Felrina, *no*."

Tears blurred her sight, streaming hot and unstoppable over her grimy cheeks. He paused, his inner conflict darkening his eyes. Then he was pulling her to his chest, his right arm enfolding her, supporting her while she cried.

"I never wanted you to know," he said. "I thought I wanted your death, too. I thought it was the correct answer for what you did, but I was wrong. Killing you was the hardest thing I've ever done."

Felrina hiccupped as she struggled for control. "I'm . . . I . . ."

"I don't hate you." Terrek's voice was gentle. "Not everyone here does. I know Vyergin doesn't. Nor does Gaelin. Avalar—I suspect she feels rage, as I do. Not hate. Remember what you told me back there? If we find a cave-in and have to dig through it, the air might fill with spores. That was a help, Felrina. You're trying, and that counts for something."

She sat back as, by degrees, he let her go. Yet still his gaze held her. "After all you suffered," he said, "this is the last place you should be, but I need your knowledge of these tunnels. Argus is a ghost. He's forgotten how it is to be . . . well, human. Roth is a troubled boy who lost his family. You cannot let their anger unravel you so, not when we're this close. I need you alert, aware, and brave like you used to be. No more of *this*." He touched her wet cheek. "Too much crying will make you sick. You're stammering, too, and you haven't done that for years."

Felrina hung her head. "That w-woman you remember no longer exists, Ter . . . Commander. She v-vanished when I—" She broke off, trembling. "Now because of me, my father . . . I c-couldn't save him, *or* your brother. I do wish that you had left me d-dead. I *do*."

Terrek drew a small knife from his boot. "No." He set its keen edge to her throat, while resolutely she shut her eyes, shivering at the steel's icy touch.

Terrek pressed ever so slightly, and Felrina shuddered, harder still, until the metal nipped her skin. She gasped at the warm trickle of blood she felt. Her eyes flew open. She clutched at Terrek's fingers with both hands, frantic to push away the blade.

Terrek let her. He drew a cloth from his pack and dabbed at her tiny cut. "You see?" he said and deliberately arched his brow. "No, you *don't*."

Chapter 50

linking, Kray looked up from where he sat at the table as Ponu charged into his workroom. Beside the little boy, the ferret, Saemson, whom Kray had been feeding, exploded into a rapid "uh-uh, uh-uh" as it dived beneath the nearest bed. "You scared him, Ponu," said Kray. "You shouldn't—"

"No!" Ponu cut him off. Then he hurried to sit on his bed and stamp on his warmest boots. "We're going," he said as he stood. His glance fell on a satchel high on a shelf, and he snatched it down, scattering jerked meat onto the floor so the ferret could forage for himself.

Kray scrambled from his chair. "Going? What?"

Ponu sighed. "Kray, we talked about this. It's time." He began quickly to gather the boy's things from under his cot.

"What're you *doing*?" Kray cried, tugging at his sleeve.

"We planned this, remember?" Straightening up, Ponu scanned his home's interior before moving to the table. Gravely he added to his ward's meager possessions the baubles Kray had earned, including the two leather-bound books he had given the child. Then Ponu froze, staring at the small crystal globe hidden between the books. Without a word, he slipped the gem into his pocket.

"I have no idea what will happen, Kray," he said, "but this cannot continue. Your people are dying! I must lend what aid I can."

"Ponu, *no!*" Quaking with grief, Kray sank to his knees.

Ponu tied the bag and placed it on the table. "Kray." Settling himself on the floor, he cupped the boy's chin and stared deep into his eyes. "You know I've been upset. Well, this will help me. Don't you want that? It will assist other humans like you, too. I promise it's not for very long. I need to take you where it's safe."

"But I wanted to show you what I found in the sky!" said Kray. "It's big and it's not on your map. I saw it through your viewer. It's *there*!" He pointed straight up.

"Did it resemble a cloud filled with stars?" Ponu asked.

Kray nodded. "Yes. You've seen it?"

"Many times, but only through my staff," Ponu said. "That is where Sephrym dwells. This worries me, Kray. What you describe should never be visible from here!"

Ponu climbed to his feet. This second visitation of Sephrym's spirit confirmed his suspicions. The great warder could sense Holram's rise to power and was preparing himself. If Holram failed to stop Ercbos this time . . . Ponu frowned. *I know what Sephrym will do*, he thought grimly.

Lifting the bag with the child's possessions, he retrieved the thick wool blanket from his bed and tossed it to Kray. "Wrap yourself up with this. It's even colder on Hothra Isle than it is here." He hesitated as the child's lips trembled. "Come now, Kray. We must all do our part!"

The boy stumbled to his feet, dabbing at his eyes with his stuffed bunny's ear. "My part?"

"Yes, this is very important, too," Ponu informed him. "If you are to become a great wizard one day, you must let us protect you."

Ponu reached for his staff, positioning himself behind the little boy and closing his eyes. More than anyone else, he knew Grevelin. He was familiar with the master's habits and haunts, and his probable whereabouts as winter dragged out on the northern isle. As Leader Second to Trentor Govorian, Grevelin had his duties, and one such chore compelled the solitary giant to venture out among people.

Ponu concentrated through his Staff of Time's crystal, focusing on the location where the giant would be.

As his magic sparked, Ponu gripped the child, steadying the boy against his hip. He smiled, seeing the small human's curiosity take over. His fears forgotten, Kray peered about him as they *transferred*, his eyes wide with wonder.

My staff is made from time crystals, Ponu recalled trying to explain to the boy—*rare round gems from the hills of Shamshedaya on my world.* Kray had nodded off as he spoke, yet Ponu had pressed on in hopes some understanding might sink in. *At first, I had to shatter one of the quartz spheres to release the power. I would then ride the blast to get where I needed to go.*

He frowned, recollecting how he had grown concerned as his supply of gems had dwindled. *My world was gone*, he had told the boy, *and my cache of stones shrinking. So I merged the finest gems I had left to form this staff. Now I don't have to destroy the stones whenever I wish to travel. Instead of ruining a crystal with a single blast, now I just push my consciousness inward into my staff and visualize my landing place.*

"*Imagination is magic*," his mother had taught him once, and so he had tried to console the boy, stressing that humans did indeed possess magic—the ability to visualize and invent. While he, reaping the benefits of his own ingenuity, could now wield his staff as often as he liked. Only as a last resort would he consider destroying one of the remaining round crystals he kept hidden in the cavern below his quarters, the cave where Kray had strayed despite his orders. He felt the little gem in his pocket growing hot in response to his staff. *It could have taken you anywhere, Kray, if you had dropped it.*

As the interior of the Ironwood Hoist Pub sprang into existence, Kray pressed against him. Standing with the child at the center of a small woven rug, Ponu stared at the huddle of giants nearby, at the muscular and yet rotund owner lifting a barrel to drain it.

The room was longer than it was wide, its peal-stone walls indented to frame rows upon rows of nautical artwork. Kneeling next to Kray, Ponu pointed, directing the child's gaze to the colorful net-entangled floaters suspended from the ceiling.

The giants sat around a table, enjoying a game of "pieces" with three many-faceted stones carved with runes on every side. Ponu counted eight males, six of them former slaves.

With bravado he did not feel, he swept them a bow. "Hail, Masters," he said in a hearty voice. "I am here for your Leader Second, Grevelin."

Scratch, the captain of a ship Ponu knew as the *Roundabout*, rose from his chair, his one stormy gray eye focusing on the child. "You bring a *human*?" He coughed through his torn throat and over the remnants of his tongue. "You *dare*?"

"Apparently so," Ponu replied. He peered at the fire in the blackened hearth, the oversized stone chairs and tables penning him in, and the Hoist's ironwood door so heavy that he knew it would take a giant's strength to open.

A tense pause ensued as the pub's owner, Rhayme, raised his club and placed it with a thud on the counter for all to see.

Ignoring this threat, the giants rose from their chairs, their big hands doubled into fists as they towered above Ponu. In their fury, he perceived the memory of whips and hunger, of chains and unending abuse. Despite his outrage at giants menacing a child, he bowed in respect.

"But this is a *little boy*, Masters! He has lost his home and everything familiar to him, because of the same evil force that once fettered you. That slaver king you abhor still exists! With no giants to torment, he attacks humans now, like this child's parents! I rescued this small one and he is my ward. None of you shall touch him!"

"They certainly shall *not*," said a scathing voice from the doorway. "Giants never harm children, and yet see you how this little one trembles! For *shame*!"

Avalar's massive uncle, Kurgenrock Mistavere, stood with his back bent, his great bearded head thrust through the doorway. With eyes that sparked like flint, Kurg snarled at the giants assembled, many of whom were of his own crew.

"They are in their cups, Captain," growled the barkeep.

"That is no excuse, Rhayme! Behold this poor child. Ponu," Kurg acknowledged. He lifted his chin and scowled at the rest. "You *lagabeds*!" he roared. "*Shame* on you! *Dawncutter*'s hull still has damage, and here you go when you finally wake up—to Hoist, of all places—for your pieces and cups! Gaming! When we sail on the morrow and '*Cutter* is taking on water! *Out*!"

The giants scattered toward their purses or sacks, jostling each other in their haste to pack up the game and scoop their winnings into pockets or satchels. They rushed for the doorway, and Kurg stepped aside.

Even Scratch, the captain still called Taneus Spadethrust by giants who did not know better, was shoving his way out, Ponu noted sadly. *All that bluster*, Ponu thought as the door slammed shut behind the *Roundabout*'s captain, *and still so crushed. As long as I have known him it has been the same.* Scratch cared for no one, or so the gossip went. He had been great among giants—the beloved friend of Thresher Govorian—until a slaver's ax had cleft his spirit as cruelly as his face.

"Grev's coming," Kurgenrock said to Ponu as the last giant vanished into the storm. He shut the iron door that had once been a galley-hatch—and forced the latch down with red, stiffened fingers. "Good night's keep to you, Rhayme Blythe," he said, bowing his head to the barkeep. "I shall cover what coin my giants still owe."

Kurgenrock, Ponu knew, had never kept a wife or even a home on solid land. His ship was his world, and the wide Misty Sea his sanctuary. As it was with many former slaves, only the endless horizon had the power to ease his heart.

Still, Ponu reminded himself, Kurg doted on his niece, Avalar. Grevelin had taken care to hide Avalar's absence from his temperamental brother, yet from the blaze of Kurgenrock's eyes, Ponu suspected that he knew.

Kurg stared in fascinated fear at the child.

"He has no family," Ponu explained, "no one to care for him but me. Yet, I have things I must do, Kurg. Suffering is wrong, and my kin from this world have done nothing to stop it."

Kurgenrock nodded. "If only my people could break free from our need for protection," he said. "I grow weary of battling magical creatures to defend the North. The Sundor Khan beasts do not slay us. So they fall beneath our swords. This butchery is not what giants were made to do! I want to live to see the day when my people remind the elves why giants came first to this world to defend all other creatures.

"Avalar is correct; we bear elven chains now. And for the sake of the world, we must toil on. But these mariners . . . threatening a *child*! What are we, if we forget who we are?"

"You will forgive me," Ponu said softly, "if I leave Kray here? I intend to ask Grev to watch him for me, and I am hoping you might help your brother, considering the hostility some giants still feel. It would just be for a few days, Kurg."

"Pardon me, Ponu," the big giant said. "But I shall be on my ship, striving to forget the ills of this world. I *will* let the rumor spread, however: what I personally vow to do to any coward who touches this boy."

The portal flew open with a bang and a blast of frigid wind. Grevelin charged in, shaking caked-on ice from his collar and scarf, bringing with him a swirl of snow. "Another whopper from the

North," he rumbled. "You may look for your giants in the cook-room, Kurg. Leader Trentor's orders—they shall not be mending *Dawncutter*'s hull today!"

As Grevelin moved to shut and bolt the ironwood door, he spotted the child and snorted. "Ponu, you bring our little friend, I see."

"Not so little," said Kray. The boy had retreated, hugging his stuffed rabbit to his chest at the sight of so many giants. He spoke boldly from behind Ponu's wings. "I'm eight years old!"

"Eight years!" Grevelin crouched low and snapped his fingers. "Come here, young warrior! Show me your muscles!"

"Grevelin—" Ponu began. He stopped, his mouth dropping open as Kray marched straight into the giant's huge hands. The Leader Second, his gaze thoughtful, cradled the boy in his massive arms.

Grevelin had been among the first giants to agree to help the human tribes in the North who, like the elves, were targeted by the Sundor Khan. *Still*, Ponu thought, *I do not believe he has ever seen a human this young before.* "Will you care for him, Grev? I will not be long. Soon, one way or another, all this will end."

"You'll come back for me, Ponu?" Kray asked.

"Of course," Ponu assured him, "as soon as I possibly can." Tapping his staff on the soft woven rug, he raised his eyes to his friend's face. "Can you protect him, Grev? I know grown giants would never injure a little boy, but you have some youngsters here that I do not trust!"

"No *true* giant would hurt a child," Kurg growled. "But do hasten back, Ponu. For many, this small human shall indeed evoke memories—pain none of us deserve."

"We must all do our part," Grevelin chided his brother. "We cannot fight as we wish, so we must aid those who can. After all, we are *giants*! Surely we can bear the memories if we must."

Kurgenrock grunted. "We defend the helpless," he agreed, inclining his head. "If I see this child in peril on the shore, I shall ward him. Yet *Dawncutter* is my first concern, and we *will* sail on the morrow!"

Kurgenrock strode to unbar the door, letting the wind swing it to smack the wall. He strode out, his body swallowed at once by the storm.

"At the least, his intentions are good!" Grevelin lunged for the hatch and, with his one free arm, slammed it shut.

Ponu smiled at Kray already drowsing in the giant's embrace. "He trusts you, Grev."

Chuckling, Grevelin lifted one of the boy's tiny fingers. "Same size as Avalar's when she was a babe."

"Don't let *him* hear you say that!" Ponu warned with a laugh. "Grev, I must go. I shut my eyes and I try to sleep, and I see innocent humans in the dark, waiting to be tortured or killed. I cannot rest. I will not rest until this is over."

"You must follow your heart, of course," Grevelin responded. "But do not forget we are bonded. I will perish if you die, and then so will the world."

"You should not forget who I am!" Ponu said as he flared his wings, waggling his brows until at last Kray chuckled. "Now stop it, Grev. No more talk of dying!"

Chapter 51

Felrina tensed as they approached the fork ahead, the tunnel splitting into twin narrow shafts separated by a wedge of mottled rock. She cocked her head at the muffled sound of water. "The river," she muttered, slipping between Terrek and the wall toward the split in the passage. Somewhere at the end of one of these paths, the Shukaia cut through the fire-mountain's core.

Avalar peered down each of the tunnels in turn. "Old magic," she muttered, sniffing the air.

Felrina squinted into the depths of the shaft closest to her. Without the ghost's green light, she was blind, staring at darkness. *If only I had my staff,* the thought intruded, *then I'd see, and I could—* She caught herself. *Oh no, what am I thinking?*

Felrina glanced at Gaelin. *He needs to bring his light closer.*

"You know this place," Avalar said. "What is your counsel?"

"I don't have any . . ." Taken aback, Felrina frowned. *I don't know,* she wanted to say. Instead, she covered her face and pointed. "There!"

"That is a wall," Avalar growled. "Care to try again?"

Felrina, opening her eyes, regarded her jutting finger. Slowly, she moved her hand toward the sound of the distant rapids. "That w-way," she stammered. "My pool got its water from s-somewhere. Yes, that must be the way." She sighed and shook her head. "To be honest, I don't know. We never used this level!"

"No, why would you?" Avalar said. "My people carved these holes, for they were laborers. *Diggers.* While the slaves you create maim and kill."

Felrina stumbled back from the giant's ire. "We don't make

slaves," she said. "We've never. . . There are a lot of things I regret. But I do *not* believe in slavery, and we never k-kept—"

"Pardon? What would you call the dachs?" Avalar demanded.

"Enough, Giant." Terrek motioned Gaelin forward. The staff-wielder padded by, his footfalls silent.

Felrina waited, watching while Gaelin dipped Mornius's heavy crown into the mouth of the first opening. Then she jumped as Terrek gripped the nape of her neck and set her in Mornius's light.

"Which one, Felrina? To get us within striking distance of Erebos, which way should we go?"

His grasp had the power to snap her bones, his fingers just as hard and unyielding as Mens's had been. She gagged, and her knees buckled.

The tunnel went uncomfortably silent. Avalar crouched in front of her with her big hand extended. Felrina clung to the giant's strength, drawing herself back to her feet.

"She already told me," Avalar said to Terrek. "The right-hand passage is best."

Felrina nodded. "I'm just guessing," she said. "I . . . don't have the B-blazenstone anymore, so I can't—"

"Why didn't you just say so?" Terrek asked. "I'm not going to kill you for not knowing the answer."

"I don't like to be *grabbed* like that!" she burst out.

"I'm sorry," said Terrek. "I wasn't thinking. It won't happen again." He gestured to his men. "Enough of this. Let's go."

Felrina stiffened when Avalar clasped her shoulder. "Stay back with me," the giant said.

Unresisting, Felrina let the big hands guide her, coaxing her next to the wall and to the coolness of the rock as she slumped against it.

"Let the others go first," Avalar urged. "You and I will take the rear. You have clung to my leader long enough. He will need his arms for battle when it comes!"

"Holram agrees with her," Gaelin quietly told Terrek. "If we want to reach the river, the right side is best."

"Good," replied Terrek. "Let's go."

Felrina watched as Terrek and the guards entered the tunnel. Gaelin, his flickering light held high, walked behind the larger men.

Vyergin hesitated, stopping in front of her. "It'll get better, my dear," he said. "Terrek's a good man. I think you know that."

Felrina jerked away from his touch on her cheek. With a soft sigh, he continued on, quickening his pace to remain in the staff's circle of light.

"That was rude," Avalar remarked. "Vyergin has only ever been kind to you."

"I *still* say he should have left you dead!" Roth snapped, shoving his face close to hers. "*Next* time we stop, I wouldn't try sleeping if I were you."

Felrina shivered as he stamped off, the force of his steps jiggling his out-of-place hat. She had nothing of value to tell him. *It's true,* she thought. *I do deserve death. Camron Florne was my friend. And Nithra! My own father!*

"Come," Avalar commanded.

Felrina pushed herself from the wall into the darkening gloom. She was too tired to resist, and Terrek's compassion wounded her, reminding her of the friend she had lost, the man who had loved her.

Her nerves were afire, painful needles at the back of her neck jabbing her as she walked. A pressure mounted in her chest. She was gasping, struggling for air.

"Easy," the giant soothed her. "Felrina Vlyn, stop. *Look* at me!"

Felrina doubled over. Then, as Gaelin's staff rounded the distant bend, the space all around them went black. "Oh!" She clutched at her chest.

Avalar gripped her shoulder, seeking to steady her. "Whoever injured you is gone," the giant said. "Lean down and breathe. Put your head between your knees."

"This is wrong!" Felrina groaned. "We're headed straight f-for *Erebos*! *He's* who we have to f-fight. The one who hurt me—he's just a t-tool!"

"We shall fight them both," said Avalar. "And he will die, or mayhap we shall. Either way, there will be an end."

Felrina sank onto her heels. The thought of Mens unraveled her, laying her flat on the tunnel's unyielding stone while she pictured him looming above and cutting her slowly. Her blood dripped from the blade of his knife when he raised it; she felt it pouring over her ribs, her limbs trembling as he savagely thrust between her legs.

"He *raped* me!" she cried. "He c-cut me and h-he...!"

Screaming, she flailed, her fists striking the floor.

The giant settled next to her on the stone. There was a pause, and then another—a long silence dragging out, filled with Avalar's soft breathing while Felrina's cries gradually faded, the two of them huddled side by side on the frigid stone.

"I know not this word '*rape*,'" Avalar murmured at last. "Felrina, we must go."

She glanced up. "You should hate me," she whispered. "The only one who does is Roth. I don't understand it."

"Felrina Vlyn, come." Avalar clasped her wrist.

Teetering upright, Felrina shambled forward, leaning on the giant's strong and steady hand. Once more her knees were failing. As she began to fall, Avalar swept her up, cradling her gently.

"No . . ." She pressed her brow to the throb of the giant's heart. "I'm sorry."

She drifted, lulled by a feeling of release. Through her lashes she caught a flicker of orange, and then she smelled smoke. Something was burning in the mountain's dead shell, the tall flames licking at the stone.

Chapter 52

Felrina glimpsed a flicker through the darkness of the mineshaft. The young giant who carried her was catching up with the rest of their companions. Shifting in Avalar's grasp, she strained to focus through the gloom. The giant was trotting now, her rhythmic strides sending tiny shocks along Felrina's spine.

"There's a tunnel above us!" Vyergin boomed. "Here, Terrek, take a look!"

Felrina nodded, remembering the labyrinth of Erebos's temple. For a flicker of an instant, she glimpsed a shadow jutting down at her face from the rock overhead, the blackness forming itself into a massive scaly muzzle with its jaws gaping, the heat of its breath searing her as she shrank back.

She batted at Avalar's arms to get her attention. But the giant's chin was up, her swift footsteps hastening them around a corner toward her friends.

"He's *here*," Felrina gasped, tugging at Avalar's sleeve below her bracer. "Erebos is here!"

Frowning, Avalar set her onto her feet.

Felrina stumbled past the staff-wielder to Vyergin, who held up his torch next to the break in the ceiling.

"I hope it's safe for the fire," Terrek murmured to her, scraping his fingernail along the rock. "There's no sign of mold. No spores."

"The toxic mold was intended as an outer d-defense," she said, "so I don't think a torch will k-kill us. We light sconces in the passageways higher up. That's one way you will know you're g-going in the right direction."

Vyergin grunted, tipping her an approving nod as she stepped closer to him. He thrust the flaming wood into the hole.

"This one's old, too," she said, catching a glimpse of cobwebs along the wall of the upper shaft. She averted her face from a pattering of grit and rose on tiptoe to see. "We d-don't use these lower levels. That's why they're so dirty. But this will get us nearer. You'll have to k-keep climbing to reach the chambers we used."

"Good girl," said Terrek. "Roth, I need a boost!"

Avalar, moving forward, caught Terrek under his arms and lifted him over the rim, setting him on his knees. "First, we must find the river," she corrected Felrina. "Or mayhap I shall go there myself if you do not. It is what the Bloodsword, Redeemer, sang to me."

"I d-didn't know," Felrina said. "I assumed you were here for Erebos, too." She held her breath as Avalar raised her through the gap to the passage above. Terrek squatted low, reaching to help her slide in beside him.

"I have my own destiny," Avalar said, looking up. "I know not what it is." Unbending her body stiffly, the giant stood tall, her chest and shoulders extending through the aperture in the floor, blocking the torchlight from below as she surveyed the new tunnel.

Shadows rushed from both directions as the narrower passageway went dark. Felrina backed away from the giant, colliding with—

Her body tensed. "Ter—"

A clawlike hand clamped over her mouth, muffling her cry. She twisted, kicking as she fought to scream a warning.

Terrek sprang to his feet and whirled, snatching out his sword. "Avalar!" he bellowed. "Get the others up here!"

Felrina squirmed as more dachs surged past her with their sabers raised, their claws scrabbling along the shaft's rocky floor and their tails curling above their wingless backs. Poison dripped down their skin from their barbed spines and streamed from their teeth as they lunged at Terrek.

Felrina bit into the palm of the creature holding her, until her mouth filled with its rank blood. The dach screeched, its grip loosening, its fangs biting at her throat. With a howl, she tore herself free.

"*Commander!*" yelled Roth as the giant tossed him onto the stone in front of Terrek. Then Avalar scrambled up, her larger bulk filling the narrow space. With a thunderous roar, she routed their charging attackers, chasing the warped humans into the darkness.

Roth's long limbs thrashed as he struggled to stand. Bending swiftly, Terrek seized him and yanked him to his feet.

Felrina dashed to help the men. She had no weapon, but she knew these creatures. Roth and Terrek stood shoulder to shoulder to battle their two remaining foes, with the blade in Terrek's hand flaking bits of rust in the torch's frail light, looking as if it might break from its hilt at any moment. Then a dach caught at Terrek and hurled him past the gap in the floor, its tail curling as it leapt to follow.

Felrina launched herself at Terrek's assailant, colliding with its scaly ribs. With all her might, she heaved against the creature, using her weight to unbalance it. It reeled, flinging her aside as it whipped around. She caught a shimmer of green at the corner of her vision— the ghost knight flitting low toward Terrek behind her.

A blow like a fist punched her off her feet. She jerked back as pain tore through her body. Beneath the curve of her breasts, she saw it— the old rusty steel dripping with her blood.

Dimly Felrina glimpsed the specter hovering, grinning as he bowed before her. He was rising or she was sinking; she could not tell and she did not care. All she knew was the agony in her belly, the deep tearing within as she tried to draw breath. Gasping in shock and pain, she watched as Silva seized the dach and rammed a dagger through its throat.

Suddenly dizzy, she began to fall.

"Felrina!"

Terrek grabbed for her shoulder as he held his sword's blade steady within her. Gently he eased her to the floor.

"Hang on!" he shouted. "Vyergin, get Gaelin up here *now*!"

"Terrek!" Felrina clung to him.

"I can't take it out," he told her, his voice raw with grief. "Not until Gaelin gets here."

"I'm sorry! I didn't mean—" Her legs were heavy and numb. An icy blanket enfolded her. "*Terrek?*" Felrina gasped.

She spat up blood. The tunnel whirled and faded, replaced by the dazzling brightness of a windy funnel and a figure within it striding toward her. It was Camron bending down to cup her face with his hands. Felrina drank in the sight of his freckled nose, his soft sparkling eyes glinting with tears.

She shivered as he kissed her forehead, his fingers caressing her cheek. *I am so sorry!* she ached to say.

Smiling, Camron nodded. "I need you to *live!*"

Felrina blinked as the light winked out. She tasted blood in her mouth. A weight dragged at her body, ripping her away from where she wanted to be—from Camron's face smiling at her. She struggled as Gaelin knelt on the stone beside her, power lancing out from Mornius's gem, flashing from his open palms.

"No!" She reached into the shadows beneath the flicker of Vyergin's torch. "Camron! Don't *go!*"

A fierce multicolored fire struck at the blade that cut through her, driving the steel tip back until, with a clang, the ancient weapon fell free.

Terrek flung it away. His glare lashed the ghost. "If you ever—"

"What?" Argus demanded. "Do you blame me? I'm just a ghost. 'I've forgotten how it is to be human!' And yes, I heard you! It doesn't matter where I am, I *hear* you when you mention my name! Oh, but I'm the evil one? You sit there coddling a murderer, and *I'm* the villain?"

"You *have* forgotten how it is," Terrek said. "And I stand by what I said." He stroked Felrina's cheek and pulled her close. Beside them, Gaelin slumped against the wall.

"Gaelin!" Terrek yanked the fiery staff from its wielder. As the Skystone dimmed, he placed Mornius on the floor and patted Gaelin's arm. "Enough," he said. "She's healed, my friend."

With a grateful sigh, Gaelin sank to his haunches.

Felrina stared at the ceiling. "I'm still linked with him," she murmured. "How else . . . ? He knows I'm here."

"Forget Erebos," Terrek said. "Don't talk, Felrina. Let me think."

She lay in his arms and savored the moment, the feel of his touch she had longed for and missed. But then she stiffened; inexplicably she began to struggle.

He released her, helping her to sit on her own as his men returned with Avalar crouching behind them, her face and hair spattered with gore. Roth bumped along the side of the tunnel, his skin ashen, blood dripping from the arm he cradled to his chest. The limb was half severed below the shoulder and flopped with his every step.

Clambering to his feet, Gaelin rushed to help him.

Felrina, averting her eyes from the two fallen dachs, stretched out her legs on the dusty floor. Across the shaft, Gaelin wilted, falling to a heap of exhaustion next to the wall. Roth settled beside him, tears streaming down his face as he fingered the shredded remains of his stovepipe hat.

"It's my fault," Felrina said. "Erebos knows I'm here."

"He knows *Holram* is here," Terrek said. "Anyway, it doesn't matter. Tell me why you called Camron's name."

"Y-you won't like it," she whispered. "You'll get angry."

Terrek sighed. "I'm too tired for that. Just tell me."

Felrina looked at him sadly. "Camron spoke to me," she said. "He was right there." She pointed. "He ... k-kissed me. I didn't want him to go."

"Neither did I," said Terrek. "And neither did Roth." Reaching out, he gripped Gaelin's arm and motioned to the dachs. "Holram wishes to restore them, doesn't he? You tell him no. You've had enough."

Vyergin busied himself digging through Avalar's pack. He tossed a rag onto Terrek's lap and then foraged deeper. "Avalar, where? Oh, never mind—here." He lifted out the vessel that contained their water.

The diradil stomach sloshed and gurgled when Vyergin passed it to Roth. "You first, son. Drink your fill. The river is close. And you next, Lady Vlyn."

"We need rest, too, not just food," Terrek said, glaring at his bloody sword.

∞ ∞ ∞

GRINNING, PONU CROUCHED below the dripping canopy of a massive tropical fern. Of all the pockets or worldlets he had designed between the various dimensions, this one was, by far, his favorite. He surveyed the human he had brought with him, lifting a brow as

Justin Tinsley groaned and thrashed awake in the lee of a large boulder. The young man squinted, then raised a hand to shield his eyes. After years underground, the gray-robe had become nocturnal.

"Once you're here for a while," drawled Ponu, "you'll find you can control the intensity of the sun. But for now . . ." He lowered his hand, and the brightness faded.

"What?" His captive rolled onto his knees, a speckling of tiny green leaves clinging to his garments. Reaching up in bewilderment, Justin picked at the corner of his mouth, drawing a thin strand of cobweb from his lower lip and neatly trimmed beard. "Where am I?"

Ponu stepped from the fern and flexed his wings. "The first morning is always difficult," he said. "But I believe, in time, you will enjoy your little prison. A tropical island! Ooh, *paradise!*"

The human climbed to his feet and turned in his heavy gray robes, taking in the world around him. "I don't understand. What is this place?"

"I call these realms between universes 'pockets,' because they're good to hide things in. In fact, there is another one right next to yours. See?" Ponu raised his hand, tickled the air briefly with his fingers, and then drew an invisible line from above his head to the ground. "Think of it like a zipper from your Earth. If you attended the old Earth inventions class at Braymore, you'll know what that is. Imparting such wisdom was part of the curriculum, I do believe. Now if I do this." He parted the opening he had made in the empty air, and the man recoiled.

"Ice!" Justin gasped.

"Not all dimensions fit tightly together," Ponu explained. "There can be pockets in the in-between, emptiness waiting to be filled. This one"—he nodded to the sliver of frozen wasteland he had revealed to the human before coaxing the air to conceal it again—"would be a fitting place for Allastor Mens if he were to live, which he will not."

"Am I dreaming?" Justin asked. "You must be an angel!" He stumbled past Ponu, extending his hand to swipe at the air.

Ponu laughed. "You cannot feel it; you have no magic," he said. "You are too heavy-handed. Besides that, you would never find it again because the pockets move. They are never in the same place for very long."

He grinned at the prisoner's blank expression. "How interesting you know the term 'angel.' Are you educated?"

Justin nodded. "I did *five years* at Braymore University," he said. "My certifications are in—"

"Yes, impressive," Ponu cut him off. "So you do know zippers." He gestured to a grassy patch of ground, and a clear rippling pool appeared. "After seeing that frozen wilderness, perhaps *now* you appreciate this temperate sanctuary I've given you. There's all the fresh water you could want, and you'll have fish in the sea—I've made sure of that—and cone mollusks in the sand. There's more food, too, if you forage thoroughly enough. Fruits and betel nuts. The grass is edible if you boil it. I would even call it tasty."

Ponu gestured to the objects beside the human's foot. "There's a fire stick there, and a pot for heating water, and a knife. I suspect until you learn how to manipulate your little realm, you may wish to modify your apparel a bit. I regret I cannot change the temperature of this place.

"And now I must be off," Ponu said, springing atop the mossy boulder. "There are others I need to capture. You're fortunate. For I am only sparing the members of your order who have not touched the bloodstones." He smiled.

Dazed, the gray-robe rubbed his forehead. "My order?"

"Whatever you call your cult these days. I suspect it might not be too late for you, Justin, and that your mind can be healed. Hopefully, your absence will go unnoticed for a while. You weren't important, were you?"

The human hung his head.

"Happily," Ponu added, "I have scores of pockets just like this one where I can isolate each of you. And while you are imprisoned, don't be surprised if you start feeling some remorse, for I have cleared your mind of Erebos's influence. Now, at last, you will comprehend all the evil you have done. And once you do, you might wish to compose your appeal, for when you stand before the elves."

Justin started. "*Elves?*"

"Guilt-ridden already?" Ponu asked. "Good. I can tell you've heard of the Seekers. Strange folk, those elves. They actually revere harmony and peace . . . can you imagine?

"They made rules for you humans to follow, too, if I recall, as a condition for you to live on their world. Which is why you're in my dungeon now. On Talenkai, things like torture and cannibalism are not allowed. But fear not, you will be spared, I am sure, for the elves do not kill. At worst, you'll end up back here, an environment you can change yourself, once you figure it out. Or you may be assigned a special task. There are a lot of orphaned children now, thanks to Erebos. Perhaps you'll do something useful with your life before your end."

"I . . . but I—"

"Oh, and that angel myth on your world. That was *us*. My people. For behold!" Ponu said, and as his grin stretched wide, he flared his white wings.

Chapter 53

elrina leaned against the wall of the shaft. They had traveled briefly, just enough to leave the smell of blood behind, and the sight of the two dead dachs. Now she reclined as the others did, her gaze on Roth slumping to the floor across from her. Beside him hovered Vyergin, holding the unwieldy diradil pouch high so Roth could drink.

The lieutenant was very pale. The fabric of his tunic sagged loosely where the dach's saber had cut, exposing his bare shoulder. And yet he barely registered the water he gulped or the gooseflesh from his arm's exposure to the cold. His attention was on the shredded hat, tears running down his face.

Vyergin moved closer, waving the bag to make it gurgle. "More!" he commanded. "You lost a lot of blood, son. You don't get to say no."

Felrina recognized Vyergin from her childhood. He had been Captain of the Enforcers while she was still playing with the Florne boys in the river alongside her cabin. She remembered well his visits on his tall black horse, and how Nithra, her father, had always respected and heartily welcomed him.

I know you, too, she thought as her gaze turned to Deravin Silva, for wherever Terrek went in his youth—and every day it was on a different mount—so did Silva on his black-tail with the funny short legs. The gray gelding had hopped like a rabbit when it galloped, its horrible conformation drawing laughter from Lucian Florne, and yet it was always the horse Deravin chose. The stocky guard had swayed proudly in the saddle with his huge goofy grin, yet always he was quick to flash his fists whenever Terrek Florne was bullied.

Her eyes moved on to Wren, admiring the gleaming black hair and high cheekbones of his native blood. She had seen him once or twice in Kideren buying supplies, and yet she knew he did not live there. He was of the Shamath Tribe, a conglomerate of native cultures—what remained of them from Earth—which had built a community of longhouses in the chain of meadows between Mount Desheya and the Shamath River. *And now you're Gaelin's guard*, she thought, smiling.

As Roth rejected Vyergin's coaxing at last, Felrina made herself look at him. *Would he really kill me if I fall asleep?*

She jerked back when Vyergin appeared next to her with a large metal cup. Felrina held it still while he filled it, shivering as the splash of cool water rinsed the grime from her hands. She mouthed her thanks and then drained the cup.

Once more he poured, grunting when he soaked her skin in his struggle to maneuver the bag. This time, shutting her eyes, she savored the musty fluid, the coolness rushing through her, reviving her depleted flesh. Sighing, she sank back, stretching out her legs as she returned to her study of Roth. *We need to talk about this*, she thought. *I can't keep worrying about what he will do.*

"Commander," she said abruptly. "How d–did you meet Caven Roth? I've never seen him before."

Terrek drank from Vyergin's bag and, catching the water in his hands, splashed it on his face. Then he rubbed himself dry with the rag he had on his lap. Clearing his throat, he answered, "He injured himself crossing Vale Horse. Riding that scatterbrained nag of his. He was trying to get to Kideren for help. But Jack the *jackrabbit* threw him from a cliff."

"I was being *chased*," Roth corrected. "You'll never guess by who!"

Felrina drew a deep breath. "I've only heard pieces of your story. I would really like—"

"Jack was exhausted. He didn't throw me; he tripped!" said Roth with a glare at Terrek. "One of your minions tried to hang me from a tree over Thunder River, but my thrashings broke the rope. I escaped and got to Jack. Your creatures followed."

"Roth hails from Cheron," Terrek explained. "He was away when your dachs hit the city."

"Yes, and Jack isn't a 'nag,' either!" Roth snarled. "He outran what no other horse could to save my life. So I could come home to find my mother and sister, Gindle, strung up like deer. Their insides were—"

"*Roth!*" Terrek cut in sharply. "She doesn't need to hear all that."

"Why the blazes not? I've heard everything about *her*. I know what she did to Camron, what she did to my family and home! She destroyed Cheron!" Roth cried. "Kideren and Chalse, too, *and* Tierdon! I can't believe you're letting it go! Unlike the ghost, I am *not* dead. Nor have I forgotten how to be human!"

Felrina frowned at the generous slice of dried racka-hare Vyergin offered. As she brushed him aside, he seized her wrist and curled her reluctant fingers around the meat.

"This again?" Terrek scowled at Roth. "First this cursed sword slips in my grasp to impale the woman I vowed to *protect*, and now this! Roth, *stop it!* Did you miss what just happened? She almost died defending me!"

Roth lowered his head. "I didn't see how she got wounded."

"Avalar tells me you threatened her, again, even after I told you to leave her alone," Terrek continued. "'I wouldn't try sleeping if I were you.' Isn't that what you said?"

Roth sat rigid. His jaw muscles bunching, he nodded slowly.

Felrina jumped to his defense. "He has every right to be angry! I knew what was happening to your towns and cities. I didn't do it myself, but I created the things that did. I held the Blazenstone and was Erebos's chosen! I k-killed people and turned them into *slaves*," she said in a husky voice, feeling Avalar's stare boring into the back of her neck. "And when this is all over, I will be visiting the Seekers, and they will *judge* me!"

Gaelin squinted at her. "Would you be able to hold another stone?"

"What are you implying, Gaelin?" Terrek asked.

"I'm sick," he said. "I couldn't change those dachs into humans again when Holram wanted me to. I barely do anything, and still I'm struggling to stay on my feet. What if I die? Who will help Holram fight?"

"*Fight?* Is that your plan?" Felrina demanded. "To let the w-warders battle each other until this mountain tumbles down around your ears? If Chesna breaks, the shield protecting the world will be gone. They'd go straight into the clouds and that—"

"Would kill us all," Terrek finished for her.

"Two dragons," said Felrina. "What we see of them in the physical realm is not what they are at all! Their presence would fill the sky!"

"*If* I die," Gaelin persisted, "Holram will need someone. He can't do this alone!"

"Someone who isn't *me*!" growled Felrina. "I'm *not* a good person. I—"

"Do you think *I* am?" Gaelin asked. "I killed an unarmed drunk with an ax! At least for you, I suspect you loved Camron; somehow you meant well. But for me, all I've known is hate, not love. And still Holram chose me. When I am no better than you!"

Felrina rubbed at her gritty eyelids. "There was love," she admitted. "Any benefits Erebos gained came from *my* pain, not Camron's. I was t-trying to spare him, hiding the fact I loved him like a b-brother! If Mens had discovered the truth, Camron's death would have been horrible!"

Terrek coughed. "We've never had a *plan*, Felrina. This was our last hope. To get here and stop him!"

"The river is the key." Avalar dropped down beside them with a thud. "I *know* it is. I would sing the song to you, but it is not in your language. The Bloodsword sang it to me when I was a child. It spoke of . . ." She furrowed her brow. "Off in the land that your people most fear, down in the pit where so many giants suffered . . . under the ground near the rock stained brown . . . It mentions a wall filled with bloodstones, and water through the rock leading the way.

"Somehow the river will fulfill my destiny, *and* mayhap yours as well. As the wind heard my call on the cliff by the castle and saved my life, so does the water heed giants. I could have quieted the sea. *Avaunt, storm* . . . and the waves would have stilled for me."

"Bloodstones," Felrina whispered to Gaelin. "Don't they kill giants?"

"I'll take first watch," Terrek announced, glancing at the faces around him. "It's not safe to stop, but I don't see any other choice. Lieutenant Roth, there won't be a third time. Enough! Let her *be*!"

Roth nodded wearily. "I didn't know she defended you, Commander. I suppose that changes things."

Terrek smiled at Felrina. "Yes, I think it does."

Argus lowered himself slowly in their midst, his green glow merging with the glints of gold from the torch. He glowered at them all, his face tight with pain.

"Something to say?" Terrek growled.

"Only that Erebos is here!" snapped Argus. "Like a winged worm, he weaves through the corpse of this rotted mountain. He's in the wall behind your backs, his jaws fixing on you! This rock becomes his limbs, and they will throttle you. I would not take rest! You must *hurry*!"

Avalar attacked the pack beside her, pulling out the remaining pieces of her leather-lined steel armor.

"Why the panic?" Argus asked. "You knew Erebos was near. My purpose is not to state the obvious, but to clarify what dangers you face. He likes to be slow. Cat and mouse is his favorite game! And Felrina Vlyn is not a concern to him anymore. He doesn't want *her*."

"Good!" Felrina muttered fiercely. "I don't want *him*, either!"

The ghost arched his brow. "You're used to Holram," he continued to Terrek. "Erebos is different. Within these tunnels, he does as he pleases—takes on any form, wolf, bear, or worse! This mountain is dead. He killed it without even trying, so it would shield him."

He heaved a sigh. "Terrek Florne, my time grows short. You brought my sword, and soon you must throw it away. Felrina Vlyn speaks truly about one thing. Camron is here. All the lives the Destroyer, Erebos, took are converging now, and your brother is among them. As a trained knight, I have become the leader of these dead; they will fight for *me* when the time comes! Together, we will break the spell that holds Arawn in this realm—and myself as well. But as for Erebos . . ."

Felrina followed his gaze toward the staff-wielder. Gaelin sat, oblivious, his body glowing in the tunnel's dim light, his skin translucent as if it burned from within. Tremors shook his narrow frame. "Holram gathers his strength," Argus observed. "He senses his foe. This will end soon, Terrek Florne. Your staff-wielder will not last much longer."

Ignoring the ghost, Terrek moved toward Gaelin and knelt to clasp his shoulder, gently rousing him. "Gaelin. What is it?"

Shivering, Gaelin glanced up. In a slow, agitated rhythm, his palms thumped the floor by his feet. "It's *Holram*," he breathed. The warder came and went in the depths of his wide stare. His mouth twitched and his brows furrowed.

"What can we do to help you?" Terrek asked.

"There's nothing you can do," Gaelin murmured. "Holram hopes to give you a gift, Terrek, and to free himself from the pit of this mountain. He seeks to heal, to . . . destroy. He's . . . here. Argus is right." Gaelin blanched as he peered around him. "We must hurry."

Chapter 54

The child prodded the hard ice of the beach with his stick, stabbing furiously at the zigzag trail filling with water. "Over here, Master!" Kray called. Confidently now, he poked with his twig to cut the creature off, and from the packed gray surface came a swift ejection of foam.

Grevelin bent beside the boy to strike with his shovel. Bracing his feet, he dug deep into the sand, seizing the slippery sea cone and dragging the mollusk out. With a squelch, the rubbery body hit the crowded interior of his lidded bucket.

"Sails!" Grevelin peered in at his catch and then thumbed the cover shut. "Your eyes are keen, little human. It well serves me to have your sight so close to the ground."

Strutting around him in a circle, Kray kept his gaze fixed on the hollows he created with his splashing feet. Abruptly he hopped onto a half-buried rock to clasp Grevelin's thumb. "You mean it's good I'm small?" he asked.

"Indeed," said Grevelin. "We make a formidable pair. Come."

The boy, clutching the stuffed rabbit Ponu had given him, jumped from the rock. As Grevelin scooped him up, Kray scaled his shoulder to straddle the back of his neck, his tiny fingers twining in Grevelin's hair.

Hoisting the bucket, Grevelin walked bent against the wind, aiming for Hothra's massive cliff and the modest stone homes set beneath its shelter. Even from here, he could tell his house from the others by the tinkling seashell chimes his daughter had hung beside the doorway.

A dark figure waited next to the porch. He recognized his leader's muscular shape, his upper body outlined by candlelight through the

frosty front window.

Trentor came to meet him, his burly arms swinging in his familiar saunter. Grevelin tensed as Hothra's ruler, jerking to a stop before him, caught sight of the child.

"There is a conclave that requires your immediate presence, Master Second," Trentor said, and Grevelin met his calm gaze. Gravely, Trentor reached up and, with a dignified nod, took the small boy's hand and shook it, bowing. "I am Trentor Govorian," he said, "the eldest son of Thresher Govorian and Tavahra Sky, and I command these giants. I bid you welcome to Hothra Hone Isle, young human."

Grevelin paused, feeling the child tremble against his neck. The boy's arms slid below his ears to hug him tight.

"He is frightened," Trentor observed. The leader stepped back, flashing Grevelin a disapproving glare. "I must ask why he is here, Master Second. You risk much, including his life. The gathering is to discuss this, my friend. Is there a safe place your guest may stay while we meet?"

Grevelin glowered. Hothra's ruler was younger than he was, and as the eldest son of the one who had freed them from bondage, Trentor enjoyed considerable respect from his peers.

"I vowed the little one would not leave my sight," said Grevelin. "He is Ponu's ward. You know how Ponu can be!"

Trentor thumped Grevelin's chest. "Come!" he urged. "Ere this tempest in the making blows the child away and us with him! Our fellows are gathering at the Hall."

Grevelin trotted across the frozen sand, his bucket of sea cones banging his thigh. Up the cliff's slippery steps, he scrambled after Trentor. The leader's unruly black hair was blown back, and as his gray wolf's cloak raised from his wide shoulders, Grevelin caught a glimpse of the younger giant's belt, the symbol of the great sword stamped deep into the brown leather.

Above the steep stair, the crystalline monument known as Freedom Hall appeared in stages as Grevelin climbed. Gazing up, he drew a breath as he so often did, fighting back tears when he recalled his escape long ago, and Trentor's father, the savior they had been forced to leave behind.

Blindingly radiant, the structure revered by his people stood tall atop the cliff, designed to be visible from all three corners of Hothra Hone Isle as a beacon of hope to the world. Its torches burned perpetually, their light intensified by the clear dome, beckoning Hothra's heroes and ships alike from the dangers of the sea.

The ice that had gathered on the building's roof during the night was melting, rippling down the hall's translucent sides. Grevelin, ascending the flight of glass steps and moving on through the arched doorway of woven crystal, trailed his superior and friend into the foyer. How he wished that he could have prepared the little boy for the hostility he was about to be exposed to, yet before he could ask his leader to spare a moment, Trentor came back across the white floor and gently addressed the child.

"Remember who you are," Trentor told him. "It is not for these great brutes to determine your identity, for they know you not! They will be angry, innocent one, but never with you. For *you* have done nothing wrong. Do you understand?"

When Kray spoke, it was almost a whimper. "Yes."

Trentor shifted his gaze to Grevelin. "I called this meeting myself, Master Second, as I wish to bury this matter at sea. I like it not, but what is necessary is often unpleasant."

Grevelin bent, setting his bucket on the pristine marble. Then he reached with both hands to catch Kray's shoulders, lifting him forward and cradling him in his arms. "Whatever happens, keep watching me," Grevelin told him with a comforting smile. "Soon this will end, and we can resume our day as we planned."

He nodded at Trentor. "We have an appointment with Stitch after we break our fast," he explained. "The tailor is a friend of mine; he has agreed to fashion thicker garments for the boy. Whether or not you allow him to remain on Hothra, the human has little to wear. Ponu is dear to me. But he knows naught of fatherhood."

Trentor snorted and gestured him through the hall's central arch into its largest chamber. Around the elaborately carved dais and leader's seat, nine white stone chairs stood in a loose circle, three each to the east, west, and south, representing the corners of Hothra Isle.

The giants rose as Trentor sauntered past them to mount the platform. Five of the attendees were the senior captains, representing Hothra's productive fisher trade. Grevelin recognized two as commanders of the isle's great warships, there to speak on behalf of the warriors. He grunted as his gaze settled on the last pair. *Politicians*, he thought, identifying both the governor of Hothra and the short, burly giant who was their sheriff.

Grevelin knew every face in the bright and airy room, yet they had changed. They shied away from Hothra's small visitor, glaring at the floor or their hands or even the walls.

"Master Second," said Trentor formally from his place on the dais. "We welcome your guest to Hothra Isle."

Trentor waited as the nine giants reseated themselves. "I have allowed this assembly so that you may judge for yourselves the human in question," he announced. "For I grow weary of these petitions requesting the youngling's removal. Now observe him. Behold, he is naught but a child. You are giants. What manner of threat could he be?"

Sledgefist Arelian, Hothra's sheriff, glanced at Grevelin. "I have no problem with the little one," he said. "But I fear for his safety, and of course, potential riots. Regrettably, we cannot reeducate every giant on Hothra. Nor do we all have the benefit of a winged elf to ease our hurt, Leader Second. For most of us, the word *human* conjures much that is painful. We think *slaver*. Many of us still feel the whip. A child without magic is no match for an enraged giant, I fear."

"I will be happy to remain on my ship," one of the fisher captains growled. Grevelin recognized him as Urphelus Churnin, the grizzled captain of the *Deluge*, Hothra's largest fisher vessel. "I refuse to acknowledge this infant now. Nor will I, ever! He is my enemy, and I do have the future of my son, Lorean, to consider. I vowed I would never again endure these unnatural abominations. This island is my home, and I should not be subjected to torture in my *home*, Leader Trentor. *No* giant should!"

Grevelin smiled reassuringly at Kray. The tiny human moaned, tears glistening on his cheeks. "This shall not be borne!" Grevelin snapped. "What a shameful thing to say. He is not an abomination, and you are all grown giants making a little boy cry! Leader Trentor, I shall take my leave of you! Kray and I have a pleasant day planned. Decide what you will. Frankly, I care not."

"Grevelin," Trentor said, rising quickly. "*Wait.*"

By the chamber's crystal door, Grevelin hesitated.

"This is not about deciding anything," Trentor said. "It is about promoting understanding. If these giants are reassured, mayhap they will pass it on, sharing what they have learned with friends and family."

Grevelin glanced at Kray. "Can I tell them something?" the small boy begged.

"You need not defend yourself, little human," said Grevelin, shaking his head. "You have done nothing wrong."

"Please?" Kray, clutching his floppy toy, looked up pleadingly. The boy's wide, teary eyes tugged at Grevelin's heart. Heavily he approached the dais, a sour taste of dread in his mouth.

"Hothra's guest requests you give him your attention," he said gruffly, glaring at the captains and politicians. Then he regarded the child he bore. "Kray?" he prompted.

The human pointed to the dais. "There!" he said. "So they can see me."

Grevelin lifted him up, setting him on the platform near Trentor.

The boy barely reached the height of the leader's knees. He wavered a moment, blinking in the shaft of light beaming through the chamber's crystalline roof as he hugged his furry bunny.

"I am Kray Middleton," he said in his piping voice. "I am a citizen of the town Firanth in the land of Thalus. I . . . my mother died defending *me*! I watched our house . . . and my mother burn up. I . . . I have been in a cave on the mountain with Ponu. He has taught me a lot about magic. He told me what magic did to . . . to you. What bad humans did with magic to giants. He says it's like when I dream about monsters, only I wake up. *You* never do."

Kray glanced back at Trentor. The leader smiled, nodding encouragement.

"I . . . I wish I had magic to wake you. *Good* magic, so I could help *you* get more fish," he said to the fisher captains. "Or help *you* to be safe," he added to the commanders. "And I'd make your gardens get big, and your sick people to get better, too. So maybe you'd see I am *good*! But I can't. I don't have anything."

As Kray climbed once more into his arms, Grevelin bowed to Trentor and flicked a scowl at the other giants, all nine of whom had risen to their feet. Ignoring their astonished expressions, he strode with the little one out the door.

"You—" Grevelin shook his head as he exited the crystal hall. Carrying Kray, he thumped down the building's outer steps, his recovered bucket of sea cones tapping again at his thigh.

"Did I say too much?" Kray asked.

"No." Gently Grevelin stroked the boy's bangs from his eyes. "You spoke well, little Kray." Stopping atop the great cliff, he peered over the edge at Hothra's U-shaped bay, its shore studded with piers along one side, the black water beyond them clogged with boats and ships. He spied *Dawncutter* guarding the horizon, its distinctive silhouette shaped like the curving blade of a sword. Majestically the war vessel floated on waves touched to gold by the fingers of the sun.

Grevelin smiled, envisioning his brother, Kurgenrock, dining with his crew and enjoying his morning meal of gull eggs, cheese, and toasted buttered bread. "Are you hungry?" he asked the child. "*I* am. I am *famished*!"

"Me, too!" Kray exclaimed. "I've never had cone mollusks before."

"Not just the cones," Grevelin said. "I make a perfect blending with onion, egg, and reef-weed!" Tilting back his head, he inhaled, savoring the tang of the salty air. "You and I are on our way to a feast this morning, Kray! Today we shall dine like kings!"

Kray threw his arms wide. "Like kings!" he shouted.

Grevelin, chuckling despite himself, began to descend the steep stairs carved into the cliff. Suddenly Trentor's voice stopped him, calling his name. "Wait," Grevelin whispered to Kray and then reluctantly turned, stepping back to the icy rim above the stairs.

His wolf fur rippling back from his shoulders, Trentor hurried up. "Good news," he said. "My giants were enchanted, Grev. I did not think it possible, but this child's spirit has swayed them." Trentor winked at the little boy. "Hear me, young man. It appears you may indeed possess some magic, for you have touched the granite hearts of my giants. After you left, they were moved beyond words when I strove to question them."

"It is as you hoped now?" Grevelin inquired. "They will let him be?"

"Who can say what giants will do?" said Trentor. "Yet I believe, at this moment, they would surrender their lives to defend this boy. Of course, that sentiment will fade soon enough. With them, such feelings always do. Their memories of the whip will guarantee that. But I suspect the sincere emotions they saw in this child today will also linger." Smiling, Trentor patted Kray's head. "You, little human friend, are welcome to stay on Hothra for as long as you wish!"

"Good!" Grevelin returned his superior's grin and, with a grunt, hefted his heavy bucket, holding it below Trentor's nose. "We were fortunate in our quest this morning. Care to break our fast with us,

Leader First?"

Trentor pried open the lid and gasped. "Hmm, indeed! An *impressive* effort. But I wonder," he intoned gravely with a nod to Kray, "will this friend of giants deign to share his kingly feast with *me*?"

Kray beamed, his eyes glistening. "Yes, I will!" he said with a laugh.

Chapter 55

aelin stared into the blackness of the void. The tight shaft where he lay on his stomach was freezing, the temperature of the granite creeping into his bones. As Avalar wriggled close behind him, the bundle she shoved in front of her jostled his feet. The scrape of her scabbard resounded in the cramped space, as did the random clangs of the blades his friends carried.

Holding Mornius near his face, Gaelin glanced at its Skystone. The gem's soft light showed him every detail of the rocky tube they crawled in, only to fade as he peered forward. *What don't you want us to see?* he thought to his warder.

The chute had ended abruptly, opening into a massive expanse. The Shukaia's roar reverberated somewhere in the cave below, the condensation from its mist gathering on their eyebrows and chins.

Vyergin, squeezing past him, had ventured out first. "Wait, I almost have it," the captain called, his raspy voice echoing in the darkness.

Gaelin heard a sharp click and saw a spark—a glimpse of Vyergin crouching on the stone with his steel and flint. Another strike and the tinder around the torch caught fire.

"Let's see what we've found, shall we?" said Vyergin, walking with hesitant steps toward the thunder. "Holram's balls, this place reeks! Watch your footing when you get out here. This red muck is slippery!"

Gaelin scrambled from the passage and lifted Mornius to illuminate what he could of the vaulted chasm. Avalar fought her way out of the crawl space next and sat on her heels, reaching her arm back into the chute to help their companions.

"Did I not say?" she asked Terrek as she drew him to his feet.

"This small tunnel would lead the way?"

"Yes, you did," he returned.

"I hear the water," said Vyergin, "but how far down is it?" He stood on the edge of the granite shelf, bending over his braced legs as he stared into the mountain's throat, the pounding rapids hidden under the misty gloom. The stone glistened below his feet as he swung the torch. Then he released his grip and the flames fell.

Gaelin strained to make out the captain beyond his warder's reluctant light. He caught the hiss of the torch striking the bottom.

"Ah, there it is," Vyergin confirmed. "Hades's blazes, that's deep. Hurry, Lavahl, bring your staff before I break my neck. Whatever this rock is covered with is nasty slick. If I take a wrong step . . ."

Catching Terrek's gesture, Gaelin extended the Skystone's brightness, the warder's fire forming a halo around his body. With Wren at his side, he advanced toward Vyergin, shuddering when the air went icy against his skin, wafting in drafts from the river to merge with the frigid breezes above. He gazed up into a darkness his staff refused to breach, the glow of its gem revealing only the broken ends of enormous teeth—huge dripping stalactites pointed at his head.

As Vyergin's elbow stopped him, Gaelin looked where the torch had fallen. He was teetering on the brink, the granite angling downward out of his sight, the black torrent spurting from the rocks below. He caught the flicker of Vyergin's torch straddling the boulders at the water's edge. Trails of pale smoke poured over the jagged bank, and the flames cast golden ripples along the Shukaia's current.

"What's wrong with your staff?" asked Vyergin. "Is your warder trying to kill me?"

"The enemy must be close," Gaelin said. "I . . . Holram doesn't want to attract attention." He turned, hearing Felrina groan near the opening they had left. Revulsion twisted her features as she stared at a damp patch of stone beside her.

"That's blood!" she gasped. "Old blood." Her voice climbed in pitch. "It's leaking from the upper levels! It m-must be from—"

Blood? Gaelin cocked his head.

Terrek stepped quickly to clasp her shoulder. "Easy!" he soothed, steering her away from the brown liquid oozing down the wall.

Deliberately he transferred her into Silva's care.

"Is *that* what we smell?" Roth squatted to examine the congealing fluid, gingerly touching it with his finger. "She's right. Ugh!"

"Of course I am!" Felrina snapped. "And I know where it's coming from, too! My pool is above us; that must be the source. This ledge we're on is rotten. Terrek! Erebos is *here*! I feel him!"

"Deep breaths, Felrina. We'll get this sorted—" Terrek stopped, his attention shifting to the giant as stiff-legged, her head lifted and her eyes staring, Avalar approached the drop-off. "Giant? What is it?"

Ignoring him, she surveyed the immense cavern. "My people have toiled in this place," Avalar said. "They perished here, for the stones drained them, as now they begin to drain me. This was the cache where the sniffers found the bloodstones. The heart of the magic is here, Leader Terrek." She nodded at the opposite wall. "Within those formations."

Gaelin, his thoughts becoming vague, shuffled toward the pungent pool beneath the cliff. There he unshouldered his sack and began to rummage in it. As Wren sidled closer to watch, Gaelin pulled out a bit of cloth and gestured for him to take the pack.

"Here," Gaelin mused aloud, and now it was Holram guiding his fingers. "Here, too." He dabbed at the slime, scooping up a quivering globule.

"That's disgusting," said Felrina. "Why in blazes would you—"

"I don't know," Gaelin muttered. "I'm not doing it." He folded the cloth around the goo and tucked it into the pack Wren was holding. "I just . . . I know he needs this, and . . . living flesh, too."

Felrina shuddered, gaping at his face. "What do you—"

Wren, his nose wrinkling, let the bag fall as he turned away. Gaelin snatched the sack from the rotting fluid, hastily wiping the gunk from its side. "That's how it happens," he explained to Felrina. "Before I know it, Holram's telling me what to do."

"But you agreed to it. Didn't you?"

Gaelin sighed. "It took me a while," he admitted. "But people are dying, and I want to make that stop. My life doesn't seem so important as it once did."

"Staff-Wielder." Terrek motioned toward a gouge in the wall at their backs. Gaelin, glancing where he pointed, spied four tiny steps curving into the darkness, a narrow stairway no wider than Avalar's foot.

At Terrek's nod, Gaelin raised his Skystone, and then he saw it—a crumbling pathway zigzagging along the surface of the towering cliff. "The footsteps of doomed children made that trail," Avalar informed them. "Now upon it we must follow."

Chapter 56

aelin studied the stalactites jutting down at him from above. Cavities dotted the cliff behind him, potential entrances to other passageways, many of them small like the one he and his companions had used. He turned, his gaze lifting as he raised his staff.

The enormous cave leaned in overhead where the fire mountain had collapsed, splitting the cavern's opposite wall and exposing its inner trove—countless formations of gnarled yellow crystal, the quartz shining green under the Skystone's light.

He glimpsed teardrop-shaped gems deeper in the gaping cleft, the crimson orbs hanging from their tapered points like seeds within a ripened fruit. *Bloodstones?* Gaelin thought, glancing at the giant. Gravely she nodded as if reading his mind, her face pale.

"Enough of this," Terrek said. "Let's go!" He paused, eyeing the giant. "You wanted to say something?"

"A word of warning," Avalar told him. "The path above us is fragile and narrow, for the deaths of so many giants here damaged the stone. We must be cautious. What little life this rock retains does not trust humans."

"*Great*," Roth muttered.

Avalar motioned to Gaelin. "Come and mount my shoulders, my friend." She smiled when he stumbled back. "I assure you, it will be well. If you position your staff in front of my throat and grip it on either side of me, you will not fall."

"But won't that choke you?" he asked.

"Not if you keep your arms loose. Yet I would rather be injured than have you die."

Mutely Gaelin surrendered Mornius to Terrek. As he stepped to accept the giant's help, he looked once again across the chasm at the wounded wall.

"Staff-Wielder?" Terrek queried.

They're watching me, Gaelin noticed as he returned Terrek's stare. *Holram, too, and he's their hope. I can't let them see fear.*

"Try to sustain your light," Terrek urged him. "We can't count on Argus to be here when we need him. You had problems earlier, didn't you? When Vyergin needed to see. I know it's hard, but if you falter again while we're on that cliff . . ."

"I won't," Gaelin said. "Holram is—I don't know, maybe he's preparing for the battle to come. But as long as I'm in control, I won't fail you. I promise." He raised his foot high to reach Avalar's proffered knee, then seized her thick braid and scrambled up, straddling her neck. Slowly he relaxed as he discovered that the pack she carried supported his lower back. He accepted Mornius from Terrek, positioning the staff as Avalar had suggested.

"You will go ahead of me," the giant commanded with a gesture to Roth. When he reddened with embarrassment, she clarified, "to scan the pathway for loose rocks."

Roth hesitated, biting his lip, until finally, with an angry snort, he approached the steep steps. Avalar grasped the stone beside him as he began his ascent. "You worry about your feet," she murmured in his ear. "And I shall remain behind you so you will not fall."

Gaelin screwed his eyes shut while Avalar guided the lieutenant. Roth was chatting incessantly, and for a time, Gaelin listened, learning more than he ever wanted to about the nervous young man. The rush of the Shukaia's current faded as they ventured upward, replaced by icy touches of wind, like fingers dancing along his skin. As the far wall angled closer, the glistening red gems leaned toward him, clusters of bloodstones uncovered by his light. *So many*, he thought. *More than I can count!*

"Is the mountain healing itself?" he asked the giant. "Is that why the bloodstones are here?"

Her shoulders shrugged beneath him. "I know not, Staff-Wielder. The blood absorbs magic, and the veins of the world carry that power to wherever there is need."

"'And water leading the way through the rock,'" said Gaelin. "Didn't your song say something like that? You mentioned the bloodstones, too. In Chesna, we have both."

Water pattered on his head from the blackness above. Lulled by the rocking of the giant's strides, Gaelin strove to stay alert and aware—to keep Mornius lit no matter how his bones ached. On impulse, he tipped back his chin, catching the drops on his tongue. The liquid ran down his throat, its metallic taste making him wince.

Avalar climbed steadily, walking upright whenever possible. Gaelin heard his companions' crunching steps behind him, the faint clicks of their buckles or gear comforting to his ears. Felrina Vlyn stayed close at Avalar's heels, with Wren, Terrek, and Silva following, and Vyergin at the rear.

How far have we come? Gaelin wondered. A flash of green caught his attention. Looking up, he saw Argus flitting between the stalactites overhead.

"Gaelin," Felrina panted. "What did you mean before? He needs living flesh? Who does? Holram?"

Gaelin grimaced. The odd little gleams brightening near Argus became eyes as he watched, unblinking orbs staring down from a legion of phantom faces, their ghostly mouths stretched wide.

Are they crying? he thought wildly. *Why can't I hear them?* A glowing mist wafted into suggestions of bodies around the Thalian Knight, a multitude of long pearly limbs with spectral fingers—then frayed once more into flickers and glints.

Gaelin buried his face in the giant's hair, his body lurching in rhythm with her strides as he held out his staff. The narrow path twisted back on itself yet again, slanting past the entrance to a passageway, and then another. Tunnels studded the wall, an untold number of holes carved into the flat gray stone.

"Gaelin?" Felrina called again. "Tell me what you meant!"

"Keep going," said Terrek. "Whatever it is, Felrina, worry about it later."

Gaelin felt like an insect upon the cliff, with escape routes above him and below, each one marking a path to places unknown. He tilted his staff, illuminating a dusty fringe of blowing cobwebs inside a long-forgotten shaft, and down its throat, a twisted heap of bones.

Groaning, he averted his face, while closer to the ceiling, the ghosts wailed. Argus floated like a king among the rest, his minions draping his form with a garment of woven light, echoes of flashes, there and then gone.

As blackness seized his mind, Gaelin's awareness expanded. He discerned bugs on the surface of the stone, and the dust motes stirred by his own breathing. He shivered when a chill entered the murk, twining with the counterfeit night between the fangs of the cavern's roof.

With a chorus of moans, Argus's ghosts splintered to pieces. Atop the receding vapor, the nothingness hovered, even darker than before. Gaelin struggled for air in the gathering gloom. He fell out of himself, becoming as a little boy, his legs too short to run.

"*Blazes,*" moaned Felrina. "He's *here.*"

"Steady," Terrek replied. "Keep your eyes forward."

Gaelin tensed. His heart labored as a shadow oozed out of crannies in the rock over his head, its massive wings solidifying, unfurling with a snap as a black sinewy neck snaked down. A dragon parted the mist, its silver talons splayed, the beast clinging to the mountain's teeth while it took form. Gaelin shuddered as its fiery eyes met his.

The world was falling, spinning him through a tunnel's unending maw until—

Shrieking with pain, Seth Lavahl sprawled on the floor in front of him, slipping in his own blood. Gaelin followed, grinning in ruthless delight. Years of fury erupted within him as he stood beside the helpless man, his legs braced.

Splintering sounds filled his ears as the screams cut short, and for the longest time, Gaelin swung the long-handled ax, the gore spattering his tunic and arms. He would erase Seth Lavahl—remove all traces of his evil from the world.

"*You and I are the same,*" a reverberating voice rumbled. "*We savor the death!*"

"No!" Gaelin sobbed against the giant's neck, while Seth Lavahl came at him once more, his brains spilling onto his stained vest, his shoulder dangling from his torso by a thread.

Gaelin shrieked—the cowardly sound that he hated so much, that so often he had suppressed in his pillow during dreams that would never let him go.

"*Staff-Wielder!*" Terrek cut in sharply. "Felrina says he feeds off fear. He's getting into your thoughts! Don't let him!"

Gaelin nodded, the iron-shod crown of Mornius swaying above him as the giant climbed. Abruptly he lifted his staff, its gem, roused by his anger, becoming a crackling ball of defiance to repel the darkness.

Teeth gritted, his mouth still tasting like metal, he closed his eyes, feeling his warder's heart embracing his frail and mortal one. Raising his head, he strode from the Skystone that had been his prison, as he had once fought his way from his stepfather's abuse, the layers of fog rolling back. His heels clicked over a sheen of liquid glass, the blue-white reflection of a turbulent sky.

Lightning flashed in time with his movements, each surge more savage than before. He stretched out his arm, and power leapt from the floor, piercing his bones, infusing his flesh.

He tipped his hand, freeing the blaze like multicolored threads of healing—a fire to weave around his friends, forming a protective dome against the cliff. Smoke rose from the stone beneath his feet. He would scour the mountain clean—bring renewal to Chesna's crippled soul. *No, we are not the same!* Holram raged to his foe.

The dragon lunged at him from its ebon lair, wings of ice slapping at his sphere, spreading lurid cracks through his defenses. The fissures spread as the dragon's tail whipped back and forth, and Gaelin howled. His consciousness toppled when the glass horizon canted, spinning him from its edge. Down into oblivion he plunged, Holram's wrath falling with him, flailing its useless limbs.

"Keep climbing!" Felrina cried. "We can't let them fight! Holram's not strong enough!"

Gaelin gasped when his warder, seizing his mind, restored his sinking awareness. He nodded, opening his senses to the pressures rising in his throat, tightening his skin as his muscles sprang taut. Here and now he would surrender his bones—fuel for the flames engulfing him.

Far in the distance, he heard Avalar scream, and he directed his force upward, away from her magic—the threat of contact with her world. With all his strength, he fought to keep his heart beating, with Holram buttressing his shield, hurling blasts from his mortal limbs down the Destroyer's throat.

His body rocked as the giant halted. Through the fire, Gaelin saw his companions ducking under her arms into a narrow, winding shaft. Her body bent low, Avalar followed.

Gaelin yelped when the giant snatched him from the cavern and his enemy, dashing his small wild sun to pieces, burning fragments skittering along the damp passage. Around a corner she raced—to slam to a stop beside Vyergin.

Sagging, Gaelin lowered his staff, the remnants of his blaze spilling across the floor.

"What are you *doing?*" Felrina grabbed Terrek's wrist. "Come on! This way! We've got to *run!*"

"Wait!" Terrek eyed a green stain below the ceiling.

"Terrek!" Felrina threw herself backward, dragging him farther down the shaft. "Erebos is *coming!* We have to run!"

Terrek pressed her against the wall, restraining her until she quieted. He pointed to the faded mark. "What is that, Felrina? What does it tell us?"

Gaelin extended Mornius, holding its Skystone away from the giant. As she swung him to the floor, Vyergin caught him. "Whew!" the captain exclaimed. "That was some light-show, Staff-Wielder!"

Leaning on him, Gaelin peered through the glow of Mornius's gem into the darkness where they had come. *I'm getting weaker*, he realized, feeling Holram's power gnawing through his body, his bones aching from the heat of it. *Maybe it should end here.*

"I d–don't *know!*" Felrina stammered. "Color marks . . ." She sucked in a breath. "Markers! That's the older system—from the slavers long ago. The lower burrows were color-coded, too. Green signifies . . . the fifth or eighth level, I think. The fourth has my pool. We use the fifth for minor ceremonies, so it would be lighted."

"Good," Terrek said, "we're getting close." Gently he tugged at her shoulder. Her body was stiff, resisting his pull. He tilted his head, his hazel eyes narrowing as he studied the giant. Then his gaze shifted to Gaelin.

You see it. I know you do, Gaelin thought. *Holram's rising in me. I don't look the same anymore.*

Releasing Felrina, Terrek swung toward Caven Roth still crouched beside the wall. "I don't like heights," Roth muttered. He clambered to his feet and Terrek took his arm, helping him down the passage after the guards while Felrina and Vyergin followed.

"My father had a hat," said Roth to Terrek as they hastened

along. "It was black. Not like mine, but close. He always wore it. I bet he would have liked the one I lost."

"Maybe we'll find you another just as good," Terrek told him.

Gaelin trailed his friends. His perceptions—Holram's—sharpened, and he shivered, hugging his ribs at the fury concealed behind them.

Chapter 57

$\mathscr{A}$s Avalar stumbled sideways, fragments of the ceiling her head had collided with pattered to the floor. She hurried past Silva when the guard stopped with a muffled curse, her gaze on the tunnel's downward-sloping roof. Once more she could hear it—a faint gurgling of liquid through the rock.

She glanced back at a scuffling sound. Silva was bent over, balancing one-legged as he tugged at the shaft of his boot. He flipped her a jaunty salute as his foot slid free. Then, grimacing, he tilted his boot and shook out a pebble. "I know," he said at her look. "I'm supposed to stay by Terrek. But did you see? I would rather walk barefoot than carry boulders like that around!"

"Pardon me." Grinning at him, Avalar rubbed her aching brow. "I fear it was I who dislodged the stone when I hit my head. This passage was not meant for giants."

She peered forward, anxious at the thought of her leader unprotected. Terrek was standing with his shoulders rigid, a flight of well-worn stairs blocking his path. The granite steps, spanning half the tunnel, vanished into a hollow above the ceiling.

"I recognize this," Felrina whispered. Slowly she knelt, staring up. "The path turns high in the stairwell before it continues on. There's a lot of rock between this shaft and m-my pool. We're closer than I thought. But I don't understand. If we're on the fifth level, why is it so dark?"

Terrek motioned to the hovering ghost. "Lord Argus," he said, nodding to the uneven steps. "If you would please guide our—"

Avalar started at Silva's scream, whirling with her sword in her hand. Gaelin, with Wren Neche next to him, appeared at her side a moment later. The light from his staff found Silva on his back, pinned by a hulking shadow. A creature was solidifying over the guard, its wolf-form stretching into the shape of a bear, a hissing fluid dripping from its open jaws. With a burst of sudden movement like a moth escaping its cocoon, the upper half of a dragon reared from the bear's shaggy bulk. The monster's body wheezed for breath as its shadow wings unfurled, its black scales fading to brown.

Snarling, the beast ripped at Silva with its claws, the guard's blood splattering the walls and floor. Its crimson eyes flaring, the dragon lowered its muzzle to tug with its teeth. Then it jerked up its head, flinging a mouthful of entrails at the ceiling.

"Silva!" Terrek cried. He thrust forward, shoving between Vyergin and Wren.

Avalar ducked as power from Mornius shrieked by her ear. Gaelin jumped to block her attempt to charge, his arm gesturing her back while he turned to face their foe. Avalar staggered, the ground lurching beneath her as the staff erupted, fire exploding from the stone.

By degrees the blast faded, its remnants flickering on the floor at Gaelin's feet. The creature was gone, its furious cries echoing down the shaft. Silva remained twitching where the dragon had left him. One half of his torso was missing below his neck, while bits of him dripped from the roof above.

Avalar's vision blurred. Beside her, Terrek silently wept.

"Commander?" Roth asked behind them. "Are you—"

"Vyergin," said Terrek in a strangled voice. "I know he's dead but . . ."

Gaelin sagged trembling against the wall after Vyergin pushed past him. "I'm sorry, Terrek," he groaned to his friend.

"You *tried*," Avalar soothed him.

"Terrek," Vyergin said hoarsely from where he crouched near the guard. "I—"

"Forget it," muttered Terrek. "We can't let this destroy us. That's just what our enemy wants."

"*Gindle!*" Roth shouted. Avalar wheeled to see him gesturing frantically, his brown eyes wide as he stared where the beast had gone. "Gindleyn's *here*! He's got my *sister*!"

"He does *not*," Terrek said. "Snap out of it, Roth!"

"*Gindle!*" His sword lifted, Roth lunged forward.

Avalar seized the young man by the collar and raised him aloft, kicking and flailing. "Watch the sword!" she cried as the tip of his blade flicked her cheek.

"Terrek Florne," Gaelin said in Holram's resonating voice. "This is not what I expected. My enemy does not behave like a warder. His ways are unfamiliar."

"Understood!" Terrek growled. Avalar waited, her attention on Roth while, his cheeks turning red, he twisted in her grasp.

"*Gindleyn!*" he yelled again as Terrek stopped beside him. "She's down the tunnel, Commander! We must help her!"

"No, she's *dead*, Roth!" said Terrek. "You found her yourself, remember?" Reaching up, he extricated the sword from Roth's desperate grip. "*Think* about it, Lieutenant. We cannot lose you, too!"

Avalar met her leader's glance as she felt Roth relax. At Terrek's nod, she set him on his feet. Then Terrek clasped his arm, steadying him.

Vyergin was seated by the dead guard. His head bowed, the captain spread a blanket over the body.

"Deravin," murmured Terrek. "My father assigned you to me on my tenth birthday. You've been with me every single day, and now you're—"

"Terrek Florne," Holram intoned. "Erebos is close. We must depart from this place at once."

"You won't heal him?" Terrek asked.

His eyes unfocused, Gaelin gazed at the floor. Yet, when Holram spoke, his voice from the staff-wielder was achingly sad. "I cannot mend a body torn to pieces," he reminded them. "I could remake him, Terrek Florne, but Gaelin is already ill, and he still has much to do."

"*Remake* him?" Terrek moved to kneel by Silva, to gently touch the upturned palm outside the blanket. He caught the edge of the wool between his fingers, lifting it to cover the guard's empty hand. "I can't imagine he'd like that."

"There are worse things than death," said Vyergin quietly. "Terrek, my young friend, let him go."

Felrina approached Roth where Terrek had left him, his shoulders quaking as he peered down the shaft. "Don't," she said, the sound of her voice making him jump. Unflinching, she met his stare. "What you're hearing now in your head is a game he likes to play. He's trying to lure you away to k–kill you. This is strengthening him, Roth. Our sadness and pain are the things he feeds on."

Avalar positioned herself behind Felrina, her body tensing as she watched Roth's face.

"I'm . . . sorry," Roth whispered. "For what I . . ."

"No!" Felrina cut him off. "I'm the one with reasons to be sorry. Not you."

"This isn't over!" Terrek told them. "He might be getting stronger; I'm quite sure he's enjoying this. But he hasn't won. Not yet."

"He *cannot* win," Holram agreed. "For I refuse to be the cause of Talenkai's death!"

Terrek scowled. "Silva would want us to keep fighting. And that is what we will do."

Climbing stiffly to his feet, Vyergin took hold of Wren Neche's shoulder, his cheeks damp as he guided the shaking young guard from Silva's body.

Chapter 58

eaning on his crystal staff, Ponu peered over the ledge above Mount Chesna, the wind at his back whipping his white hair forward. His hands trembled as, reaching with his senses, he freed his mind to delve through the Staff of Time's changeable depths.

He had removed all the redeemable humans he could find from the slavers' labyrinth. Now he faced the unpleasant task of destroying the rest when they tried to flee, as the black-robed clerics certainly would.

There is a difference, Ponu thought grimly, *between the ones deceived by false promises and the sadists who enjoy torture. I will not let the humans repeat what they did to each other on Earth!*

Through Sephrym's heightened awareness, he perceived how Erebos's attention shifted in the mountain. The Destroyer was stalking Terrek Florne and his men, and Avalar, too—invaders the dark warder intended to kill.

Ponu focused on the present, diverting his gaze from the sunlight overhead. He visualized a dungeon filled with pain, with starving men and women left to waste away in their cells. The staff's crystal clouded as he probed through its matrix to find what mattered to him most—a pocket of heat buried deep under Chesna's stone.

Calmly he inhaled, concentrating on his breathing. For this *transfer*, he would be blind, stepping off the edge of the cliff into nothingness and perhaps death.

His single reference was the ache growing in his belly, the starvation of Erebos's captives draining the strength from his muscles and bones. His searching brought a human tang to his senses, the rank scent of sweat and terror, the eye-watering stench of stale urine.

He imagined himself beneath a low roof, in a long rectangular chamber filled with sickness and death, despairing hearts both blind and cold, hungry and terrified.

All around him, voices moaned. He covered his mouth. The air reeked of feces, but still he sucked it in while struggling to stay erect. He fixated on his staff's radiance between his hands, the power of his magic upholding him.

"An *angel!*" someone whispered. "We're *saved!*"

Ponu snorted. "Notice the ears?" He brushed back his long hair. "I'm an *elf.*"

Tentative footsteps padded in the gloom, the prisoners taking care to stay beyond the circle of his light. "Is this courteous?" he asked. "I cannot see you, but you see *me* clearly enough. Do I look like one of Erebos's minions? No, I do not. I'm here to rescue you."

"Please," a voice groaned. "Don't hurt me."

"I risk much coming to this place," said Ponu. "I am not an angel. Stop labeling the things you don't comprehend! I am Ponu, one of the few survivors of my homeworld, Chorahn. Now let me see you."

A young man in gray robes appeared from out of the darkness, his bruised arms raised to hide his face. Ponu took in the shredded fabric hanging from his shoulders, the fold of flesh that had once been his ear.

"You are a novice." Ponu lowered his staff and dimmed it. "A servant of Erebos. Why are *you* here?"

The apprentice sank to his knees, his arms dropping at his sides. "Many of us are," he whispered. "I'm Gulgrin. I betrayed Erebos by aiding the woman who was training me. It was my fault she escaped."

Ponu kept his features placid, concealing his horror as the glow of his staff revealed a second figure—a skeletal-faced female accompanied by another, the two women pale and emaciated, followed by a man so frail he could barely stand. The humans' eyes were sunken in their heads, the transparent skin of their necks sheened with sweat. *There's at least two score of them,* Ponu realized. *Perhaps even more!*

As his vision adjusted, he discerned people farther back and sprawled on the floor. Beyond them, he saw a shape beside the rear

wall, a heap of rotting corpses.

"I don't understand," he said. "Why didn't they sacrifice you like the others?"

"Oh, but they have!" A man edged closer to the light, his grizzled beard standing out stiffly. "We're already dead as far as they're concerned. Starvation is their slowest method, and they've tried many. That *thing* comes among us assuming one of his forms. He strikes at random, dissolving us. We never know who will be next. Every day we're forced to witness him growing stronger as our suffering feeds him. He consumed my wife. I watched his shadow wrap around her. He knew I was there, so he made it take days. I will never get her screams out of my head!"

"I promise you," said Ponu, "he will pay. This warder will die before this is over. I'll make sure of it. Even among his own kind, he is an abomination.

"Listen," he spoke as loudly as he dared. "Come here to me. We're leaving."

The man motioned to Erebos's clerics huddled near the dead. "Surely, you're not taking *them*? Let them go to Hades's blazes where they belong!"

Ponu glared. "I mean to free every living person. No, *don't touch them!*" he shouted at the people falling on the novice priests with punches and kicks. Ponu strode toward his enemy's failed servants, his body ablaze with Sephrym's fire, tendrils of it hissing along the ceiling. At the sight of the gray-robes' injuries, he rounded on the other prisoners. "Did you do this to them?"

He snatched a breath, biting down on his rage. "Let's try this again, shall we? I want everyone where I can see you." He gestured to the floor in front of him. "And if *they* don't go," he said with a nod at the battered priests, "none of *you* go, either."

"You can't be serious!" a new voice shrieked.

"Oh, but I am!" Ponu marched to the wall where Gulgrin crouched. The apprentice whimpered at his approach. "Do not fear," Ponu told him gently. "You're coming, too."

"How can you say that?" demanded a woman. "It's *his* kind who put us here!"

"Yes, and since it is *my* kind getting you out," Ponu said, "I decide the rules!"

"He's an elf, all right," a prisoner muttered from the darkness. "Look at him telling us what to do."

"Indeed!" Ponu declared. "And as an elf with the ability to judge, I can decide only to rescue these victims of your abuse, while treating *you* in the same way I have treated the other monsters within this accursed rock! Oh, but if I did, I would be acting like you, wouldn't I? As you have been proving yourselves to be just as bad as your captors! You do realize, I hope, that by causing harm, *you* have been strengthening Erebos, too?"

He pointed at the injured priests. "Now, bring them!"

"No!" cried the woman. The other humans argued angrily, all of them talking at once.

Ponu lifted Gulgrin to his feet, then drew back his cowl from his bleeding scalp.

"*Look* at him!" Ponu held the apprentice to keep him from bolting. Gulgrin's nose was dripping blood, his left cheekbone and eye socket were shattered. An infected slash crossed his forehead, a thin trail of pus leaking down.

"*You* did this!" Ponu said. "Not the tormenters holding you, and not the warder they worship. So how are *you* any better? You beat these people and you think you have the right? Now *bring them!*"

The prisoners cowered, the strongest of them shuffling to do his bidding, their shoulders hunched as if they expected him to smite them. Tight-lipped, Ponu watched them help the novices stand, coaxing the gray-robes to come under his light.

"That's better!" said Ponu. "Now—"

He froze as jittery fingers touched his hand. He stared into an older man's dark-complexioned face, a pair of great brown eyes brimming with pain. "I dreamt about you," the human said. "You came out from the fire and you had wings."

"The Khanal elves believe you humans lack magic," Ponu said, "but in a way, you do have it, and it lives right here." He tapped the man's temple. "This is your higher self. When your heart interferes, that is when you hurt each other."

Releasing Gulgrin, Ponu opened his mind to the fearful crowd. The prisoners were silent now, clustered around him with their eyes filled with hope.

"Don't be frightened," Ponu told them. "You'll be moving quickly while standing in place, both at the same time. For this to work, you must keep very still.

"Hold on to each other, the injured, too. Huddle up and press against me. Don't get distracted. Focus on my face."

Ponu stood gripping Gulgrin. His staff flared as he raised it, flickering as it sensed his need. He visualized the temple with its domed central chamber, the reflective crystal roof above it.

He imagined himself *there* with the humans pressing close, skimming through the currents of power the Staff of Time created. He was a traveler hurling forward with a flock of wounded souls, wild birds with damaged wings longing for freedom, desperately fluttering in his grasp.

Firming his will, he held them tight. This was magic from his homeworld, a force he had mastered. By the strength of pure will, he had crossed the void to find this world. It was easy in comparison to snatch these people away from their doom and land them safely in front of the Table of Life, inside the main chamber of the temple at Heartwood.

Ponu collapsed as the humans let him go. With slow, deep breaths, he fought to clear his head.

"Thank you," said Gulgrin. "Ponu, are . . . are you well?"

Ponu planted his staff and stood. "I am," he said. "But you"— Ponu pushed back the wavy hair from Gulgrin's swollen eyelid—"are not. We will have that tended to at once. Come."

Gulgrin reached out to touch his cheek in a gesture of gratitude, his undamaged eye shining bright. Taken aback, Ponu smiled.

elrina gazed past Wren Neche at the stairs. She was glad for the delay in their plan to venture up. *I wish Gaelin hadn't collapsed, though*, she thought sadly.

She shivered, for witnessing what had appeared at the time to be Gaelin's death had shaken her to her core. Despite Holram's efforts to sustain him after battling his foe, Gaelin had folded with a gasp at the foot of the steps, with Vyergin hastening over and Wren leaping to his defense with his sword drawn. Yet now the young guard was conflicted, bracing his feet, his head swiveling as if he was determined to defend them all.

Drifting toward Gaelin, Felrina studied the stairs on which the staff-wielder lay. The brown splotches on the stone, dappled afresh with Silva's blood, were familiar. *Older deaths?* she mused as she licked her dry lips. *The people I killed?* Sitting on the steps near Gaelin, she recalled how she had waited indifferently at the edge of the pool, lost in her false ambitions, without any consideration for the lives she would take or the suffering she would cause.

Sudden tears stung her eyes as Terrek and Roth stopped to retrieve their shields.

"Well, I'm fine, *now*," Gaelin replied testily, his staff with its colorful, glowing crystal propped beside him. Leaning close, Vyergin poured more of the yellow powder into Gaelin's cup and then stirred with his finger until it dissolved.

"A few more sips," Vyergin urged as he plied the staff-wielder again with the medicine. "It really does help."

"Please," Felrina whispered, surprised to discover she had spoken aloud. Her cheeks flamed. "Don't make me go up there."

"Where else could you go?" Terrek demanded.

"Back? Or maybe just slit my throat and be done?" she said. "It would be better! Seeing Mens and the others—I'd rather die!" Felrina turned, struggling to meet his stare. "You warned me if I t-tried to run, you'd have Roth . . ."

"Don't be ridiculous," Terrek said. "We're beyond that, Felrina. But now that we're here, I thought you might enjoy a little revenge."

She pressed her palm on the bloodstained step. "For years I've walked down this stair and never noticed it before. All this death and so much worse, and I never really *saw* it."

"But today you did," said Terrek.

"No!" Angrily, she flipped back her hair. "Don't make this into a good thing. I'm a monster! I took the lives of innocent people!"

"As have I," he replied. "I slew the victims of your cult, and I did it so I wouldn't have to die, and to protect my friends and family. Doesn't some of that sound familiar? Isn't that partly why you killed?"

"No," she said. "It's because I was foolish and delusional. You would not have had to take anyone's life, Terrek, if not for what I did!"

"See Caven Roth, there? You owe it to him to climb these stairs and keep going. You owe it to him to try."

Felrina met Roth's despondent gaze. "You're right, Terrek," she agreed. "I'm sorry."

Terrek rose, holding out his hand. "You can do this, Felrina. You're not their slave anymore."

With a sigh, she surrendered, his arms drawing her to her feet. "But it's a trap," she protested.

Vyergin, standing next to her, gravely passed her his dagger. In horror, she almost dropped it.

"No, you're supposed to *throw* it," said Vyergin as Felrina examined the blade with its worn leather hilt. "My aim's not so great anymore. And who knows? Maybe you'll hit something vital!"

"But I'm a prisoner. You can't give me—"

"Of course it's a trap," Terrek interrupted. His head was raised, his words addressing them all. "And it's also our last battle." Somberly he motioned to the gear on the floor. "We'll leave all this here. If any of us survive, we can come back for it."

"Erebos wants this," said Felrina. "He wanted us in this tunnel, and he wants me by my pool. Blood feeds the wizard Arawn's spirit; this time *we're* to be the sacrifice."

Avalar lowered her oversized pack from her shoulders. "Leader Terrek, I shall go first."

"You will not!" Terrek said. "We go as a team and we fight together. That's it. Remember what you are, Giant. For the sake of your world, you must survive this. Felrina's no warrior. She'll need you guarding her back. Stay clear of any magic—even Gaelin's, at this point. I guarantee you, Holram will not be thinking about your safety if he's fighting for his life."

Avalar sniffed. Lifting her sword, she swung it, the massive blade whistling through the air.

Terrek knelt beside Gaelin, his eyes softening as he saw the resignation on the staff-wielder's face.

"If I fail," Gaelin said, "think well of me, won't you? I'm not a wizard. I'm not important like Avalar is. I never even went—"

"Enough!" Terrek reached to clasp his arm. "You've not failed at anything since we met. Nor are you what you were. You wanted to save Silva. It was you who went first with your staff to defend him, not Holram. You held out your arm to keep us back, and I saw your expression. That is not what the warder looks like when he's angry."

Gaelin fought not to shy away. In his soft brown eyes, Felrina glimpsed the child he used to be, a boy who remembered pain—abuse which so often accompanied a male's touch. Yet now his jaw hardened; he was a man overcoming his fear.

She drew a deep breath. Her pulse was steadier, for the blade in her grasp gave her strength. Closing her eyes, she fingered its leather hilt, enjoying the feel of it against her hand.

A sharp hissing sound jolted her. She glanced down as an inky shadow darted from the wall to form a puddle around her feet, the black substance thickening like tar.

"Terrek!" Felrina gasped. She struggled to jump away, but suction held her to the stone. Fiery needles stabbed through the tough hide of her boots and then her flesh, burning tentacles slicing into her calves, twining around her bones.

Groaning, she clutched her legs, rubbing at the pain burrowing swiftly into her thighs.

Terrek was by her side, helping her stand. "Felrina?" What is it?"

"It's Erebos," said Gaelin. Sitting up straight, he braced his staff on the floor.

Felrina bit her lip, her shoulders shaking as she yanked up the front of her tunic. Purplish lines climbed into view between her hips and below her belly, worming under her pale skin. Before her eyes, her stomach darkened as bruises appeared.

Spangles, bursting from Mornius's gem, descended from the ceiling like flakes of sapphire snow. Trembling, Felrina sank into Terrek's strong arms.

As the sparkling fragments covered her lower torso, the iron grip of Erebos weakened within her. Faster the healing flakes flew, their tiny lights skittering toward her. Felrina sobbed in relief as the marks faded beneath her skin, the pressure retreating back into her legs and feet. The pool of inky shadow reappeared briefly around her and then vanished.

"Someone's unhappy," Terrek observed. "We're not keeping to his schedule."

Felrina turned to Gaelin. The staff-wielder was lying exhausted on the steps, his arms hugging Mornius to his chest. "You had to use your power to fight him off," she said. "That's the last thing you needed."

Abruptly Gaelin jerked to his feet to stand on the bottom stair, his dark eyes glinting silver as he stared down at her. He was Holram, and yet still a human on the verge of failure, accepting that weakness as his own.

Raising Mornius, Holram stooped to snatch Gaelin's bag from the pile of gear. He paused, his expression puzzled as he fought with the straps. Then he wheeled smartly on his heel and marched up the steps.

"I thought you said no packs," Roth muttered.

Felrina squeezed Terrek's shoulder "We can't let the warders fight. If they do battle—"

"I know," he said. "And we won't."

Nodding to the others, Terrek set off in pursuit of his friend.

Chapter 60

Gaelin, his body caught firmly in Holram's mental grasp, watched himself hesitate. From somewhere beyond the stairwell, he heard a faint gurgle, a listless lapping of waves. As the steps curved upward, Argus's green illumination stretched along the ceiling overhead, the ghostly flickers merging with Mornius's light.

A hand touched his elbow, and he was comforted. "We're with you," Terrek said softly at his back.

Gaelin nodded as Holram lifted his foot. His lungs kept working despite the tightness in his chest, the painful knot at the base of his throat. The walls brightened as he climbed, the granite near the top of the stairs glowing red. He paused again at a murmur of distant voices, something scraping along the stone.

"No," Felrina groaned under her breath.

Gaelin sighed shakily as Holram released him. He stood on the uppermost step with his face revealed, staring into a sunken chamber, its rounded walls lined with torches. This time he had no refuge, no wolf-mother to come to his aid. With a shrug, he repositioned his pack, wincing when its straps pinched his neck.

A wave of power struck him as he straightened, a stinging heat, intense to the point of burning. He gazed down at a black circle of water in a rock-rimmed hollow. *Felrina's pool*, he thought, recognizing the basin from her description of its surrounding ledges of stone, the rear platform where she had stood.

As he peered at the tarn's greasy surface, smelling its reek of death, his stomach heaved.

"Holram?" Terrek prodded him. "Keep going!"

Gaelin shook his head. "It's me," he whispered. "Holram's

waiting to see if we fail."

"*What?*" Roth's mouth dropped open. "We don't have magic?"

"And no time to discuss it, either," Terrek said. "Keep close to me, Roth. Remember, we've come to fight! Avalar, hide here until I call."

"Leader Terrek, I—"

"Hush, Giant. You heard me!"

Gaelin faced the vaulted chamber. No one stood in front to shield him from attack, and his free hand itched for a weapon. Licking his lips, he edged out, creeping through the shadow under the flaming sconces. He looked intently at a crimson orb left beside the pool below, the fist-sized gem casting fiery reflections on the water.

He spied movement in the gloom, in a shadowy gap between the ledges. For a flicker of a moment, struggling bodies were discernable behind a low obsidian wall, eight figures striking at someone on the ground.

A gaunt, beady-eyed man darted from the darkness to snatch the gem. As he turned toward Gaelin, he raised his arm, the carnelian's light crackling between his fingers.

Gaelin stiffened when the other black-robes appeared, a cluster of wizards dragging a body. The sight of their broken and battered victim—a youth dressed in gray and barely recognizable as human— took his breath away. The man with the stone gestured, and the boy was flung to the floor, flinching weakly while his assailants tore off his clothes.

"Terrek Florne!" the head mage called, staring up. "Your winged elf ally rescued our captives, did you know? His actions force our hand; now we must slay our *faithful* to feed our god!" He grimaced, leering through the bloody radiance of his gem. "Priestess Vlyn, my dear! Back for more?"

Gaelin glanced at Felrina. *Allastor Mens*, he thought.

"Great Erebos, no!" She pointed, and Gaelin saw it—a winged apparition solidifying behind Mens and his companions. The Destroyer's dragon shape, midnight black with its eye glinting red, crouched in the shadow, its neck folded against the barbed length of its tail.

"How *dare* you speak his name?" Mens shouted. "Oh, but you've always been an insolent bitch. Wait until we're done here today,

Felrina! I have so many new things to try with you!"

The memories of his mother's death seared Gaelin's mind as the captive sobbed and fought, flailing while his attackers arched his body over the makeshift altar. Gaelin shuddered, remembering his mother on the table and Seth Lavahl with his knife. And just as in his dreams, Allastor Mens braced his legs for the leverage he would need, the curved blade of the dagger gleaming in the torchlight.

"We're not finished with our ritual, Gaelin Lavahl," Mens said. "I'm afraid you must wait your turn!"

Gaelin gasped when the cavern tilted abruptly. He lifted his gaze to the ceiling, fixing his attention on the roof's two remaining stalactites until his vertigo stopped.

Terrek, with Roth fast on his heels, lunged toward the ledges surrounding the pond. "Bastard!" he yelled, drawing Argus's sword. "Come and fight a *grown* man, coward! Leave the boy alone!"

The dragon extended its neck, the thunder of its roar reverberating through the floor, a fretwork of cracks splintering the granite behind Gaelin's head. In Mens's grasp, the Blazenstone erupted, its blast melting the rock nearby.

The black-robes charged from the opposite side of the tarn, and as they brandished their bloodstone staves, the gems magnified Erebos's fire. Gaelin reeled as the combined sheets of flame leapt at Terrek and Roth, slamming them into the wall and pinning them flat.

Mens smiled through the shimmer of his magic. He bent to his prisoner, cutting precisely with his knife below the youth's ribs, and with the same calm expression, continued to slice through the boy's navel.

Blood poured down the stone as Gaelin stared transfixed. He was helpless, hindered by memories of his mother's slaughter. The heat of Mens's power burned his face; the vapor from the water scalded him. Yet still he glared through the brightness holding Terrek, Holram's anger and frustration writhing in his gut.

Mens transferred his knife to his mouth, biting on its hilt as he leaned over the sacrifice.

"*Blazes!*" snarled Vyergin.

As the entrails emerged encased in membrane, Mens held them against his victim and cut them free, then tossed them into the pool.

"Did you tell them Arawn's magic requires blood to work?" Mens asked Felrina. "And Erebos needs Arawn for his skill!" Above him the dragon snapped its jaws, its long sinewy neck flexing as it prepared to strike.

Gaelin lifted his staff. Stepping to block Felrina's view, he risked a glance at Terrek and Roth immobilized by the wall.

"*Sick bastard!*" Roth cried, tears streaming down his cheeks.

The dragon was silent, its chest swelling as a green smoking liquid dripped from the corners of its mouth.

"*Feast*, great Arawn!" Mens, positioned in front of the warder, motioned to the stalactites overhead. "Wake now to help us slay our foes!"

"Grakan's teeth, I hate religion," muttered Vyergin.

The black-robes lowered their sacrifice to the floor. The youth lay staring, pale with shock, and still horribly alive. Mens straddled the boy and squatted, the blade of his knife vanishing below the ribcage to sever the heart. Laughing, Mens stood and flipped the corpse onto its stomach, then kicked it into the water.

"*Slaver!*"

Gaelin whirled as Avalar burst from the stairwell. Her strong hands seized Wren Neche, throwing him aside and out of her way. Sobbing with rage, she charged, taking two ledges at a time as she threw herself toward Mens. At the base of the chamber, she sprang, the sweep of her blade cleaving the fire from Mens's gem—to free her leader and Roth.

"Avalar, *no!*" Terrek howled, and his command brought her up short, the remnants of Mens's magic sluicing down her legs. Trembling, she gasped for breath near the tarn's bloody edge.

Mens stepped close to the water opposite her, the carnelian flashing in his hand. The black-robes arranged themselves at his back, their bloodstone staves raised high, the teardrop crystals pulsing as the wizards labored again to expand Erebos's power.

Mens grinned at Terrek. "Why, *thank* you, Terrek Florne, for bringing us a giant to kill! That's all it would take to create our world! Thanks to you, it'll be born today!"

"Slay her and you'll die, too!" Terrek gritted in disgust. "We all will. Your delusions will kill us all!"

"You *removed* the stone?"

Felrina stumbled forward, revulsion replacing her fear as she gripped Vyergin's knife. "Erebos needed the Blazenstone *in its staff*!"

Mens's grin stretched taut. "Erebos wanted it removed! It works better this way, having direct contact with human flesh. You should have figured it out yourself! You can add that to your list of failures!"

"Well, you couldn't make dachs and *she* could!" Vyergin countered. "You made me so flawed I still had the presence of mind to escape you! But only after you destroyed *how* many good men?"

Eyeing him, Mens snorted. "One old man? How is that a loss?"

"I have at least twenty years on you," said Vyergin. "And *still* I beat you."

Mens turned away, his face going pale as the dragon above him swiveled its head to follow his stare. Avalar stalked him along the rim of the pool, her features rigid with hate, her shoulders hunched, her sword whistling as she swung it.

"Giant!" Terrek snapped. "What did I say?"

"Call off your *pet*, Terrek Florne." Mens held up his fist, drawing streaks of fire through the air before him with the stone. "Or I promise you, I'll kill her!"

Gaelin cocked his head at the quaver in the man's nasally voice. *He's afraid*! he realized.

An emerald glow skimmed over the pool. Argus, his phantom-gray face impassive, floated to a stop in front of Mens.

"I'm tired of you," the ghost said. "All this drama, and there's nothing original about you. Your kind has been feeding off people as long as there have been people. You're all the same—mentally stunted children. But, *you*!" Flitting to the center of the tarn, Argus pointed an accusing finger at the water. "Today, my slayer, you'll learn you cannot cheat death forever! And I, Sir Nathaniel Argus, am here to teach you! You only get to endure as long as the curse you put on me does, isn't that right? Well!"

Spiraling up toward the stalactites, Argus shouted, "Throw my sword into the pool, Terrek Florne! Let its blade put an end to my slayer!"

"One move, Florne," snarled Mens, "and I'll fry you where you stand!"

Gaelin leveled Mornius at Mens's chest. "*Try* it!" he yelled, and spread his arms, releasing Holram's fire to protect Terrek.

Glaring back, Mens straddled the rock still damp with gore from his latest victim. He slapped his palm over the blood, the Blazenstone tilted in his outstretched hand toward the pool. Flames exploded from the crimson gem, striking the tarn's warped heart.

Gaelin staggered as the chamber rocked. Terrek, standing within Holram's defenses, lifted Argus's snake-handled sword. With a fierce cry, he hurled it.

Water spouted from the pond, incited by the power of Mens's stone, splashing high in all directions. Gaelin cringed as it doused his shield to nothingness, the oily fluid soaking his hair and skin. Yet he fixed his gaze on the ancient sword arcing high and spinning free. It struck a stalactite with a clang. Then it dropped with its point straight down, flashing through Argus—to vanish beneath the tarn's flat surface.

Chapter 61

At the touch of the ghost knight's sword, the pool erupted, the water tossing in a frenzy of foam and human blood. Argus, laughing, bowed in triumph to the warder inside of Gaelin as the blade flashed beneath the waves. Grinning, he whirled above the tarn to confront Mens. "Arawn's spell is broken! His spirit has reunited with the weapon he cursed. You've *lost* him, slayer! You'll never make dachs again!"

"*What?*" Mens stumbled as he approached the rim of the turbulent pool, his eyes wide. "What are you saying, Ghost?"

"Oh, but Arawn's fighting it!" Argus observed, glancing down. He rose to the ceiling and turned. For a moment, Gaelin met his stare through Holram's sight, seeing the brief look of pain the warder knew so well. Yet relief was flooding the Thalian Knight's face, his bitterness replaced with joy.

Argus dove toward the pool's churning surface, his enemy's desperate efforts to remain among the living. The dead knight opened his arms as he entered the water, spreading them to embrace his slayer.

In the green glimmer of his wake, his minions appeared, a silver bolt of lightning, a host of pearl-white bodies entwined. Gaelin glimpsed women and men, children and infants, fused together for one purpose: to form a lance of spectral wrath to follow their leader and purge the tarn.

"*No!*" Mens blasted the pool with the gem he held, the Destroyer's magic freezing the water solid.

"I have trapped our wizard's spirit on *this* world where he belongs!" Mens cried. "He will stay. And, *you*, Ghost, you'll stay also and there's nothing you can do!"

With a furious howl, Avalar sprang over the ice. In three enormous leaps, she crashed into Mens, hurling him back, slamming him against the wall. "Govorian *take* you!" Raising her sword, she scrambled after him.

Two figures cut her off, black-robes wielding their staves, the bloodstones at their crowns engorged with power, throbbing with Erebos's magic. The explosion from the stones sent her reeling, melting the mail across her chest and searing her long blond braid. In agony, she fell onto her stomach, her body rigid as she convulsed.

Gaelin sank to his knees, aiming his staff at the dragon shadow swelling above Mens, the restless ebon wings of Holram's foe. Erebos's roar shattered the chamber, the Destroyer's crimson glare shifting toward him.

You don't scare me! Gaelin thought. A power seized his heart, Holram's mental hands reaching to possess him. Sweat was streaming from his hair. He weakened, tumbling down on all fours, only to groan and clamber upright.

Forward he strode, the gray rock softening, sinking beneath him as he descended the ledges. The wizards were jumping to dodge his fire, throwing aside their staves as the metal holding the bloodstones melted under his attack. The teardrop gems, released from their crowns, rolled across the floor, then flattened abruptly into puddles.

Gaelin laughed, consumed with the euphoria of understanding, his growing awareness of who he was. He flared like a newborn sun, kindling flames within himself and thrusting them out. Soon he would burn through the mountain's shell, his name pounding the granite like a drum: *O-THEL-ion! O-THEL-ion!*

"Terrek!" yelled Felrina from far away. "The warders! We can't let them *fight*! We must stop—"

Thwack!

Dimly Gaelin knew when Terrek's dagger cut through his flame, burying itself to its crossguard in Allastor Mens's flesh.

Thwack! Thwack!

Felrina let fly Vyergin's little knife, with Roth flicking his dirk expertly behind.

Mens stumbled with his mouth agape. Three hilts protruded from his body—one from under his ribs, the others below and above his groin. The Blazenstone clattered from his hand and spun across the floor. Screaming in pain, Mens collapsed in a heap of midnight cloth.

"*No!*" roared a voice like boulders breaking.

As the dragon faded to mist, it reached with its claws to seize the red gem. Hugging the orb close to the vagueness that had been its chest, the shadow beast snapped its wings—a great rush of air swirling over the frozen pool.

The cracked ceiling split, the gloom that was Erebos fleeing into the rift. Gaelin hurried to reach the giant. All around him, the black-robes fled, their garments billowing as they hastened into the gap between the ledges, to slip out through an exit he had not seen before.

A green flicker under the tarn's ice highlighted the giant's face as Gaelin knelt beside her. "Avalar?" He undid the straps of her mail, grunting as he tried to pull the melted steel away from her charred tunic. "Giant? I can heal you if you'll let me."

Her eyes turned toward him, and she smiled. "I will mend!" Her whisper was fierce. She pointed to the splotches of crimson hardening on the floor. "Those were bloodstones! How did you destroy them?"

Terrek straddled Mens. With a brutal jerk, he tore his knife from the man's ribs. Then he seized the black-robe by his hair, forcing back his head to slit his throat.

"*Hold!*" Gaelin shouted with his warder's voice. He, too, wanted Mens dead, but Holram, possessing him, had other plans for the wizard. In growing frustration, Gaelin felt his mouth speaking the last words he wanted to hear.

"I need him to *live*, Terrek Florne," Holram said. "Restrain him for me."

Terrek stood scowling over Mens. The mage wheezed for breath, pawing at the knives still embedded near his groin.

In morbid fascination, Vyergin and Felrina drifted close to stare down. Gravely Terrek nodded. "See that, Vyergin? That was Felrina's. Would you call that 'something vital'?" Mens shrieked as Terrek jostled the hilt in question with his toe.

Vyergin whistled. Then, smirking, he bent, tugging one knife free while leaving the other. "Definitely not bad for a blind throw," he said.

With a resounding crack, the pool's icy sheath fractured at the center, the jagged pieces separating, tipping in the water. Argus's emerald aura flared deep within, his grinning face gliding along the tarn's granite floor.

"Where's the oil and blood?" Felrina murmured to Wren Neche beside her. "I can see straight to the bottom!"

Arawn's gone, too, Gaelin thought as Argus floated out of the pond in streamers of green and gold. The ghost clasped his ancient sword to his breast, his gaze fixed on Terrek's face.

"I am *free*!" he exulted. "Terrek Florne, I hereby give you my weapon to replace the one you lost. It is strong and whole again, and it should serve you well. Cherish it. For though it was not wrought by elves, the blade *is* unique. It was forged on Earth."

Terrek stepped to the water's edge, and Argus lowered the ancient sword into his hands. "I didn't know that," he said. He smiled at the ghost. "You've been a great help to us, Argus."

"Yes, I know. Godspeed and farewell." Argus snorted. "I'm not sure those are possible for me, though. It seems I have a following." He motioned toward the faint glints of silver below the tarn's surface. "Fear not, my dear!" he said at Felrina's worried frown. "Their hatred has been washed away; their haunting days are done." He flitted past Terrek to look Gaelin in the eyes. "I have a message for you, old friend. No, not *you*. Holram!"

Argus bent closer, his black gaze steady. "You need to know," the ghost said, and Gaelin felt Holram listening attentively inside him. "The old magic retains its memory; it doesn't need giants to keep it.

"I have some idea of what you're planning. You won't require Arawn's skill the way Felrina Vlyn did. You have the water. You have everything you need right here."

"Where will you go?" Holram asked him.

"I'm not sure yet," Argus replied. "Here and there, I suppose. I could become a magical creature if I can stand sparkling in a lantern for the length of an elvish year. Or maybe I'll just stay a ghost. It's not so bad, once you get used to it." He swept them a bow. Then slowly, dramatically, he straightened his shoulders and threw back his head.

Gaelin squinted at the blinding flash of green Argus left behind, leaving only Mornius's glow to illuminate the chamber.

Chapter 62

aelin, his nose wrinkling at the stench from Avalar's burnt hair, knelt beside her as she struggled to sit up. She grimaced in disgust at the charred pattern of rings her damaged mail had left on her jerkin. "I am wondering—" she began, gesturing to the mage lying supine nearby. Then she froze, her eyes flaring wide.

"Look what I found!" Caven Roth stopped before them, his arms cradling an object. "What is this? Do you know?" He squatted, grunting as he placed his discovery on the floor—a long, flat shard of crimson glass. "Be careful. It's sharp!"

Avalar gasped, scrambling backward on her haunches. "Where was it?" she demanded. "Keep it away!"

Roth pointed to the gap between the ledges, the obsidian barrier concealing the rear exit. "There's a crack you can't see from here, a split in the volcanic rock."

"'*Volcanic* rock'?" Gaelin raised his brows.

"Terrek calls it that," said Roth. "I found more stones your staff melted behind the wall. A few had leaked into the crevice to make this. I had to chip around it to get it out."

"Is there anything you can't find?" Gaelin asked, impressed.

Grinning, Roth shook his head.

Avalar rolled to her knees and crept closer to inspect the crystal. "Gaelin, could you turn it for me? It is bloodstone. It would harm me to touch it."

Gaelin stood, and with Roth's help, lifted the fragment. He set the heavy end on the floor beside his foot, then rested the tip against his shoulder. The shard was slender and flat, with parallel edges tapered to a point.

As he tilted it, Avalar bent near. "It is not unlike Redeemer," she said. "If I did not know better, I would say this *is* the blade of Govorian's sword. It has the same pockmarks at the base."

"There were some pebbles stuck to it I picked out," Roth told them. "If you want, I can wrap the glass in leather so it can't hurt you. I still have scraps from the tents in my pack." He sat in front of them, his dark eyes sparkling as he reached to feel the edge. Hissing, he yanked back his hand.

"You may do as you say," Avalar said to Roth, "but only if you promise not to do that again. I believe my leader on Hothra, Trentor, would wish to examine this object." She glanced at Terrek, her gaze lowering to the black-robe at his feet. "How is that slaver still breathing?"

"I'd like to know that myself," said Terrek. "Why the hesitation, *Holram*?" Deliberately he emphasized the name as he turned toward Gaelin. "Kindly enlighten us!"

"I gather the necessary elements," Gaelin heard his mouth say. "It is much the same as creating stars . . ."

As Holram manipulated his vocal cords, Gaelin's attention strayed to Roth. The young man raised the unwieldy shard, staggering under its weight, and carried it wrapped in his coat to the top of the ledges—to slip out of sight down the stairs.

Gaelin took in the contours of the sunken room. He spied the hollows in the ceiling where other stalactites had been and the three troughs leading from the pool. In the background of his thoughts, Holram's voice droned on: "Living flesh is matter to me, clay waiting to be formed."

"Did you get all that?" muttered Vyergin.

Gaelin opened his mouth, nodding in relief when he found that he could. Terrek, his expression grim, met his stare briefly before leaning over his prisoner.

". . . Florne," Mens rasped.

Terrek gripped Felrina's knife; as he jerked it free, Mens screamed.

Shuddering, Gaelin felt Holram take control from him once more, compelling him to crouch beside Mens. Blood streamed from the black-robe's wounded chest, collecting in the hollow of his stomach. "Perhaps you hope I might save you?" Holram asked the wizard. "I will not, for I have beheld your handiwork. You are as much a poison to this world as I am."

He straightened, pointing to the chamber's rear exit. "Felrina Vlyn. There is a staff on the steps beyond the wall. Its bloodstone remains intact. You will apply it to this man's forehead."

Holram waited, demonstrating a patience Gaelin did not share while Felrina went to find the abandoned staff. After a long pause, she returned, her expression bewildered as she halted by his side. Trembling, she glared down at Mens.

"Be at ease," Holram reassured her. "He cannot harm you."

"What will this do?" she asked.

"Absorb him," said Holram. "His life force will be drawn into the stone, imprisoned as I was in Mornius. Life is precious, Felrina Vlyn. I do not intend to waste the shell he leaves behind."

Felrina knelt, baring her teeth while she placed the crystal between Mens's black brows. Abruptly he convulsed, his bloodshot eyes staring as he spasmed on the stone.

Gaelin sprang clear when Mens vomited, a pinkish foam pouring from the wizard's mouth.

"How long?" Felrina whispered.

"Until it stops," Holram said.

Turning, Gaelin squatted above his pack, the warder within him fumbling with its straps. Mens continued to thrash, fists and heels pummeling the floor. Gaelin's gaze shied away—Holram allowing him that much—from the mage's contorted face.

"His ears and nose are bleeding," said Felrina. "His eyes, too. I had no idea bloodstones could—"

"Kill?" Holram queried. "They are lethal. Just ask the giant. These crystals are the living blood of this world. Life is power, and all magic needs energy. To survive, this very old planet will absorb all it can get through these stones. These gems drain anything; they have even slain giants.

"Flesh starts to fail once the spirit is gone. We must act quickly. Erebos is wounded by this loss; his retribution will be swift," Holram said as he searched inside the bag. "And here it is!" Gaelin, watching himself withdraw a folded piece of cloth, mentally recoiled as he recalled its contents, his consciousness slipping behind Holram's thoughts.

"Now," the warder went on, "if the flesh has quieted, Terrek Florne, I request that you remove its clothing."

"It hasn't," Terrek gritted.

Holram glanced over. "It has *enough*. Place it in the water.

"Is this distasteful to you?" Holram inquired, focusing on Caven Roth as Terrek and Vyergin disrobed the rigid body. "Have you learned at last that everyone has a story, including this man? He, too, was a victim of my foe, though unlike Felrina Vlyn, he is warped beyond my aid. Erebos's darkness and the opportunity to practice cruelty called to this man, not the cult with its false promises of a new world. His crimes are so dire I am unable to dismiss them."

He nodded to Terrek. "Place it in the water, Terrek Florne. Let us wring some goodness from this death."

"What do you mean to do?" Terrek asked with a scowl. "As you say, Erebos will pay us a visit. Staying here is the last thing we should do."

"The inevitable happens whether you want it or not," said Holram. "I am a maker. That is my purpose. The carbon in suns is also found in flesh, which is what you are. Until you open your mouth, Terrek Florne—until I hear otherwise—you are nothing to me but salt, air, and water. Chemicals."

Vyergin snorted.

"This is what I am," Holram explained. "You think of me as a spirit like Argus, possessing this human. I am not. I am energy and thought; I have never been solid. *That . . .*" He motioned toward the body. "Is matter. From it, much as Felrina Vlyn created her monsters, I shall fashion a gift for you."

"What gift?" Terrek demanded. He nudged the limp form with his boot. "From *this*? No, thank you!"

Avalar was eyeing the pool, the tears on her jaw glittering in Mornius's light. Following her stare, Holram saw a shimmer above the tarn's clear surface.

Holram nodded. "Already you sense him, Giant. Good. Your heart perceives what your sight cannot. You, Avalar Mistavere, shall be my guide. Terrek Florne?"

Sighing, Terrek slid his arms beneath the body. Bereft of his robes, Mens was pathetically thin, his shoulders and back an intricate map of self-abuse, with bruises and scars marring his skin.

Terrek waded into the water carrying the still-breathing husk of what had been a living man. At Holram's gesture, he released the twitching form.

"Avalar must remain," Holram said, as Terrek climbed from the pool. "Also you, Felrina Vlyn. I ask you to stay close as well. Terrek Florne, if you and your men would . . ."

"We'll guard your back," said Terrek. "But be quick, whatever you're planning to do. Delaying like this endangers us all." He turned to his men, murmuring softly. Then, with a faint clinking of mail and the wet slap of Terrek's boots, the warriors left as Holram had commanded them.

Chapter 63

The wizard's body floated spread-eagled in the midst of the pool. Cleansed by the fury of Arawn's victims, the tarn's depths shimmered to the very bottom. With no healthy rock to absorb it, Holram sensed the water's magic seeking an outlet. In time, it might work to restore the crippled mountain, but he needed its power now.

"What should I do?" Felrina asked.

Holram smiled. His home above the sky felt closer now. He wondered briefly if he would ever see it. "Light from darkness," he murmured. "This is what warders do." He nodded to the females beside him. "Avalar, you need to recall the one from your memories, the spirit who eased your heart when you were so afraid. Remember his voice and visualize his appearance for me. Can you do this?"

"I could never not do it," Avalar replied. "The one you speak of lives in my dreams."

Holram lifted the little cloth. "This flowed through his veins once. Now behold." He tossed the fabric into the water, watching it unfold in a fluttering dance. Slowly it circled in the pool's gentle current, sinking down. "Felrina Vlyn," he said. "Repeat your parting words to Camron Florne, if you can. They will draw him near."

Holram sat with his legs in the tranquil water. After a moment, he looked up at the light bathing his face, the colorful radiance of Mornius's gem.

Reaching into the pool, he swirled the cool liquid with his fingers. "Grasp the staff beneath where I am holding it, Felrina Vlyn, and speak the words you said to your friend as accurately as you can."

Felrina came up next to him to grip the staff. For a long, quiet moment, Holram gazed pensively into the water. He shut his eyes, letting his awareness slip under the waves, diving deep through the tarn's warming depths. On the surface, the body rotated on its back as it drifted, its blind stare fixed on the ceiling.

"Oh, Camron," Felrina said in a husky voice. "I know it hurts, but I have to believe it's for the good of us all. You'll come back; you'll see. We'll be together, you and me. We'll build our houses beside another river and . . . Why did it have to be *you*?"

From a distance, Holram discerned the echo of a response. "Don't cry, dear one. That wasn't you."

The water rose to engulf Holram's wrist, churning hot around his elbow and rising up his arm, its steam soaking the skin of his neck. He heard the rhythmic slosh of waves upon the stone.

When a scalding spray burned his cheeks, his body scrambled to its feet against his will, his reaction dragging Felrina up as well as she fought to retain her grip on the staff. Holram stepped away from the heat, his thoughts bent on reducing the pool's temperature until it matched that of his host.

Concentrating, he extended his awareness outside the cave, far away from Mount Chesna's gutted rock, and even past the sky—to harness the icy cold of the starry realm beyond.

"Why did you let them catch you?" Felrina whispered. "Why? Oh, Camron, *forgive* me!"

The pool's surface surged with the force of its currents. The mage's flesh was losing its human shape, its skin becoming transparent. Through the thinning membrane, the heart was visible now, still beating and intact, while the skeleton slid from its sheath and dropped, rolling along the tarn's floor.

"Sails!" Avalar breathed.

As Holram continued his work, remnants of sinew unfurled from the sunken bones, dissolving as veins and arteries detached from the fraying muscles, the red tendrils expanding through the froth.

"Giant," he said. "Put your hands in the water."

Avalar thrust her arms into what had become a pinkish soup, a steaming vat of pulsating matter.

Eyes closed, Holram clenched his staff. With a flex of his will, power screamed from the Skystone, striking the pond's living core. As if from far away, Felrina cried out: "No, *no*! You're doing it wrong!"

Holram ignored her.

In one great spout, the foaming torrent lashed the granite encircling the pool—to strike the ceiling and splatter, the warm liquid raining down. The veins retracted in the water, clustering again around the still-throbbing heart. Far below, the skeleton diffused into streamers of gray, the minerals funneling up.

At the center of the whirlpool, an adult-sized body formed curled in a fetal position. The unconscious figure twitched while the water upheld it, its misshapen limbs dangling.

As the pond gradually cleared, the newborn's anatomy took on definition. Now arms and legs hugged the currents, and a wavy red mane sprouted from the skull.

Felrina seized Holram's wrist. "No!" she gasped. "He's too *big*!"

Holram spied the little hairs erupting from the skin, the freckles dotting the figure's hands. He could see the fingernails growing, the fingers beginning to move.

"He's . . . !" Felrina gasped.

Holram nodded. "A giant." Inhaling deeply, he reined in his power until, bit by bit, the water settled, sloshing gently along the tarn's granite rim. As he surveyed what his efforts had wrought, the Skystone winked out.

In the absolute blackness of the cave, Holram frowned at his host's fatigue. Gaelin's waning health was wicking away his energy, impairing his ability to focus. Holram heard the ragged breathing of his companions as they waited him out, neither one questioning his failure.

"But I thought," Felrina said through the darkness, "you were bringing *Camron* back. I assumed *he* would be Terrek's gift."

"And he is," Holram told her. "The physical form has been adapted to match the spirit Avalar recalled. I assure you, he is Camron. Who else *could* he be?"

Water gurgled as something large swam through it. A hard cough filled the chamber, a fourth set of lungs snatching the air in greedy gulps.

"Where am I?" asked a masculine voice. "*What* am I?"

Holram clenched his fist, and the Skystone roused, its glow spreading in tentative flickers. Avalar remained kneeling with her hands in the pool, her eyes screwed shut. An enormous male giant climbed the tarn's hidden steps before her. Leaning down, he grasped her wrists—to lift them dripping from the water.

Avalar started. "*Camron!*" she cried and threw her arms around him.

Felrina, gasping, sank to her knees. "Camron! It *is* you!"

Terrek appeared at the top of the chamber, followed by Roth. The latter slammed to a stop, stunned. Then Vyergin burst into view, and lastly Wren Neche. Terrek stumbled as he saw the newcomer, his jaw dropping. "Blazes!" he cried, vaulting at a run down the rocky shelves toward them, his expression incredulous as he beheld the warm pillar of living flesh that was his brother.

Gaelin blinked groggily as Holram receded from his mind, his body sinking to the floor. He smiled at the joy on Terrek's face, the unbridled relief gleaming through Felrina Vlyn's tears. Roth sat near the gap at the rear of the room, digging through his pack to pull out the artwork he had kept and cherished. His expression was elated, tears glimmering on his cheeks.

Vyergin whirled at the top of the ledges to vanish back into the stairwell. Moments later, he returned, red-faced and panting, dragging Avalar's bulky pack along with the object Roth had found.

Avalar clung to Camron Florne, water rippling over her arms from his long ruddy hair. *He even has freckles on his calves*, Gaelin noted with a grin.

"He is beautiful," Felrina said. Gaelin nodded at her, and at Terrek and Roth, while Avalar helped the newborn giant from the pool.

"My brother." Terrek choked on the words.

Vyergin supplied Avalar with clothing from her pack, a tunic and her extra pair of leggings. She held them against Camron's body, frowning as she checked the fit.

"You're so *big*," she muttered. "He made you too big, Camron!"

"Holram?" Terrek asked Gaelin, crouching near.

Gaelin shook his head. "No, just me." His smile faded at his friend's worried expression. "Holram needs to rest," Gaelin explained. "I'm so sick it drains *him*."

"Well," said Terrek. "Hopefully soon you'll be rid of each other."

"Or dead," Gaelin whispered.

Roth stood by Camron's thigh, grinning while he unrolled his painting for the giant to see. "Camron, look! Remember this? I rescued it from the museum!"

Camron glanced down. "Sorry, but I don't," he said and turned away.

"Holram?"

Gaelin jumped as Felrina snapped her fingers in front of his nose. She gestured sharply at Camron. "Why did you make him a giant?"

Gaelin sighed. Across the floor, Roth lowered the canvas slowly, his eyes bewildered as he stared at Camron's back. "I'm not Holram," Gaelin said, "so I can't tell you. You were here, and I wasn't."

"Wait, I am almost done!" said Avalar to the larger giant. She sawed at her spare tunic with her knife, slitting it along its sides. His movements clumsy, Camron took it from her grasp. He struggled to pull it over his head, with Avalar guiding his muscular arms through its generous sleeves. As she knelt to help him with the stretchy wool leggings, he towered above her, flexing his massive hands.

Once more, Roth positioned himself where the newly formed giant could see him. "Camron?" he asked softly. "Don't you recognize me?"

Camron rubbed his chin. "I regret I do not," he admitted. "I don't even know who I am or if this is really *me*?"

"It's you," Gaelin called to him. "A combining of magic created you. And Avalar's memory, too."

"So I was a ghost and now I'm . . . a giant?"

"Yes!" Roth said. "I think it was an accident."

"It doesn't matter," Terrek said. "There is no better gift that anyone could have given me. Gaelin, can Holram hear me? I'd like to thank him."

Gaelin nodded. "He hears you."

Terrek went to his gigantic sibling, grinning as he peered up. "No calling *me* 'little brother,' now," he said, lightly punching the giant's wrist. "That privilege belongs to me. *I'm* still the big brother!"

Camron's brown eyes twinkled. "I doubt you'd say that if you had seen me *before* I put these on." He motioned to the leggings. "But you *are* kind of puny, Terrek." He lifted his arms, raising his undersized tunic. Fascinated, Terrek stared at Camron's exposed midriff, the unblemished skin where a navel would normally be.

"Not much to cover up with, either!" Camron laughed, tugging at the fabric around his hips. "But at least the important parts are hidden."

Terrek snorted.

"Now the boots," Avalar said, squatting at his feet as Roth heaved her heavy pack next to her.

"See, Avalar?" Roth said. "I did as you asked; I wrapped the glass shard for you!" He stepped back and beamed at Camron. "I tied it to your pack."

She smiled. "Yes, I see, *Caven Roth*," she said, glancing up at Camron to see his reaction as she spoke the boy's name. "Lieutenant, are you well? You seem out of sorts."

"You'll need to cut those in front," said Vyergin, eyeing the boots she produced from her pack. "There's no way those will fit otherwise. Here, I'll do one. You do the other."

Trembling, Gaelin turned from both the reunion with Camron Florne and the growing despair on Caven Roth's face. Holram's consciousness thrashed weakly inside him. A tingle along his spine alerted him to the mist at the back of the chamber. Slowly a power uncoiled itself, a creeping chill like premature death, the bared fangs of oblivion about to bite.

Holram thrust the single word from the pit of his chest, up his throat, and from his mouth: "*Run!*"

His cry was lost, consumed by a reverberating howl, a dragon screaming in thunderous rage amid a bright crimson explosion. With an earsplitting roar, the entire top of the chamber crashed down.

Absolute darkness ensued. Holram, crushed by the weight of the mountain, imprisoned in Gaelin's unconscious flesh, could do nothing but wait as his enemy's laughter droned on.

Chapter 64

Coughing, Avalar fumbled through the dusty darkness for her weapon. Above her, something hard and unyielding brushed her hair. Reaching up, she felt stone, floating slabs of massive rock bobbing aside when she struggled to her knees. After a pause, she heard splashes as the heavy slabs dropped into the pool.

"Camron?" Avalar spoke softly, hoping her world's magic had also shielded him. With growing frustration, she cast about in the murk. "Leader Terrek?"

Her breathing rasped as the silence in the pit dragged out. She blundered across her half-buried pack, identifying the bloodstone shard, still intact and wrapped in leather.

Caven Roth, she thought, recalling his sad eyes and forced smile—the last thing she had seen. "I wish I could touch you," she whispered to the molded quartz. "No giant will believe my tale that bloodstone can be melted. Yet here you are. I beheld it myself how Holram's staff created you—so like the Bloodsword that comforted me when I was little."

Again she coughed. "Of all the giants, the weapon picked *me*. Avalar, child of Grevelin Mistavere and Alaysha Graysquall; you may as well know my names, for I shall perish soon. The sword Redeemer bade me come here. It gave courage to our Leader Thresher Govorian after he had lost all hope. Bloodstone drains giants, but the soul of the world compelled Redeemer to *give* to Govorian rather than take. Because of that sword, Govorian had strength enough to free his people, to snap necks and shatter rock. It guided his feet and gave him skill he never had before.

"I am telling you this," Avalar said, "for mayhap the world will survive my death, and another sword might be needed.

"Bloodstone *remembers*. Therefore, the words I say now shall be imprinted in you. Perhaps one day soon you will sing to another child the way Redeemer sang to me." Avalar rested her cheek on the shard's leather covering. Softly then, she crooned Redeemer's song, the same message and tune that the Bloodsword had long ago imparted to her. The language of giants was difficult for humans, both to master and to hear. The melody was dear to her, too cherished to risk exposing it to short-lived people who could not understand.

She choked on sobs as the echo of her ballad faded. *How many slaves died in this way*, she wondered. *Buried alive and all alone?* She listened to the sounds within the draining pool, the gurgle of water spilling around her knees. A deep grinding noise shook the rock below her, an irregular groan as the huge boulders settled along the tarn's bottom.

"Avalar?" Camron's voice queried abruptly. "I heard singing. What happened?"

"*Shh!*" Avalar almost laughed in her relief. "Erebos—mayhap his shadow lingers still. He wants us dead."

"I know he does," said Camron. "I'm aware of what he wants, and what Terrek hopes to do. Being a ghost had its advantages."

She held her breath, seeing a red dot winking in the blackness. Her throat went dry as the inky splotch beside it moved. "Erebos is here," she hissed. "High on the wall behind you. See that flicker?"

As he shifted closer, she caught his scent—sweet, like a newborn babe's. For a moment, she clung to his elbow.

"What should we do?" he whispered. "I'm not good at battling things. I've never been a warrior."

Avalar grimaced. "He cannot slay us without killing the world, and if Talenkai dies, he would be forced above the sky to fight Sephrym. I think our magic protects us. We are safe for now to find our friends." Reaching out, she explored the slabs of granite piled around her.

Grief entered Camron's voice. "I'm afraid to look."

"So am I, and yet we must." Avalar felt her way to where she had last seen Terrek, steering Camron in the opposite direction. "You check over there. Be careful and watch the water!"

"Felrina?" Camron called as loudly as he dared, and Avalar heard the rip of fabric from his tight garments as he was forced to climb the rocks. She blinked, catching sight of a misty glimmer, a sliver of colorful light. She tracked it past the outlines of two stones, one enormous slab tilted against another.

"I have found Gaelin," she said. Her hand touched his chest and felt the flutter of his heart. "He is alive!"

"This one is not," said Camron sadly. "It is the young man who showed me the picture. I was distracted. I should have noticed he was upset. I used to know him, didn't I? We were friends?"

Avalar fought back her tears. "Indeed, you were. He was a true and loyal companion, Camron." Roughly she heaved at the boulder in her way to pull it down. Kneeling next to Gaelin, she lifted him into her lap. "Erebos is here!" she murmured, bending low. "Gaelin, you must rouse so that Holram may defend us."

"This one, too," said Camron out of the darkness. "I don't . . . think he's Terrek."

Avalar bowed her head. "Keep searching!" she urged.

"I hardly got to talk to him. *Terrek!* Oh, Giant, what if he's dead, too?"

"Hush now!" said Avalar. "Take a breath, Camron. We do not *know* who is—" She jumped as coughing filled the chamber.

"Felrina Vlyn," Camron affirmed.

"I'm all right!" gasped Felrina. "I think I'm bleeding, though. My head hurts." She paused. "Terrek?"

"Shh!" Avalar watched the crimson sparkle flick sideways as Felrina spoke. "We are seeking to find him, Felrina. It is my fear he is under these rocks. Now be still. Erebos is here!"

"He can hear your thoughts, you know," said Felrina. "He's linked to us now, enjoying our pain while we die."

The ominous light bobbed along the far wall. "He is waiting," Avalar observed. "I wonder what for?"

"We're *suffering*; that's why!" Felrina snapped. "We're afraid, grieving, hurt, and he's a sponge soaking it up, gaining even more strength. The moment we lose hope and stop caring, *that's* when he'll strike. I notice he has the Blazenstone. Direct contact, too."

Gaelin moaned. Her gaze on Erebos, Avalar stroked the staff-wielder's hair. "Gaelin, Terrek is in danger!" she said, scowling at the tremor in her voice. "The Destroyer is here holding the wizard's stone. Mayhap he prepares another attack!"

Holram's agitated voice spoke through Gaelin's mouth. "I cannot *move*," he said. "Erebos has drawn Gaelin's consciousness into his stone. This shell is mindless now; it will not stir."

Avalar, inhaling deeply, fought for calm. "Can you brighten your staff at least? So we may see if any of our friends yet live?"

She blinked when Mornius flashed through the gloom, its radiance spilling over a mound of shattered rock.

Now she beheld the crushed torso of Caven Roth, his surprise frozen forever on his lifeless face. Another companion lay pinned as well, with only his legs visible. Beyond the rubble, Erebos's dragon crouched, its red eyes glowing, the Earth gem glinting from one raised claw. *If Gaelin's in that stone,* she thought, *how do we get him out?*

Avalar staggered to her feet above the staff-wielder's body, confronting the thing that had slain young Roth. *Vyergin, too,* she decided, glancing again at the visible remains of the second man.

"Avalar?" Camron asked.

"Keep looking," she said. Erebos's shadow loomed closer now, his glistening black wings unfurling.

Avalar shrugged on her pack and buckled her sword belt tight over her hips. Leaning down, she scooped Gaelin into her arms, curling his fingers around his staff. "Mornius," she identified it in his ear. "No matter what happens, do *not* let it go."

Camron stared. "What are you doing?"

Avalar held up her hand, stopping him as he began to follow. "*No*, Camron! Stay here and defend Felrina. Find Terrek and take care of the others while I lead this monster from our midst! I have the staff; he will pursue me if I go."

She started climbing, her eyes on Erebos as the throb of her pulse quickened in her throat, the dragon's horned head tracking her every move.

A breeze thrust at her from behind, compelling her to hurry. She focused straight ahead, ignoring the looming shadow as she scrambled up the rocks. With all her strength, Avalar struggled to climb, ascending to where she hoped the chamber's exit would be.

Chapter 65

Through the blackness, Gaelin perceived Holram's imminent failure, the warder's power draining from him, worn down by the heat in his bones. Erebos was stronger, a fully mature warder, while Holram was not. In moments, Gaelin's flesh would fail.

He faltered and darkness seized him, tearing him from his body. His inner self flew across the room, past the giants oblivious to his plight, to slam into the Blazenstone, a void without direction, warmth, or sound.

Strands of crystal opened before him, red glassy threads beneath a mineral sky. Screaming mutely, Gaelin swung his mental fists at the crimson currents. Yet still the quartz's inferno possessed him, its flames lashing at the giants' reflections within its depths. His life force ebbed as he resisted, desperate to return to his body.

There was a lurch when Avalar started climbing, but it was Holram who rode Mornius's erupting fire, who stretched arms of power across the darkness of the chamber—the warder seeking to follow him and retrieve his spirit. An explosion shook the Earth gem when Holram pierced it, and then vibrations of a roar, the silent clash of titans as Holram threw himself at his foe.

The two dragon shapes twined at the Blazenstone's core, fangs like lightning stabbing at each other.

No! thought Gaelin, straining toward the limp figure in Avalar's grasp. Holram hurled his power again, and still again, each effort jolting Gaelin as Holram strove to shake him loose.

"*Stop it!*"

From far away, Gaelin heard his voice, felt his cry from his human throat. His consciousness recoiled with a blast of wind, flinging him back into his body. He found his staff in his hand, with Avalar's fingers around his own. At once he plunged his awareness into Mornius's gem. With his mind, Gaelin caught at Holram in the Blazenstone, freeing the one who had battled to rescue him.

He moaned as Avalar pressed him close. Blinded by fury, Holram rampaged through his flesh, for at long last the warder had seen combat and wanted more.

Gaelin opened his eyes, wincing at the pressures within him. Avalar was carrying him, holding him with one arm while she hauled herself up the rocks. "I cannot stop!" she replied, straddling a massive boulder.

"No, *run!*" Still disoriented, Gaelin grunted as Holram rammed against the barriers in his mind. *No!* he thought to the warder. *Your enemy almost killed you!*

Avalar jumped from one slab to the next. She scrambled from the rocks, then broke into a run down the stairs and into the tunnel, racing past Silva's shrouded body, the walls splintering as she went. The air hissed with the rush of indrawn breath as Erebos's dragon flung itself in pursuit, its claws outstretched, the strikes of its great wings reducing the shaft behind them to rubble.

"*Faster!*" Gaelin panted, flopping over the crook of the giant's elbow. Through the fracturing tunnel she sprinted, her breathing ragged in her throat. Light burst from his staff, brightening the passage so she could see. Erebos's dragon heaved its bulk from side to side at their backs, crushing the shaft around it, crumbling the stone at Avalar's feet.

She bounded forward when the floor collapsed, her muscles flexing, her magic lending speed and strength as she dodged the Destroyer's darting head, the heat from its wide-open jaws.

A reptilian foot shot in front of them and curled, its talons flaring as it swiped at her legs. Howling, Avalar snatched out her sword and hacked at the claw—and with a sharp crack, her weapon shattered. Dropping its hilt, she leapt over the foot as it flailed again, and holding tight to Gaelin, somersaulted out of the tunnel's mouth and onto its ledge. As she bounced to her feet, Gaelin spotted a rocky protrusion on the wall facing them, and beyond it what looked like another passage—a glimmer of hope. The mountain's throat lay before them, the roar of the river reverberating from below. They would have to jump.

"No!" Gaelin cried. As the floor disintegrated beneath them, Avalar launched herself at a flat run, hurtling across the cavern's expanse, straining for the distant ledge. Her fingertips brushed the stone; she missed her mark and fell.

"No, *no!*" cried Gaelin.

"*Avaunt, storm!*" Avalar shouted.

There was an explosion from above as they plummeted, the thunderbolt that was Erebos slamming into the wall in a hail of debris. A second detonation shook the cave, splitting the mountain's core from top to bottom. Gaelin yelped when something hard cut his cheek. He caught a glimpse of Chesna's wounded granite yawning open, the Destroyer overhead folding his wings to dive.

A deafening torrent covered the banks below, the Shukaia flooding the base of the cavern. The turbulent current surged up to meet them, punching out chunks of loosened rock.

Avalar plunged into the river and sank deep in a blur of tiny bubbles, a silvery cloud of sediment rising and roiling as her feet hit the bottom. In flashes of gyrating foam, her strong legs thrust, kicking them toward the surface.

Blackness struck the water like the fall of a mountain, the force of it driving them back down, rolling them battered and bruised along the river's floor. There was a jerk as their pursuer's teeth closed on Avalar's pack. As she wriggled from its straps and Gaelin grabbed at her shoulder, a glimmer of crimson slipped past them. The bloodstone shard shed its leather covering to spin free in the water, its razor-sharp edges glittering red. Avalar scissored her legs and pounced, seizing the crystal blade by the notches at its base.

She pulled at Gaelin as her feet gained purchase on a rock, helping him to climb as well, her waterlogged boots finding another higher step followed by a ledge. Avalar raised him onto the bank under the wingbeats of their attacker and then hastened up behind. Her nose already bloody as the bloodstone she clenched leached her strength, she lifted the blade high—to impale the dragon crashing down.

Erebos reared back, straining for escape. Yet the bloodstone held him as Avalar gripped it with all her might, the shard pulsing in her hands, gorging on the warder's great power.

Screaming, abandoning his dragon shape, Erebos threw himself back and forth, shifting from wolf to bear to slash at Avalar with his jaws. The changing forms melted into greasy tar, the warder's weight yanking the weapon from Avalar's grasp and flinging it across the stones.

Still the Destroyer fought, blackness rippling along his length as he struggled, his shapeless mass shrieking, his inky shadow sticking to the wall.

Then Gaelin saw it, how the bloodstones within Chesna's ruptured granite sucked the warder in, the countless orbs latching onto his hoarded energy and devouring it.

Rock shattered, the rift crumbling inside, dragging Erebos deeper. The warder screamed as the orbs clung to him and drank, the clusters of gems draining his strength, feasting on his frantic blasts of power.

Swaying on their tapered ends, more stones extended to ensnare their prey as Erebos thrashed against the mountain. With a shriek, the Destroyer pummeled the cavern's interior with black flame, with formless fists of desperate rage.

Stalactites dropped to pierce the water, embedding themselves forever in the river's floor. The vaulted ceiling parted down the middle, its rock splitting, radiance from above spilling in.

Gaelin trembled as Avalar clasped him protectively, his gaze raised to the blinding glimpse of sky. "Avalar, he's punching *through*! If he reaches outside the mountain, he—"

She gasped. "I know not what to *do*!"

"*Throw me!*" yelled Gaelin. He braced himself in her arms, gripping Mornius as she sprang to her feet, his attention fixed on the crimson gem throbbing at Erebos's core. "He can't focus without the Blazenstone! Avalar, I can get it! Throw me!"

She raised him over her shoulders and, with a shout, flung him at the warder. He tumbled through the air, his arms wrapped tight around his knees, screaming as the cavern went pitch-black, as a sudden burning acid tore at his skin, melting it, and flaying him alive.

His elbow hit something small and solid within the fire. He grabbed for it, striking hard with his staff, swatting it—

Mornius splintered in his hand from end to end, falling to nothingness.

Gaelin struck the river, the water closing over his head. The Skystone, released from its iron claws, capered and danced along with the current, the Blazenstone skittering and leaping beside it. He saw the red quartz flash a final echo of Erebos's spite, then vanish among the rocks.

Fingers circled his wrists, coaxing him upward. With tender care, Avalar placed him atop the rocky ledge and clambered up next to him.

He glimpsed a shadow on the wall above, a transparent tapestry of blackness fading to gray. Erebos snarled feebly at the bloodstones, the little spheres doubling in size as they fed.

Killing him.

Gaelin lay stunned next to the river, raising the lumps that had been his hands. He was shaking and could not stop, curling into a ball.

Gray flakes dotted the filtered light of the cavern, floating upward as Erebos's husk slowly dissolved.

Avalar nudged the Skystone against the charred stump where his thumb had been. "*Gaelin!*" She sobbed his name, afraid to touch him and hurt him more. "*Heal yourself!*"

He longed to blink his lidless eyes. He had no lips to form words, no tongue to taste the air wafting down. The flesh was sloughing from his bones. All he knew was the pain in his mouth, the numbness of his body as he begged with his thoughts to die.

"*No,*" said Holram's voice deep within him. "*No, you will stay.*"

Chapter 66

Gaelin squinted at the daylight flooding into the mountain's crater. There was only death for him now, and the pain it would cost to get there. All his life he had suffered in silence, for anything else meant drawing attention to himself. Yet here under the sun's eye, he was screaming frantically, thumping the stumps of his hands. Tongueless as he was, his guttural sounds did not carry. Even the river's gurgle was louder than he was.

Avalar cried for him as he lay twitching beside her. He longed for death, and though he tried to gesture toward the knife at her belt, his attempts only intensified her grief.

She'll remember me like this, Gaelin thought bitterly. *Avalar and all her people, too, for as long as there are giants.*

"Ponu!" Avalar's voice cracked as she shouted. "*Help* us!"

Her hand hovered in front of him, full of the mushrooms that contained the poisoned spores, the ones he had seen in the burrow that had led them into the mountain. The giant squeezed her hand, and a brownish liquid ran down.

"Drink this," she begged. "Please."

He swallowed, gratitude swelling in his breast that his friend was helping him to die. He tasted nothing, and still the pain in his mouth sawed on. Then Avalar touched Mornius's gem to what remained of his right palm.

He wept that his stubborn heart kept beating, the Skystone's fire pulsing in vain. Mornius existed far away now in another place. All he knew was numbness in his hands and the awareness of how helpless he was.

Through the filtered light, Avalar surged erect and stepped back. Then a pair of worn boots took her place, followed by knees dropping to the granite and a white swirl of feathered wings.

Fingers splayed in front of him. Ponu's face, frowning and out of focus, wavered in his sight. "You did well, Gaelin," the elf-mage said. Gaelin shivered at a vibration against his flesh he barely felt, a current from Ponu's palms. "But you are not alone. Others are also hurt and require healing. They need Holram to help them—through *you.*"

"I gave him this," Avalar said, uncurling her fingers to reveal the crushed fungi. "It is something I remembered. I know not why."

"Very good, Giant," said Ponu. "Your mother, Alaysha, was a skilled healer. Perhaps her memories guided you. For sleep you would need more—twice that much. But you eased his hurt. You are a caring friend. Now I need you to remove what is left of his clothing. He cannot heal like this."

"Clothing?" Avalar echoed. "Where?"

"Look closely. Fabric contains thread, while flesh does not." Ponu made his way to the river's receding edge. With his legs braced above the flowing current, he stretched his bare arm out, his palm turned to the water. The elf shut his eyes and pointed at Gaelin, who opened his charred and blistered mouth as cooling rain sluiced down. "Hurry, Giant," he urged.

Gently Avalar tugged at Gaelin, her probing touch detecting the ends of long tatters of bloody fabric and lifting them carefully away.

"You needn't worry about hurting him," said Ponu softly. "I assure you, he cannot feel it."

"I believe I have removed it all," she whispered at last, her features stark white.

"Avalar!"

The ringing call came from high above. The giant peered up from the base of the massive cliff, relief flooding her face. "Leader Terrek!"

Ponu grinned. "I was hoping he still lived. We can use him."

Don't go! Gaelin wanted to say, but his mouth was empty, his lips and tongue gone. He raised his lump of a hand in protest.

"Only for a moment," Ponu said, and Gaelin lost himself in the mage's calming gaze. "To save time, I must carry your companions down here, Gaelin. I would help you to sleep to spare you this torment, but you are so badly injured you might never wake up."

Gaelin stared at the sky. All his life he had known hurt and endured it. Yet, as Ponu drew away, the anguish was too much and he writhed, hating the pitiful noises that issued from his throat.

Ponu rose in a rush of wings, a single white feather spiraling free in the sunlight.

"*It is enough, Gaelin,*" said Holram from within him. "*You, my faithful friend, do not deserve this.*"

Make it stop! Gaelin cried mentally. *Please. I'll do anything*!

Abruptly other hurts replaced his own. The granite suffered beneath him. Mount Chesna was shrinking and near death. Glad for the distraction, Gaelin thrust his focus into the volcano's crippled heart.

His awareness found the Blazenstone in a rocky crevice, its carmine ire seeping poison into Chesna's husk. Holram, reaching through him, purified the Earth gem, washing all traces of Erebos from its depths.

"*It is solid,*" the warder whispered among his thoughts. "*Malleable minerals. A rock cannot resist me the way you do. There can be no victory here, no healing for you until you forgive yourself. You cannot thrive if you despair.*"

Gaelin moaned as the warder uncovered his deepest hurts, the torment he carried inside that dwarfed his physical pain.

"*Let it go,*" Holram said in his mind. "*Stop denying who you are. You have Jaegar Othelion's blood in your veins!*"

Gaelin bumped at the Skystone with his wrist, his burnt flesh drawing a smear of wet crimson across the floor. With his fingerless palm covering the stone, he listened to the water, the gurgling rush of life between the rocks. He imagined sweeping along in that current, washing free and unfettered through the broken layers of the mountain.

A colorful pulse soothed the stinging of his eyes, sending surges of coolness over his flesh.

Time lost meaning. Somewhere along the way, he came to acknowledge that Holram was right. He could be all the things that he wished for, as courageous and true as he had always yearned to be.

What was it Terrek said about his never failing? Yet he *had* failed many times, and he knew it. Perhaps Terrek had not noticed, but he had.

Yet there was Hawk, whom he had healed, Vyergin and Terrek, too, and Roth. He had braved greater illness to succor Felrina Vlyn, had stood at the brink of death and taunted her father.

Seth Lavahl was dead, yet not buried. His stepfather's abuse circled endlessly through his thoughts. The poisonous words had become a part of him, disguised as an old friend.

"*Hear* me," Holram said. "*They are not your friends. Let them go.*"

Gaelin nodded. He ached to embrace the freedom of the sky overhead. Beyond the mountain's shattered dome, high above the clouds, he felt Holram spreading his arms and yearning for home.

Through the warder's senses, he discovered the scattered black-robes, the fleeing followers of Erebos lying dead where Ponu had left them. He found scores of dachs emaciated and abandoned, dying in their pens.

With a single flex of power, Gaelin brought the warped victims of Erebos to wholeness, freed at last from the merciless clutches of the Destroyer's cult.

Caven Roth, sprawled dead beside the shattered pool, rose restored, his shoulders shaking as he snatched his first breaths.

Gaelin saw the massive boulder lift from Brant Vyergin, who staggered to his feet, slapping dust from his tunic and cloak.

Felrina Vlyn's cut brow—healed. As Ponu lowered Terrek onto the riverbank, Holram, with a flick of a thought, knitted Terrek's cracked skull and kneecap.

Gaelin surrendered to the warder's persistent pressure, the gentle flame of his touch. Tingles spread throughout his body, surge after surge of itchy coolness. Something firm pushed against his teeth and he tasted blood, then caught the lingering smell of sulfur.

With difficulty, he blinked, his new eyelids sliding over eyes as dry as gritpaper. Terrek crouched by his side, covering him with something—a blanket.

Tendrils of coolness stroked his firming scalp. With power-heightened nerves, Gaelin felt hair growing on his head, heard the rustle of his new mane sliding down his cheek.

"Terrek!" Camron called excitedly. "It's Caven and Captain Vyergin! They're *alive!*"

Gaelin drew a shaky breath. "We're here with you," Terrek told him, smiling.

Gaelin stiffened as cramps seized his calves. Under his muscles, his bones creaked as they lengthened. "*Just a nudge and not too much,*" Holram reassured him. "*You shall now be what you would have been, had you been properly cared for.*"

Gaelin closed his eyes, sighing in relief that he finally could. *A dream, it has to be!* he thought. *I can wield a sword and ride a horse? I can be a warrior and walk among men?*

"*It was never your size restricting you,*" Holram interjected. "*You always had it in you to be anything you wanted.*"

With a shudder, Gaelin fought to sit up. Hands pressed him flat, preventing him from throwing off his blanket.

"Wait," Terrek urged with a laugh, "there are ladies present!"

As Gaelin relaxed against the stone, Terrek continued, "Wren and Roth are fetching our gear. You still have extra clothing, I hope?"

"Yes." Gaelin grinned at the sound of his voice, at the feel of his tongue on the roof of his mouth. He raised his arms, marveling at the firmness of new muscle below the smooth skin. In vain, he searched his belly for the bumps of scar tissue Nithra's knife had left.

"Everything healed?" asked Terrek. "Erebos is gone, Gaelin. I don't know how you did it. Was it all Holram, or did Avalar help?"

Ponu descended with a flutter of wings, carrying Caven Roth. The youth's face was pale, sadness still glimmering behind his brown eyes.

"Camron didn't want to burden Ponu with his size," Felrina said. "He's going to make the descent through the tunnels, bringing the packs."

"In his mind, he's still a human, trying to be a giant," Ponu mused. "You, Leader Florne, should observe him well. And you also, Avalar. We have no way to know how changed he is."

"He is Camron Florne and nothing else!" Avalar scanned the boulders at her feet. Then, her mien triumphant, she descended into the river, flashing them a grin as she lifted the dripping shard of bloodstone she had used as a sword. "It does not drain me now," she told them. "Mayhap it has gorged enough for one day. I know this is not Govorian's weapon, yet I will keep it with me and cherish it, for it has shown me its greatness. It, too, deserves a place at Freedom Hall."

Gaelin was careful to tuck the blanket around him as he levered himself to a sitting position. He glanced at Ponu, feeling Holram's control once more take his throat.

"It would appear," said Holram, "that I am still trapped: the last of my kind on this world."

"That *is* a problem," Ponu agreed. "No offense, but I believe we all hoped that whatever force would rid us of Erebos would take *you* away as well."

Holram hesitated, and Gaelin winced at the rapid acceleration of the warder's thoughts within him. "You bear an object that will help me break free," Holram said to Ponu. "Though I perceive from your reaction this is not your intent. Come, Sephrym's Chosen, bring it forth and show me."

With a puzzled expression, Ponu examined himself, patting his vest, feeling the pouches dangling from his belt. Then abruptly he stopped.

He gazed past Gaelin into nothingness as the others gathered around to see. Slowly he delved into the pocket above his hip and, with a grim glance at his audience, drew forth a glittering crystal sphere. "This comes from my world," he said. "A young human in my care brought this out of safe hiding by mistake. It should not be here, and it is not meant for you."

Holram wrested the orb from Ponu's reluctant grasp.

"Time Crystals," Ponu explained, his features pale. "The facets are naturally occurring and random. They are a wild and dangerous magic, difficult to guide, even for me. This is *not* for you!"

"Yes, it is," Holram said, sifting through Ponu's thoughts. "I shatter the stone and the power releases on impact. One flash, and I ride its fire. White lightning, so beautiful. Will it take me home?"

Ponu nodded gravely. "Not just you," he said. With impatient fingers, he flipped back his white hair. "Gaelin also would ride that fire to the airless void you call home. He would freeze instantly and die."

"It doesn't matter," Gaelin told Ponu, shaking free of Holram's grip. "I made my life count. That's enough for me. I'm dying anyway; let me go."

"You will do no such thing," Terrek said roughly.

Camron appeared, wading around an immense boulder. He rose

dripping from the water onto the bank, his massive hands clutching their bedraggled gear.

Gaelin recognized his pack with a surge of relief. He took his single possession from the giant and quickly dressed under the blanket in the same tattered gray tunic he had worn when he murdered Seth Lavahl. The activity briefly comforted him, easing his dread.

His death was coming, yet the chill down his back was not fear. All along, he had been conscious of its advance through his flesh. Yet as he faced it at last, he had what very few others did—the knowledge that his end would protect the world.

"You won't," said Terrek. "We'll find another way."

Gaelin fingered Ponu's crystal. "How long do you think Holram will last here without doing serious damage?" he asked. "I'm sorry, Terrek."

He stood, letting the blanket crumple around his feet. Gathering his courage, he tried to smile. In his chest, Holram tensed in alarm. *"Gaelin, no. Listen to him. There must be another way."*

Gaelin watched his hand rise quickly and fall, the white explosion blinding him as the crystal struck the stone.

Caught in the heart of a whirling kaleidoscope, he glimpsed a thousand different places and moments whipping around him, with the white-speckled lens at the end rushing toward him to snatch him up.

From the mouth of Mount Chesna far beneath his kicking feet came Avalar's strident scream cut short. Somehow, he still perceived it with his warder's understanding: seized by the brilliance of the crystal's flash, the young giant, too, had winked out.

Chapter 67

*C*aught fast by alien magic, Gaelin ignored the countless times and places flashing across his sight—the remnants of Ponu's ruined crystal. Transfixed, he gaped at the starry endlessness spreading out before him.

A vision filled his mind of a pathway high on a mountain, the Companion's disk shining silver behind it to dominate the midnight sky. Snow swirled and a figure appeared, his golden eyes gleaming, his blurred features resembling Terrek's. The being held out his hand, gripping Gaelin's forearm. Puzzled, Gaelin met the other's proud stare and returned the clasp.

A tearing pain ripped through his chest as Holram let him go, breaking from him at last, abandoning him for freedom. The separation left a tang of metal in his mouth, the taste of the warder's regret.

He tumbled end over end, a feather in a freezing void, his lungs desperate for breath. He was fading fast, his consciousness fraying, his limbs stretching toward the misty barrier that rushed to meet him.

A white shield of power snapped into existence around his body, sending jolts of fire through his flesh to keep his blood pumping. The burning was familiar yet stronger than he had ever known and beyond ancient, potent and wholly mastered.

A whirling gray funnel rose from the churning clouds under him, a spout of furious wind, pale lightning licking through its core.

Still flailing, Gaelin plunged into its heart, toward a ring of distant water. Down he sank, buffeted by gentle currents. He caught glimpses of wings as ephemeral as the wind, of thick, arched necks and brilliant eyes. From the corner of his vision, he saw snatches of occasional detail, jaws bristling with fangs and diamond scales reflecting the sky. He slid from one pair of muscular shoulders to the next, and as he descended, he felt his numb body returning to life.

Thunder rolled long and loud, building to a crescendo, a massive voice speaking one word: "*Live!*"

Gaelin dropped through the storm of dragonesque forms, with one visible directly beneath him, its powerful neck thrust forward and great wings spiraling him toward the widening patch of sea.

Something floated in the circle of water far below. It grew swiftly as the great beast carried him down.

It was a ship. A very large ship, shaped like the blade of a sword.

SIGHING, TERREK LEANED his elbows on his knees and puzzled at the roll of canvas in his hands. "You're giving this to me, why?" he asked.

Roth shrugged testily. "I don't need it anymore."

"If this is about Camron," Terrek said, "I think you should wait and give him some time."

"I don't want it; that's all!" said Roth. "And it's not what you think, either. I don't care if he ever remembers me. He's alive! That's what counts."

"Good boy." Vyergin winked. "No point in wasting your days trying to control what you can't."

Grinning, Terrek nodded. "Words of wisdom," he said. "Come spring, we'll take a little trip to Marin and see if we can locate a hat for you like the one your father wore."

Roth's eyes went wide. "Really?" He beamed at them, the jaunty bounce back in his step as he ducked into the patched tent.

"Strange lad," Vyergin observed. "Life won't ever be dull as long as he's around."

"*Laori*," mumbled Terrek.

Felrina, beside him, stretched her hands toward the flames. "Ponu should be here soon," she said, glancing skyward. "Must I go to Heartwood?"

Terrek frowned at the wistful note in her voice, the glint of dread in her gaze. "Yes, and you will do fine, Felrina."

"All the other black-robes are *dead!*" She choked on the last word. "Maybe I deserve that, too."

"And you *did* die," he reminded her. "Felrina, those other priests picked a fight with the wrong elf. The same one who went out of his way to save you. You have the strongest mage on the planet on your side. I don't think you need to worry, do you?"

"I guess you're right." She paused. "T-Terrek?"

He inclined his chin. Then Vyergin rose discreetly from scrubbing the pans and, whistling, sauntered away.

"Will you and I . . . ? I mean . . ." Felrina ducked her head. "Oh, never mind."

He drew a deep breath. "*We* shouldn't obsess about things beyond our control, either. You need to go to Heartwood and endure the elves' judgment. I need to take these men home and help rebuild Kideren. *Time*," he stressed. "What you did—I can't just erase that like it never happened. I need to digest what has happened between us. And I think *you* do, too."

"And *I* think," Ponu said as he strode through the trees to join them, "all this is making me hungry." He grunted when he spied the washed dishes piled by the little blaze. "Ah, but I missed it!"

"You have not said." Terrek strode around the fire to confront the winged elf. "Has Gaelin's body been recovered yet? I would like to have him buried next to Silva at Vale Horse. I was hoping you would have word."

"Bury his body?" Ponu arched a brow. "Interesting. Is this how your people honor your heroes?"

Terrek stepped back. "Gaelin's alive?"

"Yes," Ponu said. "Very much so. I will be taking him to Heartwood soon as well, Felrina, so you might see him there."

"Why Heartwood?" Terrek asked. "Are the elves planning some kind of special . . ." He trailed off.

"Gaelin is dying, Terrek Florne," said Ponu. "It is my hope the Seeker elves might have a remedy . . . something to keep him alive at least for a while."

"Oh, Gaelin!" Eyes brimming, Felrina covered her mouth.

"This isn't a time for tears," Ponu told her. "Your staff-wielder not only rode lightening and touched the sky, he flew an *Azkharren*, too. Something no human has ever done! He has found himself, Felrina Vlyn." Reaching out, he clasped her arm. "And now, my dear, it is your turn."

Chapter 68

valar blinked to clear her sight. A rank smell filled her nostrils, the lumpy objects beneath her knees sinking under her weight. She made out the blacker darkness of the stone walls around her and caught the faint scent of dirt mingled with the stronger reek of decay. Her gorge rose as she realized there were corpses beneath her, the husks of her people in various stages of decomposition.

A repetitive crack sounded overhead and, with it, an occasional grunt or moan. Curious, dreading what she would find, Avalar crept up the side of the trench.

The tableau on the rocky shelf above her appeared frozen at first, the figure in chains motionless as she drew near. She shivered in horror as she recognized her surroundings, and knew who the giants were who lay dead in the pit.

A large grizzle-haired male in the garments of a slave knelt in a patch of unnatural light, his wrists bound by heavy links to a thick and bloodied stake. She saw his manacles first, his drooping head with its matted hair, his cheek leaning against the post.

He looks like Trentor, she thought wildly. A chill ran tingling along her spine as she remembered the paintings of Trentor's legendary father at Freedom Hall.

This is Thresher Govorian; he has to be! She ducked low when the whip struck close to her own head. The leader's spirit was clearly broken, his body nigh to death after cycles of toil. She could not tell what lurked behind him other than more gloom. Once again came the whistle and *crack*, blood spattering as the iron balls struck.

Ponu's crystal did this. I am in the past! Grimly she nodded, pondering hard. The slavers meant to strip the flesh from their unruly captive, and soon it would be Govorian lying dead on the pile below her.

He is supposed to find the sword and save his people! Avalar cringed as the hideous whip struck and cut. Govorian's eyes were slitted, his shoulders quivering as he gasped for breath. Mocking human laughter echoed from the dimness.

Dizzy and shaken from her unexpected transition, Avalar lowered herself back into the ditch. She positioned her pack beside the bodies, her eyes watering at the stench as she fixed her attention on the wrapped shard of crystal that had helped to bring the Destroyer down. *It is bloodstone—gorged on a warder's power*, she recalled, and she had imprinted it with all the knowledge the Bloodsword Redeemer had given her. *I even taught it the song.*

Carefully she unwrapped the blade-shaped quartz, its magic thrumming beneath her hands. As the relentless whip cracked on, she worked swiftly to modify the shard, cutting a wide strip of leather with her knife and wrapping the base of the crystal, twisting the hide around and crisscrossing it before tucking it tight. *Now you have a proper hilt*, she thought to the makeshift weapon. *You are not Redeemer, but mayhap you will do, for Govorian needs our aid now, else he shall not live to find the sword!*

Avalar climbed the wall of the trench, crouching as low as possible until she squatted again under the gory stake.

Reaching up, her fingers trembling, she stroked Govorian's wrist. Then, as soundlessly as she could, she worked her knife's tip between two of the links holding him and, twisting hard, pried them apart.

Govorian's gaze shifted as his pain-ridden mind registered the unexpected vibrations. In his brittle glare, fear and suspicion sparked and gradually ebbed, giving way to sudden hope as she quietly separated the links, laying the two ends of the massive chain on the stone.

"You are *free!*" Avalar whispered fiercely, sliding the bloodstone blade as close to him as she could. His eyes widened as he took in the object by his knee.

"Have courage, great Leader! Please," she said. "You are the one who saves us, and you will succeed, you will! Behold the sword! It is already filled with power; it will not drain you, it will give you strength! Escape now and free your people!"

She swiped at her tears. *If only you could have lived, too,* she thought. *You helped so many of us, but not yourself!*

She sank back as he bent, groping through the dust for the sword. Like other sires and grandsires, he would surrender his place on the last Skimmer. For the sake of the children and their mothers, he would stay behind.

"Now you can fight," she murmured as he grasped the weapon's crude hilt. "You shall defeat them, great-hearted one. You will win!"

Avalar sighed as she emerged from the memory, tears running down her cheeks. She focused on her father's worried frown, and on Trentor peering at her across the granite table.

"Because of *us*! Gaelin and Ponu, Terrek Florne and . . . and me. Because of all we did, Thresher Govorian found hope!"

"Do you remember anything else?" Trentor asked. She shook her head, her gaze on the easel that Freedom Hall's curator had set up next to them. As the artist labored over the canvas, his fine brush mirrored her vision, re-creating Govorian's ordeal with loving touches of flax-oil paint.

"There *was* more," she said at the curator's glance. She closed her eyes. In her mind, the memory was clear—Govorian's tortured body gathering itself, the great leader clambering to his feet next to the stake, his back and shoulders spraying blood as he whirled in his broken chains to face his tormentors, the homemade sword pulsing in his battered hands.

"I heard his cry," said Avalar. "His roar was like thunder; he was so angry! He charged with the weapon held high, and the shard cut through them as if they were not even there." She shivered.

"That is when I located her and brought her back." Ponu entered the hall through the arched doorway. "Thresher never caught sight of her, Master First. Your great sire beheld Redeemer; that is all. Nothing has been harmed by her journey."

"No. Were you not listening?" Avalar asked. "It was not the Bloodsword; it was melted stone. He must have discovered the true sword during the battle. Redeemer is here, is it not? In Freedom Hall. That would mean he did eventually find it."

Avalar, shaking off the painful memory, met her father's marveling gaze across the table, and Camron seated next to her, with his human features that she had loved. "Redeemer has a *gray* hilt," she said. "Petrified bottomwood."

"Avalar," said her father, his eyes twinkling. "You are correct about one thing. Redeemer does indeed rest upstairs in its case, and it has the beautiful hilt you describe, too. I suggest at the conclusion of this meeting you go and take a peek at the sword. Mayhap examine more closely the leather the quartz is lying on. Avalar, Redeemer's fancy hilt was fashioned later by a skilled crafter. The blade Govorian wielded had a leather haft."

"But . . ." Avalar sprang to her feet. "You are telling me that *I* brought him the sword?"

Camron bobbed his head and grinned. He was larger than her father, larger even than Kurgenrock, her uncle, as his ill-fitting, borrowed trousers and tunic proved. "It would seem," he said, "you are a hero now, too, and not just Gaelin."

Flabbergasted, she dropped to her seat. "*I* brought the sword! The whole time I was carrying it, I never . . . So when it spoke to me . . . sang to me when I was little, it was . . ."

"It was merely repeating the things you taught it, my dear," Ponu said. He smiled. "I suppose I should have believed you."

"And the others?" she inquired. "Leader Terrek and . . ."

"Safe and sound, Avalar," said Camron. "I was there to bid farewell to my brother before Ponu *transferred* me here. I know Terrek plans to journey to Tierdon to swap the shan for his horses. He told me that much. We didn't get to talk very long."

Avalar nodded, glaring at the table's granite surface beyond her folded hands. "But not Gaelin. He never returned?"

"Now Erebos is dead and Holram is gone," said Ponu, "and the world is safe. All is as it should be, with only Talenkai's magic here. And my own."

"Human magic too," sang a piping voice, breaking the tension. Avalar smiled at the familiar little human skipping into the room.

"*Kray?*" She gaped at Ponu. "*This* is the child you are caring for? The one I rescued?"

"Indeed." Ponu grinned as the little boy dashed to the table and climbed up Grevelin's leg. "Though, for his sake, that arrangement has changed. He's now in your father's care. Grevelin has agreed to let Kray stay here. At least until he is older."

Avalar looked from one face to the next. Everything had fallen into place, except for one thing—her future. She was back where she began, on Hothra Isle, after months of tasting freedom and learning the Swordslore from Roshar Navaren at Tierdon.

The new blade Father has promised me, she thought. *What use will it serve here?*

"Avalar, you have done well representing our people in a hostile land," Trentor said. "And this strapping fellow that Ponu brought here is correct; you are a hero. There shall be a feast in your honor tonight in the courtyard, to celebrate the one who delivered the weapon that set us all free. But still I sense a restlessness in you."

"I want more." She paused, wincing at her own impudence. "I am sorry, Father," she said to Grevelin. "Leader Trentor, it is not enough for me to just exist! I have gained skill with my weapon. I have striven very hard to master it."

"With the slavers gone," Trentor said, "mayhap the time will come when giants can return to Skythorn Valley in the south and replant our grain crops there. But you have been away, Avalar. You have not heard of the reports we have received from our ships. The Sherkon Raider fleet has been sighted near Thalus. It is my fear the pirates might try to take that land."

Slowly Avalar exhaled as she devoured her leader's every word.

"The Raiders pose a threat to us whenever we sail," he continued. "They are fierce fighters, Avalar, a greater danger by far than the Sundor Khan in the North, for the Raiders care nothing for the Circle. They live only for the hunt. They would not hesitate to slay a giant, even at the expense of the world. I will need strong warriors to protect our ships and, if necessary, defend Thalus. You are familiar with that land. I am quite sure your skills will be an asset."

"I can help, too," Camron ventured. "But someone will need to teach me to use a sword."

Avalar smiled. "I can do that. We shall commence your training tomorrow." With hope in her heart, she faced her leader. "Yes! You have my sword. If my father allows it."

"Ha!" Grevelin barked a laugh over the little human on his lap. "As if I could ever deny you?"

Avalar opened her mouth to answer. Then she stopped.

Her uncle Kurgenrock had crept in behind Ponu and bent to

whisper in his ear. At Ponu's reaction, she leapt to her feet, her stone chair flipping backward with a crash. Ignoring it, Avalar broke away from them all and hurried to the elf.

"What *is* it, Uncle?" she said. "Ponu, *what*?"

The mage pursed his lips, trying to appear serious, but as he looked past her to Trentor, his grin returned. "Leader Trentor," Ponu said formally. "I am saddened to report . . . you now have *another* human on Hothra Isle!"

"*Gaelin*!" Avalar gasped. Then she was sprinting out of Freedom Hall, down the icy steps, and across the wooden bridges to the shore. Tiny granules of snow pelted her cheeks, but she did not care.

Ahead lay the gray outline of the docks, darker smudges against the misty sea. There, floating serenely at the end of the nearest pier, rested *Dawncutter*, her uncle's ship.

The figure in oversized clothing walking toward her on the wharf was too small and too slight to be a giant. His mouth slanted up on one side, and his rusty-colored hair whipped away from his eyes.

He held no staff, yet Avalar knew him at once. She vaulted onto the pier and rushed toward him.

"You are *alive*!" Dropping to her knees, she enfolded him in her embrace. "Gaelin Lavahl! *How*? He took you into the sky! Terrek saw flashes in the clouds above the mountain."

Gaelin stepped back, smiling, and reached for her, his fingers sliding up to trace the soft curve of her brows. "Well," he said wryly, "I guess I'm not done yet. Somehow Holram knew. So did Sephrym, who wrapped me in his power when I first started falling so I wouldn't die.

"You may call me Gaelin *Othelion*, now. That's my rightful name." He patted her arm. "It's good I don't smell like magic anymore, or your uncle would never have fished me out of the sea. Look!" From his generous pocket, he drew the Skystone. "Even Mornius's heart is free!"

Tentatively Avalar reached to touch the gem's fissured surface with its shimmering layers of blue and violet. "It is beautiful," she said. "I do not fear it anymore."

"I've decided to accept Terrek's offer," Gaelin announced, beaming up at her as he pocketed the stone.

"What offer?" Avalar asked him. "I do not recall."

She beheld a different Gaelin now, a young man standing tall and strong. He lifted his chin, his jaunty smile and squared shoulders reflecting a confidence she had not seen in him before. Astonished and laughing, she returned his grin.

Gaelin's eyes sparkled. "Terrek made me a promise, Avalar. He's going to teach me to ride horses!"

Chapter 69

A smile tugged at Gaelin's mouth as he donned his oversized coat and departed the crowded hall. His mind reeled at the sight of so much food in one place, and so many large bodies packed together.

Spotting Ponu on a bluff observing him through the flying snow, Gaelin sighed. There was a tremor in his stomach that, try as he might, he could not quell. He braved the uneven steps, climbing slowly. At last he reached the top of the rocky hillock next to the ocean and stood by Ponu, shuddering at the island's bitter cold.

Ponu stepped in close. Gaelin smiled in relief when a pocket of heated air gathered around them both. Then the elf seized his wrist and examined his quaking hand.

"I was afraid of this," Ponu said sadly as Gaelin jerked free. "Your body will have to adjust, Gaelin. You have been exposed to Holram's power for many years, and now the warder is gone. The Skystone is a pretty bauble from Earth now, and nothing more."

"Did I really ride an *Azkhar*?" Gaelin asked. "These weren't huge like the ones I saw you with at Tierdon."

"Captain Kurgenrock witnessed your fall," Ponu said. "So yes, that's what they were. They were males, Gaelin, which are considerably smaller. The males care for the queens, who spend their lives mostly in the air. It's rare for any of them to fly in groups, but when they do, they create storms. '*Shathni fye*,' the giants called it when they rode them."

Reaching into his pocket, Gaelin withdrew the Skystone. "Could they have wanted this?"

"It is a beautiful keepsake to set on your mantle once you have one," Ponu said, shrugging. "Gaelin, it is from Earth. It has no magic."

"So everything I did is gone like it never happened. It made me sick, and what have I to show for it? Oh look, I have a *bauble*."

"Petulant child! In addition to healing the afflicted and sparing humankind from a future with Erebos, you also saved Avalar's life and the lives of her people. That sword would not exist if not for your staff, and the giants would not exist if not for that sword—nor would this world!

"Yes, it was Holram's power. But it was *your* actions that hurled the magic and melted the stones, and ultimately made it possible for that song to exist, to stir a child's heart and motivate her to help her leader liberate her people. Is that not enough for you?" Ponu demanded.

"Now." Leaning close, he met Gaelin's faltering glare. "If you want confirmation your actions made a difference, just take in the world around you every morning when you open your eyes and climb out of bed. They are calling you a hero. And so you are." He gestured to Govorian's Hall, its walls reverberating with the clamor of the celebration within. "We should get back inside. You are not well. But since the giants are feasting in your honor, perhaps you can make an appearance before I whisk you off to Heartwood."

Gaelin gnawed at his lower lip. "Do you really think they can heal me? Is that what you hope?"

"It is. The Seekers have healing lore the other elf tribes on this world have lost. There is very little they cannot do. *And*"—grinning, Ponu patted his pockets—"I also have a trick or two up my sleeve. I have potions and powders in mind. And when you do get stronger, I will hie you off to Vale Horse, where you will live in a comfortable home of your own for the rest of your days."

"You mean I'll have a room," Gaelin corrected. "I'm not a—"

Ponu's snort cut him off. "If I had meant 'room,' I would have said 'room.' No, you will have a *home*, Gaelin Othelion. Terrek Florne intends to have one built. You will have that freedom you have always longed for. You will want for nothing!"

Gaelin frowned. "I don't want to be pampered! I want to work and earn wages like everyone else and be normal! I want to build things and learn to ride and wield a sword."

Ponu laughed. "First, we need to get you well! And the best way to begin is to eat!" Grinning, he held out his hand. "Come, brave warrior from Thalus. Shall we rejoin the big people?"

Gaelin looked past the elf's white wings to find Avalar standing below in her formal tunic, leggings, and shiny black boots, her expression filled with concern. "Gaelin? What are you doing out here?"

Swaying on his feet, Gaelin reached for the boulder that slanted across the stairway, but Ponu's hand stopped him, catching his elbow.

"He's exhausted," Ponu said to the worried young giant. "I was hoping to bring him inside, but I think it would be better for him if we take our leave now."

Avalar nodded. "I will inform Leader Trentor that you had to depart," she said in a husky voice. "Gaelin, will I ever see you?"

"Of course you will." Ponu retrieved his crystal staff from where he had propped it against the wall.

"I shall," Avalar reassured herself. "Of course I shall. I have *you*, Ponu, and you can fly me anywhere." She knelt and pulled Gaelin into her powerful embrace. "Be strong and get well, Gaelin *Othelion*," she breathed into his ear. "I wish . . ."

Gaelin smiled as she let him go, as Ponu urged him closer to the staff. "I wish, too," he said. "Thank you, Avalar, for being my friend."

The giant nodded, tears glistening on her cheeks. As the Staff of Time bucked, Gaelin staggered, its shower of sparks replacing the giant's kind face. Ponu's magic showed him the here and now, with flashes of possible futures.

Idly Gaelin wondered in which one he would live.

Raised on a tree nursery next to Farmer Green's cornfield in Waukesha, Wisconsin, and then relocated as a child to the Pacific NW, Diane has been a dreamer all her life. She finds the greatest happiness both in nature and in far-off, imagined places—often within the pages of a favorite book.

Diane is currently hard at work on the sequel and plans to continue the adventure through future books set on the magical world of Talenkai.

A Note to My Readers

I began writing Song of Mornius two decades ago. I was in the process of trying to get the final draft published when unforeseen events got in the way. I had some battles of my own to fight, during which my computer crashed. When I finally went back to look for my story, I discovered I had lost almost all of it. I could only find a few printed chapters from an old draft.

As I worked to reconstruct my life, my creative spark returned. I began to reinvent the book, and gradually this endeavor helped me to find myself. I remembered how much I loved writing and the friends I discovered within the pages.

The process of restoring Song of Mornius represents, for me, a long battle coming to a triumphant end, and the start of a whole new journey. I sincerely hope you enjoyed the story.